One More Moment in Time

Written by author

Elizabeth Anne Ryan

A special thank you to my editing team of:

Faye Adams
Kathleen Ford
Teresa Manczyk
Susan Schmitz
Melanie Williams

You wonderful women of God are the best.

Book Cover couple –
Jenny and Justin J. Janney – Married May 17, 2008

Book cover photograph by Jill Shuman
Shuman Fine Art Photography
www.shumanfineartphotography.com

§℮

One More Moment in Time

Book 2 of the Endless Love Book Series

If you have not read – <u>Endless Love</u> (Book 1) – You can order this book at - amazon.com – buy.com - or at Xulon Press.com - Just type "Endless Love by Elizabeth A. Ryan" - in their book search section. Then read <u>Endless Love</u> first. Since this series has a mystery, do not peek in this book until you have read <u>Endless Love</u>.

Endless Love – Book One
One More Moment in Time – Book Two
Forever in His Heart – Book Three
Book 4 to be announced in Book Three

§§

"By Grace, we are saved, not of the works that we do, lest any man should boast." Ephesians 2:8-9

"I can do all things through Christ who strengthens me." Phil 4:13

"And with all his abundant wealth through Christ Jesus, my God will supply all your needs." Phil 4:19

Words of Encouragement

Y ou are about to proceed on a tremendous adventure. The characters you are about to meet will fill your heart with delightful fascination. Mark's strong will and determination get him captured into places in which his character and faith creatively move him. Enjoy the journey as your emotions ignite from the embrace of <u>Endless Love</u> and <u>One More Moment in Time</u>.

This inspiring book was written as a source for education on Aplastic Anemia and as a strong witness of God's love, forgiveness and faithfulness. Through fictional characters, this Christian novel highlights classic symptoms and contemporary procedures, which Aplastic Anemia patients endured. God's miracles are revealed through unexpected circumstances. Challenges are faced and faith matures in a curiously gripping story.

Life has quite a way of weaving an intricately incredible web, almost full circle it seems, in such a way that one would never imagine, in a way that one could not have planned, more colorful and creative than ever thought possible, overcoming more than thought could be endured.

You have such a gift of presenting this story in a tremendously creative, colorful, inspiring, entertaining way. - **Teresa Manczyk**

This book has been a huge inspiration in my life. It has shown me never to give up, and when all else fails, God will be right there to catch me. Your words have life.. It has also shown me that God has already hand picked this one person to put in my life for me to love and cherish forever. I truly hope that <u>Endless Love</u> has been an impact on you as it has to me. Miss Liz is a wonderful, God-gifted woman, who I know God has truly chosen to make a change and to use her talent to reach out to people and most importantly glorify Him. – **Erin Lambert**

I am very, very much interested in purchasing Book 2 <u>One More Moment in Time</u>. This is the most fascinating book I have ever read and believe me, I read all the time. Nicholas Sparks, Max Lucado, Lori Wick, Janette Oke, etc. don't even hold a candle to Liz. She puts some of the so-called "greats" to shame. We are so proud of her. Thanks a million, Liz, and for all your talent in writing these books, I congratulate you. They are awesome. Never have I jumped right into a story on the first page before. My sister, JoAnn Alloways, joins me in "singing your praises". She dittos everything I have said. We both want Book 2. **- Charlotte Lambert**

I don't know how to say this, I CANNOT wait until Nov. to read book 2. I need an advanced copy, like yesterday. I started this book the night I received it in the mail, and I never put it down until I finished the very last page. WOW, The Lord has given you a real gift; you are so blessed. You are a true blessing to me. I plan on sharing this with my book club this Sunday. I cannot believe I am about to say this but you are better than my favorite author, Karen Kingsbury.

I want to share this book with everyone I know. I will tell everyone about you and how truly blessed you are and how gifted you are. Everyone should be reading your books; I am making that my goal, to help get your books out there, for the world to read!!! I love you, Your Friend for life, **- Mary Fields**

Acknowledgements

§§

I want to extend my personal and sincere thanks to these wonderful people. Their constant belief in this book series has made this book possible.

To God – His constant love in my heart inspired this book. I have been amazed how He has worked through me to write this story. His unending love surrounds my life.

My children, **Robin, Justin, Bryan, and Nathan,** who sacrificed countless hours away from me while the book was being written. Their unconditional love and support gave me the strength I needed during times of uncertain decisions. I dedicate this book to each one of them. Nathan, thanks for doing all the cooking, someday you will make a wonderful chef and a great husband.

I welcome my new daughter-in-law, Jenny, and her family, into our family.

My grandchildren, **Hannah Nicole**, who was only seven when she read Endless Love and wanted me to read One More Moment in Time to her every time she came to visit me. Hannah absolutely loved my characters. She has given me her expectations of things to come for them in this book. **Madison and Stephon**, you are blessings to my life. I thank God for each of you. I love you, kids!

A special thank you to **Penny Reddick** who has graciously featured my books in her store – Main Street Jewelry and Gifts.

To my honorary editing staff – Teresa Manczyk, Kathleen Ford, Melanie Williams, Faye Adams, Suzy Schmitz, Kittie McGuire, Sherry Grooms, Debbie Edwards, and Becky Triplett. ChristianWriters.com friends, Jackie Maxwell, Joy Gompah.

Thank you from the bottom of my heart for your unwavering enthusiasm and encouragement and for believing so passionately in my work and giving up your valuable time to edit for me.

Sherry Grooms – She could not wait until this book was published and was one of my few friends who read it before it was published. I am proud to call her my Christian friend. She is a treasure to know and is a prayer warrior for me.

Thanks - Colin, Erin, Kaley, Wendy, Charlotte, Sherry Lambert.

Thank you Miss Carolyn Taylor for being a loving mother to me.

This book is also dedicated to the love between **Kay and Sebern Rigdon.** Their love lasted over 56 years. When their family saw the book cover on Endless Love, they thought the hands joined together belonged to Kay and Shorty. This couple proved that Love could last a lifetime.

To Carolyn Taylor, Betty Camby, Betty Rogers, Florence Brazell, and Daphine Reddick, my thoughts and prayers are with you.

Each defining moment of our day can be significant; life is made up of small moments that we must treasure as gifts from God. Pursue your faith and find the courage and love to grasp deep within to find your God-given strengths no matter how difficult your circumstances. Author unknown.

One More Moment in Time Chapters

§§

Next book in this series is:
Book 3 – **Forever in His Heart**

When this book is available, it will be found at amazon.com

Chapter One

Miracles of God's Blessings
ৡৡ

The magical candles burned brightly all around them in this tranquil moment where time seemed to stand still. The couple intertwined their faith as God's twinkling stars sparkled above them while they gave their hearts to each other.

As this serene moment unfolded, there was only joy in the hearts of those who had held any dreaded thoughts of Mark succumbing to his death from his illness earlier that morning. They realized with heartfelt tears there was nothing love could not triumph over in the lives of these two standing before each other in the presence of God.

April and Mark passionately exchanged their wedding kiss. They turned to face their overjoyed family and friends. Everyone stood elated and clapped in harmony as they showed their support for the young couple.

Many wept as the couple expressed their love for each other as they melted in the depths of each other's eyes. The moon smiled brightly as they embraced. They looked back at the crowd and gave thanks those most precious to them had witnessed the miracles of God's blessings upon them.

Mark noticed the group of men dressed in crisp black jackets surrounding the perimeter of the wedding guests to keep any hostile intruders from entering.

That included Paul Morgan, April's father, who had made threats to kill Mark. Mark scanned the bodyguards for detainees. Thankfully, there were no signs of Paul.

Would Paul show up and disrupt this night? Was he out there waiting for his chance to make his daughter a widow on her wedding night? Mark pushed those appalling thoughts out of his mind and turned his attention back on his bride.

Mark and April looked spectacular as the first chapter of their life together was just beginning. These two would live on the faith and love God would bestow upon them.

Mark held her delicate hand in his, interlocking their fingers. Tears of joy trickled down his warm cheeks. He knew he had been blessed more than he could have ever imagined. He was the recipient of a precious treasure from God.

I promise You, God, that I will cherish her and love her with every beat of my heart for the rest of my life.

All of the unraveling events were overwhelming. Just hours ago, no one could have imagined they would be here tonight, under the blanket of stars God provided, as Mark pledged his everlasting love to April and joined them together as husband and wife. How was it possible, other than God put everything and everyone in the right place for Mark and April tonight?

The blueness of Sunny's eyes mirrored the image of her father. The crowd witnessed the undeniable miracle of life in Sunny. God had truly given Mark his miracle by giving life to his child five years ago. This child would some day soon save her father's life. God and Sunny held the future of all there would be for this precious family, a prayer all those in attendance continued to pray on behalf of Mark.

God put His supernatural plan into action just as Mark claimed He would. Everyone stood in amazement as they absorbed the widespread glow of health on a supposedly dying man's face. They felt God's Holy presence touching Mark's life.

Would they continue their walk in faith with God as tomorrow came, and Mark was faced with what seemed like the impossible? Or would they let fear for his life creep back into their hearts? Could they embrace the firm foundation Mark laid before them that God is more powerful and mighty than anything that could come against him?

Through God, all things are possible. Mark believed that with unwavering confidence as he took April as his wife, knowing there was still a battle he and God had yet to conquer, a victory that was just one day away.

Knowing and feeling the excitement of his victory tonight, there was no reservations in Mark's mind about the victory tomorrow would bring him, when he led his team, as their starting quarterback, to an AFC Championship win. Mark made up his mind and set his feet in stone.

The thought of winning the game filled his veins with adrenaline. Mark Sanders was on a high from which nothing could bring him down. The best was yet to come tonight, that he was sure of, he thought with a broad grin, squeezing April's fingers and once again claiming her lips for a lingering kiss.

All the guests lined up to throw rose petals at the young couple as they came down from the gazebo. Mark and April exchanged another tender kiss and walked down the aisle gracefully.

All those that loved them dearly surrounded them in celebration. This was a night none of their guests would take for granted. Seeing Mark this ecstatic gave them the hope they needed to believe he indeed had the rest of his life to love the woman of his dreams.

It was as if he had wiped aplastic anemia from his mind and body. The doctor's prediction of his pending death was far from his mind. He once again proved his faith remained firm against the infringement of the enemy.

Mark and April gave Sunny a warm hug as she joined them. Mark gathered his precious family in his arms and thanked God again for this extraordinary moment in his life. He bent down on one knee and hugged Sunny to his chest. *Thank you, God, for Sunny.*

"I love you, Sunny." His moist eyes sparkled with joy. He took a deep breath and pressed his hand to his chest where his heart still hurt from missing her. Then he pushed that awful thought out of his mind. Sunny touched his face with her delicate hands and reminded him she belonged to him. God had faithfully honored Mark's prayers.

Sunny planted a soft kiss on the tip of his nose and let out one of her little giggle laughs as she claimed his playful smile with her hands. He returned her gesture by rubbing noses with her, making her laugh louder.

"I love ya, Mark!" she exclaimed, as she bounced around in his arms. "You're my prince!"

"No, Sunny ... I am your daddy ... I will always be your daddy ... for the rest of my life I will love you." His arms wrapped around her securely. He prayed silently that he could fulfill his promise to her; he would spend an eternity loving her.

Julia touched Mark's shoulder gently, and he briefly looked up into her tearful eyes. However, he made no attempt to free Sunny from the safety of his arms. He discreetly examined her for any obvious injuries inflicted on her by her kidnappers.

Noting what he was doing, his mother Julia spoke with assurance. "Sunny is fine, Mark, they did not harm her. Dan and Dr. Price have given her a complete medical clearance. Dan brought her home to us after the police found her. I will explain it all to you later."

Everyone stood quietly as Mark wept softly in a thankful prayer that Sunny was unharmed. Sunny laid her head upon his shoulder and wrapped her arms around his neck, locking her fingers together as she encased her father.

She whispered into his ear, "Mark, don't cry. I got ya ... you're safe now ... with me." She let go of his neck, wiped his tears, and kissed his nose.

If those watching were not crying before, they were now, as the flood-gates to Mark's heart spilled over. He was unable to contain the relief he was feeling that Sunny had been returned to him by God unharmed.

Sunny rescued him once again with her childlike bravery as she placed the palms of her hands over his ears and drew him to her so they were touching forehead to forehead. "I love you, Mark," she whispered.

"I love you, too, little girl." He drew back his tears with a deep breath and once again held his chest where his heart hurt. Only this time he was not sure he could catch his breath. A look of concern crossed his face as he gave his pain a second thought.

April tearfully stood in the arms of her Uncle Dan. She watched Mark claim their little girl into his heart in this tender moment of rejoicing that they would soon be a family.

If they could ever get Mark to let Sunny go for the night, Sunny would stay behind with Mark's parents, Robert and Julia, while Mark and April enjoyed their honeymoon night alone.

Julia touched Mark's shoulder again and softly spoke his name, "Mark." This time he looked up at her, and in seconds, he was wrapped in her awaiting arms as he kept one hand firmly holding Sunny's hand.

"Thanks, Mom ... I love you." His tears escaped once again from the overwhelming love he felt for his mother. She wiped them away with her silk gloves.

My tough little boy has grown up, but how can I let him go, how am I ever going to let him go? Not just yet, no, not yet.

Her body embraced him in an attempt to keep him safe with her for just a little longer. The concerned mother hugged her son as he held on to his own daughter. It was a touching sight shared by all those watching this family embrace each other in love.

Mark put on the finishing touches in this picturesque moment by kissing Julia gently on her forehead as the photographer captured them.

"Sunny is going to stay with Robert and me tonight," Julia spoke to his watchful eyes. Sunny wrapped her arms around his leg and held on for a playful hug.

Mark quickly shook his head in protest. "No, Mom, Sunny stays with me. I am not letting her out of my sight." He reached down and placed his hand on Sunny's head. He was not ready to let Sunny out of his protection.

Julia placed her fingers on his lips to keep him from speaking. "She will be fine, Son. I promise; Robert and I will keep her safe with us. You and April deserve this night together alone. Sunny and I have already talked about what is going to happen tonight and tomorrow and she understands," she reassured him with her warm maternal eyes that he could not refuse.

Mark felt her trusting eyes touch his soul and knew he had nothing to fear. Sunny would be safe with his parents.

Robert touched Mark's arm letting him know Sunny would be safe in his care. "Son, let us do this for you," Robert's tender voice reflected his esteem for his son as he captured Mark's gratitude for him.

Sunny looked up at Mark with seemingly wishful eyes. "Can I stay with Nana and Granddaddy tonight, Mark?" she unselfishly voiced. Truthfully, she really wanted Mark's arms wrapped around her tonight. *Just one night and Mark will belong to me*, she thought, remembering the talk Julia had with her earlier.

Mark was pleasantly surprised Sunny had already chosen names for his parents. Just a week or so ago, she formally called them Mr. and Mrs. Sanders. Julia had gotten her answer to prayer: Sunny was her granddaughter. Mark stood humbled at how God had brought them all together.

Sunny grinned as she folded her hands and squeezed her fingers together as if in prayer. "Please, Mark, pleeeeease." Mark's cheeks lifted into a smile as Sunny charmed her way through his resistance of giving her up, even if it was for just one night.

"I guess … thanks, Mom and Dad." He let his parents gather a delighted Sunny in their arms. Satisfied, he turned and gathered April in his arm as he extended his other hand out to Dan.

"Thanks, Dan … thanks for bringing my daughter home safe." Dan emotionally claimed Mark in his arms and bear-hugged him.

"I am so happy for you, Mark. I love you, Son." With that said, the two men who had shared an entire lifetime together exchanged an understanding look that told everyone Mark was indeed the son of Dr. Dan Morgan, maybe not by blood, but by the union of their hearts.

Chapter Two

A New Beginning

𝕾𝕭

April could not believe her eyes as Mark escorted her to the sidewalk. The football players formed two lines and held out their sparkling candles. She covered her mouth with her silk-gloved hands and let out a bubbly sigh. "Oh, Mark, it is absolutely beautiful."

A white horse-drawn carriage covered in white and pink miniature roses and flowers awaited them. The driver was poised on top, dressed sophisticatedly in his black and white tuxedo, white gloves, and an Abe Lincoln top hat. It was an eye-catching scene straight out of the *Gone with the Wind* movie, except Rhett Butler did not hold a candle to her strikingly handsome husband, Mark Sanders.

Mark gave a gracious bow to his princess. He took her gloved hand and helped her up into the carriage. He gallantly climbed up and sat beside her on the soft luxurious velvet bench. She gave her grand approval as she thanked her thoughtful and honorable prince with a tender kiss.

The couple waved to all their guests as the carriage took leave. Sunny blew them a kiss and waved with both arms as Robert and Julia stood waving beside her.

April was undeniably feeling like a princess; her face was glowing with joy as she blew a kiss back to Sunny. Mark gave a captain's salute to his teammates. Noting Sunny was safe with his parents. Mark relaxed against the seat and turned his attention to his beautiful bride.

Mark was glad he finally had April alone as he thoughtfully covered them with a soft blanket. They were off for a romantic ride around the entire moonlit park. The miniature snowflakes fell softly on the canopy above them. The magical wintry evening was perfect. He knew he could never have planned anything as wonderful as what God's masterpiece provided for them tonight.

They cuddled comfortably against each other as they consumed the love that surrounded them. They were so addicted to each other, they did not notice anything else around them.

April leaned her head against his shoulder as they held hands. Mark slipped her gloves off, and lifted their hands together as one. He joined their sparkling wedding rings side by side, admiring the symbols of their *endless love* for each other. Gazing into her eyes, he held their hands against his heart making it official.

Their eyes were trapped in the depth of their love as their hearts beat to the same melody. He leaned his head down and captured her amazing lips. God placed the twinkling stars in the sky above them but neither noticed the magic surrounding them.

Mark let go of her hand and slid his hand between her jacket and her gown. He wrapped his arm around her tiny waist and pulled her to him. Saying nothing, he held her close as if he never wanted to let her go. He absorbed the gift that had been given to him with an understanding of God's faithfulness. He put his trust in God and April was his reward.

She laid her head tenderly against his chest. He kissed the top of her soft hair as he basked in the pleasure of knowing she was in fact his wife. She was a priceless treasure from the God above them.

Neither of them spoke words; there was no need. Their hearts spoke the truth of their feelings as they melted together in this serene moment. Only the sounds of the hooves of the horses against the pavement were heard as they came to the end of the ride.

Mark told the driver to go around the park again. He was not ready to share her, not yet, as he found her incredible lips and blissfully saturated them with his own.

April jokingly asked if they were going back to their blanket by the pond. Mark laughed. Knowing his family, the park just might be the only private place they could go tonight to be alone.

The air was getting cooler and the snow was falling heavier; the comfort of the penthouse would have to do, he disappointingly told her with a sparkle in his eyes of things to come tonight.

It was eight o'clock when they arrived at the front of the penthouse lobby. Mark carefully helped her down from the carriage. He gathered her in his arms and began kissing her tenderly as they stood in front of the luxurious hotel.

The doorman held an umbrella over them to keep the snow from covering them. Neither one noticed him, as they continued to share in this heavenly moment of standing there in the moonlight, kissing affectionately and making a memory on this crisp night.

They had the warmth and comfort of each other as they wrapped their bodies together in their arms. Mark touched her face with his fingertips and whispered his love for her, as his lips pressed tenderly against hers.

Her scent was subtle and alluring as the moonlight. He was savoring every breath he took of her neck. Mark wanted to pick her up in his arms and take her away with him so they could get lost in their love for each other. She was all he wanted. He would have gladly skipped the reception and gone straight to the penthouse.

"Sir, the guests are waiting," the door attendant hesitantly interrupted Mark. Reluctant to end this moment, Mark looked over at him with his sly grin and raised his eyebrows in disappointment. April gave him a consolation kiss on his cheek, took his hand, and led him to the door. The attendant held the door open as the two walked through.

The guests were waiting in the ballroom, eager to greet them. The room was lavishly decorated. Mark and his mother had taken care of every intricate detail with the wedding planners.

The announcer presented them to the guests as Dr. and Mrs. Robert Mark Sanders, the third. April gazed at Mark's elated face. She was Mrs. Mark Sanders, she thought with growing excitement. She glided into the room, as if in a dream, holding onto her husband's bent arm. Everyone applauded as they exchanged warm congratulatory hugs with the happy couple.

Mark realizing Sunny was not with his family, quickly scanned the room searching for her and was relieved when he saw her safe with Sister Jessica and Katie. Sensing his presence, Sunny waved to him and returned to her conversation. Mark chuckled at her independence.

As they took the dance floor, the song began. The two passionately danced as if no one else was in the ballroom. The moment was so magical, just as it had been that very first time they had danced here together six years ago on Mark's birthday.

Mark was so strikingly handsome, as he held April gently in his arms, making her feel dreamingly beautiful and light on her toes. His sturdy arms grasped her to his warm body as they swayed elegantly to the music and floated into their own secluded miraculous world.

She felt safe as she closed her eyes and eagerly accepted the warm kisses Mark feverishly placed against the sensitive skin on the back of her neck. Nothing could ever take them away from this romantic moment; she shuddered as he continued to cause warm sensations to travel throughout her body, making her light-headed.

They kissed, each kiss sending waves of joy to her heart. His crystal blue eyes sparkled in the light from the chandeliers above them. Forever she would remember this magnificent night with the man she loved. The memories of this glorious moment would stay in her heart forever.

She touched his warm cheek with the palm of her soft hand, turning his head to meet her awaiting lips. She became dizzy as he gently pressed his smooth face against hers and whispered sweet words of love into her ear.

"Mrs. Mark Sanders, you are the most beautiful, kind, compassionate, devoted woman that I have ever met. I love you with all my heart."

"Mr. Mark Sanders, I will love you forever."

He was thankful God blessed his life with her three times and now forever. Her heart belonged exclusively to him, and he would bestow on her everything her heart desired.

They would soon become a family and make a lifetime of precious memories. That very thought made him smile as he keenly kissed her fingertips.

They were intensely lost deep in their love as they circled around and around in the arms of each other. The power of their love spread throughout the entire room as couples gathered closer to each other and shared in their renewed love.

Mark could not wait to tell April what he wanted them to do. Telling her would have to wait until they were alone upstairs in the privacy of the penthouse. For now, he would wholeheartedly shower her with his love as he drew her closer to him and planned never to let her go. She felt his heart so close to hers as he touched her lips and they melted together as one.

Mark looked over her shoulder and frantically scanned the room as they circled the dance floor. He could not shake the uncertain feeling he needed to keep a closer eye on Sunny. The thought that she could be *kidnapped* again sent chilling waves down his spine.

He spotted Sunny with his Grandmother Ella and Rebecca's two young sons, Brad and James Robert. They were keeping Grandma Ella entertained; the vision of them together brought relief to Mark's face.

Charlie sat down beside Ella and handed her a glass of punch. Content that Sunny was in good hands, Mark relaxed and turned his full attention back to his bride.

26

The softness of her curves sent his mind on an endless journey of expectations of things to come.

Chapter Three

Not So Amusing

❦❦

Dan, Jeff, and Dr. Stevenson were sitting at their table watching Mark and April dancing, admiring the love they shared for each other. Yet Dan and Tom's faces showed apprehension as they thought about Mark's declining health.

True enough, Mark looked to be in perfect health as he snuggled against April, indulging her with his breathtaking kisses. The glowing tan on his face hid the truth that beneath his muscular frame existed a very sick young man.

"We have to tell Mark about tonight," Dr. Stevenson spoke to Dan and Jeff with deep concern in his voice.

"Tell him what?" Jeff was focusing his playboy attention on Ashley and the other appealing nurses surrounding her. Bachelorhood suited him just fine.

"The honeymoon night can't happen. Mark needs to continue with his treatments," Dr. Stevenson announced, knowing they needed to collect Mark's stem cells before tomorrow's game. They would have to do it tonight.

Jeff's head swung around in confusion and he faced Tom straight on. "I thought we agreed I was going with them to the penthouse to give Mark his nightly medications and to keep an eye on him until tomorrow. What are you talking about?" Jeff questioned, noting the profound concern on Dr. Stevenson's face.

Jeff was unaware of the caution Mark's cardiologist, Dr. Megan McGuire, gave the other two doctors earlier at the hospital when she found out his intentions to marry April tonight.

Dr. McGuire opposed Mark's decision to play in the football game. When Tom and Dan informed her Mark was getting married that evening, she put her hands on her hips and said, "What? A wedding, tonight? You have got to be kidding! What is Mark thinking? Oh, that's right; the problem with Mark, he does not think! I'll just wait for you two doctors in the emergency room tonight. That way I'll already be there when you two bring in Casanova after he has a heart attack making love to his new bride."

Once Megan calmed down, she devised a game plan with them to prevent a premature visit to the ER before the game. Nevertheless, her warning had been clear; Mark was treading on thin ice, and at any minute, he could crack through it. She made a quick call to her nurse practitioner, Vivian Wiggins, telling her to be prepared to come in to the hospital if she needed her.

"Look at the two of them. Mark's blood pressure has to be elevated. He cannot take the chance of increasing it anymore. He cannot go through with tonight. It is not safe. Dr. McGuire warned us about keeping Mark as calm as possible." Tom's voice never wavered as he agreed with Megan.

"Are you serious?" Jeff smirked.

"You know what that means as well as I do, Jeff," Dan said with apprehension. He thought of Mark's enlarged heart and the warning Dr. McGuire gave them after Mark left the hospital.

Jeff's eyes widened. "Uh … let me just call Mark over here and let you tell him that piece of unwelcome information," Jeff chuckled, knowing exactly how Mark Sanders would respond to their … uh … awkward news.

Jeff comically grinned at them as he got up and went to Mark. *This is going to be good*, Jeff chuckled, even though he knew deep down maybe he should be taking this matter a little more seriously. He could not help it as he chuckled again and felt his cheeks turn a fine shade of red.

We'll just see what "Mister Stud-man" Mark Sanders will have to say about this, he chuckled again, as he remembered the discussion the two of them had while they were in med school about their expectations of their honeymoon nights and the final ending of their bachelorhood.

Mark is definitely not going to welcome the warning Dan and Tom plan to enlighten him with, that is, if I can ever get him away from April.

Jeff smiled again, thinking Tom and Dan were just overreacting, and Mark was about to wipe the floor up with them when they told him that, uh, well uh . . . He laughed again, as he stood behind the glamour boy's bride.

According to *Gentlemen's Illustrated Magazine*, the glamour boy was none other than Mark Sanders: sportsman of the year, striking physical good looks, irresistible alluring qualities, and desired by women all over the world.

Wasn't that the article Mark used for firewood after he read it? Jeff laughed again. *And lucky me, I am his best friend.* He felt another blushing grin return on his face.

The dance song ended, and the bride and groom locked in a kiss as everyone clapped in their honor.

Jeff stood impatiently waiting for the kiss to end ... to end ... to end. *This is going to take awhile,* Jeff shook his head and grinned. *There certainly isn't anything wrong with Mark's heart; it is going full speed.*

After what seemed like an eternity, Mark opened his eyes and saw Jeff standing behind April. Jeff had his arms crossed and was giving Mark that keen look of his.

"What?" Mark asked, looking confused. Mark was still holding April in his arms and dancing slowly to the new song. Mark knew it could not be good news from the humorous grin on Jeff's face.

"The guys over there ... would like to have a word with you," Jeff informed Mark with amusement as he pointed to the doctors and gave them a comic wave.

Mark looked over at the twosome staring in his direction. They did not share the same amusing look as Jeff. In fact, they gave the impression they were rather annoyed at Jeff. Mark swallowed the lump forming in his throat.

What is their problem? he wondered, yet sure, he really did not want to know what they were thinking.

Against his better judgment, Mark excused himself from April, giving her a kiss on her forehead. He reluctantly walked over to the table with Jeff.

Jeff plopped down, leaned back, crossed his arms across his chest and grinned at Mark. *What is up with him?* Mark wondered as he stood over them with his hands on his hips.

"This better be important," Mark warned them. He did not like the seriousness on their faces; it could only mean one thing - trouble.

"Have a seat, Mark; there is something we need to discuss with you," Dan replied.

Mark could tell by the look on their faces he did not want to hear what they had to say. Only Jeff's face showed amusement. Mark decided to remain standing in case he needed to escape.

"What is so important you took me away from my bride?" Mark asked, irritated at them for interrupting his precious time with April.

"We need to talk to you about your honeymoon tonight," Dan said seriously, his eyes firmly planted on Mark.

Silence fell. Mark looked surprised. His cheeks lifted as he blushed. "I certainly think I can handle that, guys," Mark assured them with a bashful grin, thinking this was some sort of joke they were playing on him.

"Mark, let's look at this situation medically. You have to be careful not to overexert your heart," Dr. Stevenson affirmed.

"What?" Mark asked with amusement, not sure exactly what they were trying to say or if they were joking. "What are you talking about?"

"You can't make love to April tonight, Mark. That's what they are trying to tell you," Jeff humorously blurted out.

Mark's expression showed disbelief when he heard those striking words leave Jeff's lips. His eyebrows came together.

"What? Did I just hear you right? You've got to be kidding, right!" Mark was agitated. He could not believe they were discussing this delicate subject with him. No one spoke.

He scratched the top of his head with his fingers, giving them his disapproving look. "What is going on here? Have you guys, lost your minds?"

"Sit down, Mark, this is serious," Dan told him as he pulled out a chair for Mark. Mark scrunched his eyebrows together and shot them his well-known "*off limits*" look.

"You can't be serious. You really expect me to stand my bride up on her wedding night?" Mark smirked. He did not know if he should laugh at them or knock them out of their chairs.

"Just postpone it," Dan suggested.

Now Mark was really getting aggravated, stress lines formed on his forehead. "To when?" Mark snapped back. "Monday at eight o'clock you are ripping my spleen out, followed by chemo. Then I will be in isolation for eight to ten weeks. I do not think so. I am not going to make her wait that long." He grabbed at a breath of air to refill his lungs. "I am not going to wait that long."

"Look, Mark, we have taken care of everything for tonight. Jeff has a medical bag completely equipped with everything he could possibly need if you have a problem with your heart or your spleen," Tom explained.

"You're kidding, right?"

"No, Jeff is staying in the penthouse with you and April tonight. You and April can cuddle on the bed while you get your medications and stay on oxygen. When she falls asleep, you can come to the hospital for the rest of your treatments." Tom was firm about this well thought out plan of his.

Mark, on the other hand, was not buying into his plan. "Oh, really! Jeff is going on my honeymoon? Why don't you all just come?" Mark offered with annoyance. "Let's just make it a party," Mark sarcastically said as he gave them his "*I am about to kill someone*" look. They had crossed over the line; this was not even remotely funny.

Jeff came to the rescue. He remembered his promise to watch Mark's back for him. "Mark, honestly, that wasn't exactly the original plan. I will be there just in case something happens, say, like if you flat line; April can come get me. If not, I'll just watch TV all night. You and April, hey, you guys can do whatever you want, no problem. I got your back, buddy." Jeff was trying to lighten up Mark's mood.

Mark and Jeff exchanged looks at each other, as they contemplated their next move together against these two over-protective men. The stress was on and they were about to go into overdrive to override it just as they had always done in the past when things got too serious for them. Jeff could not help it as he chuckled and hid his face with his hand, trying not to laugh out loud.

"I don't believe you two; you have lost your minds?" Mark shook his head at Tom and Dan in disbelief. Then Mark cracked a slight smile as Jeff continued to entertain him with his wacky facial expressions.

"Your heart is not up to any of this. You know the danger we are talking about, Doctor Sanders. Now sit down and hear us out!" It was apparent Tom was dead serious and not about to give an inch with these two comedians.

Dan was glaring at Jeff, sending him a direct message to knock it off with the joking around. A swift kick under the table and Jeff grabbed his ankle in pain.

Mark slid down into the chair. *Tom just had to call me doctor*, Mark thought defeated. Mark knew exactly what they were talking about, but he was not claiming any heart attack; his heart was fine.

Darn them, he had planned everything out but this slight problem. He took in a deep breath. He would have to think about this for all of … five whole seconds. His smile returned to his face as he looked at Jeff for support.

"What if you have a fatal heart attack, or your spleen busts while you are with her? How do you think that will make her feel?" Dan warned sympathetically, realizing Mark's dilemma.

That statement caught Mark's attention. *Dan just had to put the knife in there and twist it,* Mark thought with frustration about the whole situation. *This just really stinks!*

Jeff was feeling sorry for his best friend at this point. Mark's honeymoon was not something he would give up after all he had gone through to make this special night happen. Not to mention the way Mark and April loved each other. Most of all, Jeff knew what Mark was planning to ask April tonight.

None of this was fair. Mark deserved to have a normal honeymoon and Jeff would do everything in his power to make that happen for Mark. The bottom line, what if Mark died without ever knowing the pleasures of loving his wife? Jeff dismissed the knot in his stomach and the fear in his heart, and he placed a smile back on his face to encourage Mark.

"Go for it, Mark. I'll be right there; I got an A+ in heart resuscitation," Jeff said with humor. Jeff saw the stern looks from the other two doctors. He moved over to the other chair out of Dan's kicking reach.

Mark smiled; leave it to Jeff to lighten the tension. "Look, guys, I've come this far, and God has watched out for me all night. I have Sunny and April; I have it all right now. I am not going to have a heart attack. I am in perfect health. I am not sick; remember that guys. What happened to your faith in me? I thought we were on the same team?"

He knocked the fight out of them for now. Mark looked them straight in their eyes and smiled. "God's got me in the palms of His hands tonight, trust me. And guys, I do plan to have it all tonight, all of it."

Mark revealed his plans to them with a wide grin on his face as he winked at them. Then he got up and walked back to April. *I cannot believe those guys,* he thought as he playfully shook his head in disbelief and laughed.

Dan and Dr. Stevenson exchanged unconvinced looks. Dan reached over and punched Jeff in the shoulder. That wiped the smirk off Jeff's face. "You weren't much help," Dan told Jeff sternly. "I am going to go have a talk with April." He stood up, but Jeff firmly grabbed his arm to stop him. Jeff was serious now, his eyes on fire.

"No way, don't tell her anything. If Mark goes through with this tonight, she would wonder with every kiss if it was going to be their last one. You cannot put fear in her heart. This is their night; let them have it. If tonight happens, it happens. I will be right there and the helicopter will be on the roof. We've got it covered, so leave them alone. Don't ask Mark to die without loving his wife!" Jeff pleaded. Still Dan and Dr. Stevenson did not look convinced.

"Have faith, men, in God and in Mark. I have his back; I am not about to let anything happen to him. Mark is not going to have a heart attack unless the two of you get him all stressed out," Jeff declared as he got up to go find some more interesting seating companions. He'd had his eyes on them all evening. Mark was not going to be the only one with someone in his arms tonight.

The team of doctors planned everything to the last detail. Mark would not be out of their sight until Monday morning when they had him on the operating room table. Jeff would spend the night at the penthouse with the life-saving equipment. All three of them would be on the sideline during tomorrow's game.

Would Mark teach them another lesson in faith?

Mark returned to the dance floor, his eyes melting as he saw the charming vision of the little girl standing there waiting to have the next dance with him. This little angel won his heart the very first moment he met her. Now she belonged only to him, or *so he thought.*

A wide smile crossed her face as she stretched her arms out to him and waved her fingers, eager to grasp the man that had claimed her heart. He was her prince, and this time, she wanted to be the princess in his arms. He glided over to her with a glow that lit up the entire room and gathered her tiny fingers in his gentle hands.

"My little angel. God, thank You for giving her to me." A special place in his heart exploded with love as she danced in his arms. No other thoughts filled his mind as she swallowed him into her heart. He twirled her around; her long blonde hair flowed away from her body. Then she stepped up onto the tips of his boots and with each step Mark took, his little daughter followed along with him.

The sight of Mark with his daughter drew tears from many who stood watching them bask in the love they had for each other. All knew Mark had been given a miracle. Sunny would be the breath of air that would save this young man's life.

Someday this father would dance with his daughter at her wedding, but in this magical moment they shared, her heart belonged entirely to him, which was emphasized in their *one more moment in time* together.

He picked her up and held her tightly as he continued to dance with her. She wrapped her arms around his neck and laid her head down on his shoulder, her legs wrapped around his waist. He could have easily rocked her to sleep with the gentle swaying of his hips.

Sunny's prince held her in the safety of his fatherly arms. No longer would she ever have to fear anything in her life as long as she had Mark to provide her with moments like this one.

God had supplied all her needs. She placed her head on his shoulder and tenderly whispered a tiny thank you to God, as she reached up, took a hold of Mark's earlobe, and rubbed it between her two fingers. She closed her eyes and whispered, "God gave you a wish come true."

"Yes, Sunny, He did. He gave me you." Tears welled in his eyes once again as the softness of her body in his arms sent another sea of emotions straight to his heart. He remembered the time Sunny told him to close his eyes and make a wish. "I wished for a little girl, just like you, and God granted me that wish." Sunny giggled and twisted Mark's earlobe in agreement.

As the song was ending, Mark danced over to April. They embraced in a group hug and expressed their words of endless *love* for each other. Life was beautiful; could it get any better than this minute?

Jeff, Carlo, and the rest of Mark and April's friends took the stage. Jeff got everyone's attention. He told Mark and April to take the dance floor; they had a song they wanted to sing to them.

The football players formed a large circle around Mark and April as if they were in a team huddle. They stood at attention to honor their team captain on the most important day of his life.

The game tomorrow could not even compare to this special moment they shared with him. April was officially accepted into their elite group as the inauguration dance began. Carlo gave Mark a wink and a "thumbs up" to show his approval.

Mark and April danced their last dance of the night to the song their friends performed. All those watching admired their elegant moves and lifted the couple up in prayer.

It was here Mark first gave his heart completely to the woman he held in his arms now. It was in this very room they shared their first kiss with each other. Mark beamed with love as he looked into April's face and knew his life was just beginning.

Mark had taken his jacket, vest, and tie off a long time ago. April thought he looked stunning in his white starched shirt and black pants. She admired her majestic husband as she felt his warm skin through his shirt as she held him.

Mark picked up Sunny and held her as they danced together as a family. She giggled when he teased her. They laughed together as Mark sang the remainder of the song to them. Sunny joined him; she had inherited her father's superb voice.

Mark remembered when he first met Sunny that he thought she sang, "You are my Sunshine" like his sister, Rebecca, sang when she was younger. Now he knew why her voice sounded like her Aunt Rebecca's.

As the photograph of them was snapped, he declared he would forever love his family as much as he loved them at this very moment.

They deserved this moment in time of happiness. Mark was without a doubt the happiest man in the entire universe. As the song ended, his lips joined hers to seal their destiny as husband and wife.

They cut the cake and sipped from their wine glasses. It was time to toss the wedding bouquet and they would be off. April tossed it high in the air and Ashley caught it. Ashley smiled wishfully at Jeff.

Jeff blushed as Mark pointed his arm straight out at him. "Look out, Buddy, you're next!" Jeff did not receive that message. He quickly left to find something else to do. Ashley was too much of a temptation. He did not plan to be next in line any time soon. He was not about to stick around for Mark to shoot him with April's garter belt.

The reception had been short and elegant. Mark planned to spend the rest of the night alone with April. His guests would enjoy a feast in the ballroom while he and April enjoyed theirs alone in the seclusion of the penthouse.

Mark and April received congratulatory hugs from all of their friends. All five million of them, Mark thought impatiently as he kept looking at his watch. Mark had waited long enough. He picked April up in his arms and carried her out of the room.

Everyone cheered and clapped, as Mark and April escaped *and set out for a night of romance.*

Chapter Four

A Test of Patience

ᔕᔐ

Mark gallantly carried April to the elevator. He gently set her down and pushed the up button. He drew her close to him while they waited. They were finally on their way to their secret paradise.

Mark had hired four wedding companies to get everything perfect. They had done a superb job with the wedding and reception. However, the best was yet to come. Mark was eager to spend this time alone with April.

When Mark opened the doors to the penthouse, they saw the spectacular flower arrangements that filled the entire grand room. He picked her up in his arms and carried her into the luxurious room.

She was breathless, as she looked around at the romantic area, aware of the meticulous setting Mark had prepared just for her. "Oh, Mark," she gasped at the beauty surrounding her. The room was definitely the finest room she had ever encountered.

"I take it you approve."

"Yes, I love everything." Mark held her in his secure arms and kissed her tenderly. "Thank you for making our night so special."

"You're welcome." He gently put her down and hand in hand, they walked over to the dining table.

Dinner was prepared for them on a small elegant table. It was beautifully set with fine china on top of a white silk-laced tablecloth. Glowing candles and an elegant flower arrangement made it warm and cozy. Martha finished putting the meal on the table and went into the kitchen.

Mark thoughtfully held a chair out for April. Once she was seated, he bent down and gently lifted her chin in his tender fingers and kissed her. "Mrs. Sanders, I am totally in love with you."

"Mr. Sanders, my heart belongs to you," she whispered as he knelt and kissed her again before he took his place across the table.

Mark gathered her hands in his, and together they prayed over the meal as Mark acknowledged and honored God's blessings upon them.

April nibbled at the scrumptious meal as Mark sat and admired her. They enjoyed these few tranquil minutes to themselves as they relaxed over candlelight, with soft romantic music playing in the background. He was truly thankful he finally had April all to himself.

Mark had never felt healthier. He sat there and admired his beautiful wife, taking in every aspect of her. His heart completely healed the minute she said "I do," and gave her heart to him forever. Her appealing mouth tasting the savory flavors of the food on her plate conquered his mind as he felt himself falling prematurely weak.

Tonight was not all about what would happen physically in his bedroom later. He planned to spiritually celebrate and take pleasure in the woman he loved. He intended to plan a future with her and their children as a godly man that would be pleasing to God.

The heartache of losing Sunny was gone and replaced with the fulfillment of knowing he had his family to cherish for the rest of his long life. He and April would grow old together and have many more children to carry out all their dreams.

He would have insisted Sunny stay with them if it were not his honeymoon night. As much as this was his moment to be alone with April, his heartstrings were thinking of Sunny. He thought of his little angel dressed in her long flowing white dress. The memory of her quickly brought a humbled smile to his face. His affectionate smile extended to the mother of his child sitting across from him.

Sunny and April would be the reason each day would bring him new life when the devil would try to steal his life away. No matter what happened from this moment on, the very memory of this day would be etched in his mind, and he would draw on it to bring him out of any darkness he would face.

April noticed Mark had not touched anything on his plate. She cut her roast beef, stuck a piece of meat on her silver fork, leaned over the table, and held it out to him.

Mark looked deep into her eyes and leaned forward to accept the fork into his mouth. He approved of the flavor of the meat with a smile. He bent over the table and found April's lips to share in the moistness of her mouth.

The door opened and Jeff came in with his overnight bag hanging off his broad shoulder. From the pile of bags already in the corner, Mark thought Jeff brought the entire ER with him. Sometimes Jeff could be annoying, but knowing better than to put the blame entirely on Jeff, Mark knew Dan and Dr. Stevenson must have put him up to it. Those two were the real cohorts.

Debbie merrily came in with an overnight bag for her younger sister, April. She expressed her delight in the decorated grand room as she came to the dainty table where the couple sat with star-struck eyes for each other.

April has definitely married into wealth. Wow, and not to mention the honorable and gorgeous man sitting across from her; he is the real treasure. Oh my, Mark is positively worth keeping.

Her little sister had walked right into a fairytale storybook, Debbie thought with gratitude for all God had accomplished in the life of her younger sister.

Debbie stood and talked and talked and talked to April about how wonderful the wedding had been. Mark was growing impatient as Debbie continued to babble.

Mark was rolling his eyes as Debbie continued to talk; he was hoping she would get the message to exit. April gave Mark a disapproving look. Her influential eyes were telling him to stop with the rolling of his eyes and to behave. At last, Debbie bent and kissed April, and then she stole a quick kiss from Mark before leaving.

Mark sat up straight in his chair, took April's hand in his and kissed it. His repenting eyes were begging her for forgiveness for the way he acted. She smiled tenderly at him as she unconditionally forgave him. They were just getting back into their romantic mood when the door opened again.

Robert and Julia brought Sunny in to say goodnight to her new parents and to make sure that everything was just right. His mother checked out all the rooms to make sure everything was completed to her satisfaction.

Sunny loved the gala of flowers. She fell into Mark's arms for a lingering hug. Then she hopped off his lap and climbed up in April's lap. Mark reached his hand across the table, and Sunny wrapped her tiny fingers around Mark's thumb.

Mark talked to Sunny as his mother checked out the entire penthouse. Of course, she did not miss one flower arrangement as she pondered each one and commented to Robert on how wonderful they were. Robert looked bored but he politely accommodated her.

Mark beamed his eyes at his dad and gave him his best rival look, hoping Robert would interpret the meaning and speed Julia up so he and April could be alone.

Then he slumped back in his chair, looked at his watch again, and frowned as he crisscrossed his arms across his chest and let out a loud annoyed sigh.

Thomas came in with Mark's luggage and headed to the bedroom. Martha came out, refilled their water glasses and went back in the kitchen. Mark ran his fingers through his hair and resisted the temptation of letting his true feelings show.

Thomas came back out and pretended to straighten the photographs on the grand piano. He spoke in a hushed voice with Julia and Robert.

Mark leaned sideways in his chair watching everyone come and go. He started tapping the table with his fingertips. *What do you bet, Dan and Tom come next*, Mark thought frustrated.

Up to this point, he had been polite, but if one more person came through that door, he would have something to say about them interrupting his honeymoon. They were stealing his precious minutes to be alone with April, minutes he could not afford to give away.

April was reading Mark's very thoughts from the look on his frustrated face. She smiled at him and teasingly tossed a cloth napkin at him. He looked at her with a frown, and she smiled and gave him one of her well-known *"have patience"* looks. She had often given him the same look as a child when things were not going his way. Nevertheless, she did not blame him; she wanted to be alone with him, too.

Julia and Robert came back into the dining room. Julia was pleased with everything and asked if they needed anything. Mark wanted to say something, but he held his tongue. Instead, he painted a smile across his face and glanced at his watch. April politely told them everything was perfect. She gave Julia a warm thankful hug.

Julia bent and kissed Mark on the cheek. She stood back and admired her handsome son. She just wanted to cry. *My little boy is all grown up and married*. If only she could stop time by lingering here, she would have kept him right there, safe from all harm, safe from the uncertainties of tomorrow.

It would take everything she had inside of her to give him up and walk out the door. She would have gladly given him to April if they had a future beyond tonight … but not even April could protect Mark from tomorrow.

Tears formed in her eyes as she bent, touched Mark's cheek with her gloved hand and·kissed Mark on his other cheek. That kiss was all it took for Mark to forgive her for intruding on his time with April.

Robert extended his hand out to Mark and congratulated the couple on their marriage. He bent and kissed April's cheek as he gave thanks for his beautiful daughter-in-law. April would fill the void that had been missing in Mark's life since his grandfather died.

Mark knelt down on one knee, kissed Sunny, and gave her a big teddy bear hug. It felt so good to have her in his arms. If only he did not have to give her up so soon. She would spend the week at the ranch with Thomas and Martha, while his parents were at the hospital with him during his surgery on Monday and his recovery the following weeks.

"She will be fine, Mark." Julia spoke softly to him as she touched his shoulder, knowing Mark's apprehensive thoughts about leaving Sunny were pulling at his heart once again. Mark twisted a lock of Sunny's curly hair between his fingers.

"Sunny is going to sleep in the west wing with her cousins tonight. Charlie set up the teepee for them in the playroom; he will camp out with them." Julia enlightened Mark, knowing how much Mark loved and trusted old Charlie.

"Sounds like my Indian princess is going to have lots of fun, but don't keep Aunt Becky up too late," he whispered. "She needs all the beauty sleep she can get."

Sunny laughed at Mark's joking around. He placed a final kiss on the top of her forehead and pushed her hair off her shoulders neatly.

"I won't. Good night, Mark ... you too, April. Have fun tonight." Sunny half-waved goodbye to April, with a slight hint of jealousy.

"I love you, Sunny," April tearfully spoke. She noted Sunny's attention never wavered from Mark even when she spoke to her.

"I love you too, Sunny." Mark held back his emotions, wishing with all his heart that someday soon Sunny would call him, Daddy.

Sunny suddenly felt a frightened feeling rise up in her stomach, and the thought of being separated from Mark caused her to tremble. She held back her urge to reclaim his neck. Not wanting to mess up his night with April, she remained silent and bravely took Julia's hand and left with his parents.

It hurt Mark's heart to watch the door close behind them. He stood contemplating going after her. He felt a sting in his heart and for a second it hurt to breathe.

The warmth of April's hand touched his, and he slowly turned his partial attention back to her. She read the sadness on his face, knowing he missed Sunny already. He glanced back at the door as if Sunny was going to reenter and rush back into his arms.

The only regret Mark had was not having Sunny stay with them. He planned to give Sunny his undivided attention for the rest of his life. He would make up for the years they had lost. At this moment, the only thing that consumed his mind was having his family safe with him. If he took just one step forward, he would be running out the door to bring her back.

April reminded him quickly why they were in this room as she claimed his firm waist in her arm, reached up, and placed the warmth of her palm on his cheek. Mark leaned his head down and flashed her a teasing look before his lips received the softness of her mouth. He cradled her head with both hands as the passion rose for her in his heart.

Once again, they were interrupted as Thomas came through the room. They sat back down to finish their romantic dinner.

Mark's full attention was now on the desirable woman sitting across from him. He watched as she took a bite of her roll and teased him with her playful eyes. *Oh what she does to me, Lord,* he grinned, proving he was definitely not going to follow the advice of the two overprotective doctors when he finally got a chance to be alone with her.

Jeff came through the room in his jeans, body shirt, and barefooted, on his way to the kitchen. He came out with a can of soda. He stopped to say something to them, but Mark shook his head in disapproval, letting Jeff know he was not welcome to invade their privacy. A stern look from Mark sent Jeff packing to the guest room.

There was a knock at the door and Thomas answered it. Whoever was at the door was smart enough to stand out of Mark's view. Mark frowned; he exchanged a restless look with April.

Martha came back out with the water pitcher and refilled their already full glasses. She picked up April's overnight bag and took it to Mark's bedroom. She removed April's nightgown from her bag and placed it neatly on the bed.

Thomas left the door open and headed to the guest room and knocked on the door. Jeff reappeared and headed with Thomas to the door. They stood in quiet conversation.

Mark was about to take April back to the blanket in the park. If they stayed here, nothing would happen tonight. Was that everyone's plan? He looked at his watch again and frowned.

Well, he would show them! He grabbed a dinner roll, took aim with his quarterback arm and was ready to throw it at whoever came through the door next.

April continued to give him that disapproving look of hers. *She should have been a teacher*, he thought as she pointed firmly at the roll and then pointed at the basket.

He sent her a look of his own as he slowly lowered his arm and gave in to her request. She watched the frown on his face gradually lift into a good-humored smile as he tossed his dinner roll back in the basket. April giggled at him just as Sunny would have done.

The commotion at the front entrance caught his attention again and just as he predicted, Dan and Dr. Stevenson came in the room. Mark turned and saw them. He grabbed the napkin out of his lap and slammed it down on the table.

"That's it!" He stood up to give them a piece of his mind, but before he could, April quickly stood up in front of him and lightly pressed her hands against his chest to hold him back.

Mark gave in once again and sat down with a thud. April joined him by sitting on his lap. At least he could not hit anyone if she was sitting there. She teased the hair on the back of his neck to calm him down, but that only made him more anxious to get on with what he had in mind for the two of them.

The two doctors stood talking to Jeff. There was somewhat of a disagreement before Dr. Stevenson handed Jeff a small bag. They waved goodnight to Mark and April; however, Mark did not wave back. Jeff took the bag and quickly exited back into the guest bedroom.

Martha returned from Mark's bedroom and winked as she passed by him. Thomas smiled, gave Mark a "thumbs up" and followed Martha into the kitchen.

With the "all clear," Mark kissed April. She stood up, took his hand in hers and smiled. Their eyes met as Mark picked her up in his arms and carried her to his bedroom.

Once in the room he locked the door.

He was not about to be interrupted.

Chapter Five

Emotional, Physical, and Spiritual Love

§§

Sparkling candles blazed everywhere. Bouquets of flowers graced the entire room. Tiny rose petals were scattered on the king-size bed. The entire back wall was made of brilliant glass windowpanes with French doors leading out to a private balcony. The view of the city lights filling the skyline was absolutely magnificent from where Mark held her in his arms.

He put her down, and hand in hand, they walked out onto the balcony. They looked out at the splendid view of the twinkling city lights. Everything about this night was so romantic. April felt like a princess standing there in awe.

Could this really be happening or was this just a dream? She felt him in her arms. She felt his passionate kiss on her lips. *Oh please, do not let this feeling go away*, she prayed as her blood flowed warmly through her heart.

Then he lovingly looked into her affectionate eyes and asked her if there was any possible way they could conceive a child tonight as they consummated their marriage. It was what he wanted, but he would leave the final decision up to her.

His desire was evident in his soft teary eyes. They told her how important it was to him for them to conceive another child. She understood why his wish needed to be fulfilled tonight.

She had already made up her mind she wanted this for him. Her eyes filled with happy tears. It would be the perfect time if they did nothing to prevent it; she already knew that.

She knew his chemo treatments could prevent them from having any future children. *chemo* … tears welled in her eyes as she thought for those brief seconds of the chemo, and her voice stilled. Unable to speak, she buried her face in his shoulder to absorb her tears.

If she should lose him, she would have his child growing inside of her for comfort, just as Jessica had done. She loved him so much; he had made this entire night special for her. She owed it to him to cherish every second they had with each other. Just days ago she thought he would never know how it felt to love her completely. Her inspirational thoughts of the man she loved making passionate love to her in just minutes diminished all other thoughts in her mind.

There was nothing she wanted more than to be with the man she loved. She would take pleasure in conceiving his baby tonight as her wedding gift to him. She lifted her elated face to his, kissed his amazing warm lips and told him, yes. "Yes, Mark, tonight we will conceive a child."

He celebrated her answer with another emotional kiss as he gathered her closer to him, and whispered through his tears of joy, "Thank you, April." It was at that heartfelt moment that his once silent joyful tears began to consume him, as he could no longer restrain them from falling.

Mark absolutely believed with all his heart he would be healed. He looked forward to being a husband and a father. He was not dying, he was living; his love for God and his faith had confirmed that. He was ready to accept God's favor and His many blessings as he shared his life with April.

The tranquil thought of them having a baby reaffirmed his faith and hope of a new beginning for his life. Tears continued to fall softly down his cheeks as the emotions of his ecstatic heart spilled over.

"God, I love you, April," his tender voice spoke directly into her heart. "God, thank You for this wonderful woman."

April placed her hand behind his head and gathered him to her just as if he were a small child. Then she cuddled his tearful face to her breasts and spoke soft words of her devoted love for him. He drew strength from her encouraging words, wiped his tears and claimed his victory as they melted into a passionate kiss under the star-filled sky.

It took a genuine man to show his sincere emotions like Mark passionately did when things touched his heart deeply. She admired every faithful attribute Mark had within him. God had supplied all her needs. *Yes, Sunny, you were right. God gave me more than I could have ever dreamed of having*, April thought as she brushed away a few of her own warm tears.

They went back into the room. Mark turned the lights down low and turned on soft romantic music on the stereo. He did a few talented dance steps as he came to her. Her face lifted into a cheerful smile as she warmly admired how dashing he was as he entertained her with his charm.

Mark sat on the bed and removed his boots. April sat next to him. As their bodies touched, they knew the moment had come that would forever bring them together as one. He took her fingers and held on tight, and then he brought them up to his lips and kissed them.

"I love you, April, more than my own life. I will always love you." He lifted her hand in his and softly placed the back of his hand against her cheek and was met with her eyes of approval. She was ready to love him in the seclusion of this romantic atmosphere.

He slid off the bed, and knelt in front of her. He gathered her hands in his, bowed his head, and prayed over the two of them, asking God to place a blessing upon them as they joined together as husband and wife. He sincerely prayed that the miracle of their union would be blessed by a child.

They believed God would honor their request and bless their faithfulness to Him with a baby. The time had come to discover the gifts that God intended for them to enjoy as husband and wife.

Mark slid her shoes off carefully. He kissed her feet as he massaged them. He would cherish every inch of her body with his deepest respect.

The entire time his fabulous eyes did not leave her affectionate eyes, as he positioned himself in front of her on his knees, as she sat watchful of his every move. He undid the back of her gown and slid it down to her waist. He passionately kissed her soft shoulders and her neck.

She placed her hands on his shirt and nervously unbuttoned it. He helped her slide it off. But as she did, she exposed the catheter bandage below his shoulder. She felt a pang in her heart seeing it there, and she had to take a quick breath to recover.

Before she could let the disheartening thoughts of his illness sink in, he stood up and held his hand out to her. She stood up; her gown fell to the floor around her ankles and she kicked it away.

He pulled the comforter open on the bed and moved their bathrobes and her nightgown to the end of the bed.

He gathered her in his strong arms, kissed her splendid neck, and smelled her sweet fragrance. He unpinned her hair and let her soft silky hair fall over her slender shoulders. He gently brushed her hair away from her neck and kissed her softly and slowly.

She wrapped her arms around his neck and kissed his chest. She could hear his heart beating for her as she laid her head against his bare chest. She loved him so much. There was no need for words as she melted in total submission into his arms as her body felt faint.

Later that evening, when her tears of joy fell, he knew that they had reached eternity. He kissed her tears away from her cheeks and embraced her into the safety of his masculine arms.

She felt his strong heartbeat and held her hand over his chest as she sprinkled soft tears against him. She had his heart in the palm of her hand and forever they would be inseparable.

"Why are you crying, April?"

"Because, Mark, I love you … with every beat of my heart. I love you so much it hurts to breathe sometimes. Tonight we became one, joining our hearts forever. *Forever you will be in my heart*, Mark. I love you."

This time it was Mark who was in total submission as he melted compassionately into her arms and whispered his endless love for her.

He helped her into her silk nightgown. Then he continued to hold her, kissing her hands, her fingers, and her forehead, playing with her soft hair, consuming every inch of her amazing body. He gave her his life and love. She closed her eyes and let him shower her with his love, as she peacefully fell asleep in his protective arms.

Mark's life was now complete, with such fulfillment. He thanked God for his wedding and wedding night. He promised to love April forever the way God intended.

He placed his hand over his heart and felt his strong heartbeat and grinned, a wide sly smile crossed his face as he thought about what Dan and Dr. Stevenson had said. He laughed softly in victory.

As much as he hated it, he knew he had to surrender to the care of those two overprotective men. They were waiting for him at the hospital. He had given in and agreed to meet them there tonight after April fell asleep.

He carefully slid his arm out from under April's neck and pulled the comforter up over her shoulders. He took a bathrobe and put it on. He quietly went out of the bedroom and went to find Jeff.

Mark would have to have his treatments. He knew Dan and Dr. Stevenson were right, as he rubbed his hand across his sore ribs. He was thankful for the rib block he received just hours ago.

Jeff got the bag Dr. Stevenson gave him. He pulled out the syringes, and injected them into Mark's central line. They quietly placed the large oxygen machine in the bedroom. Mark would use it later when he came back from the hospital. It was important he keep his blood cells oxygenated for tomorrow's game.

When Jeff saw April sleeping, he winked at Mark. Then they manly embraced in unconditional friendship. Mark thanked Jeff for running interference for him earlier.

The undeniable significance of Mark's marriage to April emotionally moved them to tears. Their future friendship would include many more shared moments like this. Jeff's own marriage, the births of their children, their medical careers, the joys and heartaches in their lives were just beginning for these two men who embraced supportively.

After tonight, Mark's life would travel in a new direction, but it would always include his best friend in more ways than Jeff could have ever imagined.

Jeff empathetically thought back to his promise to take care of Mark's family should anything happen to him. *Is Mark thinking the same thoughts?* Jeff wondered with sadness, as he felt Mark's embrace strengthened just before they parted from each other.

Jeff's compassionate eyes fell on April, and his tender heart gave thanks God had given Mark the woman that would love him forever.

Please, God, give them forever, heal Mark and make him whole, Jeff silently prayed as he watched Mark attentively place his pillow gently against April's back.

The touching sight of Mark attending to this simple act of tucking April safely against his pillow inspired Jeff with a deeper understanding of just how much Mark loved this woman. It was a love like he had never witnessed before. But then, it was a love that was meant to last them a lifetime.

If only ... if only Mark had a lifetime. No, I can't think like that ... stop it ... I've got to think positive ... Oh, God, help me believe there will be forever for this couple...

The last thing Mark wanted to do was leave April behind. He would have given anything to stay in her arms. *I have to do what I have to do; the choice is not mine.* He had to surrender to aplastic anemia on his wedding night.

Mark turned and mournfully faced Jeff. Their eyes shared a deep understanding of their unspoken words to each other. Jeff knew what Mark wanted. He wanted him to take care of his wife, not just for tonight but forever. Jeff fought back new tears as he nodded his head in agreement to Mark's unselfish request.

The reminder of how things really were for Mark would come all too quickly. In a few minutes, Mark would go to the hospital to have his stem cells removed.

He asked Jeff to sleep in the living room in case April woke up and found him gone. He had not told her about the treatments, as he did not want that to overshadow their night together. April never would have allowed him to go to the hospital without her if he had told her.

Jeff left the bedroom. Mark stood over April watching her sleep so peacefully. He moved his other pillow up against her back. This was probably the first peaceful sleep she has had in days. *God, let her sleep until I get back.*

His affection for her was overwhelming. He knelt beside the bed, gently picked up her hand, and kissed it. Then he prayed as he held her hand to his heart. He emotionally thanked God for her.

"I love you, April Sanders," he whispered. Then he quickly dressed and left behind his bride.

Thomas was waiting in the library for Mark. He would take him to the hospital. It was after midnight. Mark thanked him kindly for waiting on him.

During the quiet ride to the hospital, Mark was deep in thought about everything that had happened that day. God had blessed him with a fabulous woman and he had married her.

Sunny had been safely returned to him. She was no longer just another child but his very own child. It was no accident he found Sunny that day in the park. God sent her to save him. Mark received twice the blessings, just as the Bible promised God would give him. God fulfilled his deepest dreams of having his very own family.

Tears formed in his eyes as his heart felt overwhelmed with the love he was feeling for April and Sunny. He promised God he would love these two women for the rest of his life in a way that would honor Him.

That was one promise he vowed never to break, but would tomorrow shatter that promise?

Chapter Six

Memorable Moments

D an and Dr. Stevenson met Mark at the emergency room entrance and both joined him in a warm hug. They were thankful Mark seemed to be in good health and he was not mad at them for giving him their unsolicited advice at his wedding reception.

Just like Mark, he had not even given what they had done to him a second thought. Mark was quick with his temper, but he was just as quick to forgive. It was not in Mark's nature to hold a grudge, no matter what someone had done to him.

If only they could wipe the grin off Mark's face, maybe they could get him to be more serious about his treatments before the game started in less than fourteen hours.

Mark would spend the next three hours in the hospital. He hated the thought of being away from April. He knew they needed to get his stem cells from his bloodstream tonight, so when the chemo destroyed any remaining stem cells, he could replace them with his own.

Mark would have to survive chemo to get his transplant from Sunny. If they could harvest enough of his own stem cells, those cells could possibly help him survive chemo. The key to their success depended on retrieving enough of them from this procedure tonight. However, both men knew it was a long shot and were counting on another miracle for Mark.

Dr. Stevenson was relieved Mark's body had settled down from the reactions to the medications they had given him earlier. Mark had a slight fever, but no more stomach cramps, hives, or a painful headache. This is how most AA patients respond to their medications. Why did Mark go from one extreme to the other?

Dr. Stevenson listened to Mark's heart and lungs and was surprised they were normal. Mark continued to grin, making it hard for Tom to keep a straight face. "Ok, Mark, you win this time, but just take it easy when you get back to the penthouse."

"Sure, whatever you say," Mark mischievously smirked. Tom was not buying into Mark's answer. He playfully punched Mark in the shoulder and laughed. Tom prayed Mark would keep his sense of humor throughout the rest of his illness; he would need it.

Then Tom hooked Mark up to the machine and prayed they could retrieve enough stem cells. They would give him additional blood and oxygen while he was there. All that was left to do now was pray, and Tom and Dan planned to do a lot of praying before the game.

Mark wanted the lights turned down so he could sleep during the procedure. He turned over on his side and fell asleep quickly. Dan pulled the blanket up over him, touched his arm, and prayed over him.

"God, please protect Mark from all harm tonight." Then Dan and Tom left the room to get a cup of coffee and begin their prayer session. It was going to be a long night.

Marty tiptoed into the room, snatched Mark's water jug, and took it into the bathroom. Once again, he slipped something powdery into the container before filling it with fresh water. Then he placed it on Mark's table next to his bed.

Lewis had called Marty earlier and told him the police had picked up Sunny; their plan had *temporarily* failed. Lewis reported that his girl-friend, who was also Marty's sister and *a nurse* on Mark's floor, had told him Mark was scheduled to be back at the hospital later that night. They had one last calculating chance to stop Mark from playing in the game.

Marty was just about to reach up to Mark's IV, when Christy came in the room and was surprised to see him there.

"What are you doing in here?" Christy questioned Marty with a demanding yet hushed voice.

"Uh … I just finished cleaning the bathroom. I was just leaving."

"Why are you in here so late?"

"We were short-handed today … uh … the flu. I am running behind."

"Tell your supervisor the nursing staff will keep this room clean from now on."

"I will." He nervously backed out of the room under Christy's watchful eyes. There was something about Marty that made her feel uneasy. Christy turned and looked around the room. Everything seemed in order. She checked Mark's IV drip and the machine. Then she saw the water jug sitting on the table.

Dr. Stevenson must have filled it for Mark, she thought as she moved it closer to Mark so he could reach it. She checked Mark's pulse and once she was satisfied that he was fine, she left the room.

Downstairs in the cafeteria, Dan and Tom continued to cover Mark in protective prayer.

Three hours later Mark slid under the warm sheets and placed his arm under April's head. April stirred; she sleepily looked into his warm eyes and smiled. Realizing she was not dreaming, she kissed him tenderly. "It's true, Mark, we really are married. I wasn't dreaming."

"Yes, we are married. It's too late to change your mind now."

"I really am, April Sanders, and I intend to stay that way."

"You say that now but wait til' you have to live with me."

"Stop it, Mark, you are spoiling the moment."

"I'll show you who isn't spoiling the moment."

He brushed his lips against hers and passionately kissed her as he gathered her into his ambitious arms. They would not be going back to sleep any time soon.

The treatments went well. Mark was feeling great, maybe too great. He laughed as April teased him with her warm inviting hands. *Hmmmmmm, what did Dr. Stevenson tell me.* Mark grinned as he conveniently forgot and was thankful he had just received three hours of oxygen and pain medication.

At eight a.m., there was a soft rap on the door. Martha came in with a tray of breakfast foods and served the couple in bed.

"Martha, would you mind getting our bath ready? She smiled and gave Mark a playful wink before leaving the couple to enjoy their meal.

Martha went into the bathroom, closing the door behind her. She grinned and giggled to herself. Mark and April's clothes were still lying all over the floor in the bedroom.

"My little Master Mark is all grown up, and I'm going to miss him," she whispered to herself. *He belongs to April now; she will take care of him.* She wiped away a tear. *Mark will be a wonderful husband to April.* "Thank you, almighty Jesus."

She took a bottle of bubble bath from her pocket that she had gotten from Julia and Robert's bathroom and generously filled the tub.

April deserves to be pampered before she has to face the rest of this day with her new husband. When Martha finished in the bathroom, she went back out and closed the door to Mark's bedroom. *I will pick up the clothes later*, she thought with a bighearted smile.

Mark handed April her bathrobe. He put his on, came around to her side of the bed, and reached out his hand to help her stand up. He led her into the bathroom.

Rose petals covered the counters. The garden tub was filled with rose-colored bubbles. Surrounding the tub were shimmering candles, making it so romantic. She turned to face her husbands glowing face. "Oh, Mark, you did all of this for me?"

"Just for you. I plan to spoil you for the rest of your life." He slid her bathrobe off her shoulders; it dropped to the floor. She fell into the warmth of his bathrobe. He pulled it around her so they shared the same one.

"I love you so much, Mark." She caressed his chest. He felt feverish. Alarmed, she stepped back and questioned him. "Mark, you have a fever."

"The only fever I have is for you." He alleged with one of his crafty smiles, and to prove his point his hand slid up her neck and around to the back of her head to bring her closer to him for an engaging kiss.

When she pulled the bathrobe down off his shoulders, she saw his catheter covered in heavy gauze pads. She knew he had lied to her and gone for his treatments during the night. She knew he had a fever from his reaction to the drugs they had given him. The pads would protect the catheter in today's game.

She smiled up at him as if he was an overgrown child but decided not to expose his secret. He seemed healthier and stronger than when they had first started dating. Whatever the doctors did to him last night worked. He was glowing with happiness.

She would cherish everything he did to make her laugh, and they would enjoy every opportunity to have fun in their relationship. After all, that is what Mark wanted to be remembered for, bringing cheer and joy to all those around him.

He took her hand and helped her into the tub. He would have slid in under her, but he knew he could not get the catheter wet without causing an infection. He took a plastic covering and placed it over the bandages.

Then he slid onto the step so he was not submerged in the water above his navel. She moved over to him and teased him by blowing bubbles off her hands at him. He laughed and claimed her wet arms as he gathered her into his arms as they fell into the suds.

They enjoyed their splendid time in the tub as Mark washed her back and hair with the bubbles. Their magical moments continued, as they got lost in the tenderness of their love for each other, laughing, having fun, and making a memory on this spectacular morning.

When it was time for them to get out of the tub, Mark took one last deep refreshing breath as he held April close to him. She smelled so wonderfully sweet of the rose petal fragranced bubbles.

However, his enjoyment of her aroma was short-lived as a disturbing thought came to mind, and his eyes widened. *If she smells like a rose bush, what do I smell like? Oh no, no way!*

"April!" he panicked, "I've got to take a shower! There is no way that I am going to the locker room smelling like a flower garden! Do you know the kind of torment the guys would do to me?"

April burst out laughing, as Mark jumped out of the tub, covered in bubbles. They dripped down his legs all over the floor as he offered her his hand to help her out.

"Come on, hurry up and stop laughing. This is not funny. Help me get this ridiculous smell off of me!" She tried to keep a straight face but he was such a sight. She laughed so hard she had tears in her eyes.

"Do you want me to call Martha and have her bring you some tomatoes?" She laughed, thinking about the time he and a skunk had a run-in when he was seven.

"Oh, you think you are so funny," he grinned remembering the same memory. "A lot of help you were."

They got into the shower to wash off the scented bubbles. April gently washed Mark's body with a sponge filled with his manly smelling soap. They would need to buy some his-and-her towels and his-and-her soaps.

Her amusing thoughts ended abruptly as soon as her hands touched him. She realized the significance of just being there with him, as his wife, feeling his body against hers, and suddenly her heartfelt thoughts of him took her to a quiet place as she thought about their future relationship as husband and wife.

He is mine; he is my husband. Feeling his strong shoulders against her hands made her believe he was indestructible. *No sickness will take him from me. I will never allow that to happen.*

She closed her eyes tight, not wanting to allow the reality she had been blocking out to seep back into her mind. *I will care for him. No one will ever touch his body but me. I will nurse him back to health when he is sick.*

She had not thought about what the rest of this day would bring them. At this moment, nothing mattered. He was blooming with love and she belonged to him. His magnificent body against hers, warm and wet, was all she wanted. She never wanted to let him go. She laced their fingers together and leaned against him to accept whatever he had to offer her.

But she soon realized what did lie ahead for them. When they stepped out of the shower, she realized their magical time together was about to end. Suddenly her heart was throbbing and she became increasingly scared for him. She wanted him to stay right there with her, away from all that could harm him. *Oh, Mark, I can't let you leave me today.*

She trembled as she watched him standing there wrapped only in his towel, shaving. *Just one nick and he could start bleeding.* She watched him be ever so gentle with the razor, careful not to cut himself, knowing that he should be using an electric razor.

"Let me do that." She took the razor from his hand and took over for him. Noting her nervousness he gently took her hand in his and together they glided the razor until his face was smooth. She took a damp towel and gently wiped the shaving cream off his face.

Everything they did from this point on would lead them closer to the time she might have to let him go, she thought with such heartache.

Was he thinking about the football game? Did he know his love for football could take away all they could share together in life? Would his commitment to his team take him away from her?

Mark did not show any fear as he slapped on his after-shave lotion. He seemed so at peace and happy. He acted as if this was going to be the second best day of his life. She did not share in his excitement as she gathered him in her arms.

She kissed his tender face and smelled his after-shave. "I love the way you smell." She touched his face, felt his smooth skin, and claimed his lips for a kiss he was not likely to forget.

"You smell pretty good, too." He gathered her closer in his arms and held her.

She felt his heart beating strong as she laid her head on his bare chest. She kept repeating: *no sickness will ever take his heart from me. His heart belongs only to me.*

"Debbie packed a bag with clothes for you to wear at the game. You will need to change clothes at the church after the church service. We will not have a chance to come back here before the game. I have to go to the team luncheon right after church. Dan will take you to the restaurant where everyone is meeting before they go to the stadium."

He gathered some of his things off the counter and put them in his travel bag. "After we win the game, I will have to give an interview with the reporters. I want you to come back here and wait for me. Dan will drive you. Then we'll go out to the ranch and get Sunny."

She nodded her head slowly. He had everything planned out. There was no doubt in his mind that everything would go according to his plans.

As they went into the bedroom, she looked at the bed where they had shared their tender most love for each other. She wanted to pull him to her and fall back into the safety of the covers.

How could she tell him how she was really feeling? Would he give up the game for her? Could she ask him to make her his only love? Would that be selfish of her?

He seemed content as he started to dress. He continued to show no fear as his hands steadily buttoned the front of his dress shirt. He was having no regrets. He was the one who believed he could have it all. He was the one who was strong, when all of them were weak.

How could she tell him her feelings? Not now, she would let him have his faith; she would bring him no reservations. She would somehow find it in her heart to join him in his faith and believe she would never have to let him go.

She went to him, held him close in her arms once again, and whispered her words of love to him. "Mark … I love you so much."

He lifted her head up and bent his face down to meet hers and then she kissed his smooth face. He answered her with an all-consuming kiss. She felt his heartbeat against hers, their hearts beating as one. She closed her eyes to keep the tears from falling and then she let him go.

He was in God's hands.

Chapter Seven

Through the Eyes of Love

⚜

They dressed for church. Mark looked dashing in his dark blue suit. It made his blue eyes shine like the heavens above. April was dressed in a beautiful white satin dress with tiny straps that held it up on her shoulders. It hugged tightly around her waist showing off her perfect figure and her slender legs.

Debbie had excellent taste in choosing clothes for April, although this time the dress she chose seemed rather formal to be wearing to Mark's church. For a brief moment, April pondered that thought. No wonder Debbie sent her clothes to change into after church; she certainly could not wear this formal dress to the football game.

Mark was standing in front of the mirror adjusting his tie as she came up behind him. He saw her magnificent reflection in the mirror. He turned around to face her. They looked at each other with mischief.

"April, you look … so beautiful. You take my breath away."

"Well, Mr. Sanders, maybe I can help you with that problem."

April took his tie in her hand and pulled him to the edge of the bed. He pushed her over onto the bed with him. He caressed her face with his hands and kissed her. She consumed him with her enchanting eyes. If only there was more time; he would take her back to eternity, he thought as he looked at his watch.

He was not going to let his life pass him by today. He was going to find a place in this moment that she would remember. She gave him a reason to breathe; she made him feel whole. She could have him and satisfy her hunger to love him for a time without end.

After they left this room, it would be eight to ten weeks before their bodies were joined as one again. Mark was not in favor of that thought as she nestled next to him and teased him unmercifully. He was not willing to give her up just yet, and she was now more determined than ever she was never going to let him go, at least not for the next few minutes, as she slipped the tie from around his neck and deliberately tossed it onto the floor.

They rode to the church in the limo. They were running very late. Thomas checked his watch and peeked in the rear view mirror. He blushed when he saw Mark and April kissing as they cuddled together. They clearly were unaware of their surroundings.

Jeff was looking out the limo window trying to pretend he had not noticed that Mark and April were engaged in loving each other in the seat across from him.

Deep down Jeff gave thanks Mark had found someone like April who would love him through his illness. She would be his reason to win the battle he was facing. God sent his best friend an angel from heaven.

Jeff would never forget the promise he made to Mark on that awful day in the hospital when Mark had laid on the bathroom floor thinking he might die. Mark had asked Jeff to promise him he would take care of April if he died.

Mark had loved her first, but he would unselfishly give her away to his best friend, Jeff, should he die. Jeff looked at them and held his heart intact. He already loved her. He would keep his promise to Mark.

Martha was sitting up front with Thomas. She felt the atmosphere of love in the limo, reached over, grabbed Thomas' hand, and winked at him. Thomas stole another glance back at Mark and April and then he smiled at Martha. Mark had a way of bringing out fresh love in everyone.

Julia and Robert invited all of Mark's teammates, coaches, hospital staff, friends, and family to their church for the special church service they planned. Their pastor would call Mark to the front of the church at the end of the service, and everyone would lay hands on him.

They would ask God to protect him during the game. They would ask for the healing of his body. Then they would turn him over to the Lord to do His will in Mark's life. They would celebrate Mark's life with him here in his church, with all those who loved him.

There would be no memorial service tomorrow. That is how Mark wanted it if he did not survive today. If God called him home, he wanted everyone to be rejoicing, not grieving. He would be dancing for the Lord.

He had told them that only because he felt it needed to be said, not because he believed tomorrow would never come for him.

The guests arrived early to surprise him. Robert and Dan waited outside for the limo so they could protect Mark from all the reporters and paparazzi that had gathered to capture a picture of Mark before the game. The police showed up and escorted the paparazzi away from the main entrance to the church.

When the limo pulled up, cameras flashed wildly around them as the couple got out of the limo. Dan and Robert shielded the couple, as they quickly walked up the steps to the entrance.

Sunny came out from behind the pillars and jumped out at them. Mark grabbed her up into his arms and kissed her. April bent to get her kiss. Julia leaned over and claimed her kiss from her son.

They went inside and stood in the lobby with Miss Carolyn the greeter. Carolyn was in her late sixties but she was adventurous and was definitely young spirited at heart. Mark admired her energetic positive outlook on life, and her Christian walk was undeniably genuine.

Mark gave Carolyn his usual peck on her cheek and teased her about having to find a new boyfriend since he just gotten married. Carolyn appeared heartbroken and Mark slyly grinned at her. He reached in his jacket pocket, pulled out three VIP passes for the football game, and gave them to his biggest fan.

Carolyn reached up in delight, pinched his cheek, and stole a kiss from him. Mark accepted the kiss and charmingly returned it with a warm hug. Then Carolyn hurried to tell her sister, Bette, and her husband, Clyde, they had tickets to the game.

Mark put Sunny down and took her hand in his. Sunny looked up at Mark with eyes filled with excitement. She could hardly contain herself as she knew the secret that was about to unfold in the church sanctuary. Mark thought she had ants in her pants from the way she was fidgeting and pulling on his hand to enter the sanctuary.

Together the family walked into the sanctuary. Everyone stood up and faced the couple standing there in awe at the scene before them.

Mark's face lit up. He pointed his arm straight out at the football players and pointed with his finger, just as he did in the football games when he was about to take the snap from the center.

The wedding march melody began playing as Sunny led them up to the front of the church. The end chairs were decorated in white bows and flowers, with a sparkling hurricane candle in the center. The flower arrangements from last night's ceremony filled the church along with several decorated candelabras graced with glowing candles.

April and Mark looked at each other as they walked up to the front, each shook their head no. So who had done this magnificent arrangement for them?

Mark's pastor asked them to come forward and stand before him. "Your families wanted you to have a church wedding," he told them as his heart reached out to the young couple. His prayers for them had been answered, and he had taken great pride in performing the ceremony last night and again today.

Mark and April looked into each other's eyes, then turned around, and smiled at each of their families. Debbie stepped forward beside April and Robert took his place beside Mark.

April saw her mother, Tammy, sitting next to Debbie's family and her heart dropped. Her brother, Todd, was also there sitting beside her grandparents. Tears formed in her eyes as she thought of the missing figure who should have been sitting beside her mother. She placed her hands up to her face to hold back her tears as sadness flooded her heart.

Mark took April in his comforting arms and tenderly rubbed her back with his hand, trying to bring her comfort. He knew April was thinking about her father. He wondered when it would finally cause April distress that her father had not given them his blessings. He searched her moist eyes and prayed she would find the strength in their love to continue with the wedding.

Mark had assigned Dan the job of telling Paul about the wedding. Mark prayed Paul would search deep within his heart and realize that he loved his daughter enough to put his unforgiving feelings towards him aside and give them his blessings in this significant time in April's life.

Dan tried to reason with his hardhearted brother; however, it was impossible to smother the fire and outrageous hatred Paul had for Mark. Fearful Paul would execute a revengeful attack against Mark; Dan was determined more than ever to keep Paul away from the weddings.

Dan had an uneasy feeling that Paul would have the last word in all of this and whatever that attack was it would not be good. Dan joined forces with Robert to plan a safety net for Mark should he need it.

Then a promising thought came to Dan's mind. All Paul had to do was get to know his new son-in-law. Anyone who spent time with Mark instantly liked the honorable man that he was.

Maybe, just maybe, Mark would be the one to lead Paul to God. That was certainly something to start praying about, and at that very moment, Dan hit his knees with both hands joined and prayed God would open up Paul's heart by using Mark as His messenger. He prayed that in the mean time, Paul would not do something stupid to harm Mark.

April clung to Mark with both her hands on the lapel to his sports jacket. She lifted her face to his concerned face and spoke softly.

"Everyone I love is here, Mark. Will you marry me?" she asked through her tears. Mark's face brightened; his heart leaped for joy as he forgot they were standing in the front of the church. He promptly claimed her soft lips to his to remind her how much he treasured her.

"Uh, Mark, we haven't got to the part where you kiss the bride yet." His pastor laughed and everyone clapped in recognition of the love the couple had for each other.

Mark gave April one more reassuring kiss and then he humbled himself before his pastor to receive April as his precious wife for a second time.

Chapter Eight

Saying Goodbye to their Hero

⧸⧹

The wedding began, and the guests were soon tearful as the romantic couple exchanged their words of love. They lit a single candle to show they were united as one. They knelt as their pastor placed his hands upon their heads and blessed them. He pronounced them as husband and wife and they sealed it with an affectionate kiss. Mark had married the woman of his dreams twice; he felt blessed beyond words.

Everyone clapped and cheered as they stood up to honor them. Mark thanked them with a wave of his hand. Then he and April took their seats in the first row beside Sunny and Mark's parents.

April rejoiced; her dream of marrying Mark in the same church in which they had given their hearts to Jesus as teenagers had been fulfilled.

Mark's face was glowing with happiness. Other than yesterday, he had never felt this great in his entire life. April had taken his breath away and he was speechless as he cuddled her next to him. He quietly rededicated his life to God in a prayer of thanksgiving for all the miracles he had received.

His pastor preached on God's grace and mercy. Then Pastor Evan and the praise team sang. Mark requested praise music to uplift and witness to those there. Mark came forward, took the microphone, and sang a solo with a heart filled with the Holy Spirit. Soon everyone was standing and singing praises to the Lord along with him.

Mark rejoined April and Sunny when he finished singing. He felt so in tune with God. His joy was overflowing as he lifted his arms up high in agreement to the words that his pastor dedicated to him.

Mark felt on top of the world, with Sunny and April beside him worshipping God. His heart was spilling over with excitement. This was living life to the fullest. He could have stayed there all day praising God with the songs that were pouring from his heart.

One at a time, God continued to fulfill all his dreams. What was next? Mark knew the precise answer as soon as he asked himself that question. He was more than ready to carry out the next degree of his accomplishments with God. It was a vision he had dreamed of since he was ten years old. As an NFL quarterback, he would take his team all the way to the Super Bowl and "God willing" they would win it.

After a few more songs, Mark's sister, Rebecca, came forward and took the microphone. Rebecca looked fondly at Mark and said, "This one is for you, little brother."

Everyone sat down as Rebecca emotionally sang, "Wind Beneath My Wings" to her little brother. She sang with such heartbreaking emotions as she remembered the times they had spent growing up and knowing Mark's time with her could end today.

Julia was soon crying on Robert's shoulder as the song touched her heart deeply. Mark could hear his mother's sadness. He took a slow deep breath, unable to look in her direction, knowing he could not emotionally handle her tears for him.

Mark began to feel uneasy as he watched his sister tearfully sing. He loosened his tie and squirmed in his seat as Rebecca's emotions strangled him. April wrapped her arm around his and tried to offer him comfort, as she understood what was happening. It hurt her heart deeply for Mark that his joy of worshipping was gone.

Dan had flashbacks of the times he spent with Mark as a child. He remembered the time he laid on the bed with Mark after Mark's grandfather died. Mark had only been a small child. Now he was a young man fighting for his life. That thought was inconceivable.

Dan thought of the secret he and Julia had kept for twenty-five years. Would it have mattered if he had told Mark the truth?

Just weeks ago Dan's heart had been crushed when he was reminded of the past. He glanced over at Julia and wished he could take away her pain, just as he had done when Robert had not been a husband to her or a father to Mark and Rebecca.

It was Mark that brought his father to his knees when all of them had failed to bring Robert out of his destruction.

Dan glanced at Mark. He was so proud of the man that Mark had become. Mark had walked in his career path. Dan was thankful he had been able to be a mentor to Mark all these years.

Yet burning deep down within his soul there was still something left he needed to say to Mark. Dan bowed his head and began praying God would show him what he needed to do.

Mark's grandmother, Ella Sanders, was thinking about all the times Mark spent with his beloved grandfather. She remembered Mark's outburst at his grandfather's funeral; he bluntly told everyone to go home. She wiped the sad tears from her eyes with a handkerchief Mark gave her when he was six.

He had told her, "Grandma, use this handkerchief to wipe away your happy tears, 'cause God wants us to be happy." She had kept the handkerchief all these years to remind herself of that.

"Only happy tears are allowed, Grandma." Her tears fell softly as her broken heart spoke to Mark. *I am sorry, Mark; today I have sad tears.* She dabbed at her tears for the grandson she loved dearly.

Mark wanted no funeral should he die. *How can he ask that of us? Mark, you are too young to be suffering or dying. Happy tears, Grandma,* she reminded herself again.

Would Mark and his Grandfather meet again soon? Would tonight Mark fly home to be with the God he loved so much? Ella wondered tearfully, clinging to the handkerchief tightly.

Next to Ella, Julia's parents, Everett and Victoria Tate, held hands and bowed their heads in quiet prayer. They were begging God to spare their grandson's life. Victoria remembered Mark's first step when he fell and got up without shedding a single tear. *God, please hold him up when he cannot take his own steps today,* Victoria prayed. Everett thought about how proud they had all been when Mark graduated from medical school.

Pedro and Maria were thinking of all the times Mark had gotten into mischief as a youngster. Pedro remembered the time Mark had fallen into the mineshaft. They tried to protect him from harm, but Mark's adventure for life had proven to be more than any of them could handle. They never dreamed an illness like aplastic anemia would claim him away from them.

Thomas and Martha thought about the many times they caught Mark with his homeless pets in his bedroom. Mark filled the house with joy; even when he had a mischievous spirit, he brought them laughter.

Master Mark, the loving child, always trying to save and protect things. *Please, God, save him from all harm today,* Thomas prayed.

Charlie was thinking about the many times he watched Mark sit on top of Thunder and ride across the pastures with his hair flying wildly in the wind. Mark had to have his freedom. *Take away his broken wings. Give him new wings, God, or let him fly home to You in peace.*

The little boy who was loved by so many people was a gentle, meek, kindhearted man. They were all so proud of whom he had become. Rebecca looked at her brother. She loved him the very first day he came home from the hospital as a baby. He was her real live baby doll. He was such a good brother. He was a gifted, compassionate doctor. He was now a father and husband. He was her hero. There was no way she could go on living without him, she thought as the tears flowed and her voice became shaky.

Mark has so much to live for. Let him have no more pain. Let him have the glory today. Let him be our hero. Let him come home to us tonight, Lord, Rebecca prayed as she continued singing. Mark saw the tears falling softly down the sides of his sister's cheeks as she looked sadly at him. He stood up and went to her side to offer her comfort.

He looked out and saw all the long tearful faces. His heart hurt and his eyes sunk in misery. This was not what he wanted. He did not want tears; he wanted joy! He took a hold of her hand as she sang. He was suffocating in their grief. When she began struggling with the words, he took the microphone from her and sang the third verse as she wiped the tears from her face. "You're everything I wish I could be."

However, Mark soon found himself absorbed in the tears of his family, and as his voice faded, she rejoined him and together they drew strength from each other and sang as they focused only on their eyes. There was nothing the two of them could not do when they joined hearts.

Julia and Robert thought they were seeing their children together for the last time; they both were softly crying. Robert thanked God that he had been saved in time to love his son. God had given him the extra years to make things right with Mark. *I am not done being his dad*, Robert thought with regret, wishing they still had more time.

Mark mistakenly looked back out at his family again. It was worse than before as they were all crying. He wanted them to stop all of this gloominess. How could they give up on him, he thought with heartache as they tore his heart in two. He held in his emotions as he swallowed the lump in his throat, yet he was unable to continue singing the end of the song. His last words would not come.

A sudden movement in the unused balcony at the very back of the sanctuary caught his full attention. He saw the unwelcome figure standing there alone.

Although the lighting from the front of the church only dimly lit the balcony, they were still able to make harsh eye contact. Instant fear

70

crossed Mark's face as he saw the hateful man reaching for something. The thought of what was about to happen when Mark saw an object in the man's hands sent his heart racing out of control.

Rebecca had just finished the song. She was unaware of Mark's attention on the balcony as she strongly embraced him in a hug. Fearing for her, Mark tried to push her away from him. Just as they parted from each other's arms, Mark's chest jerked, forcefully pushing him backwards. Rebecca grabbed his jacket in fear that he was falling. "Mark!" she screamed in horror.

Suddenly Mark thought his heart was going to bust from the sharp stabbing pain he abruptly felt.

"Oh God!" His hands folded across each other as he held his chest and curled up as he tried to remain standing. His pained face turned white and sweat formed on his forehead.

Dan quickly jumped up and yelled at Jeff to get the emergency bags. *Fear pierced Dan's heart as he watched his son grasping for one more breath of life.*

"Oh, God, please, no ... let my son live!"

Chapter Nine

Unthinkable

ৡৡ

Mark slowly slid from Rebecca's arms and sat down on the step holding his chest tightly. April rushed to him and swiftly removed his tie to make it easier for him to breathe.

Dan was quickly at his side. Mark wanted to tell him whom he had seen, but with April there he could not say anything without upsetting her. He glanced up at the balcony and was relieved when he saw no one. Mark held his trembling hands out in front of him. No blood stained them; he had not been shot.

Mark closed his eyes in thankful prayer, knowing God had intervened with His protection on his life. He opened his eyes slowly and took a slow, painful breath of air as he tried to gather his alarming thoughts about what had almost happened. He was still in a state of shock, unbelieving, confused, wounded, and beaten down.

He looked into April's concerned eyes as she removed his jacket, and he knew he could never reveal the secret he now shared with a man so filled with hatred for him that he would risk everything to kill him. What had driven the man to that point?

Mark's soul filled with mercy for the man. A forgiving spirit came over him. Tears filled Mark's overcast eyes as he felt pity for the man who was so desperately lost that he was driven to do what he had done. *God, please intercede in this man's life, help him find peace where hatred has imprisoned him.*

Mark looked at April; his heart broke for her. How would she ever recover if she knew the truth? Mark vowed he would protect her at all cost.

Jeff ran in with his emergency bag. All the doctors were up front trying to assist. There was no need to call for medical help; all the doctors were there.

Mark assured them that he had just gotten too hot. He tried to convince himself he was suffering from a severe panic attack. The song Rebecca sang, the tears of everyone, the emotions, and the unwanted figure in the balcony threatening his life, all had contributed to the attack.

Then a chilling thought crossed Mark's mind. God sent him the chest pain to protect him from the bullet.

If I had not fallen on my own, then ... no, no, oh, God, please tell me that he never would have pulled the trigger. Tell me he only wanted to scare me. Tell me he only wanted me to know that his daughter still belonged to him. Please, God, tell me there was no gun at all and that it was all my imagination.

What could have driven Paul to do what he had done? There had to be more than the fact that he had gotten April pregnant.

It took a very desperate man to act out his revenge in a church where his daughter was ... Mark grabbed his chest again, alarming all those around him. However, this time he knew why he felt pain. His breathing labored as his thoughts continued.

I should have told Paul I was sorry. I should have understood how he felt and asked him to forgive me for what I did to his daughter. Does Paul still think I raped her? What was going through his mind? Mark placed the blame of what had happened on his shoulders.

If Lewis had harmed Sunny, I would have killed him. Paul was just trying to protect his daughter; how can I blame him? Mark could not blame him; he had to forgive him.

Tears threatened the corners of his eyes as his heart ached for the woman he loved, knowing what this would do to her if she ever found out what her father had planned to do to him on her wedding day.

"Oh, God!" Mark could not catch his breath as his eyes widened.

"Mark, look at me!" Jeff spoke, fearful of the distant look on Mark's face. Mark slowly shifted his gaze to Jeff and caught his breath. Jeff placed an oxygen mask on Mark's face. When he did not refuse it, Jeff knew Mark's condition was worse than he was letting on.

Had all the excitement of last night hurt his heart, Jeff wondered and regretted the jokes he made at the wedding reception.

Pastor Evan placed his hands over Mark's head and prayed. The men of the church surrounded him and laid hands on him. Members of the church reached their hands out to him and prayed. The chattering prayers continued and Mark accepted the prayers offered into his heart.

He said his own prayers for April and her father. His next plan was to go to Paul and ask him to forgive him. He would make things right between them.

Mark was very quiet and pale; he seemed lost in his thoughts. April worried, as time seemed to stand still while Mark took in the oxygen with slow deep breaths.

Mark kindly waved everyone away from him, as he continued to assure everyone he was fine. He wanted them to stop fussing over him, but no one moved away.

The craziness had to stop; he had to get control of this situation before it got out of hand. There was nothing more he could do about Paul. But there was something he could do to turn this day around.

Mark looked at his watch, removed the mask and firmly told his teammates it was time to head to the stadium. "You guys are going to be late for the luncheon. I will come in a few minutes."

"Are you sure, Mark," Carlo wanted to know.

"I promise, just give me a minute to catch my breath. Go on, get out of here." He placed the mask back on his face.

Reluctantly, the team left the inside of the church and boarded the team buses for the team luncheon. Mark's seat on the bus remained empty, as empty as the players felt in their hearts for Mark. Not a word was spoken as the buses pulled away from the church without Mark.

Mark moved to the front row and sat beside Sunny. She climbed in his lap and claimed his neck with her arms. He remained on oxygen but he took it off to kiss her and let her know he was fine.

She looked sad as he wrapped his arms around her. She did not want to take her arms away from his neck. All deals were off. She changed her mind, she wanted to stay with Mark and not go home with Maria and Pedro! She grabbed the tip of Mark's earlobe and rubbed it between her tiny fingers.

Mark took a slow deep breath, grabbing at his heart again as he felt another sharp pain. Sunny was breaking his heart with her pitiful grip on him. April realized Sunny was making Mark uncomfortable and leaned forward to take her from him. She untangled Sunny's arms from around Mark's neck. She placed Sunny on her lap and spoke tender words to bring her comfort.

Mark's parents came and knelt in front of him and told him they would see him at the game. Mark gave them each a hug and thanked them for the surprise wedding.

"Mark, I want you to know how proud I am of you. A man could not have asked for a better son than you have been. I will be cheering for you. Throw a touchdown pass or two for your mom and me, okay, Son?"

"You got it, Dad, thanks." Their concerned look for him burned Mark's heart. He saw their pain, knowing he was the reason for it.

Sunny resisted when Robert took her from April and held her in his arms. "Mark, do I have to go?"

"I love you, Sunny. I will see you after the game. Be a good girl for Pedro and Maria today, ok, sweetheart."

"But I want to stay with you, pleeeease!" she begged, sending Mark emotionally over the edge, as he regretfully shook his head no.

"Sunny, Mark has to play in the football game today, remember? You will get to see him on TV, and then he will come and spend the night with us before he goes to the hospital." Robert reassured his granddaughter tenderly.

"No, I don't want to go. Please, Mark, can't I stay with you?" She did not understand why, but somewhere deep inside of her soul she was afraid she would never see Mark again. Her insecurities of her past reinforced her feelings.

"Mark, Sunny will be fine. We explained everything to her last night. She is just tired from all the excitement," Julia informed him.

Sunny reached out her hand for Mark. He reached up and touched the edges of her fingertips as his father stepped back, preventing their union. Robert knew if the two joined hands, Mark would never let her go. Sunny put up a fuss, and Mark could hear her crying for him as his parents took her out of the church. She wanted her Mark. It took everything he had not to run to her.

He took another deep breath as the day became even more complicated with emotions that threatened to take him down. *God, You have to give me strength.*

Rebecca's family came next and Mark hugged the boys. Rebecca touched his face with the palm of her hand, and in response to her, he reached up and touched her hand.

"I'm sorry, Mark. I sang that song to honor you as my hero. I never thought it would hurt you. I'm so sorry." She bent and kissed him; her tears dropped in his lap as she leaned over and hugged him.

"Rebecca, you are my hero. You made me into everything good that I am." His eyes watered as he looked into her distressed face. He took a deep breath to suck the tears back in and keep them from falling.

"Uncle Markie, if you make a homerun, I'll yell yippy so loud you can hear me all the way from the ranch," James Robert added as Mark tousled his hair and gave him a high five.

Six-year-old Brad gave him a hug. "Uncle Mark, I'll take care of Sunny for you ... you don't have to worry about her."

"You're my man, Brad. Take care of your mom, too ... she's my best friend, got that?"

"Got it. Oh, and bring me the winning football, so I can show it to all my friends."

"Sure thing, Buddy. I'll even sign my name on it."

Brad and James Robert clung to their father's legs as Steven stood over Mark.

"You and I have an appointment in the OR tomorrow morning. Don't be late; got that, Mark?"

Mark nodded his head in agreement at his brother-in-law, the surgeon. Surgery was the last thing on Mark's mind. He hated being reminded he had to surrender himself to the knife of Steven and Dan.

Thomas came next. "I put Miss April's bag in the ladies' room for her. I got what you wanted and put it in her bag. No need to worry, Sir, I will take good care of your parents for you."

"Thanks, Thomas, thanks for everything."

Martha, Charlie, Grandma Ella, Everett, Victoria, Maria, and Pedro each got a hug from him. There were no smiles, just concern for him as they spoke softly to him. They had all given into the gloom of the situation.

They walked down the aisle and outside. Everyone got into the limos that would take them away from the church. Sunny wrapped her arms around her new granddaddy and felt safe in his arms. If she could not have Mark, at least she had Mark's daddy and mommy.

"Granddaddy, did you ever play football?" Sunny looked up at Robert with her crystal blue eyes. He laughed as he looked over at Julia and took her hand as he thought back to their high school days when he was class president.

"No, Sunny, I was a bookworm. I wanted to be the President of the United States someday. Your daddy definitely got his athletics from his Uncle Dan." He leaned over and gave Julia a warm kiss.

"Your granddaddy was the best looking president of our school. He won my heart the minute I met him." She smiled affectionately at the man she had loved for over 35 years.

Robert's heart spilled over with love for Sunny. She would give him the chance to make things right with Mark. If only he could have been the kind of father to Mark, he knew he was going to be as a grandfather to Sunny.

Time is a precious thing – each minute can only be lived once.

Chapter Ten

The Wooden Cross

Just as Mark's family and friends pulled away from the church, the ambulance and paramedics arrived and quickly entered the church.

Hearing them arriving, Dan went to meet them in the foyer. Dan told them to wait until the rest of the group waiting to speak to Mark had left. Then Dan went back into the church and headed upfront where he could keep a close eye on Mark.

April's family came to her and offered her their love. They wished Mark luck in his game before they left. This was not the time to reunite with her mother. April's thoughts were only of Mark. Nothing could distract her attention away from him.

April had not notice that her brother, Todd, disappeared after Mark collapsed. Debbie reassured her everything was under control; she would take care of their parents. She freed April to concentrate on Mark.

They all told him goodbye while he was still alive. A tremendous ache overwhelmed him. Was the pain he was feeling from his heart failing him or from his tormented emotions? He had not wanted tears today. He had longed for rejoicing. He had prayed for them to believe in God's favor over his life. He wanted them to trust God and claim his healing. They had drained his energy and drive out of him to do what he was destined to do.

Mark's pastor came and spoke reassuring words to him. "I know your family is upset, Mark, and it may seem to you like they have lost faith in God, but you have to understand, they are only human. They love you so much their hearts are hurting for you. You must understand that a lot has happened to you in the last few days, and they have not had the healing time to sort out everything in their hearts." Mark shook his head in agreement.

"Pray for God's grace to work in their hearts. Continue to be an example of your faith to them, Mark. When they see you out on the golf course, goofing around next week with Kenny and me, they will believe you are going to be just fine." He patted Mark on the shoulder, and they laughed.

"I plan on it, Evan," Mark smiled with his usual keen grin as he spoke. "You better start praying I don't win all of your money, because you're going to need prayer if you plan to beat me at golf next week."

"You got it, Mark; now let's go win an AFC Championship Game, kid." They gave each other a high five.

"I will see you on the golf course Friday at nine a.m. sharp." Surgery on Monday, golf on Friday, that sounded like a good plan to him. Pastor Evan made Mark smile. At least Pastor Evan believed without a doubt Mark was already receiving his healing from all the prayers that were just lifted up for him.

The church was empty now except for the three doctors. Dan listened to Mark's heart while Dr. Stevenson took his blood pressure. Mark's eyes told them not to say anything with April in the room. She was anxiously attached to his other arm.

Dan whispered to Mark, "The paramedics are here to take you to the hospital." Mark objected with a shake of his head and spoke softly from deep within his soul.

"No, Dan, I have to finish what I started. I have obligations I have to keep. I'm fine. I am not going anywhere but to the stadium. Tell them to leave. Please, Dan, do this for me." The unwavering sad look on Mark's face told them he had to finish out his life the way it should have been. He would not surrender his belief he owed it to his teammates to play today.

Out of their respect for his unselfish decision, the three men were silent as they acknowledged they would support Mark's final decision, if he agreed to let them help him.

April bit her lip and bowed her head, avoiding the words that just wanted to cry out. *How can you even think about playing in the game? Mark, you have to go to the hospital. You are not going to the stadium!* She felt his hand squeeze her tense fingers, sending her a silent message. She turned to meet his tender eyes. He removed the oxygen mask and placed a kiss softly on her lips. Still her mind screamed out but no words left her lips.

The doctors exchanged information with each other. To their surprise, Mark's heart rate and blood pressure were almost normal. Jeff got into the medical bag on the floor. Dan left to speak to the paramedics.

They were extremely worried about Mark, but they each understood his conviction to continue his life the way it should have been. Besides, it had all been hammered out. Even with the transplant, there was no guarantee Mark would survive.

Tom remembered what Mark said while they were at the hospital. "We are just doctors; we do what we are trained to do. I want you to remember that God has the final say in my life, not us. I am living according to God's covenant with me."

The debate ended when Mark's discouraging lab reports arrived on Dr. Stevenson's desk that morning with the stem cell count results. Tom met with Dan and discussed the results. Both decided not to release the results today. Mark's family had enough to worry about, and there was no reason to put more stress on Mark. However, now there was every reason to let Mark play in the game today. He had nothing to lose.

Jeff motioned for Mark to follow him with the turning of his head, before he headed to the bathroom. Mark told April he was going to go splash his face with cool water. She gathered his tie and jacket and followed Mark to the door. He kissed her before he went into the bathroom.

Since Mark's catheter had already been prepared for the game, Jeff did not want to undo the gauze. Jeff unbuttoned and removed Mark's shirt. He listened to Mark's heart and lungs. Satisfied with what he heard, he gave Mark his medications in his left arm. "This should help get you through the game."

They embraced; each knowing it might be their last moment together. Jeff held back his reserved feelings. He promised himself he would be strong for Mark as he bit his lip in an effort to maintain his composure.

Jeff helped Mark put on his shirt. Nothing was said about what Mark should do about the game. Jeff's concerned face expressed all his unspoken words straight into Mark's torn heart. "I'll be outside if you need me." He left the room, unable to continue this emotional scene with the man he considered his little brother.

Mark splashed his face with water over the sink. He looked up to see his reflection in the mirror. *If only they could have faith that I am healed. I would not have had the panic attack if they had been rejoicing, instead of thinking they were at my funeral,* he thought sadly.

The door opened slowly and in walked a young man about twenty. Mark was not sure who he was. They stood facing each other. Mark felt the uneasiness of the man's demeanor as he built up the courage to speak to him.

"I'm Todd, April's brother. I told my dad about the wedding. I thought he should know. Paul really is not a bad person, Mark. He just loves April. She was all he had left and you just took her from him. Listen here, I found this up in the balcony where he was sitting. I guess it belongs to you and April now."

Todd handed Mark a six-inch wooden cross. Mark looked down at it and stared. His heart rate increased; his hands trembled, as he understood the significance of the cross.

"April made it for Dad in Vacation Bible School, when she was eight," Todd told him as he watched Mark's downhearted face stare at the object.

Mark already knew that. He had a cross just like the one he held in his hands. He had made it while sitting beside April in Vacation Bible School, just days before he fell into the mineshaft. That day had been the first time he had declared his love for her, there behind the church building where they met every Sunday after church.

Mark emotionally turned the cross over and read what April had written on it so long ago. "My heart belongs to you, Daddy, but is it ok if I love Mark, too?" Tears streamed down Mark's face as he looked up at Todd.

"Dad found it yesterday at our old house. That is where I met him last night while you were marrying my sister. Maybe he planned to give it to April today. I don't know. He was pretty upset yesterday, but he's gone now."

Mark held back the tears. "You found it in the balcony?" Todd nodded yes, and instantly Mark hit the floor on his knees in thankful prayer stronger than he had ever prayed before.

"Are you okay, Mark?"

Mark grasped the cross between his fingers and held it up to Todd. "Give it back to your dad, Todd. Tell him I said that he hasn't lost a daughter ... he's gained a son." Todd left the room.

Paul held the cross in the balcony, not a gun. Never had a burden been lifted off his shoulders as it had been at this very moment as God worked out yet another miracle with a simple wooden cross. It was a cross that once declared a little girl's heart for her daddy and for the boy she would someday marry.

Mark knew God placed the cross in Paul's path last night to bring him to his little girl's wedding today. Mark continued to receive the miracles God placed before him.

Mark knew he needed to do something to bring April out of her fears for him today. He rewashed his face with cold water, turned, and faced the door. He took a deep breath, placed a smile on his face and opened the door to deal with those waiting for him.

April was anxiously waiting for him next to Dan and Tom. Mark saw Todd leaving the church. April noticed Mark's attention on her brother and wondered what the two of them talked about in the bathroom.

Mark reassured April he was fine. He was smiling and talking with good spirits. She guessed the conversation had been a good one, but something told her Mark was only pretending he was feeling better.

Mark and Jeff did their comedy act together and were soon laughing, but April's face remained taut. There was nothing comical about this moment. She knew they were both faking their smiles. "April, it's time to change your clothes," Mark told her after he looked at his watch.

April's eyes met Mark's with reservations. It was time; her final moments alone with him had come. Her feet stood still. *No, I won't do it,* her mind screamed. *If I change my clothes, Mark will leave me behind with Dan.* She hesitantly shook her head, no, as her mind filled with uncertainties. *No, I can't do this, please Mark, don't make me do this,* her mind spoke, yet no words left her lips.

She was thankful Jeff had Mark's attention; otherwise, Mark would have seen the torment on her face as she forced herself to move. April drew from her unselfishness as Mark's wife and surrendered her feelings to give Mark what he wanted. She went to the women's room to change her clothes.

She had just closed the door and stepped out of her shoes, when the door unexpectedly opened and her heart stopped beating.

Chapter Eleven

One Heart

§§

April looked up to see Mark standing there wearing his mischievous face that she loved. "Mark Sanders, what are you doing in here?" she exclaimed, embarrassed that their pastor might still be around and wonder what the two of them were doing in the bathroom. After all, they had just gotten married.

Mark continued with his brilliant, "*up to no good*" face as he glanced at her. She was not sure what he had in mind. There was no way to predict what that look of his would produce.

"I always wondered what was in this room." Mark pretended as he looked around. Then Mark turned and claimed her into his masculine arms. "I thought maybe you could use some help undressing," he laughed and she smiled. His plan had worked; she was smiling and soon relaxed in his strapping arms. He ruffled a lock of her hair around his finger. "Don't worry, Jeff is guarding the door."

"Mark?" she blushed as he kissed her.

"I just wanted to hold you one more time before the game and let you know how much I love you."

Her smile faded as her vulnerable feelings and tears threatened to spill. "I can't, Mark, I can't change my clothes, not if it means ... I have to leave here ... without you." There was no taking back the words she tried so hard to suppress.

Mark felt compassion for her as he lifted her up, sat her up on the counter, and leaned over her. She wrapped her arms around his neck and wiped her tears on his shoulder. "I am so sorry, April, please don't cry." He lifted her chin upward and kissed her tenderly on her moist lips. He stepped back so they were face to face.

"I want you to remember that today is about living, not about dying. You and I will always be. I will always love you. I do not plan to miss one of your glorious smiles or one of your sweet kisses on my lips. We have so much to be thankful for already, and God has more in store for us. I need you to have faith for us both. I need you to be strong for me. I have no regrets about playing today. I am at peace with all of this. I want you to find peace when you see me step on the field today. This is something I have to do," he told her from his heart, hoping to bring her comfort and the understanding of what he had to do.

Then he looked deep into her eyes for the reassurance their hearts were still joined as one, which was the only way he could make it through this day. The key words April heard from Mark's lips were, "*have to do.*" The words he unintentionally let slip out, stabbed at her heart as she read into his mind. *He has to do this! Playing is not his choice any longer, making it impossible for him to share how he is feeling about today with others, including me.*

Her heart raced. She understood now; he could not hide what he was thinking from her. She had always been able to read his mind when they were growing up together. She knew every emotion, every expression on his face. She was as much a part of him as he was of himself.

Suddenly she felt selfish; all she considered were her feelings. Yet it was Mark who was in torment right now. It was Mark that was only doing what he had to do. It was Mark that had to step on that field today because he had to. He was her hero, her unselfish noble hero and she loved him. She fell into his arms and let him hold her. In this moment, she held him against her breasts and joined their hearts and souls together just as he requested. "Oh, Mark, I love you so much."

There was no one in the world that could take her breath away like he did, as he kissed her neck and ran his fingers through the back of her hair. He held her head to his for an unyielding kiss that seemed to linger forever. No one would ever love her as much as he did. She would hold on tight to that cherished thought.

If she could not find the strength in her heart to undress for the game, he would be her strength. In an act of love, he unzipped her dress and carefully lifted it over her head. Her affectionate eyes watched as he gently lifted her silk slip off, exposing her amazing body. His tender eyes travel over every inch of her exposed skin as he touched the side of her face with the palm of his hand to remind her that he was her husband and she was his wife.

"Tonight, April Sanders, I will take pleasure in loving you. That's a promise I intend to keep." His warm hands caressed her bare shoulders, making their way around the back of her neck as he pulled her to him. He softly whispered her name and sampled her engaging lips, sealing his promise to love her with an enchanting kiss.

Then he pulled a sweater from her bag, helped her put it over her head, and pulled it down to her tiny waist. He pulled her hair out from under the sweater and smoothed it out across her back. Taking advantage of his nearness to her, he parted her lips with his and revealed his unending love for her.

His mind filled with wishful thoughts of taking her back to the penthouse where time would stand still as they loved each other and finally they could put this day behind them. If only ... he closed his eyes and pushed the thoughts invading his mind out. He opened his eyes and proceeded to do what needed to be done.

He handed her a pair of jeans, helped her step into them, and zipped them up as his eyes soaked up the love pouring from her eyes. He raised his eyebrows up and grinned at her, tonight he would take pleasure in unzipping these same jeans. She read his thoughts and blushed.

"Mark Sanders ..." but his lips silenced her.

He leaned over and took one more item from the bag. With a big smile, he pulled out his own football jersey and placed it over her head.

"Now we share the same heart, the same number, and the same dreams. Remember this, April; I am on your team no matter what. You are my whole world; don't ever forget that." Tears formed in his eyes as he stood back and thought how wonderful God had been to him. He had one more surprise for her.

"I hired a photographer to take pictures of us, in our wedding outfits, at the ranch next week after I get out of the hospital. It will remind us where our love began and where our love for each other will always be as we begin our journey together as husband and wife."

He took her hands in his, bowed his head against the top of her shoulder and prayed. The passion of his words filled her soul and gave her the peace to give his life over to God and she let him go.

Mark passionately kissed April goodbye on the top step of the church behind the pillars where the persistent paparazzi could not steal a picture of them. She hugged him with everything she had in her heart. She would not tell him to stay there with her. She would set him free and let him fly and do what he had to do.

The minute he stepped into view, cameras flashed, and he was surrounded as the paparazzi ambushed him. The few remaining police officers unsuccessfully tried to hold them back. Dan and Tom took Mark by the arms and safely led him to the limo.

A reporter yelled out questions to him. "Mark, we want to talk to you! Why aren't you with your team? Are you playing today?"

Mark turned around, took one last look at April and waved goodbye to her. Then he took his place beside Jeff in the limo and it sped away.

April closed her eyes as his limo pulled away from the curb. One by one, the tears escaped from the deepest part of her heart that already missed him. Dan gathered her in his arms; he knew exactly how she was feeling. His own heart was aching for a miracle.

Dan and Tom sheltered April as the cameras and questions turned on her. April realized then just how much the public owned Mark. They entrapped him; they possessed his personal life. Her heart understood more than ever how it felt to have someone else in control, and there was nothing one could do about it.

She would ride to the restaurant with Dan and Dr. Stevenson. They would eat with the Sanders' family before going to the game. April knew she could not possibly eat anything. Her stomach was in knots, and her mind needed more time to absorb what Mark told her in the women's room.

She clutched onto his jersey as if she was holding onto him, praying that somehow she could keep her promise to him and believe with all her heart that tonight he would keep his promise.

Chapter Twelve

Choices to Make

ৡ৶

Mark and Jeff rode to the stadium in the limo. Mark sat silently as agonizing thoughts filled his troubled mind. He lacked the peace he felt hours earlier. *God, if this is meant to be, then give me peace.*

The vision of April's heart-stricken face had a tremendous effect on his mind during this hushed time as he searched deep within his soul for answers.

I cannot get out of the fight and give up now. The devil wants me to waver and give in. He tossed that thought around, but it only pulled the knot in his stomach tighter. *The team needs me; I have to play.*

He focused his thoughts on the morning worship service. He thought about his two incredible weddings. He thought about his remarkable romantic night with April. He thought about how much he loved Sunny. He smiled when he imagined the child they would have in nine months. He found peace in those treasured thoughts.

He thought about how his family had arranged the church service to tell him goodbye while he was still alive. He was not ready to tell anyone goodbye as he did not plan to die today.

It upset him they did not hold stronger to their faith after all the times he had shown them God was moving forward in his life. He shifted in his seat and ran his fingers through his hair in frustration. He leaned back against the seat and closed his moist eyes. *The devil has a stronghold on my family. He has taken their faith and replaced it with fear. They believe I am going to die.*

He was a doctor; medically he knew what would happen to him if he played and his spleen ruptured or his heart failed. But he was not living medically; he was living under God's protection. At least, he thought he was, until doubts invaded his mind.

Mark remembered what his pastor said. "If you jump off a building, you are going to feel pain. God cannot protect you from the law of gravity; you are mortal. God cannot stop you from your bad choices that produce severe consequences. God gives you free will. A fool will die before their appointed time. The devil would like to end your life over one foolish choice. The enemy is looking for any chance to kill you."

Hmmm. Would playing with an enlarged spleen qualify as a bad choice? Well, maybe. Ok, so there is a strong possibility that it could rupture. Mark bit his lip; he seriously needed to think about that staggering truth. *Talk to me, God. Why do I think I am indestructible if I am going against Your wisdom?* That thought pierced his mind.

Maybe I am taking this situation out of God's hands. Whatever happens to me will be my doing, not God's. He opened his eyes, stared out the limo window, and thought about that credible truth. Mark knew God was speaking to his heart at this very moment. He sat up straight against the seat and gave God his undivided attention.

Things were different now. He had a family. He wanted to live. Even if he could not have it all, he had April and Sunny. They were more than enough; his life was complete. His whole outlook on his situation was changing as his thoughts with God continued. Never had he felt God's presence as strong as he was feeling Him now.

If my transplant works, I can have a normal life. What, what did I just say; of course my transplant is going to work. Today is not my last football game. I have years to play football. What have I been thinking? This game is the flood and if I play, I will drown in it.

He knew God had given him a way to live, by giving Sunny to him. *She's my lifeboat and it is up to me to grab on and get in. It was no accident I found my own child in the park that night. God sent her to heal me.* Mark sat up straighter as he thought about that realistic truth. In the very beginning, when Sunny first came into his life Mark promised God, *"Whatever it takes, even my pro football career, I will give it all up for her."*

"Thank you, God, for reminding me!" he spoke aloud as deliverance filled his soul. Jeff turned and looked straight at him. Mark was on the edge of his seat and busting with joy. He finally found his peace. "I choose Sunny and April. They are my whole life, Jeff. I don't need anything more than I need them. I don't owe anything to anyone but them."

Mark's smile brightened as he told Jeff his new plans for the football game. Jeff let out a holler of relief and hugged him. Jeff was so excited for Mark he could hardly contain himself as he celebrated and encouraged Mark to stick with his new plan.

Peace and freedom swept over Mark, as he knew without a doubt God had given him the answer he had been seeking. He wanted to live. He wanted to be a father and a husband more than anything else - including football. *God had once again saved him, just in time, before he did something unwise to end his life.*

With distressed faces, the team had gathered in the locker room. They had witnessed the seriousness of Mark's condition at the church and begged the coach to pull him out of the game. Again, the coach told them Mark would have to make that important decision. Now they paced the floor waiting anxiously for Mark to arrive.

Mark made a heartfelt decision on his way to the stadium. The only thing left to do was to tell his coaches and teammates. He talked to his coaches first. Then Coach Walker called the players to come to Mark's locker. Mark stepped forward as all eyes fell on him. "First off, I want you to know I love all of you, guys. Thank you, for all that you have done for me and for my family." He took a long breath.

"This is the hardest thing I think I have ever done. ... I won't be playing today. I have new responsibilities other than this game I have to consider. I am a husband and a father. Now that I have a perfect bone marrow match, I can survive this illness and come back next year to play with you guys."

The team broke out in cheers. Mark did not have to finish his speech. They had accepted his news unconditionally. They shook his hand and told him he made the.right decision.

"April is far better-looking than us. I can understand how you would choose her over us," Justin teased him.

"She is worth it, Buddy. Your life is more important than this game," Carlo confirmed with a playful punch to Mark's shoulder.

Mark smiled as he watched his selfless friends dress out for the game. Mark would not dress out, except for wearing his team jersey. It felt strange to be the outsider. But he knew he made the right decision. Now he would have to tell his family and his fans his decision. He hoped his fans would be as understanding.

The pre-game activities were going on outside. Coach Stuart Walker told the players to line up. He gave them their last minute instructions. Stuart asked Mark to pray. Mark gave them all a blessing; he put his whole heart into the prayer. His prayer touched them deeply as he spoke.

When the prayer was finished the team huddled together, put their hands in the center of the circle, and gave a loud cheer. They lined up. Mark would walk out on the field with the coaches.

The crowd had been anticipating this game all week. Mark's picture had been all over the newspapers and on every sports show and news station. The fans knew the risks if Mark was to play. The question still remained: would Mark play?

The morning newspaper quoted Mark as saying, "Don't come to see me die, come to see me play the best game of my life." Mark included information on the magnitude of giving blood and encouraged readers to donate. The fans waited in anticipation for him to make his appearance. Heads were turning in all directions, hoping to get a glimpse of him before the game.

April held Robert and Dan's hands. They would have to hold her up throughout this game. She had not asked Mark to give up his dream. She would never take this day away from him if this was what he wanted or if this was what he felt obligated to do.

There was still the chance he would not survive the chemo or an infection would take his life. She remembered what he said, "This game is on my 'to do list' not on my 'end of my life list.'"

He had given her the night. As spectacular as it had been, there was still this game to conquer and in Mark's heart, he knew he could do it all. He trusted God when none of them did. If he had any fears, he never admitted them to her or to anyone. He made them smile through it all, April thought.

Mark was so excited that morning, taking everything in stride, just as he did for all of his games. He showed absolutely no apprehension when he left her at the church.

He gave her the memories she asked for, and now she would give him this chance to fulfill his dream, if this was still his dream. She knew his heart. She knew he loved her. She knew if he had any other choice, they would be back at the penthouse right now, starting a lifetime together with their daughter and the baby she prayed was forming within her womb at this very minute.

She touched her tummy and thought of the night she and Mark conceived Sunny after he won a State Championship Football Game. No matter what happened today, she would always have a part of him in the smiles of their children. She would always love only him.

She strangely remembered what he had written on a wooden cross he had made when they were eight years old. His words were, "I love You, God, but I will always love April, too."

Thank You, God, for honoring Mark's prayer that he placed upon Your cross, she thought.

A warm smile crossed her lips.

Chapter Thirteen

Honoring His Word

ৡৡ

The announcer welcomed the crowd to the AFC Championship Game. Then they introduced the two teams playing. The visiting team took the field and lined up on the sideline as they were introduced.

They announced Mark's team next. His team came running out and took their places. The crowd was cheering loudly, chanting Mark's name in high-pitched voices that penetrated the entire stadium.

"Where is Mark?" They searched the lineup of men, but he was nowhere to be seen. Mark had missed the pre-game warm-ups. No one was saying anything about what had happened to him.

When Mark came onto the field, he scanned the sideline in search of April. Spotting her, he jogged over to her, took her hand in his, and gave her a tender squeeze. "April."

The minute she saw Mark was not in full uniform her heart soared, and she bounced up and kissed his cheek. "Oh, Mark, thank you!" She held his hand, tangling her fingers in his, not willing to let him go. Excitement filled her veins. She felt as if she was soaring; as she floated out with him onto the field and proudly stood by him as his wife.

Her fears were gone and she filled her mind with the anticipation of taking Mark home with her tonight to the safety of their bedroom. *Mark belongs solely to me now. He will make love to me as soon as I can get him home*, she thought and smiled in anticipation. She could barely contain the joy she was feeling. Her lips ached to claim his in a lingering kiss.

"I love you," she whispered, and watched his approving smile dance across his face.

The announcer spoke. "Ladies and Gentlemen, let's welcome your Quarterback, Mark Sanders." The crowd stood and cheered as Mark took April's hand and led her to the center of the field.

A hush fell over the stadium when the crowd realized he was not in full uniform. A lone fan yelled out, "Is Mark playing?" They waited for an explanation. Mark nervously took the microphone, uncertain how his decision to sit out the game would be received by those expecting to see him play.

"Welcome, thank you for coming out here today. Thank you for being such loyal fans. I know you have heard I need a bone marrow transplant, which was true, I did. I want to thank everyone who was tested on my behalf. Hundreds of lives like mine can be saved if people would be tested for a bone marrow donor. Someone out there may be waiting on you to save their life," he challenged passionately as moisture filled his eyes.

"As you know, doctors tried to tell me I would not make it off this field alive today if I played. But without a bone marrow match, I was willing to risk that slight chance." He took a deep breath to hold back his emotions.

"I did not want to die in some hospital knowing I could have played today and fulfilled my dream of playing in a championship game like this one. I love my teammates, my coaches, and you guys, my fans . . . but I love someone else more." Mark turned and looked into April's radiant face. This was a big moment for them. He smiled in gratification of her support of him. He turned to face his fans again.

"Last night, the woman of my dreams became my wife." He glanced at April with a fulfillment that flooded his whole inner being. "I want you to meet my wife, April." He proudly held her hand up with his into the air just as he did when his team scored an exciting touchdown. Cameras flashed from all directions.

The crowd roared their approval and clapped. The scoreboard screen was flashing the sentence: Mark loves April, with firecrackers blasting in the background.

"I have one more announcement to make." Mark waved at the crowd until silence once again surrounded the stadium. "I know the newspapers and tabloids will get a hold of this story and make it into something it is not. Therefore, I am going to tell you the truth right now. I am also the father of the most beautiful daughter in this entire universe." Mark's voice cracked as he touched his fist to his heart.

Not a sound was heard, except the heartbeat pounding in his chest, as Mark deliberately stepped out of his protective box, uncovering his personal life, and exposed the truth to divert anything the tabloids might lie about later when they found out about Sunny.

"April and I had a child when we were very young. She just came back into our lives. Her name is Sunny. Sunny turned out to be my perfect bone marrow match. God sent us Sunny to save my life. Tomorrow I will have surgery to remove my spleen and then I'll start treatments to prepare for my transplant." Mark heard gasps and people commenting to each other. Then they turned their attention back to him.

"My odds of coming off this field if I play are not too good, but the odds of my having a successful transplant are better. I have chosen to live for my family. I will not be playing today. I will stand by my teammates and cheer them on. Before I close, I just want to ask you to please give blood." He felt April's hand tense up in his.

"On the wide screen over there, is information on how your gift of blood could save someone's life. Please do it . . . my life . . . and millions of people ... depend on blood donors . . . so please . . . just do it. Be a blessing to someone . . . it's that simple. Thank you . . . I love you all." He waved to the cheering crowd as he choked back his emotions. It was final; he was not playing today.

April turned to him and gave him a hug and a touching kiss. Today she owned him; the public could not have him. Mark had put her first in his life.

Mark gave his fans one more parting wave as they clapped in support of their hero. There were no indications of their displeasure from his decision not to play. Many were reading the screen on how to give blood.

Mark and April headed back to the sideline where Mark took his place beside his teammates. He wrapped his arm around April's waist and was content because *God had already given him the best victory of all.* It felt so good to have him standing next to her. *Tonight we'll have one more night to cherish each other before his surgery,* April thought with excitement. She could not wait to take him back to the penthouse where she would share her deepest love with him.

The announcer asked everyone to stand for the National Anthem. Mark glanced over his shoulder to watch the singer take the field. To his surprise, it was his mother, Julia Sanders, escorted by Robert Sanders. She sang beautifully, her tribute to Mark, bringing tears to Mark's eyes.

It feels so good to be alive, Mark humbly thought, counting all the blessings that God had abundantly showered him with in the last few days.

The Air Force F-16 Fighting Falcons flew over the stadium when the song was finished. Mark looked up into the sky and admired the magnificent jets. *Someday, I am going to learn to fly*, he thought with a meek grin, as the team walked to their places and the game began without him. *Would Mark get his wings and fly?*

Chapter Fourteen

Dedication to Others

§❧

Mark stood beside April on the sideline at the beginning of the game. She tugged at his jersey the entire first half when he was getting too involved in the game.

She would have to remind him to calm down as she grabbed him by his shirttail and pulled him back to the bench where he was supposed to be sitting with the rest of the injured players.

Dan, Jeff, Dr. Stevenson, and Robert stood close behind him. They were keeping a close watch on Mark. They did not want a repeat of what had happened at the church. They were ready at anytime to assist him.

Another botched play happened, and Mark jumped up off the bench and was at the coach's side discussing what they needed to do next. It was hard for Mark not to pretend he was the quarterback on the field. When Kevin's hand went back to pass, Mark had his arm up to pass. He winced when Kevin was sacked. "Come on guys, block for him!"

He jerked as if completing an evasive maneuver. April would gently remind him to stop. Getting him to sit back down proved impossible.

The twenty-four year old was like a ten-year-old child in a candy store. Mark did not want to taste the candy. He wanted much more; he wanted to make it.

He would give April a reassuring smile and tell her she was being silly. Then, unable to resist her charm, he bent and kissed her. It was a kiss all of America saw on the broadcast, as the camera captured their private moment on the sideline.

Mark was excited to be a part of this crucial championship game. The magnitude of Mark's knowledge from watching films of the other team was evident as he went over the plays with Kevin. In key situations, Mark would send the plays out to Kevin to be executed.

Several times, Mark left April's side to cheer on one of the players running with the ball. He would wave his hand toward the goal line as he ran along the sideline shouting, "Run, go!"

The doctors would cringe when he came back to April out of breath. Jeff had clearly given Mark way too much pain medication, Dan thought, as he watched Mark overexert himself. Dan quickly put the matter to prayer and turned Mark over to his heavenly Father to deal with.

When halftime came, a flustered Doc reported to Coach Walker that several players were extremely sick to their stomachs. Doc was not sure if they ate something bad that morning or if it was the flu.

Whatever it was, it was reaping havoc on the sick players. Their other back-up quarterback was so sick Doc sent him to the hospital. It was up to Kevin to finish out the remainder of the game.

Mark and Kevin were going over the vital plays for the second half of the game in the locker room. Kevin was eagerly listening to the valuable information Mark gave him.

Coach Walker and Doc stood back and watched the two men conversing over the second half strategies.

The men were extremely concerned Mark had been exposed to whatever the players had that was making them so violently sick. They worried Mark would undoubtedly be sick soon. They stood there watching the faithful leader of their team preparing Kevin for an undeniable rough second half.

Their fear set in deeper as Mark coughed several times and took a swig from his water bottle to clear his throat. Mark had been in the locker room all afternoon with the guys. If they had something, Mark had already been exposed to it. With his low blood counts, he was sure to catch it.

"It will not be this game that kills Mark, like we all thought. He'll die from a stupid virus!" Doc said angrily. "Mark has given up his dream of playing in the game for nothing." Those were not the words Dan wanted to hear.

Then five minutes before the team was to take the field, Kevin threw up. Now their fear Mark would get sick was confirmed. Mark had spent entirely too much time with Kevin not to already have what Kevin had. It was just a matter-of-time before Mark got sick. Only for Mark, he would not be able to fight the attack on his body with his blood counts so low.

Dan gave Kevin something to settle his stomach. Mark anxiously stood back and watched Kevin continue to vomit. He knew as a doctor that Kevin would grow weaker. Not once did the thought cross Mark's mind that he too would soon be sick. Mark was too concerned for his teammates to be thinking of himself.

The locker room was busting with wild confusion as more players dropped to their knees sick. The pressure was mounting on those who remained healthy. Somehow, they would have to hold the team together or this team's dreams of going to a Super Bowl would be abruptly over.

Mark stood silently as he listened to the distressing comments made by his fellow teammates as they tried to regroup in the last few minutes before they had to take the field.

As their leader, Mark provided encouraging words. "Stand strong and believe in what we have to do out there to take this seemingly impossible situation and turn it around in our favor. Do not let Satan rob us of our victory today. We have worked too hard to give in now, so turn to God and rebuke the devil. Start depending on God. God knows our hearts, so get right with your thinking and He will honor us."

Mark spoke the words, needing to hear them in his own heart as he pumped the team back up and gave them hope. When it was time, the remaining team went back on the field. Only this time, Mark remained behind, went to his locker, and sat down on the bench.

Mark became withdrawn and subdued. He was in deep thought trying to figure it all out. He did not welcome the thoughts attacking his mind. It had been different when it had been his choice to play, but that was no longer true.

He loved April and could never leave her or take the chance, not now. His heart and chest had hurt all morning. He knew his heart was working extra hard because of his lack of red blood cells.

His lovemaking sessions with April all night had not helped it any. He rubbed his chest with his fist, took a deep long breath, and took another swig of water.

The game was on the TV in the locker room. It did not help that the commentators were stressing the need to have Mark in the game. The guilt Mark had about letting his teammates down was creeping back stronger than ever.

The camera operators were searching to find Mark on the sideline. The commentators continued in panicked voices, "The only prayer this team has left is if Mark Sanders takes over as quarterback. Has anyone seen him?"

Mark watched Kevin struggling and prayed he could hang on and finish out the game.

Jeff came in the locker room to check on Mark. The others waited anxiously outside the locker room. After Jeff saw Mark sitting on the bench, he went and told the others to go back and watch the game, but April insisted she wait outside.

Jeff went back in and sat down beside Mark. They did not speak. Jeff knew what Mark was contemplating as he sat there and watched the game with him. Mark was agitated and anxious as the team began falling apart before his eyes.

The fourth quarter came and Kevin was barely holding on. The camera focused on Kevin as he sat on the bench with a wet towel over his head. Mark shook his head in disbelief as he watched and listened.

"Kevin Brown looks bad, Howard. What is this team going to do if they get the ball back?"

"I don't know. Where is Mark Sanders? If he is watching this, he must be asking himself what he needs to do."

"Mark would have been the youngest quarterback to take his team to the Super Bowl. Talk about pressure on a guy so young. He's got to be going crazy right about now."

"Stan, Mark made the right decision not to play. After all the media frenzy this week about his illness, I was concerned he would try to play today. It took a lot of courage to face his fans today and decline his position as quarterback."

"Sure enough. The game is not over, Howard. Let's just pray Mark has already left the stadium. There will be other Super Bowls for that young man and his team. I just hate it had to end like this for them."

"A real shame. If I know Mark Sanders, he is pacing the floor right about now. The way his team is playing ... their only prayer is that he takes the field."

Dan and Jeff were busy helping Doc with the players who had become sick on the field. It seemed to be just the ones who had eaten at the buffet that morning. Most of them were second-string players. Kevin had been one of them, and they were not sure how much longer he could play. He had already been sick several times in the trashcan by the bench.

Mark got up, went into the trainer's room and turned on the TV in there. He took the oxygen mask off the wall and turned it on. He sat slouched in a chair next to the table and put the mask on his face.

Jeff went out and told April she could go in and sit with him. He asked her not to say anything, to let Mark be alone in his own thoughts. She understood; this was a decision only Mark needed to make.

April went in and saw Mark through the window. He was keeping a careful watch on the game. As the team struggled, he began pacing back and forth.

She decided to stay outside of the room and pray for him. She feared for him as she held her hands together. She thought of their life together and wondered if it would all end soon. She knew Mark; he would do whatever he had to do for his team. He would give his life if necessary.

The score was tied going into the fourth quarter of play. With five minutes left, Kevin threw an unavoidable interception as he was tackled hard from behind. He did not attempt to get up.

Mark turned and watched the monitor. He intensely watched the trainers help Kevin back to the sideline, where he fell on the ground and rolled around in pain. It was clear Kevin could not continue playing. The camera zoomed in on Dan and Doc who were at Kevin's side treating him.

The coaches were going crazy on the sideline. The players were devastated as they stood over Kevin. How could they finish the game without a quarterback? Everyone's dreams of going to the Super Bowl would end right here. Mark saw the disappointed looks on the faces of his teammates, as the cameras zoomed in on them.

Mark's chest felt heavy. His team would not go to the Super Bowl if the other team scored again. There was still time for Mark's team to get the ball back and take the lead.

They had to have a quarterback that could handle this kind of pressure to score in the last few minutes of the game, and he knew *he was that quarterback.*

Mark knew what he had to do; he had done it several times in other games. He was known for his fourth quarter miracle comebacks. He owed it to the team to do it this time, too. He flung the oxygen mask off and hurriedly turned off the machine.

He quickly went out into the locker room. He was unaware April was standing there. He opened his locker and quickly began to undress as he mentally concentrated on what he needed to execute once on the field. April stood and watched him as he undid his belt and removed his dress pants, flinging them on the bench by his locker.

Fighting back her tears, she watched her husband, her precious Mark, getting dressed. How handsome he was in his uniform. Any other day but today she would have been captured by his physical appearance. However, at this moment, she hated that uniform that encased his fragile body, with a passion, knowing it would take him away from her.

Just before he was ready to go out, the other team kicked a field goal. They were ahead now by three points. Mark's team would have just over one minute left to play. Mark's heart started beating faster, as he looped the last string on his cleats.

The coach and Doc bent over Kevin, but he was so sick he could not stand up. They would have to send him to the emergency room. Doc quickly got players to carry Kevin to the locker room on the backboard.

Mark took his helmet in his hand and hurried toward the exit. He stopped short when he saw April standing there waiting. She did not say anything. As their eyes met, April managed a fake smile. She knew in her heart Mark had no other choice; he had to do this and she would support him.

This time he had not made the decision to play; it had been made for him. Just like Mark, he was always doing the noble thing, no matter what the cost to himself. She wanted him to know she supported him. Before her stood the bravest man she had ever met, and she was proud of him as he came to her.

"I love you, April, you know I do. I can do this. You have to believe with me." He kissed her and gave her a hug. He took her hand in his and together they hurried out of the locker room. They would face this together as one.

Mark gathered his thoughts with God and asked Him to forgive him for taking this game out of His hands. He asked for favor and safety.

As they were going out, Kevin was being brought into the locker room. Kevin saw Mark dressed out and knew what he was going to do. Kevin screamed, "Mark, don't do it! Mark! Someone stop him!"

Mark gave Kevin the "thumbs up" and his reassuring grin. The two friends shared a look of understanding.

"God be with you, Mark," Kevin said to his friend.

Chapter Fifteen

One Moment in Time

§♭

The opposing kicking team finished their kick-off to Mark's team, and they returned the ball to the twenty-five yard line. Coach Walker was frantically trying to figure out which player to use for quarterback. The crowd was anxiously standing on their feet, waiting for something to happen, praying this was not the end of the season for their team.

All of a sudden, the crowd started cheering, and just like old times, they chanted Mark Sanders' name. "Sanders! Sanders!"

Mark came out onto the field with April at his side. The fans were still standing on their feet, waving, screaming, and clapping, yelling his name. Mark would unselfishly give them what they wanted.

This was his stadium; it would be all up to him. He felt total peace sweep over him. He got pumped and mentally ready to do what he had to do. He was not afraid. This was his destiny, his *one more moment in time*.

He stood tall, waved at his fans, and gave them the "thumbs up." He turned around and around, taking a good look at the entire stadium. The stadium lights were shining so brightly they made him feel completely at home. "I am in God's house tonight. God is shining His lights down on my team. Let's get this done, Lord."

He gave April another kiss and touched her cheek with his gentle hand as he looked straight into her eyes and joined their souls together. She held her tears; she knew this might be goodbye. Her heart was broken, but she refused to expose her true feeling. She would not take this opportunity away from him.

Dan came out onto the field and took April's hand. Her other hand slowly slipped out of Mark's as Dan escorted her off the field. The crowd realized, at that emotional moment, Mark was sacrificing his life with his family for them, his fans, his teammates, his friends. They stood quiet in admiration for him.

Mark rushed over to the huddle. The players all told him he did not have to do this. But he was optimistic and ready to win the championship with them. He felt great and keyed up for this challenge. His whole body was energized and ready to get the job done.

"Mark! Mark!" The crowd started yelling again, demanding a victory. "We want a touchdown. Touchdown!"

Mark strolled toward the referee and spoke to him. Then the referee went to the other team and relayed the message. The referee gave them a few minutes to think about what he said.

Mark had instructed the referee to tell the other team he was not holding back so they had better not hold back either if they wanted to win this game. In other words, Mark gave them the freedom to sack him. Just like Mark to make the odds even, knowing the other team knew he was sick and might hold back from sacking him unless he did something. Besides, Mark did not intend to let them sack him. Mark was ready to give the best performance of his life.

Dan, Jeff, and Dr. Stevenson quickly talked to each other. They knew what Mark had told the referee. April stood faintly in the arms of Robert. Her heart was heavy with the thought that in just minutes, Mark would no longer be hers. "Oh, Robert, I'm … scared for Mark."

"You must believe in him, April. He needs us to speak words of victory over him." Robert was right. This was Mark's destiny, to be his very best. He wanted it all, he had the plan to make it come true, and she would join him with her heart and faith.

She closed her eyes and thought of their life together. *How many times has he cheated death? He will do it again*, she convinced herself. She stood tall and yelled out chants to the man she loved. "Go for it, Mark! You can do it!"

The referee's whistle blew. The clock began to run.

Mark gave his final thoughts in the huddle and called the play with authority. The players lined up and listened to Mark yell out the play. The ball was snapped back to Mark. He dropped back to pass and threw it forcefully to Craig, who ran for 5 more yards before going out of bounds. They had gotten 20 yards on the play. First down!

"He's doing great!" April gave Robert a quick hug and clapped her hands. "Go, Mark!" Mark looked great on the field. He was in total command, his professional appearance was back. His feet remained steady as he avoided tackles. Adrenaline flooded Mark's veins as he moved with the grace of an athlete.

April stood proud as she watched her husband take control of the game. "We want a touchdown!" The cheerleader in her yelled out just like she had done for Mark in high school.

Once again, the ball was snapped to Mark. He dropped back in the pocket looking for his receivers; no one was open. The pressure mounted as Mark ran around the corner, jumped over a block that was made in front of him. He ran for 9 yards before he was forcefully knocked to the ground where he quickly signaled for a time out. He got up quickly and flipped the ball to the referee.

He was playing with all he had; he could taste the win. Nothing would stop his team. He raced to the huddle and quickly called the play. "Get out of bounds and stop the clock!"

The crowd was screaming. The lights were shining down on him. He was so pumped. He felt great; he always did when he was under pressure.

This time he stood back away from the line and was tossed a high hike. He jumped up to catch it. He looked for an open receiver down the field; no one was open. He ran sideways, then he flipped the ball to his running back, Carlo, and they got another first down on the 35-yard line.

Mark had been tackled to the ground just seconds after he handed off the ball to Carlo. Relief filled the stadium when he quickly jumped up to his feet and headed down the field for their last huddle.

The red zone was in sight. Fifteen seconds left, first down, with thirty-five yards to go for a touchdown. The coach gave Mark the signal to continue; they would go for the win. The coaches did not want to go into overtime and risk Mark playing anymore of this game.

Mark's last huddle with his team took place. If they did not get the touchdown on this next play, they would have to kick a field goal to tie the game. Mark wanted the touchdown. The pressure was on. He had to accomplish the touchdown in less than a mere 14 seconds or call a quick timeout so they could go for the tying field goal.

They prayed together as they held hands. Mark called the play with total confidence. All players held their eyes on their faithful leader. He gave them his reassuring grin. They broke huddle, clapping their hands loudly, and took their positions on the scrimmage line. Mark took a deep breath. He looked out over his players and pointed to the goalpost. "It's mine!" he declared.

The crowd was standing on their feet. The noise in the stadium was deafening. They were yelling Mark's name. "Sanders! Sanders! Sanders!"

Mark loudly called out the numbers to his teammates. The ball was snapped into Mark's steady hands. He dropped back, looked for his receivers; he ran to his right to avoid a tackle. The clock was running down as he scrambled in the backfield desperately looking for an open receiver.

The middle was open; he thought for just a second about running up the center. The sharp pain in his side told him that he would never make it. The crowd was screaming the seconds on the clock. Five … Four …Three …

At the last second, Mark saw Carlo open in the end zone and with every-thing he had, he threw the perfect pass into Carlo's hands. "Touchdown!" Mark jumped up three feet in the air for joy, holding his hands high in the air in victory.

They had done it; they had won the AFC Championship Game! Mark continued to jump in happiness, shaking his fists in the air. "Yes! Yes!" How great it felt to have finished. The crowd went absolutely wild, screaming his name!

This time the team knew not to touch him and shook his hand or gave him high fives instead. Everyone was loudly celebrating with excite-ment. Mark's team would go to the Super Bowl! He had fulfilled another dream!

Mark hugged and shook hands with his opponents' quarterback and briefly spoke to him as reporters surrounded them. Fans were running on the field.

Colorful confetti drifted like snowflakes from the skies in celebration of the win. AFC Championship caps and t-shirts replaced helmets and jerseys on the players already standing on the sideline. Robert grabbed a cap and shirt for his son and headed in his direction.

Mark looked over at the sideline where his family stood. He smiled at them and gave them the "thumbs up."

Robert was proudly heading onto the field to congratulate his son and give him his well-deserved championship apparel. Dan and Jeff followed him. April followed behind them, anticipating her hug from Mark. It was finished; now he would be safe, they all thought. Mark had fulfilled his destiny.

Mark excitedly headed toward his father in anticipation of a hardy hug. Mark held his helmet up high in the air and waved to the crowd to acknowledge his fans who were still chanting his name. The security guards held fans back.

Joy was written all over Mark's face. Life was good, he thought, just before he felt it. His chest jerked sideways as the relentless pain hit. He felt

his life being sucked out in that dreadful instant. The pain was unbelievable. His entire face cringed as an ominous sounding moan escaped from
his tense mouth.

He knew exactly what that pain meant. *Just let me make it off the field,*
he thought desperately as he pulled deep within, gathering all the strength
he had left.

His ears no longer heard the deafening noise from the crowd. Nor
did he acknowledge the reporters being held back by security guards. His
attention focused on his next painful breath.

Robert saw Mark's pained face and instantly ran faster to rescue his
son. "Please, no!" *Let him have this moment to celebrate, do not take it
away from him.* "Mark, hang on!"

Mark was staggering now, trying desperately to stay on his unsteady
feet. He was unsuccessfully grabbing at his life; refusing the certain death
he knew in his mind was minutes away.

He held his hand up slowly and waved a sorrowful goodbye to his
family as tears filled his eyes with regret that he was losing his battle to
live. Then he felt as if he had been shot in the chest, confirming the inevi-
table. *There is a time to live and a time to die.*

His football helmet slipped from his hand, and as if in slow motion, it
fell to the ground and bounced back up. The pain was excruciating as he
clenched his chest with his arms.

The illuminating lights in the stadium were spinning rainbow streams
around in his mind, as he began his slow descending fall to the ground. One
of his teammates tried to hold him up, but Mark fell onto the unmerciful
ground. Mark was devastated as he tried frantically to hang on, desperate
not to give in and let the earth claim his body.

Robert reached Mark and dropped to his knees in front of him. Their
eyes met as if Mark wanted one more look at his father's face and then
Mark collapsed into his father's arms. "I love you, Mark ... Son, I love
you!"

"Dad ... April ... take care ... of April," Mark spoke weakly to his
father as his eyes searched for April. He wanted to feel her arms wrapped
around him one more time. He could not die without saying goodbye to
her.

Robert cuddled Mark to his chest and rocked him. "Mark ... please,
God ... not now."

Dan and Jeff made it to them; the sight of Mark dying was inconceivable. April took a hold of Mark's arm as she fell to his side. "Oh, Mark,

no!" she screamed out as Dan and Jeff removed Mark from his father's arms and gently laid him on the earth.

Ten more feet and he would have made it off the field, just ten more feet, Robert thought. He turned and waved the people back away from his son. "Keep them back!"

The crowd went absolutely silent when they saw what was happening to Mark as they viewed the large screen. It was as if everyone had stopped breathing. Tears of disbelief were seen throughout the stadium when they saw Mark lying on the ground. The security guards held reporters back to shield Mark from their flashing cameras.

A father and his two teenage boys stood up, joined hands, and began praying. Then whispers of prayers were heard throughout the stadium as the fans realized Mark's life could end right here on his football field.

All celebration ended as teammates realized what was happening to Mark. Both teams knelt down on one knee and held their helmets in respect for Mark. Mark's friends could not believe they were about to lose him. They began praying, heads bent down as each player took a turn to plead for Mark's life.

Carlo, Justin, Jerk, and Craig stood over Mark. Rebecca and her mother forced their way through the crowd and came to Mark's side. Carlo held Julia in his arms. Craig held Rebecca in his. Justin knelt on one knee near Mark as tears streamed down his face.

The coaching staff came on the field near Mark and stood in shock. Had they made the wrong decision to let Mark play, they wondered with deep regret. They had given him just one minute to play. It was the longest minute of Mark's life; would it be his last?

Those at the ranch quickly got together and prayed when they saw what had happened to Mark on the TV. Everett held Victoria and Ella in his arms as the rest gathered around them. Thomas went to the phone.

Martha picked up a tearful Brad. "Did Uncle Mark die?" Brad buried his face in her shoulder and wept. James Robert, who had been playing in the room, looked up. He was too young to understand what was going on and went to view the TV for himself, to get answers.

Sunny had lost interest in the game since Mark was not playing. She was in the stable with Thunder and Charlie. She had found herself a cat to play with. The phone in the stable rang and Charlie answered it. There was no need to tell Charlie. He already *felt* it in his soul that something had happened to Mark. He watched Sunny innocently playing and felt compassion for her. *Would she ever recover from the loss of Mark; would any of them?*

Dr. Stevenson grabbed some of the medical equipment bags, leaving behind what Dan and Jeff were in charge of carrying and quickly ran out to Mark. The trainers grabbed the backboard and rushed out on the field.

The medical team knew they were in a race against time. Each second that passed by could mean the difference in saving Mark's life. Dan sent the trainers back for the rest of the equipment bags they needed.

The four carefully placed Mark on a backboard. This was the only time he would scream in pain as they moved him. The instant April spoke to him, he calmed down. Her soft words went straight to his heart as he held on to his life for her.

"Sun ... ny," he faintly voiced to April as he reached his hand out in search of his child. "Sun ..." His heart-wrenching voice tore through those surrounding him. "Tell her ... I love her."

"No, Mark . . . you tell her ... you have to tell her."

Jeff quickly cut Mark's jersey off and got his shoulder pads off. Tom undid the gauze padding over Mark's catheter and exposed the lines going directly into his heart.

Dan listened to Mark's heart and lungs. "Decreased breath sounds!" Dr. Stevenson felt Mark's spleen and shook his head in disgust. They compared notes and began immediate treatments, injecting medications into his chest catheter. Tom started another IV in Mark's arm. They knew exactly what the other would do and worked with preciseness. They prayed this would buy Mark the time he needed to survive.

Mark should have been in extreme pain, but he lay peaceful now with April near his head. The only movement he made was with his hands and the words he expressed with his eyes. He could hear the commotion around him but could not respond. His mind filled with thoughts of fighting his pending death. He chose this final moment to spend talking to his Lord.

Mark turned his life over to God. *Thank you, Lord, for letting me finish out this game. Thanks, God, for my life with April. Lord, thanks for my family, friends, and for all those I have loved, and for those who have ... loved me.*

He saw himself standing in the sun and felt peace and warmth as he worshipped. *Now he was free. He was in God's hands and he was not afraid.*

Chapter Sixteen

How Do I Live Without Him

৪৬

April knelt behind Mark, and gently lifted his head and cradled it in her lap. She ran her fingers through his hair and kissed his forehead repeatedly, tearfully telling him how much she loved him.

"I love you, Mark. I can't live without you … don't leave me!" she cried as her heartbroken tears streamed down her face. As her teardrops trickled onto his face, she would kiss them away with her warm lips. She absorbed his cheeks desperately trying to wash his pain away with her tender touch and keep them connected as one.

"Oh, please, Mark … don't leave me … I can't live without you… you can't die on me." Her whole world was crashing down on her as her life with Mark was abruptly ending. Her fingertips claimed every inch of his skin on his head as she gathered him in her hands.

Mark was conscious, his pain subdued by April. He turned from his thoughts with God and concentrated on her touches. His weak eyes stared up at hers as he surrendered his mind to her.

There was so much he wanted to say to her heart. "I will … love you … forever … April." A tear trickled down his face and she kissed it.

"Oh, Mark …" She bent her head so their moist cheeks were touching. "I love you, Mark," she whispered softly into his ear, as her heart succumbed to their last few minutes together.

He weakly reached his hand up and held her face to comfort her. She kissed his fingers as she took his hand in hers, interlocking their fingers.

"I can never give you up." Her heart was breaking into a million pieces. Her chin quivered as the floodgates of her heart broke open, and tears streamed down her face.

"April ... I choose you ... I don't want to die ..." His words strained as he felt his chest tighten as the blood surrounding his heart and lungs began suffocating him.

His eyes closed and he saw a *dove* in the bright light that filled his mind. "Grandfather ..." he spoke as his face softened. "Papa ...

April's heart stopped. "Nooo ...!" She looked up above Mark's head as if she saw someone standing above them. "Please ... Mark loves me ... let Mark stay with me ... we belong together."

Mark fought to open his eyes to join April's request. He did not fear dying. His broken heart spoke out. He could not leave April behind without him. His breathing labored as his left lung collapsed.

The portable oxygen arrived. Jeff handed April the oxygen mask, and she held it in place over Mark's nose and mouth. "Breathe, Mark, please ... for me." Her hands were trembling as she placed the strap around Mark's head to hold the mask in place, as she prayed the rest of the emergency equipment with the intubation kit would arrive.

Mark's hand lifelessly dropped behind his head. Pain crossed his tense face as someone touched him. He shut out the panicked voices of the others as he concentrated on the woman he loved. *April, I love you so much. God, please ... I can't ... leave ... April behind,* he agonized.

April bent forward so her face was next to his cheek. She continued to speak words of her amazing love for him through her tears, her eyes cloudy, as she rocked his head in her lap, pleading with God to spare him.

"God, please . . . please . . . leave Mark with me."

Mark was now unresponsive, unable to speak to her. He fought desperately to hang on, to hear every word of her *endless love* for him. He struggled to keep his eyes open, unable to bear the thought of losing her forever. That desolate thought brought fresh tears to his eyes. Her heartbeat speaking to him encouraged each painful breath he took, as her words kept him from descending closer to the death waiting on his surrender.

"I love you, Mark. Our hearts are one. You are not going to . . . die on me."

Finally, the defibrillator and intubation equipment arrived. Jeff placed the leads to the defibrillator on Mark's chest and watched for electrical activity. Dan hooked up a saline bag and ran it at maximum rate. The team of doctors were quickly doing all they could.

"Respiratory rate 30, come on, Mark, don't do this!" Jeff hollered at Mark as their eyes met for that split second. "Mark, you have to fight, Buddy ... just fight, please!"

Mark's lips were a faint shade of blue as his right lung denied him oxygen, diminishing his battle to remain conscious. Jeff ripped open the sterile wrapping around the intubation equipment.

Mark pulled strength from deep within, reached up again for April and tenderly touched her face with his open palm. She found his tearful eyes. Then he pulled the mask down and whispered what he knew would be his last words to her.

"I love you …" The tears fell one at a time down his face as he looked compassionately at her but with such regret, such sorrow. He had broken his promise to her. He would not be taking her home and loving her tonight.

"I … am … so … sorry," he said weakly. He slowly closed his eyes as he unwillingly surrendered to the light shining above him.

"Mark, no!" April touched his bare shoulders, wanting to embrace his body next to hers, to give him her life.

"Let him live through me," she tearfully cried, searching the sky above her. "Let me breathe for him!" she begged God as she watched Mark fade away from her.

"Give me your unending love, Mark Sanders! You promised me!" The floodgates to her heart split open and consumed her with gushing tears. She kissed him repeatedly on his face, anything to keep him as hers for *one more moment in time.*

The alarm sounded sharply! April's whole body jerked as the sound exploded in her soul. Mark had stopped breathing! His heart had stopped!

"Mark!" April screamed his name and fell over him, shaking him with both her hands. "Nooo! Noooo! Mark, don't do this! Please, Mark, stay with me!" she begged him tearfully. "I can't live without you! Mark!"

Carlo bent down and forcefully pulled her away so the doctors could work on him. She put up a struggle, reaching her arms out to Mark, screaming desperately for him.

"Mark, I love you, Mark!" Her whole body was shaking. "Mark!" She was heaving tears. "Let me hold him, please, let me hold him!" she cried as her body shook uncontrollably.

"Please, God, please…" Deep gut-wrenching convulsions attacked her body, doubling her over and causing her to gasp for air. Carlo held her firmly, as her tears ripped his heart straight down the middle.

The second the alarm sounded the doctors quickly got into position. Jeff swiftly moved to the front and tilted Mark's head back, intubated him, and forced air into his lungs. Dan started CPR.

Rebecca knelt down as if in a state of shock, yet drawing on her instinct to care for Mark as she took the ambu bag from Jeff, and continued to force air into Mark's lungs. Her baby brother's body was lifeless in front of her. She whispered in his ear her deepest love for him.

Just as she had done as the big sister, she told him to quit fooling around and get up. But he did not respond. "Mark, please," she begged him. "Why won't he listen to me, why?" she cried as her heart broke in two.

'Oh, God, no," Julia muttered as she placed her hands together over her mouth and nose. Craig grabbed Julia fearing she was about to faint and held her securely in his arms. Julia could not even speak the words of love she wanted to say to her son. Her chest tightened so stiffly she could barely breathe.

April buried her face into Carlo's shoulder and beat her fists against his chest. The pain she felt was unbearable. She twisted around and glanced back at Mark's lifeless body. She shook her head in disbelief that she was watching him die right there in front of her, and there was nothing she could do to stop him from leaving her. "Oh, M a ... r k."

Dan bent over Mark's chest. Frantically he did chest compressions, but he could not bring his son back. Emotionally drained, he turned the resuscitation over to Jeff.

Dr. Stevenson took the defibrillator paddles and covered them with gel. "Stand back, everyone!" He placed the paddles on Mark's chest and jolted him. Mark's body violently jerked upward and then fell back down. They watched the machine, no change; they fanatically shocked him again.

"Mark! Oh, God, Mark!" April screamed as they continued to shock him. It was unbearable to watch them shock his body. Each time Mark's body jerked up, it tore her heart. She ripped at Carlo's uniform with her fingers trying to get free of him.

"Stop it! Stop hurting him!" she screamed at them. She pleaded through her tears. "Just let me hold him. If he has to die ... let him die in my arms ... in peace."

"He has too much blood around his lungs and heart. We have to tap him now, we can't wait!" Dan yelled at them. Doc arrived and opened the surgical kit and got everything they needed ready. He helped Dan put on a pair of plastic surgical gloves.

Jeff frantically continued chest compressions. "Come on, Mark, come back to us!" His voice pained with grief; sweat dripped down the sides of his face as he pounded on Mark's chest. "Mark, don't do this! I'm not losing you, too."

Dr. Stevenson took the long cardiac needle and inserted more medications directly into Mark's heart. Doc hung the second bag of blood and showed Robert how to squeeze it. They watched the monitors for any signs of life, nothing.

Dan quickly scrubbed the side of Mark's chest with an antiseptic. He thanked God Mark was unconscious. Doc handed the scalpel to Dan. He made an incision into Mark's chest wall, and then he placed his finger into Mark's pleural cavity and opened the incision up to insert the chest tube. The tube quickly filled with blood.

Jeff continued the chest compressions. They waited impatiently for the blood around Mark's lungs to drain. Finally, Mark's heart started beating. Jeff said an exhausted, "Amen."

They knew Mark's spleen had ruptured. Jeff opened the cooler and got the platelets out. He handed the bags to Justin to hold. Jeff hooked the lines up to the other catheters and pushed the platelets into Mark.

They watched his heart rhythm improve. They were winning the battle for now. They were determined not to let him bleed out and die. They had enough units of blood to get him to the hospital. The sound of Life Star arriving echoed through the stadium.

April broke away from Carlo, went to Mark, kissed his cheek, and rubbed his hair with the palm of her hand. "Fight, Mark! You promised me you could do this!" she reminded him tearfully. Fresh tears burned their way down her swollen cheeks.

Mark was stable enough to be transferred to the ambulance. It would take him to the life flight helicopter outside the stadium. Steven would be ready to do emergency surgery as soon as they arrived at the hospital. Dan had arranged for all their top surgeons to be on hand for their arrival.

They put all their equipment on the backboard. Justin stepped forward, asked if his teammates could carry Mark off the field, and they came forward and carefully lifted him up.

"You did it, Mark. You won us the game." Justin lightly placed his championship cap on Mark's chest. "Don't give up the fight; hang in there for us . . ."

Jeff took over Rebecca's job and continued to force air into Mark's fragile lungs.

Carlo helped April up and when he saw her feet were unsteady, he picked her up and carried her in his arms to the ambulance.

Rebecca noticed Mark's cleats and his torn jersey lying on the field. She tearfully bent and picked them up and held them to her chest. She was numb, in a state of shock, her mind shutting down as she tried to block out the reality of this scene and pretended she was not there.

Rebecca thought, it was just like Mark, leaving his football stuff all over his room. "Don't worry, little brother, I'll pick them up for you." She had tried all her life to keep him from harm, to protect him. She had failed.

The crowd remaining in the stands had been quiet the entire time. Those standing on the field stood silent as they waited and watched the large screen for information. They cheered as Mark was carried off the field to the ambulance on the sideline. The screen was displaying information on how to give blood, with a picture of Mark Sanders to the side of the information. The caption read, "Give Blood, Save Mark!"

Robert joined Julia and Rebecca. Rebecca stood taut with Mark's things against her chest. She was too emotionally destroyed to walk on her own. Robert wrapped her under his arm and escorted her and Julia off the field. They headed for the exit. Their helicopter would take them to the hospital.

Mark's team had won the game and would advance to the Super Bowl, but at this devastating moment, not a single player cared. The cost of their victory had been too high. The two teams knelt on the field in a circle and prayed together. Mark's buddies for life were heartsick.

The crowd heard the sound of the two helicopters starting up their engines. The noise echoed throughout the stadium. The fans stood at attention, their eyes on the sky waiting for a glimpse of the helicopter that would take away their beloved hero.

Soon the sound of the two helicopters lifting into the air was heard. Mark's teammates rose to their feet and stood at attention as the helicopters flew overhead. When the helicopters were directly above them, they held their championship hats into the air. "God be with you, Mark!" a single voice shouted out.

They turned to each other and tearfully hugged one another. The post game celebration was of no interest to them, and they asked the reporters to leave them alone.

The sound of the helicopters faded. Mark was gone.

He had his wings and was flying.

The players needed time to absorb all that had happened. Just last night they shared joyfully in Mark's wedding. They prayed with him that morning in church and watched as he gave his heart in song to the God he loved. They watched him give his life to April and Sunny in another celebration of marriage. Would tomorrow they share in his funeral?

They slowly walked to the locker room with their heads hanging downwards. Not a word was spoken as they gathered around the locker room in disbelief their friend was dying. Reporters were banned from the locker room. On the overhead TV, the players viewed scenes of the team owner and coach accepting the championship trophy. Mixed emotions brought the players to tears.

Justin took notice of the sign they had placed over Mark's shower. Mark had given them memories they would never forget.

Mark's church clothes were lying on the bench in front of his locker. The doors were still wide open. Mark's boots were on the floor. Justin started to close the doors, but Carlo took his hand and stopped him.

Carlo turned to face the players who were watching. He picked up Mark's boots and held them up. Through his tears, he took a deep breath and spoke.

"This locker stays open! Mark has not finished putting his stuff away. Do you hear me? He is coming back!" He neatly placed Mark's boots on the bench. Then he brushed the tears from his eyes and quickly went to get dressed so he could go to the hospital.

Before Carlo left, the coach handed him the Championship trophy. "It belongs to Mark." Then he went into his office and cried. Not a word was exchanged, as the players dressed so they could go to the hospital. On the way to the hospital, Carlo wrote Mark a poem.

God planted Mark's dreams in his heart.
God granted the Hope, the Faith.
Now a chapter in Mark's life is over.
Mercy and Grace
God has not forgotten his son.
He has placed Mark in the arms
of His protective Angels.

Chapter Seventeen

In the Palms of His Hands

April sat between the two pilot seats, facing Mark's head. Dan and Jeff were seated across from Mark. Dan hooked Mark up to the oxygen in the helicopter. Jeff hung the bags of blood. They kept a close watch on his vital signs. Mark was shirtless, only having his football pants still on.

Mark stirred and slowly opened his weak eyes. He could not talk because of the tube in his throat. However, his thoughts ran rapid.

April leaned closer so he could see her. She gently brushed his hair away from his forehead and kissed him there. Their eyes connected.

"Oh, Mark . . . I love you . . . so much."

Her downcast eyes and her unsteady voice told him her heart was breaking. *I love you, too, April. If only I could tell you how I feel. It is all right, don't be scared for me. I will get through this.*

Jeff placed Mark's hand in hers and she locked their fingers together as one. Mark's hand was warm, a good sign, she thought. His eyes showed no fear; he seemed at peace. *Does Mark still believe in his God?* She knew he did.

Have faith in us, April. Look in my eyes and see how much I love you.

April recognized his undeniable love for her as he spoke to her with his gentle blue eyes. He had given her that same look when they were eight years old. Mark let her know he was still fighting for them; he had not given up. He wanted to keep every promise they had made to each other.

If only I could take away her tears for me and remind her to have faith in God and in me. I did not want to give you up and play in that game. I chose us. God, tell her I chose us. A look of regret strained his face.

April knew what he was thinking. "I understand, Mark; you did what you had to do. I am so proud of you … you are my hero … we did it together … out there on the field today … now we are going to finish this … you and me … we will always be …" Tears overcame her; she turned and brushed them away, praying she could be brave for him.

Please, don't cry, April. You are breaking my heart, seeing you like this. We will be together, I promise. Hold me; feel me in your arms so I can comfort you. With you by my side, I can beat this. With our hearts joined as one, we can do anything. Remember that, April. Remember how much I love you. I am truly in love with you and I know you are truly in love with me.

She faced him again. "I'm sorry, Mark. I am trying so hard to be strong for you, but I just cannot stand seeing you like this. I do believe in everything you told me at the church. Really, I do. I am just … hurting for you." Again the tears fell, despite her attempt to hold them back.

Humbly he spoke to God and worshiped with Him. *Please, God, bring her comfort. Help her put her trust in You. I love her so much, Lord. If only I could get up and hold her in my arms, Lord, I would never let her go. You joined us together, this morning, as husband and wife and that is what I want, Lord, to be her husband, forever.*

April hushed his thoughts as she spoke to him. She put her cheek next to his and cradled his other cheek with her fingers. She reminded him of their night together and told him he was not finished loving her. He squeezed her hand in agreement, and she tenderly kissed his fingers.

"Oh … Mark, I love …"

Suddenly his body jerked, and his face contorted in pain. He squeezed his eyes tight to fight through the pain. *Oh, God, please, pleeeeease, make it stop,* he begged.

"Jeff, he's in pain. Give him something!"

"Hang in there, Buddy." Jeff took a syringe of morphine, he held it up and squirted out some of the liquid to get out any bubbles, and then he injected it into Mark's IV. "You will feel better any minute now, Mark."

Dan reached out to hold April steady as they came in for the landing at the hospital. Jeff got everything ready for them to take Mark out of the helicopter. He covered Mark up with a heavy blanket to shield him from the weather.

Robert's helicopter had already landed, and he and Dr. Stevenson ran over to them. Julia helped Rebecca walk to the entrance of the hospital.

Medical staff was waiting there with a gurney. Carefully they lifted the backboard with Mark on it and put it on the gurney. They strapped him securely to it, and then they rushed him into the hospital.

"Dr. Martin is waiting for Mark in the OR!" There was no time to take him to the ER to prepare him for surgery. They would have to do it in the OR.

Mark was still conscious but foggy. He heard the muffled voices of Robert and April speaking to him as they held onto the railing of the gurney.

He felt them racing him down the hallway. Jeff was at the front, his feet riding on the bottom railing of the gurney. He continued to squeeze air into Mark's lungs with the ambu bag. "Hang on, Mark, we are almost there!"

Mark watched the ceiling lights blur in front of him as they ran down the corridor towards the operating room. The doors swung shut behind them. Robert stood with his hands against the door looking helplessly in the window. April followed Mark into the OR.

The operating team was ready for Mark. On the count of three, they quickly transferred him to the operating table. His facial muscles tightened in pain as they moved him. His weak grip on April's hand strengthened briefly as pain shot through his body.

Oh, God, not again, no more pain. Don't let my eyes show pain when April looks into them. Please, I can't let her see me in pain. I have to regain control. Let the morphine work.

Mark turned his pain into prayers and the pain disappeared. *Thank You, God, thank You, for everything You are about to do in this operating room. Thank You, for my healing, for my life.* His eyes found the man who had always been like a father to him.

One of the nurses took April aside and quickly draped her with a surgical gown and handed her a facemask and gloves. Everyone was in a hurry to get Mark ready for surgery. They started cutting away his remaining uniform, scrubbing his chest. He was completely defenseless as they worked on him.

"Look at me, Mark. Focus on my voice." Dan spoke in an attempt to distract him from what was happening. "You are in good hands. Our best surgeons are all here to take care of you," he reassured him. "I love you, Mark. I always have. From the day you were born, you have brought such joy in my life."

Mark shook his head in agreement. Mark gave him the "thumbs up". Just like Mark, he would never give up his humor to encourage others even in such a traumatic situation.

Mark's eyes turned from Dan to search for April. She moved closer to him and held his hand until Dr. Faye Wilson, the anesthesiologist, gently took his hand from her and strapped his wrist to the table. April reclaimed his fingers in hers as she moved next to him where he could see her face, while Faye strapped his other wrist.

Faye was very fond of Mark. In the last few months, he had been trying to set her up with Dan for a real date. She warmly thought of Mark's bold statement while they were at the church social. "It's time you two take this long time friendship of yours to another level."

She looked sympathetically at Dan wondering if he would ever be able to let Mark go should he not make it through the surgery.

Dan had spent his entire life dedicated to Mark's family when Robert had not been around to take care of them. Mark wanted Dan to have a chance to love someone just like his mother loved his father.

Dan deserves to find happiness with a special woman like Faye, God. Do You think maybe You can arrange that for me? Mark thought, as he watched Faye and Dan exchange a look of empathy.

Jeff patted Mark on the shoulder, and they exchanged a look of deep friendship. "I love you, Mark. I got your back, Buddy." Jeff held back his tears and then he left the room.

Would Jeff have to keep Mark's promise and love his family for him? As much as Jeff loved April, he could never give up Mark to take care of her.

Please, Mark, hang on tight and fight. I just cannot do it. I cannot take your place in April's heart, Jeff thought tearfully. Memories flooded his mind of his little brother's last hour of life in this exact operating room a few years ago. Would the outcome be the same for Mark?

As Mark felt the nurses touching him in their rush to get him ready for surgery, he felt his stomach tighten. He was a doctor; he was aware of everything that was about to happen to his body. His anxiety intensified as he heard a nurse tell Dr. Martin they were ready.

They are going to cut me in half. Oh, God, can we skip that part? I am ready to go back to the penthouse.

His operation was imminent and there was no turning back. Just as a twinge of fear unsettled his nerves, Dr. Wilson spoke to him. "God is standing right here, ready to guide the hands of these surgeons and give you healing." Mark blinked his eyes at her to acknowledge he agreed.

Faye made sure his airway was correctly positioned. "April, honey, it's time to put Mark under. You can kiss him goodbye."

"What?" April's heart dropped at the same time Mark lost his self-control on the situation. *Goodbye* was not a word either one of them wanted to hear.

No, April, don't tell me goodbye! This is not goodbye! Don't leave me, April. Mark responded in a panic by trying to pull his wrists out of the restraints. Rejecting all thoughts of never seeing April again, he shook his head no. Alarm was etched on his frightened face. They both knew Mark did not want April to leave his side.

Dr. Wilson sympathetically asked him if he wanted April to stay with him, and he nodded his head yes as his grip on April's fingers tightened. Faye patted his bare shoulder to calm him down. "It's ok, Mark, calm down. April will stay right beside you until you fall asleep."

Don't leave me, April. Don't leave me alone in this room. I cannot do this without you. Stay with me. I cannot close my eyes and let you go. I need to know you will be here with God and me.

April read his tormented face. "I am here, Mark. We will do this together. I love you." Her soft words calmed his racing heart, just before his vital signs became dangerously unstable, drawing the attention of everyone in the room.

Dr. Wilson bent over him and quickly prayed with him. She told Mark that God had him in the palms of His hands and that God was already at work restoring his body. Mark relaxed and winked his eye at her when she finished.

God, I know You are here with me. Mark envisioned himself healed through his eyes of faith. He was grasping at every word God promised him about healing. His heart soaked in the belief and fervently claimed it.

I trust you, God. I am not afraid. Please comfort my family ... calm their fears for me . . .

Dr. Wilson allowed April to stay while she injected the sedation into Mark's IV line.

"Mark, I'm staying right here. We are going to do this together. Remember, I am on your team," April whispered in his ear, keeping one hand on his and her other hand on his cheek. "When you go to sleep ... think of last night ... dream of us loving each other ... remember when you wake up ... we will be together, forever."

Mark struggled to keep his eyes focused on April. *April, I love you ... April.* He did not want to drift away from her, but he finally gave in as his eyes became heavy. He let sleep take him from the woman that he loved.

"I love you, Mark." Tears filled her eye as she watched him drift into a place she could not enter. "Oh, Mark, come back … to me."

Dan took April by the shoulders and led her out of the room. He assured her Mark was with the best doctors. They went out into the hallway. There Dan held her in his arms, wishing with all his heart he could take her back to her wedding day in the park and *give her back the man she so desperately loved.*

Chapter Eighteen

Covered by His Blood

Dan led an unwilling April to the waiting room. She wanted to turn around and stay with Mark in the OR. She was currently an ER nurse, but she had trained six months in the OR and six months in the ICU. She felt she should be with Mark. She had vowed she would take care of him.

She was not prepared for what she saw in the room when she entered. Rebecca was sitting in a chair in a trance. She thought of Mark's childhood days. He was so full of life and adventure. She remembered holding him as a child in the safety of her arms when he was scared. *Is he scared now, does he need me to hold him, to wipe his tears?*

Rebecca's arms felt empty; she needed to hold him and rock him. Her heart was heavy. She wrapped his tattered jersey around her arms like a blanket. Slowly her tears fell one at a time down her cheeks onto his jersey, as her world faded away. Her brother's life rested in the hands of her husband. *God, lend Your hands to Steven, use him to bring Your healing upon Mark.*

Julia cried softy into Robert's shoulder as he held her, both wondered how they would survive if Mark did not make it through surgery. Robert's thoughts turned to Sunny; she might never get to know her daddy. How could this happen? Mark would have made a great father to Sunny. He thought of his own inadequacies as a father and was overcome with guilt.

Julia's emotions were drained. She was still in shock from the scene she had just witnessed on the football field. Her son had lost his life briefly to a painful death, while she stood there unable to move, unable to make it all better for him. She had watched as they had pounded his chest, inserted long needles in his heart, forced blood in his veins, cut him open with a scalpel. It was a nightmare she would never forget.

Jeff sat on the floor against the wall with his legs drawn up to his chest, his face buried in his knees, his arms wrapped around the top of his head. He was exhausted and filled with grief. His wrists ached from trying to beat life back into his best friend.

He softly repeated, "Come on, Mark, you can beat this." Repeatedly the words stumbled from Jeff's lips. He tried to talk himself into believing Mark would somehow conquer what seemed like the impossible, knowing Mark was bleeding uncontrollably internally.

The hospital and team chaplain, Rev. Rick Smith, was praying with the players that had arrived.

April stared at them, stunned they seemed hopelessly lost in their grief. "What are you doing?" She became angry with all of them, "How can you give up hope for Mark? You are claiming defeat for him. Stop it … all of you!" she screamed from the pit of her stomach. If Mark's family gave up on him, what hope did she have he would survive?

Mark's pastor walked into the room. April ran to embrace him, and searched his face for hope. "Tell them Mark is covered in the blood of Christ, tell them!" she screamed out as Pastor Evan held her against him and spoke to her gently.

Mark was no longer able to be their spiritual believer; April would do it for him. She would lean on his faith; she would not claim his death. She would claim his life. Mark had to live. She wanted everyone in the room to stop mourning him. They had to have faith. Hadn't Mark taught them they had nothing to fear? Hadn't he proved to them he was still full of life when he stood before God and married her just yesterday and again today?

"Mark is not dead! He is alive; claim his life!" she demanded, as she ran from the room, unwilling to be surrounded by their worry.

Debbie and Tammy arrived just as April came into the hallway. April fell into their arms for an embrace; the grip she held on them broke her mother's heart.

Tammy was shocked the day before yesterday when Debbie called to tell her April was getting married. Tammy had succumbed to unbelievable tears when she learned that she had an amazing granddaughter. She caught the first flight out that night to be at the wedding the next morning. On the plane, Tammy had a lot of time to think about what Paul had wrongfully done to their daughter April.

All these years, Paul had been deceitful to her about the baby, her grandchild. *How could he have done that to April and me?* Tammy's heart was shattered, as she thought about the baby that April had carried. Then she remorsefully blamed herself for letting Paul send her away while April was still carrying her baby. She felt the guilt rising up, knowing she should have stayed and helped April with her pregnancy.

She believed Paul when he told her April had miscarried the baby. She wanted desperately to fly home and comfort April, but Paul insisted April was coping just fine. April refused to talk to her about the baby on the phone. Thinking April wanted to put the loss behind her, she agreed April should move on with her life and go to nursing school. Neither of them ever brought up the loss of the baby again.

Tammy understood what it was like to lose a child. Little Allison would never be forgotten, even though she never talked about Allison after that tragic night.

How awful it must have been for April to carry this heart-wrenching secret all these years. *What kind of mother was I that my own daughter could not tell me what had really happened to her baby?*

If only I had the courage to stand up to Paul for once in my life, she thought, but knew that was impossible. Paul was her husband; she had been an overly submissive wife and would continue to live under his powerful authority.

She loved Paul and she knew in the innermost part of her heart he loved her, and he really was a good man. Oh, how she wanted to believe that. Her fear of standing up to him blinded her to some of the unethical things she knew Paul did. Their daughter had been one of his victims, a fact she could not overlook, her heart cried out.

Debbie told Tammy Paul was already in town somewhere and he had made threats against Mark's life. Chills instantly struck her as she remembered the threats Paul had made when he found out April was pregnant.

She was deeply afraid of what Paul might do now that he knew Mark was the father of April's child. Fear overwhelmed her mind that Paul would keep his word and carry through with his threats. Mark needed protected against Paul; that she could not deny.

Sunday morning, the Parker, Morgan, and Johnson families had gathered at the Parker farm, and Dan told them the whole incredible story before they went to the church.

Tammy pulled Dan aside and exposed her fears for Mark's life, begging Dan to protect him. "Paul will find a way to harm Mark," she insisted.

The only one who objected to not allowing Paul to attend the wedding was April's twenty-year-old brother, Todd. Although close to his sisters, he was extremely loyal and closer to his father. The sisters feared Todd was going to take over their father's role when he graduated from the university. Now they feared Todd would betray them and side with his father. Todd could not be trusted either.

The whole family was in a whirlwind of emotions. What Paul had done was inconceivable to the entire family. They all intended to chastise him when he showed up. No one knew where Paul had gone after Dan warned Paul to stay away from Mark and April's wedding in the park. They had a feeling Todd knew something he was not telling them.

Debbie was frustrated with Tammy because she had never stood up to her husband. If Tammy had, April could have told Mark the truth about the baby, and none of this mess would have happened. After the wedding was over, she planned to have a long eye-opening discussion with her mother.

Debbie was shocked April never confided in her about her pregnancy. She remembered when April used to call Mark from her house when they were in high school. She had kept that information to herself. They had always shared their secrets, so why hadn't April come to her about the baby? What had her father done to her little sister? The thoughts were unimaginable.

Little Sunny was just precious, but would she warm-up to the Morgan family, Debbie wondered. They had tried to talk to her at the wedding, but she seemed insecure and shy. They were thankful she seemed comfortable with the Sanders' family, and there was no doubting her intense love for Mark. She seemed happy with April, but her eyes remained on Mark the entire evening.

Robert hired security guards to keep Paul and the paparazzi away from the wedding in the park. He had not counted on the large number of press that had shown up at the church.

Blanche and Lewis were still out there lurking somewhere. No one would breathe easy until they were in police custody. Sunny needed guarded until her kidnappers were located and put behind bars where they belonged.

April broke away from the arms of her mother and wiped her tears as she told her mother and sister she had to go see what was happening to Mark.

April raced to the observation room with her Uncle Dan. She would attentively watch Mark's surgery from there. She stood against the glass window with both hands reaching out to Mark and prayed the words of faith Pastor Evan gave her moments ago.

"Feel me, Mark. I am here for you," she whispered in love. "You belong with me, Mark ... stay with me, Mark." She closed her eyes and could feel him touching her hands. She felt her heart beating as she dreamed he was embracing her in the warmth of his arms at that very minute.

Fear instantly took over her thoughts. Was Mark standing behind her, holding her? Had he left his earthly body and was saying goodbye to her one last time.

No, Mark! If you are here, go back! Fight for us, Mark! Don't leave me behind without you. She closed her eyes tightly and hugged her arms close to her body, praying it was only her imagination that Mark was standing next to her.

She had flashbacks of them embracing, kissing, riding in the carriage, frolicking in the tub that morning, kissing in the bathroom at the church, and standing on the steps to the church. Mark was dressing in the locker room. They were walking hand in hand onto the football field. Their last kiss flashed through her mind as if she was watching a filmstrip.

Mark made her a promise to love her forever, yet she stood there alone, his heart separated from hers, as one more moment in time passed by them.

"Mark ... dream of me ... hold me close to your heart ...hang on, Mark ... for us."

Chapter Nineteen

Mark's Bench

§ઢ

Mark had massive bleeding. Dr. Steven Martin had no choice but to cut Mark's chest from under his breastbone to under his navel. Blood poured down the side of his body and dripped onto the floor. They inserted two more drainage tubes in an attempt to suction the blood as they rushed to get Mark's bleeding under control.

His heart rate was slowly dropping. The shrilling alarm sounded, unnerving all of the doctors. Dr. Wilson let them know Mark was becoming unstable as she turned the volume down a few notches. She relayed Mark's dangerous vital signs to the doctors.

Panic filled the room as the doctors joined together to get the bleeding under control. Steven shouted instructions as a nurse wiped the sweat beads from his forehead.

They could not get Mark's blood to clot; blood was everywhere. They frantically removed his shattered spleen, as his vitals continued to plummet. Alarm showed on all the doctor's faces as they desperately tried again to get everything under control and stop the massive bleeding.

Unit after unit of blood was hung and forced rapidly into his body in a desperate measure to save his life.

April knew what she had to do to save her husband's life. She quickly turned and left the room. She frantically dashed back to the OR, with Dan following close on her heels.

Dan pleaded with her to stay out of the OR. "April, you can't go in there, honey!" He was met with her unwavering eyes and the frantic shake of her head.

"No! Mark needs me. I have to go to him!" *No one will separate me from Mark.* She grabbed a mask and gown, put them on and burst in the room where her husband lay dying. Her determined eyes met Steven's, letting him know she was not leaving the room.

"Don't try to stop me, Steven. Mark is not going to die in your operating room!" Steven gave a sympathetic nod of approval. No one else dared to fuss at her for coming into the room, how could they? If these were Mark's last moments alive, then let him be with the woman that loved him. The doctors were doing all they could. Mark needed a miracle at this point; she might be it.

She took Mark's face in her hands and spoke compassionately to him. She kissed his face, removed the net on his head, and brushed her fingers through his hair. She would do anything it took to let him know she was fighting for his life. "Mark, feel my hands, I am right here."

April prayed with him, her strong unwavering words spoke encouragement. She touched his shoulder, rubbing it with her hand until it was warm. She kissed his forehead repeatedly through her mask, wishing her warm moist lips could touch his skin. She believed her presence would enable him to fight harder to stay alive.

She continued to talk to him with such love and passion she had Dr. Wilson weeping in tears. "Mark, squeeze my hand ... I love you, Mark. Hold on tight and don't let go ... choose us ... choose me."

Then she did the unthinkable. She gathered every ounce of strength she had left, and she sang their wedding song, "Endless Love" to her husband in a soft voice. She claimed the words she sung deep from within her heart and let Mark know their hearts belonged as one. No death would separate them as long as they had each other.

Mark's stats slowly rose. The more April sang and prayed the more he responded. She continued to let him know she was there with him as she cuddled next to his cheek. She took her fingers and softly rubbed his earlobe to remind him of their precious daughter.

"Sunny needs her daddy, Mark. You have to live for Sunny." April cried softly and whispered in his ear, "You promised me, Mark ... you promised me a ... baby." Her warm teardrops melted between their faces. "A baby, Mark, please ... I want a baby."

The doctors were astonished at the response Mark gave April. His heart rate increased and his blood clotting improved. Steven stood back for a second to gather his breath as he realized Mark's fight was not over, it was just beginning.

April's embrace somehow lets Mark know she is here fighting for him. How is that possible? Is the room filled with God's angels? Steven wondered. The tension on his forehead was replaced with peace when he

134

realized his answer was yes. God was right there performing this surgery through his hands.

Finally, they got the blood suctioned out of his abdomen and started to suture him up. The worst was over for now; they had won round one. Relief filled the room as they placed a sterile strip down Mark's abdomen to cover his long incision. There was no denying they had just seen a miracle happen before their eyes. "Amen" was the word spoken by all.

The doctors stood back as they watched Mark's stats continue to get stronger. There was not a doubt God answered April's heartfelt prayers. God was in the presence of this OR touching Mark and breathing life-saving breaths of air into his fragile body.

April stepped back as they lifted Mark carefully onto a gurney. Once he was settled, she took his hand in hers as they transferred him to the recovery room.

Steven went to speak to the family. They were overjoyed, as they hugged and praised God. Only Mark would cheat death and live. It was just like him not to play by the rules. They thanked God together as they joined hands in a circle. They made the fantastic call to the ranch.

April went to the recovery room. She washed her hands and put on a new gown and clean gloves. She was determined she would take care of Mark. When she entered the room, nurse Sherry Grooms, who was attending to Mark, respectfully stepped aside and let April assist in Mark's care with her.

No one else would ever touch his body again, April vowed. He belonged to her and she belonged to him. Together they would take care of each other. Emotions overwhelmed her. She slid into a chair in a heap and wept, thanking God for giving Mark back to her.

If the doctors had not been on the field with all the special equipment to begin treatment so quickly, Mark would have bled out before they had gotten him to the hospital. Their expert planning, down to the very last details of having specially prepared blood available, the helicopter already at the hospital on standby, and having the surgeons waiting in the OR for Mark, had saved his life.

But more importantly, God had been with Mark. They knew all of the credit truly belonged to God. God had undeniably been merciful and spared Mark's life, otherwise Mark would have died on the field just as they had predicted earlier.

Still Mark's family and friends refused to leave the hospital until they could see for themselves that Mark was going to live through the next critical 24 hours the doctors had placed over Mark's life.

Mark's grandparents, staff, and friends gathered at the ranch to lift Mark up in prayer and wait for word on his condition. They were heartbroken when they saw the media coverage play brief clips of Mark dying at the game.

They were careful to shield Sunny from knowing what happened to Mark. Charlie kept her out in the stable as long as he could before taking her inside to wash up for dinner.

However, at dinner, Sunny sensed something was wrong by their hushed voices and everyone's long faces. As the hours passed and the rest of the family did not come home, she knew. She knew in her heart that something awful happened to her new daddy.

There was no consoling her once she over-heard the staff in the kitchen say Mark died on the football field. She hysterically darted from the room, running straight into Maria, nearly knocking her down. Maria grabbed the frightened child, but Sunny fought her way out of Maria's arms. "I want to go to the park! Please, take me to the park!" she tearfully begged Maria.

"Why, Sunny? Why do you want to go to the park?"

"I have to talk to John! Please, can we go right now?" She jumped up and down in a frightful, desperate way.

"Who is John, Sunny? Why do you want to see him?" Maria was struck by Sunny's desperate behavior. Her face expressed deep concern for the distraught child.

"He's the boy in the park who can make all of this go away! John can bring Mark back to me! Take me to the park!" she screamed in a high pitch. "Take me to the park! John will bring Mark back to me!" She was screaming in her desperation to leave now, afraid that as each minute passed, her Mark would not come home ever again.

"Oh, Sunny, John cannot help Mark," Maria cried out confused, and then it suddenly occurred to her: had someone told Sunny about Mark? "Sunny, oh, Sunny, what is wrong?"

"Yes, John can! We will sit on 'Mark's bench' and Mark will come … he won't leave me … alone."

Her tears streamed down her soft little face, her heart breaking. The only thing she knew was the safety of the park where John always watched over her. The park was where Mark rescued her.

She was convinced Mark would be waiting for her there by *their bench*, and he would take her home to his apartment and things would be just fine. Her Mark was not dead. She fell to her knees. Tears poured into her hands as she held them over her face and leaned over her knees.

Just two days ago, Sunny had been kidnapped. She only knew the safety of the park and Mark's apartment. Although she had visited the ranch with Mark, it was not her home. As much as everyone doted on her, tonight they were all just strangers to her. She wanted Mark.

"My Daddy is not dead!" she cried out angrily.

Maria knelt down to her. Her mind was swirling with emotions of her own. Then she suddenly realized that this desperate little child, sitting on the floor, had just said the word 'daddy' for the very first time, and she was referring the word 'daddy' to Mark. "Oh Lord, she thinks she has lost our precious Mark."

"Oh, Sunny, Mark isn't dead. He is very, very sick, but he is not dead." Maria tried to gather Sunny in her arms to comfort her but Sunny pushed her away.

"No, I want Mark!" Sunny continued crying. She did not believe Maria. She had heard the staff; Maria was lying to her. Everyone was lying to her. She had to go to the park and find Mark.

"Take me to the park!" she screamed at everyone who came running when they heard her frightening screams at Maria. Everyone was distraught when they saw the heartbroken child in a heap on the floor crying uncontrollably for her daddy. "Oh, please ... I just want ... Mark."

Maybe if Julia or Robert were here she would feel more secure, Maria thought. Sunny's frightful tears and her desperate need to be in the park overwhelmed everyone who tried unsuccessfully to calm her down.

"I want Mark ... M a r k ... take me to Mark!" It was Old Charlie who was finally able to calm her downpour of tears when he promised to take her to the park. She climbed in his tender arms, held tightly around his neck, and whimpered as he gently patted her back.

The entire family and staff got into the limos and took Sunny to the park. There they gathered at *"Mark's Bench"* and prayed for him with Sunny as a *dove* appeared and sat still on the lamppost.

John too appeared like an angel. He sat next to Sunny on the bench and talked to her as the others watched nearby. Whatever John said to her, his soothing words calmed her down as he rocked her in his sympathetic arms.

"If I stay here, then Mark will have to come get me, right, John? Mark will have to come back. Mark can't die, John, he just can't die." Fresh tears sprinkled down her face, and John tenderly wiped them away.

"Sunny, God is watching over Mark. You have to believe in God right now. Mark would want you to stay with his family tonight, where you will be safe. God will help you when you are feeling sad and missing Mark, I promise."

John's compassionate voice spoke encouraging faith-filled words as he took her hand and helped her stand to her feet. He had the entire family spellbound by his strong words of faith. Maybe Sunny was right; John was an angel. Sunny seized his neck in a hug before she let Charlie carry her back to the limo.

Sunny wanted to see Katie. Katie had always held Sunny in her arms when she was scared at night. But there was no one at the children's home. It had a sign on the door saying it was temporarily closed. Sunny burst into tears. "I'll never see Katie again."

The hour was getting late, but Sunny insisted they go to the church and find Sister Jessica. "She will pray to God for Mark." No one answered the door to the rectory. The note on the door said they would be back on Tuesday.

Poor Sunny, everyone she loved and needed comforting from was unavailable. Her heart poured tears again, and Maria made a frantic call to Robert at the hospital and explained what was happening with Sunny. "We don't know, Robert, what more to do for the little girl."

Robert and Julia rushed to the hospital lobby and met with the family in a private family room. There they lovingly reassured their granddaughter her daddy was going to be just fine. But their faces told a much different story, and Sunny was not convinced they were telling her the truth.

Sunny wanted to see Mark for herself. She tearfully begged to see Mark. "Sunny, Mark is still in surgery," Julia softly explained to her as she glanced at her watch.

They promised her that as soon as Mark was out of surgery they would come home to be with her. She could sleep with them tonight, and tomorrow she could see Mark. It took some convincing before Sunny believed them and agreed to go back to the ranch and wait for them.

Before they got back to the ranch, Sunny fell asleep in Grandma Ella's arms next to Charlie. He carried her into Mark's bedroom and gently laid her on the bed. Grandma Ella lay next to her. Charlie sat Indian style on the rug and prayed. Something in his heart told him Mark needed more prayers. Hopefully, Julia and Robert would be home soon to comfort poor Sunny.

However, her grandparent's promise to come home would have to be broken, as Dan came to them with word on Mark's deteriorating condition.

Chapter Twenty

A Message Received

§♥

Unfortunately, the danger for Mark was far from over, as the devil continued to test the faith of those who wavered. Within an hour of surgery, Mark's temperature rose, his blood pressure dropped, and his heart rate was increasing. His drainage tubes filled with blood.

The doctors feared internal bleeding and decided to return to the operating room to find the source of his bleeding.

Their decision overwhelmed April. She was not thinking like a nurse. She was thinking as his wife. Her agonizing grip on Mark held strong. She was not about to be separated from him again.

She could not imagine the thought of the doctors reopening Mark's abdomen a second time through the same incision they made earlier. She was absorbed in the pain he would have to go through when he woke up later. His body was her body; if it hurt him, it hurt her.

"Jeff, I cannot do it. I can't ... I can't give Mark up." Jeff approached the bed that held Mark. April tearfully collapsed into Jeff's arms as Dr. Martin and Dr. Morgan prepared to move Mark back on the gurney.

April's hand remained tightly wrapped in Mark's hand as she stood her ground that no one was moving him. She was not ready to give him up to the surgeons standing in the room waiting on her to let him go.

"Yes, you can, April. Mark is depending on you." Jeff took her hand that held Mark's hand and started unlocking her resisting fingers.

"No, Jeff, please. I can't let them operate on him again. I cannot bear the thought of his body going through another surgery! Please, all I want is to take Mark in my arms and hold him ... to love him. Not this, Jeff, not this," she cried as the doctors quickly freed Mark of his many monitors.

Jeff would have given anything to give into her heartbreaking demands, but he knew he had to set aside his own feelings and do what had to be done. Mark was slowly drifting away to his inadvertent death as they stood there; every second counted.

Jeff firmly took April by both shoulders, looked directly into her distraught face, and told her Mark needed her to be there with him and she needed to hurry and dress for surgery.

"I'm sorry, April. I know how you feel, but you have to let these doctors help save Mark's life." Then he gathered her in his tender arms and spoke soft comforting words into her ear. For a brief moment, he distracted her while those behind them lifted Mark's unresponsive body and slid him onto the gurney. April turned when her hand became disconnected from Mark's fingers.

"No, you are not taking him anywhere without me!" The doctors frowned at her request, but there was no time to waste disputing her demand, especially since Jeff already promised her she could attend Mark's surgery.

April went through the motions and got herself ready to be at Mark's side. Her whole body ached as she prayed for the strength she needed to fight another battle for Mark's life. Mark was her entire life. She could not exist without him and was not about to give up on him no matter how bad things looked. She did what Mark would have wanted her to do. She continued to pray.

Once again, she stood at the head of the operating table beside Faye and spoke compassionately to him. His eyes were closed, but she believed with all her heart he heard her. She continued to speak words of her unending love to him, as her gloved hands took possession of his upper shoulder.

Jeff and Dan sat quietly in the observation room and watched the dramatic events unfolding below them. Dan's heart desired to be in the OR with Mark, taking total charge of his care, but right now, he was too emotionally close to Mark. He was feeling like Mark's father, not like one of his doctors.

Jeff sat stunned on the edge of his seat as he watched them place Mark back on the operating table. He quickly stood up and left the room when his emotions rose up in his churning stomach. He knocked into Tom's shoulder as he exited the room, but no apologetic words were exchanged. Tom joined Dan; neither said a word as they focused their attention on Mark. Instead, silent prayers filled their minds.

"Let's begin," April heard Steven instruct the surgical team. April closed her eyes and took a long deep breath, praying she would not faint.

142

She focused back on the touch of her hands on Mark as she gently ran her fingertips along his cheeks.

She would be strong for him. She prayed with her whole soul. She truly believed God was right there with them. Mark was in the arms of God's angels as they surrounded him in their protection against this attack on him.

Once again, Mark unbelievably responded to her voice and touch. No one could explain why Mark survived the first surgery, let alone the second one. Those without faith were astonished Mark was alive; it was just not possible. Only God could be the answer.

The doctors were able to get the bleeding under control and for the second time they sewed him up. The second loss of blood would make his recovery even more difficult when they factored in his anemia.

The blood bank only had a few bags of blood left that were prepared especially for Mark. They would make another plea for O negative blood from Mark's list of volunteer donors. Dr. Stevenson cringed at the amount of blood Mark had received. He knew each unit given to Mark posed a threat against the successfulness of his upcoming transplant. *The odds just continue to stack up against him*, he thought with discouragement.

Dan stood in tears because he was unable to help Mark. He could not give Mark a single drop of his blood. He was crushed when he found out he was not a perfect bone marrow match. It did not matter now; Mark would always be his son, no matter what the interpretation of the test results revealed. Mark had been his son for 24 years; that fact would never change in Dan's heart.

Jeff came into the observation room again. "How is the surgery going?" His voice was painfully heavy, as he briefly looked down into the OR while trying to keep his composure.

"They are closing Mark up right now. He is going to be fine, Jeff. They found the source of his bleeding," Tom told him as he held his hand on Jeff's droopy shoulder. He knew Jeff was reliving the death of his brother as he watched over Mark.

"Mark's teammates are still here. They want to give blood. I told them to come back tomorrow and give. I'll go tell them Mark is ..." Jeff swallowed the lump, took a deep breath, and walked away.

Mark would be honored to know so many of his fans came to pray for him. They held candles as they stood outside the hospital waiting on word of his condition.

Many decided to return to give blood the next day. From his tragic situation, Mark started a public awareness, which could save many lives.

Dan knew it took a lot of courage for Mark to make the speech he did at the football game.

A painful but true fact came to Dan's mind. Mark's verbal message about giving blood was meaningful, but not as meaningful as when he succumbed to his illness right there on the field where everyone watching saw firsthand how important it was to donate blood.

People could not ignore what they saw happen to Mark on the football field, and that is precisely why they would line up outside the hospital the next day and give blood when the bloodmobiles arrived.

When there is a tragedy in America, the American people respond with compassionate hearts. Mark nearly died on a football field in front of millions of viewers across the country.

Because of this, Mark had opened hearts throughout America. His message had been received; people wanted to donate blood. The hospital switchboard was overwhelmed with callers wanting to know when they could donate blood in honor of Mark.

They moved Mark back to the recovery room. He would spend the rest of the night in there, just in case he had to be rushed back into surgery. Steven, Sally, and Sherry planned to camp out in the recovery room with April. Jeff and Dan would come in and out as needed.

After getting Mark's CBC report, the doctors decided not to send him to the ICU in the morning with his white blood count so dangerously low. There were too many critical patients in ICU with contagious conditions. Mark needed to be in isolation; they could not chance an infection. They would have to take every precaution to ensure that he was not exposed to anything.

It was determined that Mark would go to the Bone Marrow Unit in the morning under the care of a former ICU nurse, but only after they established he was stable enough to be transferred.

During the last week, his father had a room remodeled for him in the Bone Marrow Unit. It was much larger, and it had glass pane walls to bring in the outside world to him. It had all the state-of-the-art ICU equipment in it they would need to care for Mark. It was even equipped with a video monitoring system so the nurses could keep a close watch on Mark from the nurse's station. It was finally ready for him to use. The room would remain his home for the next few months.

Steven briefly allowed Julia, Robert, and Rebecca to see Mark from the doorway of the recovery room. However, much to their disappointment, they were not allowed to come to the side of the stretcher and touch him.

April was exhausted as she tended to Mark. Jeff finally convinced her to leave Mark in the care of Sally Johnson and Sherry Grooms, while he took her to lie down in the Unit for a few hours. At first, she protested but Jeff was able to convince her that she needed her strength for later.

"I know the secret you and Mark have. He would not want you to get sick and lose that little secret. Come with me and get some rest, April." Jeff was right; she had to take care of herself if she was going to give Mark the baby he so desperately prayed was forming in her womb.

When they came out of the Surgical Unit, April was greeted by Mark's teammates who were lined up on both sides of the hallway. Jeff held April firmly as her legs gave way when she saw all the men who loved Mark, standing there with their long faces. They were not just there for Mark; they were there for her, too. She was part of the team now and she loved them for all the kindness they showed her.

Carlo and Justin came forward, she fell into their arms, and all three of them cried. The teammates offered their prayers and asked her if she needed anything. She politely thanked them for their kind support.

"How are the other players? Are they feeling better?" she thoughtfully asked. Carlo told her Kevin was dehydrated, and so were most of the other guys. He said something about *spoiled eggs* at a privately catered party the second string players went to that morning before church.

April tried to concentrate on Carlo's words, but her mind was consumed with thoughts of Mark. She wanted to turn around, go to him, and wrap him back in her empty arms.

Jeff led her down the hallway and into the elevator. All she could think of was the elevator ride going up to the penthouse when Mark held her in his arms waiting impatiently to begin their honeymoon.

If only time had stood still for them that night, she would not be in this elevator without him. Instead, she would be holding him securely in her arms and making love to him under the skylights of the city.

Chapter Twenty-One

Supernatural

§§

Absolutely no family or friends would be allowed to enter Mark's room in the Unit. Only the nurses and doctors, in full gowns, gloves, and masks could enter the restricted area. Dr. Tom Stevenson was not taking any chances of Mark getting an infection.

Christy would be Mark's nurse at night. Beth Moran would be his nurse during the day. Beth had been an ICU/surgical nurse before transferring to the Bone Marrow Unit. Beth was married to Robert's pilot, Tony, so she and Mark already knew each other. Again, Tom considered Mark's need for confidentiality to protect his dignity from outside sources eager to expose private information about him.

April showered and changed into a set of scrubs. She lay down on Mark's bed and cuddled his pillow to her chest as if she were holding tight to him. Tonight would have been their second honeymoon night, but she lay alone, lost without her husband. She drew her knees up into the fetal position. Tears trickled down her face as she thought of him.

Jeff covered her with a blanket before leaving her alone so she could release her inconsolable tears for the man she loved. Last night he watched Mark care for her; now that job was up to him. *Mark, she does not want me; she wants you.*

April would be the only one allowed to touch Mark's body besides the medical staff. She would be Mark's only normal link to the outside world while he recovered. They put an extra bed in his room so April could sleep in it. After hours of watching the hands of the clock tick by, and numerous calls to check on Mark, she let sleep mercifully claim her as she dreamed of Mark right where she was, in his bed.

Early Monday morning Mark was stable enough to be moved to the Unit. April impatiently waited for him. At six a.m., Tom, Steven, Jeff, and Dan wheeled Mark in on the gurney, and with the help of Christy, they transferred him onto his bed.

Christy hooked Mark up to all the machines and monitors. Once they got him settled, Steven took ownership of the couch against the wall. Steven thought it would be better if they let Mark's sedative wear off. Mark would be the best one to judge his own condition if he was having any medical problems. They would slowly wean him off the sedative and wait for him to regain consciousness before removing the breathing tube from his throat.

April attentively responded to Mark's needs with preciseness, fearful of causing him any additional pain. Dan and Christy stood at April's side as Dan watchfully eyed the monitors.

Robert and Julia stood outside his room and anxiously watched from the glass door. Julia's arms ached to hold her frail son and comfort him. When Tom came out of Mark's room, Julia tearfully begged him to allow her in the room so she could hold Mark.

"Not today, Julia. Mark's blood counts are extremely low. We cannot take any chances. I'm sorry, Julia. I promise as soon as Mark improves, you can touch him. It would be better for Mark if everyone stayed at the ranch for the next few days instead of coming here. I am afraid if they visit, Mark will want to see them, and right now, it is imperative no one go in that room." There was no budging in his voice.

"Can we call him?"

Tom shook his head, no. "Julia, Mark needs uninterrupted rest. I will let him call his entire family when he is stronger. Please, ask everyone to wait for Mark to call them. It is crucial Mark have adequate time to heal." It was time for him to be the doctor and not the family friend. He had to stand firm with them. Mark's life depended on his strict rules.

Tom was met with tearful eyes. "Julia, today is Monday, and thanks to the good Lord, we will not be going to a funeral today. Let's focus on that miracle. Mark has been given a second chance at living, and I am going to do everything in my power to keep your son alive."

It was true just days ago Tom had given them no hope, but things were different now. Tom had seen one miracle happen, and he was sure God had another miracle waiting in store for Mark.

Mark stirred for about 40 minutes but refused to open his heavy eyes. He would attempt to respond to April if she asked him a question by moving his head from side to side or lifting his hands off the bed. She repeatedly asked him to open his eyes, but he turned his head as if to say, "no, not yet" before drifting back to sleep for a few more minutes.

The cycle repeated itself until finally he regained his senses. He was unable to speak to her because of the breathing tube in his throat. He opened his drowsy eyes and looked into her warm inviting eyes. The joy he felt covered up his extreme pain. He closed his eyes and thanked God for sparing his life.

Jeff came in the room and was glad to hear Mark was awake. He volunteered to take the next shift with April so Steven could leave the room and get some much-needed rest in his office.

Since Mark was in the Unit and no longer in the Recovery Room, Steven wanted to keep a doctor on hand in case Mark's condition required immediate attention. Steven planned to stay at the hospital until he felt Mark was out of the woods. The doctors would rotate so one of them was always nearby.

Jeff gently touched Mark's shoulder, and Mark slowly opened his eyes and looked straight into his best friend's solemn face. Mark's weak eyes showed gratitude as thankful tears formed in the corners of his eyes. Jeff bent and gave Mark an affectionate hug, careful not to touch his injured body. When Jeff's tears came, he backed off and went into the bathroom, removed his mask, and washed his face in cool water.

April followed Jeff into the bathroom, wrapped her consoling arms around his arched back and held him. She planned to comfort him but her touch melted his heart. His quiet tears turned into sobs as he fell back against the wall and wept into his hands as April held him. "I can't lose him, April." Jeff turned and looked into April's face, and without having to speak the words that were tearing at their hearts, they understood how the other felt as they supportively embraced.

Two hours later, Mark woke up again, and just as Jeff predicted, Mark wanted his breathing tube removed. It was reassuring to have Mark acting like his old self. Jeff called the respiratory therapist, Tonya, to evaluate Mark's condition. Once Mark was cleared to breathe on his own with additional oxygen, Jeff removed the tube with April's assistance. April placed the oxygen mask on Mark's face. Jeff gave thanks Mark still had some fight left in him.

Mark's first audible word was "Sunny." He anxiously wanted her brought to him. "I want to see … Sunny."

"Mark, if Sunny saw you like this, it would frighten her. She is better off with Charlie and Grandmother Ella," Jeff spoke convincingly.

Mark reluctantly agreed for the time being. He thought back to the memories of her at his wedding. She was his little angel, his gift from God. Tears formed in his eyes thinking of her.

April sat on Mark's bed and ran her fingers through his hair. He watched her with sleepy eyes. He could not believe she was his wife. He drifted in and out, opening an eye to see if she was still there and then going back to sleep.

A few hours later, he woke up and held his hand to his raw throat. His throat was sore from the breathing tube. April put the bed in a semi-sitting position to help him breathe easier. She held a pillow to his aching abdominal muscles where his incision ran down his entire abdomen. She encouraged him to continue coughing and to breathe deeply. He handed her back the incentive spirometer she had given him. Then she spoon-fed him some ice chips from his hospital water jug.

Jeff crashed on the other bed from exhaustion. They looked over at him and smiled at each other. Mark removed April's facemask and his lips found hers as she leaned in for his kiss. She willingly let him have his way and gave him one simple kiss she thought was all too short, before he drifted back away from her into a deep relaxing sleep.

When he woke up again later he was drowsy and fought to remain conscious so he could bathe himself in April's love. She carefully lay down next to him, avoiding the several sets of drainage tubes impelling his chest and abdomen, careful not to get them in the way of their bodies touching.

She put her arm under his neck and laid her head down on his pillow. He reached his hand up, caressed her face, and peacefully fell asleep knowing they were safe in each other's arms. April closed her eyes; it had been another long day. She had so much to be thankful for, she thought. Christy finished her assessment of Mark and went to the nurse's station to update the nurse taking over Mark's care.

Christy stopped by to tell them she was going home. She stopped short when she saw them sleeping. Instead, she stood in quiet prayer for the two of them. Dan approached and reviewed Mark's chart before entering with Beth to assess Mark's progress.

An hour later, Mark moved in his sleep and cried out in pain. His loud groans woke April. Mark remained unconscious, moaning and restless, his eyes closed but his face wrenched in agony.

April got up and requested his pain medication. Beth slipped it through a drawer in the wall that went from the outside into his room. She spoke on the intercom. "April, I have to go downstairs for lunch. If you need anything, the other floor nurse on duty, Eve, can help you. Dr. Stevenson is in his office."

April was not sure she felt comfortable with Eve. They had briefly met Eve when Mark was first admitted to the Unit a week ago. Eve seemed rather rigid and inhospitable when she was introduced to Mark. Mark said she needed to go to charm school and learn a few things about dealing with the public.

April injected the medication into Mark's central line and waited for it to take effect. Mark began to stir. What had they done to him? He felt as if he had been butchered. Once the medication took the edge off his pain, Mark opened his eyes and stared at her in a daze.

She sat on his bed beside his waist and held his hand in hers. He was still too stiff to move without sending sharp waves of pain down his entire abdomen, but that didn't stop him from undoing the strings to April's facemask and pulling it away from her face. A satisfied smile crossed his face.

Once he gathered his thoughts about the game, he thought about his teammates: Kevin and the guys. "What happened to them?" he weakly asked April with concern. She told him they were still downstairs getting fluids for dehydration. They had eaten *spoiled eggs* at a private party that morning from what she could figure out from Carlo.

Mark forced a smile on his pained face, and April puzzlingly asked him why he was smiling. He grinned and explained to her that he was thinking about the passionate breakfast the two of them had shared.

She blushed and told him to behave. His hands were not listening. They claimed her waist with intentions of enjoying the softness of her curves. He withdrew them when he felt the pain of his movements. He grabbed the pillow on his chest and held it tightly. He let out a moan as a sharp pain briefly took his breath away. He was thankful for the pain; it meant he was alive.

He had risked his life for the team, but he was not proud of that decision at this very confusing moment as his mind raced with thoughts he did not welcome. He realized he could have lost it all. He humbly thanked God for standing beside him even though he had gone against His will and taken matters into his own hands. God was a merciful God, Mark acknowledged with a grateful heart. Mark could feel God's presence and knew he was lying in the presence of greatness as he closed his eyes in a solemn prayer.

Mark thanked God for His favor on his life and for fulfilling his dream of an AFC win. Mark opened his eyes and admired April, his greatest gift of all from God. *God, please let her be pregnant*, he thought as he placed his hand gently on her stomach. Then Mark closed his eyes and fell peacefully back to sleep. April curled around him, claimed his same prayer for a baby and fell asleep.

When Jeff woke up during the afternoon, he checked Mark's vital signs. Normal. Mark was receiving his supernatural healing; there was no other explanation. Mark had received God's miracle upon his life. There would be no funeral tomorrow.

Jeff was a believer. He stood watching Mark sleep soundly beside the woman he loved. Mark's faith never altered as he fought his battle. Mark spoke healing and he received healing.

God rewarded Mark for his faithfulness. Tomorrow was a new day. The sun would come up, and Mark would be able to bask in the warmth of it thanks to the Father that created the heavens and the earth.

Thanks to the God that surrounded Mark with His shield of protection.

Chapter Twenty-Two

The Mod Squad

§ℰ

Mark would spend the next few days drifting in and out. April worried Mark was unable to wake up completely. Tom assured her Mark's body needed the extra sleep. The meds they gave him were making him sleepy. "Mark needs to give his body time to heal," he stressed. "He will have his good days and his bad days for the next few weeks."

Mark lost a lot of blood during his surgeries. They were quickly trying to replace his blood volume. Mark's blood counts were a tad higher from the many units of blood transfusions they continued to give him. His white blood cell count had them all concerned.

Removing his spleen would help with the transfusions, but his battle was not over. Removing his spleen had its own complications they would have to address soon. He was a living target for infections and left with no immunity against bacterial infections.

Because of his aplastic anemia, Dr. Stevenson elected not to vaccinate him against pneumococcal pneumonia. The risk was too high with his counts. In Mark's case, he would have to remain on long-term treatments of antibiotic drugs to prevent post-splenectomy sepsis.

His unstable heart rate was a concern for Dr. McGuire, who wanted him closely monitored. She assigned her nurse practitioner, Vivian Wiggins, to Mark's case. However, Megan came in and out of his room several times a day to check on him personally. She was convinced Mark had not had a panic attack at the church. It had been more serious than they first thought; he had angina caused by his anemia.

Because Mark was so weak, Tom would not be able to continue any of Mark's treatments for his aplastic anemia, due to the fearfulness of Mark's former reactions to the drugs he needed. If only Mark would respond to them normally, Tom thought as he stepped out of Mark's room. What could they do to make that happen, Tom questioned, as he passed Marty in the hallway.

Tom continued to worry about the amount of transfusions Mark had received so far and all the ones he would need later to keep him alive while they waited for him to recover from his surgery.

The transfusions would make his bone marrow transplant less successful. Complicating things even more were the devastating results from his unsuccessful stem-cell removal. Tom and Dan had yet to share that information with anyone other than Steven.

The doctors learned one important fact, as long as April was in his arms, his blood pressure stayed normal. If she left his side while he was asleep, he would wake up in a panic. Her reassuring touch was enough to calm him back to sleep. If Mark was afraid, he never expressed it or explained what caused his need to have her near him. But April knew the reason. When they were apart, their hearts were separated; his half would not work without hers.

Julia and Robert came every day and stood at the glass door to Mark's room with the hopes of being able to go inside and touch their son. As the days passed, Julia felt more desperate to have Mark in the safety of her protective arms. It did not matter Mark was a grown man, he was her son, and her maternal instincts were stronger than ever as she struggled with her need to take care of him.

Rebecca continued to work on the third floor even though Dan volunteered to let her work in the Unit and care for Mark. Her visits to the Unit to see Mark were few. Steven worried about her emotional state, but she insisted she was coping just fine with what happened to Mark.

Doctor Martin put Mark under the care of two of the hospital's finest physical therapists, Teresa Taylor and Kathleen Naper, who just happened to be sisters.

Normally Steven would have gotten his patient up out of bed soon after surgery. Mark's case was different. They could not risk him falling or bumping into anything with his low blood counts. Steven gave strict instructions for Mark's care to Teresa and Kathleen. He said he would seriously pray for them; they would need it. "You might want to double team Mark when he gets stronger," Steven added with a shake of his head, knowing how hardheaded his brother-in-law could be.

Teresa and Kathleen had heard rumors about Mark's past hospital visits. Mark was about to meet his match with these two sisters. They gave each other a supportive grin and welcomed the challenge of Dr. Mark Sanders.

As Mark became more alert that morning, he struggled to move around in the bed. He wanted to gain control of his body, but he was still too weak and any movement caused him extreme pain. Just sitting up took all his energy. Beth helped April arrange the pillows around Mark to make him more comfortable and he fell back asleep.

Beth volunteered to sit with Mark while April went to take a shower. April had not let Mark out of her sight since he was brought to the Unit, but she was exhausted and a warm shower was just what she needed. She gave Beth a warm hug and took her up on her offer.

Beth was warm, soft spoken, and thoughtful. April knew Mark was safe with her. Beth replaced her hand in Mark's as April removed hers. The switch of hands did not fool Mark; a minute later, he was awake. Somehow, he knew April was missing. He waited for her to come back into the room before falling asleep again with her in his arms.

Teresa came in his room that morning after her talk with Dr. Martin. Mark was semi-awake and she briefly spoke to him. She found him frustrated he could not move; his entire body was stiff. She tried to make him understand what he was experiencing was normal for someone who had just undergone major emergency surgery like the one he endured.

Mark liked her the minute they met. Her soothing voice and her compassionate demeanor were just what he needed. He felt extremely helpless lying there in his bed imprisoned by all the tubes and wires. But most of all, Mark liked Teresa's encouraging laugh when she talked to him.

Teresa was in her early forties, with dark brown shoulder length hair and deep brown eyes. She was not very tall but she was strong for her petite size. She had a warm disposition and plenty of patience when it came to working with her somewhat temperamental patient.

Mark could barely keep his eyes open as they spoke casually. She explained to him what she was about to do, but by then, his eyes stayed closed. April attentively checked his oxygen prongs in his nose, rearranged the lead wires to the heart monitor, and adjusted his pillow.

Teresa's compassionate heart went out to the young wife knowing exactly how emotionally straining it was to care for someone you love.

Dr. Martin had explained the entire situation to them about Mark's current condition and his background history as a patient. Mark was fighting an uphill battle, and if he was going to be successful, it would take all of them caring for him to give him his final victory. Teresa thought back to Sunday night, when her own family had been saddened over what had happened to Mark.

Sunday, Teresa's husband Pete had been at the game with her two teenage sons, Joseph and Nicholas. They had never experienced anything as overwhelming as watching their favorite quarterback dying on the same field in which he had just boldly won the AFC Championship Game seconds before his tragic fall.

Her household remained quiet later that night. The next day the only sound was the TV, as they listened for updates on Mark's condition, just like thousands of people across the nation. They re-watched the events of the game, including a replay of a tender kiss April and Mark shared on the sideline during the game. The report ended showing the doctors desperately trying to resuscitate Mark while his wife stood horrified.

"Just hours after taking a bride, quarterback Mark Sanders, seen here with his new wife April. Who is this April anyways, what have we found out about her …?"

"We were there, Mom, this is history, like, where were you when the space shuttle blew up, we were there when Mark Sanders threw an incredible pass with 15 seconds left in the game and we won the championship! So why did they have to show us the pictures of him dying? It's not right." Joseph expressed as he reenacted Mark's winning touchdown pass with his arm while he was telling his mother what happened.

Teresa got up and turned the TV off; that was enough. It angered her that the news media had invaded Mark's privacy by airing something so tragically personal to Mark and made it available for public viewing.

She prayed for the Sanders' family. It was beyond comprehending how they were feeling tonight. She prayed they were nowhere near a television where they would have to relive the moment their son almost died, all over again. She planned to write a letter to the station and tell them a thing or two about the coverage they had shown.

Mark's teammates had stood around Mark on the field to shelter him from the view of the fans and to keep the press and cameras out, but they forgot about the blimp above the stadium. The blimp had captured the entire event.

Just as Mark had feared, he was the main headline on all the scandalous newspapers the next day. "Sanders marries after finding out he is a father." "Mark Sanders fathers a child six years ago." "Sanders nearly dies after AFC win." "Sanders makes plea – give blood." "Mark Sanders tells all before AFC game." "Sanders made history with last minute pass for AFC Championship Title." "Dreams of a Super Bowl for Mark Sanders end ..."

Teresa called her office at the hospital Monday morning to see if she could find out how Mark was doing. Then she headed to the hospital, unaware Mark Sanders would be her patient the following day.

When she arrived at work, she was surprised to see hundreds of people standing in line to give blood. Flower arrangements and large poster-size get-well cards lined the entrance to the hospital. The entrance was blocked-off by police and barricades, as news crews stood in rows; many camped out in lawn chairs. It was a mass of confusion.

She wanted to go over there and tell the media and paparazzi off. They needed to leave this devastated family alone and let them grieve without this entire invasion of their privacy.

The major networks and the local networks were showing appropriate reports on Mark. They recognized his accomplishments, highlighting his winning touchdown throw. They replayed his speech before the game. They showed scenes from the hospital showing the people lined up to give blood in honor of Mark.

A press conference was shown later that day with Mark's coaches, Dr. Martin, Dr. Morgan and Dr. Stevenson. They carefully selected the information they released and made a statement for the media to respect the privacy of Mark and his family during this difficult time.

Teresa was even more surprised Tuesday when her phone rang, and Dr. Steven Martin requested a meeting with her to discuss Mark Sanders as her new patient. She felt honored to be able to help Mark regain his life.

Teresa watched Mark sleep as she firmly stretched his leg muscles out where he had complained they were cramping up on him. She continued his treatment of stretches while he dozed. Occasionally he opened his eyes to protest when it got too painful for his abdominal muscles.

She continued with a smile and encouraged him with her laugh to keep trying to move his legs on his own even if they were tight and painful. She showed him how to pump his feet up and down, as if he was pushing on the accelerator of his car. She did not want him to get any blood clots in his legs. She checked the surgical stockings on his legs and made sure he had no spontaneous bleeding under his skin.

He opened his sleepy eyes and looked at her so pitifully. Mark wanted more; he wanted to sit up so he could stand up. The door opened and in walked a bubbly Kathleen. She came over to the bed and smiled at Mark.

"Hello, Mark, I am Kathleen. I will be working with Teresa today." Kathleen calmingly touched his shoulder as Mark wrenched from a sudden shot of pain in his abdomen. He reached up to shake her hand, and then he closed his eyes for a brief second to contemplate his thoughts. His throbbing pain did not stop his determination as he opened his weak eyes and surprised them all by his soft pleading words.

"I want out of bed ... I want to walk ... right now," he said weakly as he lifted his head slowly off his pillow. They knew he meant what he said, when he painfully twisted his shoulder up and wrenched again in pain, scaring April half to death.

"Absolutely not, Dr. Sanders. I do not believe, Sir, that you will be going anywhere today," Kathleen told him firmly as she dared Mark to disobey her with her powerful brown eyes. Mark closed his eyes and fell back against his pillow as April attended to him with extreme concern.

The women helped him turn on his side and bent his legs to relieve the pressure on his abdominal muscles. April surrounded him with soft pillows.

April did not leave his side even after he fell back asleep, and the morning turned into the afternoon before his eyes opened again. Beth came in with a food tray and encouraged April to eat something. She checked all Mark's vital signs and made notes in his chart.

Vivian and Sherry came to monitor his heart. Mark eyed Sherry as she placed the stethoscope on his chest, while Vivian looked over Mark's chart.

During Teresa and Kathleen's next visit, Mark was more alert and he poked fun at them, calling Teresa the good cop and Kathleen the bad cop as they worked together to keep his muscles strengthened and the blood circulating in his legs. Because of his aplastic anemia, his doctors could not give him the drugs he needed for blood clots so he was under a careful watch by his entire team of caregivers.

Teresa indulged him and Kathleen challenged him, a balance that worked well when it came to dealing with Mark, the doctor; need they say more about their hardheaded patient?

Mark was referring to them as the "Mod Squad" by the end of the day. He was convinced Dr. Stevenson had hired the women to police over him and keep him in line while he was a patient.

"Mark, you need to stop worrying about sitting up on your own. It's too soon; let's just concentrate on building up your strength one day at a time. Your body needs time to heal. You cannot force your body to do what you want it to do right after major surgery. That is why I am here. I will do it for you." Teresa fussed over him.

"Mark, you put one toe on that floor without us, and I will personally handcuff you to this bed." Kathleen smiled warmly as she lifted her eyebrows up at him and teased him. Just the same, she let him know who his boss was: Mod Squad rules!

Kathleen reminded Mark of his sister Rebecca: she was caring but firm when it came to taking care of him. Kathleen had a smile that was contagious and Mark planned to test that smile out as often as possible, just so he could hear Teresa laugh.

Nevertheless, the minute Teresa and Kathleen left the room; Mark tried repeatedly to sit up on his own, falling back against the bed in an exhausted state, unable to sit up on his own without the support of the bed behind him. He continued all day long in his determination to conquer this simple task.

April tried to encourage Mark to be patient, but that was one thing Mark Sanders lacked as he continued to struggle to sit up so he could stand. "I am an NFL quarterback; I can do this!" He ended up exhausting himself and fell asleep for the next several hours, just to repeat the same process again when he woke up later.

The once vibrant and muscular man found himself unable to do the simplest things and it frustrated him. He did not want anyone to touch him physically but April. He was determined to regain all he had lost as soon as possible.

The "Mod Squad" came daily to treat Mark and to show April what to do with his legs and arms to keep his muscles functioning while he was restricted to his bed.

Mark knew his "Mod Squad" was his only hope of staying physically fit so he welcomed them into his room at least three times a day, encouraging them to push him to another level of movement. His workouts were one thing he took very seriously.

They quickly learned Mark had no limitations on his expectations of getting back in the best physical shape possible. His anxious thoughts of having Sunny in his arms would be his driving force to get better quickly. They would have to watch him carefully so he did not hurt himself trying to do things too quickly on his own.

Was the "Mod Squad" up to the challenges of Mark Sanders?

Chapter Twenty-Three

Challenges to Face

§∂

Mark desperately wanted to hold Sunny. He called his parents and begged them to bring her to the hospital. Dr. Stevenson remained firm. No visitors and absolutely no children could visit Mark, and unfortunately, that included Sunny and his parents.

Mark felt deeply depressed as more and more things were taken out of his control. He felt stripped to the bone physically and mentally, and it was not a pleasant feeling.

But the implausible truth was the state had come in and wanted to remove Sunny from the ranch until the whole situation with custody could be heard in the courts.

The restraining order issued to keep Mark away from Sunny was still in effect. Robert did not have the heart to tell Mark his own daughter could not visit him.

From what they could gather, Blanche took Sunny to a motel after she informed Blanche that Mark was her real father and April was her mother. Blanche's brother, Lewis, joined her there. Sunny did not know she was in any danger until she saw the missing child report on the TV while Blanche and Lewis stood outside the room secretly talking.

She thought Blanche was taking her to a new foster home. "I don't wanna go to another foster home! Mark is my daddy! Why can't I live with Mark?"

Sunny remembered the fight she had put up as Blanche took her from the children's home. Now she realized Blanche was not taking her to another foster home. Blanche was kidnapping her. But why? None of this made any sense to her but she knew she needed to find out what to do.

Sunny called the front desk and tearfully told them she was the child that was reported missing on the newsbreak she had just seen on TV. Then she bravely locked the door as instructed. She put a chair up against the doorknob so they could not get back into the room. When Blanche and Lewis heard the sirens, they fled, leaving Sunny behind when they could not get back into the room to grab her.

Captain Grant Nelson contacted Dan, and he immediately picked Sunny up from the police department under the supervision of Mrs. Wilson. They took Sunny to the hospital to be examined. Dan filled in the missing pieces surrounding the kidnapping of Mark Sanders' and April Morgan's daughter to Mrs. Wilson.

Dan asked Dr. Gina Price to examine Sunny's mental state. Both exams thankfully revealed Sunny was just fine. Dan reported the wonderful news to Robert and Julia in the donation room.

With Julia and Robert at her side, Sunny was tested for the HLA match for Mark. Once the test was finished, Robert and Julia were allowed to take her home with them, since the children's home would be closing.

Julia began planning the surprise dinner party for Mark and April at the ranch. Julia planned to surprise Mark and April with Sunny. It was to be Sunny's homecoming party, as she reunited with her parents.

However, Mark called Julia and informed her of his plans for the night. His wedding plans had been a welcomed change. Julia could hardly believe what Mark was telling her over the phone as joyful tears consumed her. With less than four hours, the family came together to make Mark's dream of marrying April in the park that night happen.

So far, Robert had prevented the state from taking Sunny from the ranch. Mrs. Wilson had allowed Robert and Julia to be temporary foster parents. After all, what choice did Mrs. Wilson have? The children's home had been closed and there were too few foster homes to house all of those girls.

Mrs. Wilson had shown them favor for now, but the judge refused to change the court's ruling to allow Mark visitation with Sunny. More specifically he stated Sunny could not be alone with Mark at his apartment. He set up a court hearing to determine custody, since the Stanley's were still insisting they wanted custody of Sunny. The whole situation was one giant mess.

Robert failed to mention to Judge Thompson that when Mark was released from the hospital he planned to live at the ranch with April and Sunny. Therefore, the complicated legal issues and the battle for custody were just beginning. But the facts remained: Sunny was a ward of the state, not the daughter of Mark Sanders or April Morgan Sanders.

Robert had not told April or Mark the problems they were facing. In the end, Robert knew they would win their custody case. He would stop at nothing to give Mark back his daughter, and knowing Mark, it had better happen soon.

Sunny was getting more and more depressed as she missed Mark and April. Julia was home schooling her during the mornings, and in the afternoons she would stay in the stable with Charlie and Thunder and her pet cat, Hannah and her dog, Madison.

The staff grew weary looking into Sunny's downcast eyes knowing nothing could cheer her up until she was in Mark's arms again.

One morning, Charlie came rushing into the house all excited and wanted Sunny to come with him to the stable.

"You gotta see this, little missy."

"What, Charlie, what is it?" She jumped up and down.

"Just you follow me." He grinned and gave a wink to the staff standing there waiting, as impatient as Sunny was to find out what old Charlie had in the stable.

The staff followed on their heels to the stable. What a funny sight they made, chasing after Charlie and Sunny, in a long line.

When Sunny got there, she discovered Hannah was now a momma. Sunny was overjoyed. This gave her something to look forward to every afternoon when Charlie came and got her. "Oh, Charlie, they are so cute. I gotta go tell Mark the news."

Sunny would spend hours in the stable playing with the kittens as Charlie and the ranch hands watched cautiously over her. All understood the kidnappers were still out there. Pedro increased security at the front gate to the ranch. Robert hired a bodyguard, Anthony, to accompany Julia and Sunny whenever they went out of the home.

Charlie had become attached to Mark's ambitious little girl. She reminded him of her father when he was a boy. She had the same high spirit for life. Sunny was easily winning the hearts of the entire family, staff and ranch hands. Grandma Ella spent hours with her each day just as Mark had spent time with his grandfather.

Debbie and her mother, Tammy, visited Sunny, trying to develop a bond with her. Sunny still seemed preoccupied with her thoughts of Mark. Although she was pleasant with them, something in her distant eyes told them she only wanted her father's attention. Sunny did not seem as concerned about missing April, and this worried them.

When Tammy spoke to Julia about her concerns with Sunny, Julia reassured her Sunny's attachment with Mark was deeper because he was the one who rescued her from the park, and she lived with him at his apartment. Sunny only knew April as Mark's girlfriend, or her big sister, not as her mother.

"Sunny is more concerned about Mark because he is so sick. She is afraid of losing him. Just give her more time. I know she loves April," Julia encouraged them as she hid her own reservations about Sunny's distant relationship with April.

Dan made it a priority to visit Sunny and fussed over her just as he had done with Mark when he was a boy. Sunny called him Uncle Dan which was fine with him, as long as he owned a part of her heart, and he could be her stand-in grandfather, too. Sunny's growing attachment to Dan was no surprise to anyone. She saw her daddy in Dan's gentleness.

If only Dan could give Sunny what she really wanted, he would have wrapped her up in his arms and taken her to Mark.

Better than that, Dan would have given anything to bring his son back home where he belonged, with all those that loved him.

Chapter Twenty-Four

Unwavering Determination

§♦

The next day, Dr. McGuire reported that Mark's heart appeared to be stable. They were sure Mark was in God's hands as he continued to show rapid improvements.

They were not giving Mark any supportive drugs, except for his daily cocktails of antibiotics and medication for pain when he needed it.

Mark was able to tolerate a unit of blood without being as sick as he was before, so Tom decreased the amount of Mark's Benadryl and prayed he could wean Mark off it.

Mark received Robert's fresh platelets that morning and ran no fever. Dr. Stevenson could not explain why Mark was responding so well. His reactions were completely opposite of what they had been before his surgery. *What was the difference? It had to be God.*

When Beth brought in Mark's breakfast tray, he uncovered the plate, looked at the soggy disgusting-looking *eggs*, placed the lid back on the plate with a loud clang, and pushed it away.

"Looking at those eggs makes me want to throw up," he declared with conviction. He continued to refuse to eat anything they brought him from the hospital cafeteria.

When his "Mod Squad" showed up, his face brightened, thinking he had charmed them enough they would give in and let him out of bed.

"Let's go for a jog." He flashed them one of his irresistible smiles. *I got them eating out of my hands.*

He was wrong. They stood there with their arms crossed and stared at him firmly, reminding him the "Mod Squad rules."

"You are not going anywhere, Mr. Sanders," Kathleen told him. *He thinks he's so cute he can railroad us. Not a chance, Mark, you have met your match.* She looked over at Teresa and winked.

He jokingly swiped the bedpan off the nightstand and watched it hit the floor.

"My mother would have made me get up out of bed and get it myself. How about it? Do you want me to get it for you?" He smiled at them, thinking he was pretty clever as he slowly swung his legs over the edge of the bed, ready to take his first steps.

"Not a chance, Mark, but if you do that again, I am personally going to spank you like I would my own son, Matthew," Kathleen grinned at him and shook her head at her sister, Teresa. "Lord, help us," she sighed, as she picked up the bedpan and took it out of the room.

April thought she was going to die of embarrassment. She would have to give these two women an honorary award for winning the heart of her husband and for putting up with him when he took great pleasure in giving them all he had to offer in his version of "good-humor."

April thanked God for the smile on Mark's face, and then she prayed Kathleen and Teresa would also find a smile as they continued to work with Mark.

Mark soon proved he was all work and no play when it came to strengthening his stiff muscles. After they were finished, his gratitude for them showed on his humble face.

He smiled. "You guys have been promoted to the 'Charlie's Angels' … or no … no … let's just call you two, 'Mark's Angels.'" He laughed, thinking if they were his 'Angels' then he was in full control of them.

"Yes, Mark rules again!" He proudly held his hands up high over his head to indicate a touchdown. That victory was short lived as he grabbed his abdomen in pain from over-extending his muscles.

From that point on, when Teresa and Kathleen did what he wanted, he graced them as the "Angels" but when they refused to give into his demands, he demoted them back to the "Mod Squad."

Kathleen looked at Teresa, and Teresa looked at Kathleen, and Mark knew he was in for some serious trouble when the two of them joined forces.

"Lord, help me," he whispered under his breath, and they all laughed.

That afternoon things took an unexpected turn. Mark developed a slight fever and slept off and on for the remainder of the day. After refusing to eat the lunch meal and sleeping through dinner, Tom put Mark on IV nutrient supplements.

Although it was somewhat of a myth, patients have a rough third day after surgery, Mark was no exception. His fever rose and his pain increased.

Tom reminded April that Mark would have his bad days. There were issues with the amount of transfusions he had received, and unfortunately, he was at a high risk at anytime for an infection.

When the hospital pharmacist, Diane Freeman, personally delivered Mark's medications, she took time to explain the residual effects of the drugs they had given him to increase his stem cells, which explained the painful tightening of his muscles.

When Diane heard Mark's odd history with the different medications, she became concerned. Something about the way he responded to them had her suspicious there was something else going on. She planned to do some research of her own on the drugs Mark was receiving.

When Teresa and Kathleen came, Mark slept right through their treatments. Both eyed each other as they silently worked on the stiff muscles in his legs. The room was unnervingly quiet. Both knew they would have gladly let Mark throw bedpans at them or cleverly do something mischievous or humorous.

It was difficult watching him lie there motionless, with sweat covering his forehead, moaning in pain. He was put back on the same monitors from earlier.

Poor April sat in a heap next to his bed praying, as she held his hand in hers to keep them linked together.

Early the next day, Dr. Martin used extreme caution as he took Mark back into surgery to remove all the drainage tubes. Bleeding was more than usual, but they were able to control it.

They undid his surgical dressings and cleaned out what appeared to be the beginning of an infection. That explained his fever. The thought of a rapidly growing infection caused a moment of anxiety in the OR. Steven looked up to the observation window to see if April was still standing on her feet beside Dan.

The good news: Mark's CBC report indicated Mark's red blood cell counts continued to rise. Tom ordered all blood transfusions stopped to see how Mark would do on his own. There was still no change in his white blood cell counts.

When Mark woke up from surgery an hour later, he wanted out of bed. His "Mod Squad" had only allowed him to sit up in bed. There was no stopping him from trying to move around more in his bed now that they had removed the drainage tubes, and he was back on pain medication.

April helped him put on his sweatpants and a football jersey. Mark told her to throw his hospital gown in the trash. He was ready to resume his life as a doctor and a temporary ex-football player.

He worked out with "Mark's Angels" that morning, and they indulged him because of how sick he had been yesterday. They told him he was quickly becoming their favorite patient. Mark told them not to tell anyone. He did not want them to ruin his "bad boy" reputation. For that brief moment, the three shared a welcomed laugh, glad Mark was back to his humorous self.

Once Mark was unhooked from the heart monitor, they helped him stand by the bed as they held him tightly. April stood in front of him in case he fell forward.

Mark felt discouraged when the blood rushed from his head causing his knees to buckle, and he ended up falling back on the bed. It was humiliating to him, but he was not willing to stay in bed because he had failed.

His next few attempts were unsuccessful as he was too dizzy to stand alone, and they put him back on the bed before he hurt himself. He rubbed his hands across his forehead in frustration as he tried to calm down his rapid breathing.

"I have to ... do this," he exhaled a breath of air.

"Mark, you just had surgery a few hours ago, and the anesthesia is still in your system. Let's wait until tomorrow to stand." Teresa broke the news, and Kathleen bailed out when she saw the disagreeable look on Mark's face. She would save her lecture for later.

Mark would not accept defeat and continued to challenge himself to stand without their helping him up. "Let's try it again," he persistently instructed the two women, as they stood ready to catch him if he fell forward. "I can do this; I have to do this!"

It broke their hearts watching him struggle repeatedly, until finally he fell back on the bed too exhausted and in too much pain to move. He softly asked them to leave him alone. Once again, the room grew quiet as hearts became heavy. Kathleen gave a tearful April a hug and promised she would come back later and check on Mark.

Teresa played the bad cop this time and told Mark he better stay put until they came back to try it again. She had hoped to get one of his witty comments back, but he remained silent. Teresa gave April's hand a squeeze before she left with her sister.

April gave Mark an injection of pain medication and prayed he would go back to sleep so he would not hurt himself.

Mark laid still as desperate thoughts screamed in his mind. He convinced himself his legs were strong enough for him to stand. It was his head that was confused. He realized he had made his healing all about what he could do and not about what God could do for him. He repented with a heavy heart, and then he asked God for His help.

"God, I need Your help. By Your power, help clear my mind, help me walk across this floor."

Well, Teresa might as well have spoken to the doorknob, because 15 minutes later Mark was sitting up with his feet hanging off the side of the bed ready to stand up on his own.

April and Jeff tried to talk him out of it, but to no avail; his mind was set. He was going to walk with God.

"Mark, it is still too soon for you to be walking around on your own." Jeff got a stern look in return for his unsolicited advice.

"If God can make a man walk on water, He can help me walk on this cold floor. I am trusting God." With that said from deep within his heart, he put his feet on the floor and took his first steps with God.

Once he mastered the art of standing, he slowly moved around the room for five-minute periods at a time without the "Mod Squad" as he held on to his faithful IV pole and other objects in the room to keep his balance.

A fearful April was always there to assist him until his weak sea legs were grounded firmly on the floor. Jeff offered a hand, but Mark was determined to walk unassisted and told Jeff to go chase after some nurse who wanted his opinions. April was beside herself. Mark was going to drive her and everyone insane.

He was like a baby. When he was asleep he was so cute they all wanted to wake him up and play with him, but when he was awake, they all wished he would go back to sleep and be cute again.

Nevertheless, she loved him for everything he was and everything he was not. She understood how humiliating it was for him to be in this hospital and have to depend on others for everything.

His dignity as a man, as a colleague, as a professional football player, and as a husband, depended on those first few simple steps across the cold floor.

He held onto his faith that was planted firmly in his heart, and he claimed another victory with Jesus as he walked across the room.

Chapter Twenty-Five

Inventive Strategy

৪৬

After Mark fell from a sudden dizzy spell, just before lunch, Dr. Martin gave Mark strict orders he could not get out of bed unless someone was at his side. Steven was not about to let Mark fall again and injure himself.

Mark did not take this order with good humor, but said nothing, respecting Steven as his doctor. Dr. Martin was regretting treating his hardheaded brother-in-law and went to consult with Teresa and Kathleen about Mark's therapy.

Later, Mark wanted to see his friends, but again Dr. Stevenson and Dr. Martin provided a firm no. "I am not about to let you fool around with your friends and get hurt." Tom agreed with Steven, before Mark could voice a protest.

The gang would gather outside Mark's sliding glass door and drive him crazy. But it was not the same as having them in the room with him. "I don't see why I can't go out there. Tom and Steven are just being over-protective. They need to get a life and let me enjoy mine." April humored him with a smile.

The players showed up with pizza, from Bryan's Pizza Joint, in Mark's honor for winning the championship game. They met outside in the lobby across from Mark's room at lunchtime.

Even the owner, Bryan Janney, came to wish Mark well. Mark desperately wanted to go into the lobby. Eve quickly kicked his friends out of the lobby so Mark would not be tempted to join them. Beth brought Mark a slice of pizza, to smooth his disappointment, and in less than five minutes, she had him smiling again. However, her attempt to get him to eat failed.

She hooked up his IV supplement and gave April his cocktail of medications, as she wrote his vitals in his chart.

As long as Mark was improving, Dr. Stevenson was not taking any chances. Mark's counts were still not high enough to fight off infections. The doctors were surprised he was feeling strong enough to get out of bed.

The drug they had given Mark to cause his stem cells to leave the bone marrow continued to cause Mark's muscles to cramp. Tom reinforced with "Mark's Angels" that Mark could not leave his bed without someone holding onto him.

If only they could get Mark to eat the hospital food, maybe he could regain his strength even faster. Understandably, the drugs were taking away his appetite, but it was mostly Mark's refusal to eat that was the main problem. Tom planned to be stricter on Mark's refusals to comply with all of his doctors.

Mark watched the news reports daily about his condition on TV. The reporters were still camped outside the hospital. He had to stay away from the glass windows to avoid them getting a picture of him. Robert ordered a window coating to go over the windows so Mark could keep his privacy intact.

"If I want to know how I am doing, all I have to do is turn on the news," Mark sarcastically remarked to April with annoyance, wishing his private life could be restored.

When they showed his team on the news practicing for the Super Bowl, Mark quickly sat up straight and looked at the TV.

The players were wishing him well and waving at him, giving him the "thumbs up" and telling him to hurry up and get out of there. "We need you, Buddy," Jerk teased as he pointed his finger at the camera.

Mark felt homesick for them and yearned to be back on the football field where he belonged. *I hate this room*, he confirmed as he twisted his *medical alert bracelet* on his wrist, contemplating the up-coming game. The pit of his stomach hungered for the taste of a Super Bowl game.

Mark looked over at April who was reading a book while sitting sideways on the recliner. *If only I could get out of here.*

She had been observing his fidgety reactions to the news reports and knew what his scheming mind was concocting. She gave him a disapproving look in hopes of diverting his noncompliant thoughts of disobeying his doctor's instructions even more than he already was.

Mark received her look, shot her an unruly face and thought with knitted eyebrows, *she doesn't know who she is dealing with. You just wait.*

The Super Bowl is only ten days away. I will be running laps by then, he manipulatively thought as he began to plan his clever escape from the prison of the four walls surrounding him.

The more he thought about it, the more he wanted to do it. *California is only an airplane ride away*; he smartly smiled as he turned in April's direction.

"April, sweetheart, I was thinking. We need to take a vacation before I have the bone marrow transplant, you know, take Sunny somewhere nice...

"Like California?" she smiled at him and gave him that insightful look of hers.

"Ok, you think you are so smart." He fell back against the pillows on his bed. *She is going to be hard to fool*, he thought with new determination to get the better of her.

"What about our honeymoon, sweetheart?" he asked with passion, sure he would melt her into submission.

"Not a chance, honey," she said without looking up from her book. He thought he heard a giggle escape from her.

Ok, this is war! He gritted his lips together, wondering if he had married a wee bit too soon. This was going to take a great deal more planning than he was used to doing, he thought as he punched his pillow with one fist.

"Forget it, Mark, you are wasting your time thinking about it." She put the book down. "You aren't going anywhere until your absolute neutrophil count (ANC) is up to at least 900, for three days in a row," she reminded him with those big teacher eyes of hers.

"That's only 600 away. Sure, like that is going to happen anytime soon," he said in frustration and hit the pillow again. "I'm out of here when they reach 500. I don't care what Tom wants."

Already the room was driving him crazy. Getting out of bed today had helped, but now he wanted to go beyond the walls.

"April, marriage is about giving and taking ...

"You're right, Mark, I am giving you orders and you are taking them," she smiled playfully at him and laughed.

"Real cute response there, Babe." He let a resisting smile form on his now softer face. His mind shifted off the game onto a more inviting thought as he absorbed her beauty into his aroused mind.

April was not being much help in that department. She would not fool around with him in any form. He could barely get a kiss out of her. This was definitely not the honeymoon he had dreamed of having with her. There were certain curves on her delicate body he was yearning to explore.

Dr. McGuire had brainwashed April and drove it in her head that his heart was still not stable enough to let him exert himself in any way. This time Dr. McGuire came right out and said it, "No sex until I medically clear him."

If Mark could get April to come over to him, he would show those doctors whose heart was unstable and it certainly was not his! His heart was working overtime, looking at the amazing vision across the room. April was driving him wild with her soft luscious hair that fell softly over her shoulders, and her silky smooth leg that she had dangling over the side of the recliner as she swung it back and forth, pointing her toes downward, topping off his longing desires.

"Oh, God, have mercy on me," he said under his breath as he had uncontrollable thoughts about what he wanted as her new husband.

She continued reading her book, knowing his thirsty eyes were craving her attention. She let a smile escape as she pretended she had not noticed.

"April, I need more ice," he cunningly asked her.

"You haven't touched the ice I got you thirty minutes ago," she said without looking up. It was true, he asked for the ice and she had Beth bring it to him.

"I need another pillow," he informed her with a sly grin, waiting to snatch her in his arms the minute she came to him with the pillow. She reached up, got one off her bed, and threw it over at him. *Darn her,* he thought as he caught it and pounded it with his fist. He held it up to throw it back at her.

"Mark, put the pillow down, honey," she said without looking up and turned the page in the book. Mark stuffed his fist in the pillow and chuckled at her wittiness to beat him at his own game.

She is asking for it, Mark thought with growing annoyance. He snatched up the pitcher of ice and clumsily chugged down several pieces at once. He soon regretted doing it as he began choking on the ice as it went down his windpipe. He started coughing and struggling with his breathing. The coughing pulled at his abdominal incisions and sent him into extreme pain.

At first, April ignored him, thinking he was pretending. But when she looked up and saw his eyes watering and his lips turning blue, she jumped up and rushed to him. She hit the button on the wall to let them know she needed help.

April could not slap him on the back. She handed him a drink of water, placed pillows against his abdomen, and held them tight. Beth came rushing in but there was nothing more she could do for him. Finally, Mark coughed one last time and caught his breath.

Beth lowered the bed and together they helped him lay back. Beth listened to his lung sounds and to his heart, as April held her breath until Beth gave her the ok Mark was fine.

Mark was exhausted and in severe pain. He held the pillows against his abdomen and moaned as he continued to cough off and on.

Dr. Stevenson arrived in a panic wanting to know what had happened. He felt Mark's abdomen and ordered an x-ray to see if he had pulled out his internal stitches and was bleeding. He pulled back the strips of tape on the gauze where the tubes had been removed to check on those stitches and discovered they were bleeding. He held pressure on the incisions until the bleeding stopped.

Mark protested the pressure of Tom's hands with mini groans. He held the palms of his hands over his forehead as his face wrenched from the pain. Tom ordered pain medication, and Beth went to get it as April gathered one of Mark's hands in hers.

"Hang on, honey. Beth will be right back."

Once Mark had received the pain medication, they brought in the x-ray machine and took films of his chest and abdomen. Dr. Stevenson was relieved when they showed no internal bleeding.

Dr. Stevenson put an exhausted Mark back on oxygen and hooked him back up to the cardiac monitor. "No more ice or anything else he could choke on." Tom gave strict orders. Mark had to stay in bed for the next twelve hours. He was deeply concerned Mark's blood had not clotted as fast as it should have. Until they could raise his counts, they could not risk any type of simple injury.

Mark gave a weak protest about staying in bed. Tom looked him firmly in his eyes and with an unwavering voice; he let Mark know he was serious. "You put one foot on this floor, Mark, and April is going to reintroduce you to a Foley catheter, you got that Mark!"

Oh, yes! Mark got that impacting message loud and clear. He would not be touching the floor after that threat. Poor Mark, life could definitely get better than this horrible moment.

Tom called Dr. McGuire and asked her to check on Mark's heart. Then he had Beth withdraw blood from Mark's central line for a CBC.

Mark was not very responsive. The choking had taken a toll on his already weak body. The pain was making it difficult for him to breathe. He lay quietly on his side with his pillows cuddled against his chest and drifted off to sleep from the drugs they had given him.

Dr. McGuire came into the room. She gave April a comforting touch on her arm before turning her attention on Mark. Since Mark was lying on his side with his pillows cuddled next to his chest, she slid her hand and the stethoscope between his chest and the pillow and listened. Then she listened to his breath sounds by placing the stethoscope on his back. She gave April a reassuring smile before she left the room.

April lay down beside Mark. She was feeling guilty for not paying attention to his every need. She knew it would be extremely hard for Mark to watch the Super Bowl on TV and not be there with his buddies the day of the game.

This week he had already won his own Super Bowl. He had lived when no one else had given him any hope.

That had to be enough, but knowing Mark Sanders, he would be on a plane heading west with his team.

Chapter Twenty-Six

Mixed Emotions

ॐॐ

Sister Jessica arrived that afternoon to visit Mark. She hesitatingly stood outside the room with April and explained what had transpired over the last several years.

She had hoped she could talk directly to Mark. She was afraid he was mad at her for not telling him the truth about Sunflower. Her mission was to have Mark forgive her. April was not her main concern.

Back in high school, April secretly confided in Jessica she was pregnant and made Jessica swear she would never tell a soul. April's confession came as a complete surprise to Jessica and was not a secret she welcomed knowing.

In fact, Jessica was furious at April and blamed her for seducing Mark. Mark was supposed to be hers alone. That ended their so-called friendship. Mark was no longer the pure man Jessica wanted him to be for herself. The sight of Mark at school reminded her of what he and April had done.

Shortly after their conversation, April moved away, and Jessica quit school and became a nun. Their lives headed in directions neither had planned to take. Sister Jessica's first assignment was at the children's home to be a big sister to the girls.

Jessica explained, "I was at the children's home the day Sunflower was left there in a basket. I read the hidden note and knew somehow the baby in the basket belonged to you."

Jessica stood polite and cordial just as she had always done in the past with April. "I thought you were back in town. I went by your old house but no one was there. When I didn't hear from you, I just figured you went back to California without your baby. I thought you gave Sunflower up because of your father. Honestly, April, I didn't know where to find you, to ask you. So I did what you asked me. I didn't tell anyone I knew the real truth about the baby."

Thanks to God's intervention, Mark had found Sunflower in the park. Sister Jessica knew Mark was Sunflower's father; April had told her. But Jessica was afraid to tell Mark the truth because of what April had told her about her father's threats against the father of her child.

April had begged Jessica never to tell anyone it was Mark who fathered her child. So she remained silent, and besides, she would never risk Mark's life for certain deep-seeded reasons of her own.

"I was in shock when Mark walked in the church on Christmas Eve with Sunflower. I couldn't believe the Christmas miracle he had found his own daughter."

What April did not know was that Jessica traded Mark for God way back in high school after she shared her secret with Jessica.

The shock of Mark resurfacing and walking into the church that night with Sunflower flooded Jessica with feelings she had fought so hard to forget over the last several years. Mark changed everything for Jessica when he found Sunflower and came waltzing back into her life. She realized then how much she still loved him.

She had already forgiven him for his mistake with April years ago. And deep down, she hoped someday they would run into each other and develop a friendship of their own and then maybe more.

Once Mark fell in love with Sunflower and wanted to adopt her, Sister Jessica knew God worked out a plan for the father to raise his own daughter without anyone knowing the truth, just as with baby Moses. That is why Jessica told Sunflower the story that night in the apartment while Mrs. Brown was babysitting Sunflower.

Jessica had hoped someday in the far future, Sunflower and Mark would eventually find out the truth about each other. But if they didn't, that was fine, too, since they would still have each other.

Truthfully, Jessica never wanted Mark to know it had been April who conceived his child on that night long ago. *Let Mark think I had been the one to conceive his child. After all, Sunny looks just like me. I doubt he will ever remember what happened at the party with me.*

Her first plan was to have Mark fall deeply in love with her. And then, it would be too late for April to come back into his life. After all, Mark would have no memory of April, if she ever did come back to town. April would be just another woman, bidding for Mark's affection and this time she would be too late.

Mark would have Sunflower and her, the perfect family. Jessica had convinced herself of that possibility, as she thought about trading God back for Mark. Her love for God was strong, but her love for Mark grew stronger each day as she began planning their future together. With their common interest in Sunny, Jessica thought she could have God and Mark in her life. It was a plan she hoped to implement.

Unfortunately, for Sister Jessica, she did not know April had returned to town, stealing Mark away from her, until Katie called her and spilled the whole story. But the worst part was that Sunflower had been kidnapped.

Jessica's heart was devastated. Tears consumed her mind, as she feared for Sunflower's safety. She wanted desperately to run to Mark and tell him everything. But how could she? She was sure he would hate her. He would blame her for Blanche taking Sunflower, because she had not been truthful with him.

Mark was wiping April's tears, not hers. How unfair all of this was to her. Sunflower was more her child than April's.

Did Sunflower ask for April when she had been rescued? No, she asked for me! Sunflower loves me, not April.

She had Sunflower's love, but her heart was overcome with hopelessness that once again she would lose Mark out of her life forever. She turned her wayward thoughts over to her God and prayed He would give her direction.

"I thought you were out of Mark's life for good, and Mark and Sunflower could go on living without you. Even if they never knew the truth, they would still have each other and that was all that mattered."

Tearfully, Jessica asked April for forgiveness for not telling Mark the truth about Sunflower. Jessica was welcomed into April's forgiving arms, yet April sensed the hug between them was oddly cool on Jessica's part. Unknown to April was the fact Jessica's tears had nothing to do with seeking her forgiveness. Her overwhelming sense of loss she felt for Mark caused her tears.

Jessica's eyes were studying the sleeping figure on the bed inside the room. It was clear to her at the wedding that her dreams so long ago involving Mark would never come true. That, after all, was why she had to become a nun in the first place, because once again, April had won: she had Sunflower and she had Mark.

Jessica held out on taking her final vows as a nun, hoping Mark Sanders would one day love her. Tears filled her eyes; she knew that would never happen. Mark was hopelessly in love with April, not her.

All she had left was God. God had been clear when He answered her. She could not covet another woman's husband. Would God forgive her for forsaking Him and seeking Mark? Could God once again fill her heart and drown out her love for Mark? Only time would tell, but right this minute, standing before April, her heart was not receptive to anything.

Jessica felt the satisfaction of knowing she had the memories of Sunflower's early childhood. She was the one who raised Mark's child, not April. April may be Sunflower's mother, but she would always have that special bond with Sunflower April could never take away from her. Sunflower was her child as if she had come straight from her own womb.

The jealousy she secretly felt for April returned. Once again, she thought about how her life would have been so different, if April had never come back to town. Her eyes once again claimed the man that still had a strong impact on her heart.

She had one memory of Mark Sanders that belonged solely to her. Even Mark would never know of their stolen moment together.

Chapter Twenty-Seven

Climbing Unforgiving Mountains

§§

At four o'clock, Tom got back Mark's CBC report and called Dan and Steven for an urgent meeting. Mark's blood cell counts showed his platelets were still dangerously low. His ANC count disappointedly dropped to 250. Mark was unable to maintain his blood cell counts on his own. It was apparent his body's immune system was still attacking the transfused blood. They had to shut down his immune system.

After much discussion, they decided they would begin giving Mark a new drug to try to increase his white blood cell counts. Tension filled the room. The doctors realized their choice could have serious complications on Mark's already compromised body.

April stood next to his bed in prayer. *Please, Lord, let this work for Mark. He's been through so much already.*

Beth came in with the new medication and hooked the saline intravenous drip up to Mark's central line. Then she injected the new medication into Mark's hip.

Tom stood ready beside Mark's bed in case Mark experienced any type of a reaction. Dan and Steven stood just outside the room, pacing the floor in prayer they had not made the wrong decision to give Mark this potentially dangerous drug.

Mark was beside himself when he heard his counts had fallen. There was no way Tom would let him go home with an ANC count of 250. Tom increased the strength of his IV antibiotics, which meant an increase of Benadryl. Mark didn't want to sleep. He wanted out of bed, he wanted to play football and most of all, he wanted to start his new role as a husband to April and a father to Sunny.

To make matters worse, Dr. Stevenson informed Mark he could not go home until he started eating the hospital food. "You have to eat and keep the food down before you will ever see the outside of this hospital."

Since Mark had missed lunch, Beth called down to the cafeteria and ordered him a snack from Willy.

The longest fifteen minutes passed as the doctors waited for Mark to have a reaction to the new drug. Other than Mark seemed uncomfortable and restless, he had no immediate reaction. They were surprised but thankful Mark was tolerating the new drug. This was a great relief, finally a break for Mark.

Beth came in the room with a bowl of jello and set it down on the table in front of Mark. She handed him a spoon.

He viewed the firm yet slimy texture and put the spoon down. He was determined not to attempt even the slightest bite of it. *I am not going to eat this stuff!* And that was all there was to it, until he heard Tom stress.

"I want you to eat every bite of this jello. No fooling around, Mark, or you will not be going home anytime soon."

If looks could have killed, Mark was definitely trying his best to eliminate Dr. Tom Stevenson with his expression of evil eyes and scrunched eyebrows. Well, at least he hoped to drive Tom out of his room with his killer look.

However, Tom did not budge an inch; instead, he gave Mark a stern look of his own. "Start with picking up the spoon, Mark."

Mark ran his fingers through his hair in growing frustration. Tom was backing him into a corner, and Mark was not happy about it. How could he possibly eat with his stomach so messed up already? But then, Mark remembered; no one knew how messed up his stomach really was. That was one of his unvoiced complaints. There was a good reason why Mark was refusing to eat.

Tom gave April an encouraging grin, left the room, and joined the other two doctors.

"If they had a pill for stubbornness, I'd give Mark the whole bottle," Tom jokingly told them. They joined him in a laugh, as the tension lifted.

The three doctors felt confident Mark was going to respond normally to the drug after all. They left him under the watchful eyes of April and Beth.

Beth stood firm and pointed at the bowl of jello. "Mark, you heard the doctor's orders. Now be a good guy and eat your jello."

Mark took a long deep breath and snatched up the spoon like a rebellious four year old. Reluctantly, he forced himself to taste a spoonful of the jello from the *open bowl* that had been sent up to him from the hospital cafeteria.

The raspberry jello tasted stale to him. *This jello tastes like it was left over from a week ago!* Mark shook his head in disgust.

My dog wouldn't eat this garbage, he thought. *Better yet, I wouldn't force my dog to eat this nasty stuff,* he rebelliously thought, as he wanted to gag.

Beth winked at April and left the room. It was a good thing they could not read Mark's unruly mind.

April frowned at him and handed Mark his bottle of water to wash down the bite he still had swirling around in his mouth. He was dreadfully wishing he could spit it out in the washbasin sitting on his table.

With obstinate defiant eyes beamed at April, he forced the bite down his throat. "Yuk, that was horrible! I will definitely die from food poisoning, if I have to eat this awful stuff!"

"Oh, Mark, really." April shook her disapproving face at him and told him it was all in his imagination. She encouraged the next bite, but he shook his head no, and pushed the bowl away.

"This stuff belongs in the toilet!" he raved, "This is exactly the kind of lethal food that keeps this hospital in business!" He wasn't kidding as he made his hostile stand against the jello.

April cracked a smile at his childlike behavior.

"Mark, you heard what Dr. Stevenson said. If you want to go home, you have to start eating real food."

"Yeah, if I want to go home in a body bag!"

"Mark, stop it. You are being childish." April wasn't sure how to react to his strong-minded statements, as she tried not to laugh at his silliness. Her cheeks rose and she giggled.

"I don't care. I am not eating that jello!" He turned over on his side and that was the end of their conversation.

"Oh, Lord, help me," April prayed out loud, wondering what kind of ill-tempered man she had just married. For better or worse, she had married him. She gave him a tender kiss to cheer him up, and true to his form, that was all it took to change his mood.

Fifteen minutes later, Mark looked desperately at April and headed quickly to the bathroom and violently threw-up. April had Beth get Dr. Stevenson and Dan.

When Tom arrived, he shook his head in disappointment as Mark continued to be extremely sick. "How is this possible?" He questioned the absurdity of the situation with a bleak face as Dan joined him in Mark's room.

For two hours, Mark threw-up, even with nothing in his stomach. Mark's throat and stomach burned. He ran a high fever, sweated profusely, was lightheaded, and had a horrible headache. He complained of a *bad taste* in his mouth. He was sure he was going to die from the severe pain in his stomach. Mark adamantly blamed it on the jello.

"I told you the jello was going to kill me!"

Nevertheless, Tom and Dan knew it was another one of Mark's rejections to the drug Beth had just given him. Why had the drug taken 30 minutes for Mark to have a delayed reaction to it, they wondered.

Beth brought in a fresh hospital gown and gave it to April. Tom and Dan told April they would wait outside the room. Beth sympathetically helped April remove Mark's sweaty football jersey. Then Beth handed April a container of warm soapy water so April could give Mark a sponge bath.

Knowing Mark's mind-set about his privacy, Beth kindly volunteered to wait just outside the room with the doctors until April was done bathing Mark.

"If you need me, I am right here," she promised as she left the young wife to tend to her husband.

Mark was exhausted and laid there quietly as April gently wiped the sweat from his body. If only they were back at the penthouse where she had given Mark his first bath, she thought with sadness.

He had been her rose petal scented husband, strong, vibrant, and full of life. Now he was lying here, unable to bask in her love as she touched him gently, claiming what belonged only to her. Her tears touched his bare skin as she washed him. She would do for him what he could not do for himself.

When she finished with the bath, she kissed his lips and touched his cheeks with the palms of her hands.

"I love you, Mark Sanders. We can do this together, you and me, I promise."

He weakly lifted his hand up to hers and tenderly brought her hand to his mouth and kissed her fingers. That would be the extent of their expressions of love for each other as he felt sick to his stomach again and cradled his stomach with both hands.

With tears streaming down her distressed face, April quickly went to the door to get help from the doctors and Beth.

Beth unfolded the gown and together they lifted Mark's arms and pulled them through the sleeves. It was finished; he was back where he had started from, encased in a gown that claimed him as a patient.

No longer was he a doctor, or a football player, he was a man searching for a way home. But would his home be in the distant sky above them where he would finally find peace at his heavenly Father's feet?

Mark took up the fetal position and held a pillow against his stomach as April placed cool washcloths on his forehead and massaged his tense shoulders. Dan handed her the oxygen mask, and she placed it on his face.

Tom and Dan anxiously waited for Mark's face and throat to swell, or for a rash to appear, but neither happened. Tom was confused with this unusual reaction to the new drug. He concluded Mark was an unfortunate victim of the drug's extremely rare side effects, what else could it be?

Tom gave Mark a medication to calm his stomach and more medications to counteract what he thought were Mark's reactions to the drug. To prevent dehydration, Mark was given several bags of IV fluid over the next several hours.

Dan stood next to his bed and watched over Mark. He would have given anything to take away Mark's pain.

Why is this happening to him? This is not how Mark was supposed to live his young life. He should be downstairs in the ER treating patients, saving lives with his skillful hands, and winning souls for Christ.

When Dr. McGuire came to check on Mark's heart, she was quickly disturbed by the irregular heartbeat she heard. She put Mark back on the heart monitor and increased the amount of oxygen he was receiving.

Her concern deepened when sure enough, he had ventricular arrhythmias and prolonged QT-interval. This was a typical reaction to a drug poisoning, she thought strangely. She wanted Mark admitted to the CICU.

Megan called the CICU to see if Sherry Grooms was available to monitor Mark's heart in the Bone Marrow Unit. She came right away and instantly took over Mark's care.

Megan gave Sherry orders for a new heart medication to correct his heartbeat. She ordered new guidelines for his strict care.

"No ... more ... drugs," Mark grimaced, as he pulled the oxygen mask from his face and begged despondently, as he watched Sherry inject Dr. McGuire's order into his IV. *They are giving me too many drugs.*

Mark was not happy he could not get out of bed, and the medications she gave him seemed to make him sicker. He flashed April a look of distress, his weary eyes begging her to protect him, to bring him solitude.

Sherry took his hand, leaned close to Mark's face, and spoke encouraging words she knew God wanted Mark to hear. She replaced his oxygen mask and watched the monitor.

They put him back on his pain medication, and he was able to fall asleep for one short hour before he was sick to his stomach again. Was it blood he was throwing up or the jello? Mark knew the answer but said nothing.

April sat on his bed, cradled his head in her lap, and rubbed her fingers softly through his hair as he slept in a fetal position. She silently prayed and brushed back the tears that escaped the corners of her sad eyes. Just when she thought he was over one hurdle, he ran straight into another one and crashed.

"God, why? Why is this happening to Mark? Make it stop, oh, God, please make it stop." Her moist tears rubbed against his face as she bent her face to his and pressed her lips to his cheek. "I love you, Mark. I love you…"

Sherry wiped her own cheeks and continued in quiet prayer for this young couple. Julia and Robert arrived and watched Mark from the glass door, as he suffered through another episode of rejections.

This time, Julia was not taking no for an answer to be with her son and comfort him. She pestered Tom, until finally, Tom reluctantly let them dress in scrubs and enter Mark's room.

Tom hoped their visit with Mark would improve his irritated mood and bring him a tiny bit of peace until the effects of the drug wore off.

Sherry hugged Mark's parents and stepped aside so they could be next to their son. April traded spots with Julia and went to take a shower. What she really sought to do was cry in seclusion. The sound of the water drowned out her sorrowful tears, from Mark, as she sobbed uncontrollably.

If only she could save him from all this pain, she would have done it in a *heartbeat*. Again, she continued where she had left off with God. This time she bargained with God to take her life and spare Mark's.

It was the most self-sacrificing prayer she had ever spoken, as it flowed from the deepest love within her heart, for the man she loved. "God, take me. Sunny needs her father."

It was at this delicate moment in thought she decided to draft a letter.

Robert pulled a chair up beside the bed, took Mark's hand in his, and prayed for him. "God, be merciful to my son," he began, but was unable to finish the prayer aloud without the crackling of his anguished voice unnerving Julia into silent tears.

When Mark opened his drained eyes, he focused on his parents and felt a brief moment of peace. Then he closed his eyes tightly again, as a wave of nausea invaded his defenseless stomach. Sherry wiped his forehead with a cool washcloth.

"Where's April? I need her."

"She's taking a shower. She'll be right back, sweetheart," Julia said as she kissed his forehead.

Thoughts of Sunny ripped through his heart, as the need to have her in his arms pulled at his heartstrings. "Sunny ... I am coming home," he mumbled, "where's Sunny ... Sunny?"

Julia was overprotective and pampered Mark until finally he begged her to quit and go back home to be with Sunny. "I'm fine ... I need ... you ... to take care of Sunny ... go home to Sunny."

He closed his eyes briefly as if he was going back to sleep. His body jerked and he opened his frightened eyes. Yet he seemed off in a distance, unaware of where he was. He pulled his oxygen mask off.

"I want you ... to bring me ... Sunny," he pathetically begged them weakly. "Please, Mom. I want ... to hold ... Sunny."

Julia and Robert exchanged an uncertain heart-stricken glance at each other as Mark looked desperately around the room for Sunny.

"Sunny, where is she?" They could not give Mark what he so desperately wanted. According to the state, *Sunny was not his child.*

He lifted his head off his pillow as he searched for Sunny. "Something has happened to Sunny. I can feel it!"

"Sunny is fine, Mark. She is safe with Charlie," Robert tried to reassure him.

"Call and make sure. Please, Dad, call Charlie."

Sherry stepped in to calm him, as she kept a close eye on the heart monitor. "Mark, honey, I need you to calm down. Let's lie down and take a few deep breaths."

Mark gently grabbed Sherry's arm as she helped him lie down. His eyes focused on her compassionate eyes, and he calmed down and let her help him get comfortable. She placed his mask back in place.

"You are going to be just fine, Mark. Your mom and dad are right here. Sunny is fine and April will be here in just a few minutes."

Julia combed Mark's hair between her fingers and fought back her tears. "Shhh, Mark, try to sleep." Her soft voice tried to keep him calm. Robert stood behind his wife and gathered her frail body to his to offer her strength.

Rebecca came for a few minutes and watched from the window. She said nothing; she just stood there and then she walked away. *I am not going to do this,* she thought as a tear warmed her face. *I am not going to watch my brother ... die.*

Mark had just opened his eyes when Rebecca turned and started walking away. "Rebecca!" His heart felt heavy.

What have I done to her? Is she so scared of losing me that she is afraid of opening her heart back up to me? A lump filled his throat, as he reached out his hand in her direction. "Beck, come back ..."

Mark felt somewhat better that evening but refused to eat anything. He was convinced the hospital cafeteria staff was trying to kill him with their sorry food.

April shook her head and humored him. He tried to convince her that all he needed was to go home. The sooner the better, he contended with growing frustration. April thought he was suffering from *delirium.*

Mark kicked everyone who was hovering over him, out of his room. He put on his headphones, closed his eyes, turned on his side and listened to a tape of his pastor preaching. His distorted mind was not receptive to the words of his pastor as his enemy challenged his faith with continual waves of stomach pain.

Mark knew the drugs altered his behavior. *I can't let them have this kind of control over me. This is not me. I can't do this. The drugs have to stop. I have to go home before this hospital kills me.*

April paced the hallway in prayer. *How much longer can Mark stay in this hospital without going insane? Something has to give before Mark loses it.* Her prayers to take Mark home with her were stronger than ever.

Just as she was about to lose it, Rev. Smith came for a visit and offered her comfort. He reminded her God was in control over Mark. "God keeps every promise He makes. He is like a shield for all who seek His protection. Proverbs 30:5."

Tom and Dan met and discussed Mark's treatment options. The first thing they did was call the blood bank for two units of blood. They hooked his central line up to the first unit of blood.

They decided they had no other choice but to try the same drug again at one-fourth the dosage and slowly build up Mark's tolerance to the drug. They had to do something to build up Mark's blood cell counts as they were running out of options.

A bacterial infection was lurking nearby just waiting to claim his life. Without raising his counts, there would be no way the transplant committee would agree to his transplant.

Tom called Diane and asked her to prepare the new dosage for Mark. Diane looked at Mark's medication record. Five different doctors had placed orders for him. She called her husband's pharmacy to consult with him.

Dr. Stevenson brought in the smaller dose of the new medication that evening. Mark was sleeping on his side in his usual position. April pulled the cover off his hip and pulled his boxers down off his hip, swabbed the area and injected the medicine under the skin in his hip.

Mark briefly opened his sleepy eyes, as the needle pierced through his skin and the medication caused a burning sensation, and then he closed them.

Tom handed April the syringes of medications to counteract any reactions from the first one. Mark moved his leg away after the first one entered his thigh muscle. Tom held his leg in place as April injected the other two, then she tenderly massaged the area, feeling as if she had betrayed him.

Thirty minutes later, Mark ran a slight fever, was dizzy and nauseated, but he was not violently sick like before. Tylenol brought his fever back down to normal, and the pain medication helped relieve his pain. Mark appeared to have tolerated the drug in this smaller dosage.

April fed him ice chips from his hospital water jug, before tucking him in for the night.

Could it be he would finally get a break?

Chapter Twenty-Eight

Finding Light in the Darkness

❧❧

The second dose of the new drug during the night was not as well tolerated, as Mark broke out in chills, was sweating intensely, had difficulty breathing and a massive headache. The injection site was swollen and warm to the touch. Mark rolled around on the bed; he was uncomfortable and miserable. He was still convinced the jello had made him sick.

April was beside herself. Fearful Mark would stop breathing; she called Dan to come stay with them during the night. Dan claimed the couch after giving Mark a round of medications to combat his reactions. He included the drugs Dr. McGuire prescribed for Mark's heart.

Dan twisted his fingers together. Mark moaned in pain while lying in the arms of April. She tried to comfort him. Dan called Christy on the intercom.

Christy came in and gave Mark a sedative to help him sleep. April got up to go to the bathroom. Dan stood up and went to the side of Mark's bed.

Mark weakly lifted his hand up for Dan to take. Dan's heart overflowed with empathy. He bent forward, gathered Mark's head into his shoulder, and held him as he prayed. Just as he had done when Mark was a small boy and he needed comforting.

"I don't want to be here," Mark spoke weakly, "take me home ... Dad."

Dan shook his head confused. *Mark called me Dad. What is he saying?* Dan lowered Mark's head so they were face to face. Mark's despondent eyes were evident. *He knows I am holding him.* At least Dan thought Mark knew. *Did Mark know something? Did he overhear a conversation between Julia and me?*

"I love you, Mark. There is something I need to tell you …" His words ended when Mark fell asleep. Dan held Mark's slumbering head back to his heart and then laid him gently back down on his pillow just as April reentered the room.

She reclaimed her position beside Mark, wrapped him in her arms, and closed her tired eyes. Her thoughts returned to their tender night in the penthouse, wondering if they would ever have that kind of love between them again.

At four a.m., Christy came in with Mark's third dose of the new drug and injected it in his thigh. She followed up with a mixture of drugs to counteract any side effects.

Mark developed a fever and pain in his stomach shortly afterwards, and Dan increased his pain medication. By five, Mark was asleep again. Dan went to take a long hot shower and get an hour or two of sleep.

At six a.m., Christy came in and hooked up Mark's cocktail of antibiotics. She noted Mark laying there staring blankly up at the white ceiling. He never acknowledged her presence in the room. "Mark, are you alright?" she whispered, but her question remained unanswered.

As soon as she left, Mark disentangled April from him and disconnected himself from the heart monitor and oxygen mask. April sleepily turned off the buzzing machines that alerted Christy urgently back into the room.

"Mark, what are you doing? It's too early to be up," April questioned, but she was soon aware something was definitely not right with her husband.

Mark threw the sheets off and untied his hospital gown, pulling it off angrily, and flung it on the floor.

"I thought I told you I was never going to wear that stupid gown again!"

"Mark, what are you doing?" April asked frightened, confused by the way he was behaving. He never laid around in his thin boxer shorts in front of Christy. It was obvious he did not care in his mood.

Christy stood near the door, not sure what she should do. "What can I do to help?"

"Give me my sweatpants and a shirt!" he demanded in a firm but hoarse voice. His throat burned.

April quickly obeyed and got a fresh set of clothes from the cabinet. She understood why he wanted to be back in his clothes, as she knew how much he hated wearing the gown, but his demeanor seemed odd to her. He let her help him put his sweatpants on over his boxers, but he left his shirt lying on the bed, leaving his torso bare.

Mark was weak and unsteady as he got out of bed. He pulled his IV unit with him and started packing up his stuff in his team duffle bag to go home.

Christy and April stood stunned as they watched him fling his clothes carelessly in the bag.

"Mark, what are you doing, honey?" April warmly asked him as she placed her hands on his to stop him from packing. He was scaring her with his abrupt behavior.

"I'm going home," he informed her as he continued in his mission to leave. He nearly fell, as he got lightheaded.

"Mark, you can't go home, honey."

"I said I was going home." He turned and faced her briefly, but it was as if he looked right through her, as he blinked back the fog from his eyes.

He unhooked all the IV lines with all the medications he was receiving and threatened to pull the central line out of his chest when Christy moved closer to stop him.

"Mark, what are you doing? You need to get back in bed." April continued to struggle reasoning with him. It would be so much harder to keep him in the hospital when he was feeling this anxious. "Mark, you are scaring me."

He ignored her. Something was definitely not right by the way he was acting. He clumsily put his jersey shirt over his head, pulled his arms through it, and pulled it down. "Mark, tell me what's wrong so I can help you."

"Help me pack my stuff, so I can get out of this place." She didn't respond to his request.

He erratically paced the floor like a caged animal, holding his hands firmly on both sides of his head trying to block out the ringing and the persistent pain.

"Mark, please, come sit down." April tried to calm him with her touch, but he just got even more frustrated when she would not listen to what he had to say.

"I am going home, now!" he exclaimed as he went in search of his cowboy boots. "Where are my boots?" Neither of them would tell him and that made him even angrier. "Fine, I will leave here barefooted if I have to."

April was turning pale, frightened that he was going to fall and hurt himself. "Mark, please, just let me hold you and make this better for you." Her words were unheard as his mission to be free increased.

"I am going to go call his doctors. Try to calm him down."

Christy went for reinforcement, and Mark's doctors arrived shortly to face off with their aggravated patient.

"What's going on, Mark?" Dr. McGuire sympathetically asked him, knowing something was terribly wrong with Mark because of the way he was acting so detached from them.

His labored breathing had her full attention. Her first thought was that he was having a full-blown panic attack that would lead to a serious cardiac problem.

"Mark, I need for you to calm down."

"I will calm down . . . when you all leave!"

He picked his chart up off the table and angrily flung it across the room. The doctors were stunned at his violent actions.

"How can I calm down? My head is killing me." He grabbed both sides of his head with the palms of his hands and spread his fingers apart.

"Christy, get Dr. Price up here, stat!" Tom told her.

"You give me one drug to cure me, and it takes five drugs to counteract that drug, so it doesn't kill me! I am sick of these drugs!"

At this tension-filled moment, he was very perturbed; he wanted everyone out of his room. He held his arms straight out to hold them away from him.

"Get out of my room and leave me alone!"

"Mark, please, try to calm down." Steven held his hand out to Mark with his plea.

But Mark sternly eyed them all and shook his head angrily, as his breathing increased and he had to cough to catch a breath of air.

Dr. McGuire wanted him back on the monitors.

"Mark, I need you to get back on the heart monitor. You are having trouble breathing. I am concerned about your heart."

Dr. Martin wanted him back in bed. "Mark, you are going to fall. Let's get you back in bed before you rip your incisions out."

Christy was trying to get him to eat something. "I ordered you some biscuits and gravy. Maybe if you would eat something, you would feel better."

Dr. Stevenson wanted to hook him back up to his IV's and continue with the drugs. "Mark, we need to hook you back up to your medications. I will increase your pain medication, if you get back in bed."

"Mark, please listen to everyone, honey. We all want to help you."

Mark's mind was in a whirlwind of voices demanding things from him he could not deliver. He grabbed the sides of his head with clutched fists to shut them all out. He had a killer headache, and they were all demanding things from him. He just wanted them to hush.

"Hush, be quiet! I want to go home! Just let me go home," he pleaded as he collapsed onto the recliner and held his head between his knees, as the spinning continued. April was immediately at his side and held her hand on his leg as she fought back her tears.

"Mark, it is okay, honey, let us help you."

"Just let me go home." His voice was barely audible, as his emotions seemed to have drained his energy level as he tried desperately to gain control over how he was feeling.

However, Dr. Stevenson refused Mark's requests to go home. "No more special treatments, Mark. You are the patient, not the doctor, and you are too unstable to leave this hospital." That was not the direct message Mark wanted to hear and his anger rose in his face as he stared at them.

Mark was very aggravated and in an outburst he told them he was healed. "I don't care what the stupid test results showed; I am healed!" He contended, "I do not need this crazy hospital any longer. This hospital is what is making me sick! I want to go home to recover, and I want to go home today!"

April had never seen Mark act like this before. No matter how upset he had been, he had never taken his anger out on other people. His behavior right now was not typical of Mark's demeanor.

April was convinced he had delirium. *Were the drugs he was taking causing his uncommon behavior?* she wondered.

Dr. Gina Price arrived with a syringe in her hand and gently approached Mark. He saw the syringe; his face remained taut. Gina knelt down on the other side of him, their eyes met and softly melted together as they connected. She prayed Mark would trust her intentions of calming him down.

Before she could speak to him, he surprised them all, as he voluntarily held his arm out to her for the injection. All stood quietly, as she gently pulled up his shirtsleeve. Then she swabbed his arm and injected the medication as he willfully submitted to her. Mark allowed the injection he knew would alleviate his pain as it knocked him unconscious.

"I don't know what's wrong with me. You have to make it stop," he tearfully uttered to her and she tenderly embraced his forehead in her arms and let him succumb to his feelings of hopelessness. "Make it stop. Make my pain go away. I can't stand it anymore."

Gina motioned for the others to leave her alone with him and they backed away. She knew she had about two minutes before Mark would be too drowsy to speak to her.

"Mark, what's wrong? Tell me what you are feeling."

Mark told her he felt helpless and overly restless. "My head is spinning out of control." He could not explain why he could not get his frustrations under control.

"Not even my prayers can calm me down. Gina, the drugs are taking away my healing from God. It's not a panic attack … it's something more … something is wrong with me … I don't want to feel this way … but I can't stop it … make it stop… make it all go away."

His grave appeal stopped the hearts of all those still in the room, as they watched him tearfully drift off to sleep in her arms.

Mark's bizarre behavior concerned Dr. Price. It was not like him to show such an unpleasant outburst towards those he loved. *He actually does seem to be suffering from delirium, but what is causing it?*

As April cuddled Mark in her arms, Gina went in search of an answer by looking carefully through his chart. She discovered all his doctors together had him on eleven different medications. She concluded his aloof behavior was from the combinations of all the drugs they were giving him. *What else could it be?*

The doctors moved in on their now defenseless patient. They carried him over to the bed, removed his shirt and checked his vital signs. They hooked him back up to the heart monitor, placed him on oxygen, and placed a pulse oximeter probe on his finger. April stood back and watched as her heart broke for her husband.

"Stop it!" She would take over for Mark and fight for him. "No more drugs! Mark cannot tolerate them. They are seriously changing his personality." She took the IV tubing and held it in her hands firmly as Dr. Stevenson gave her his full attention.

"No more drugs, Tom, not today. They are killing him. This is not how I want Mark to live the remainder of his life." Tears swarmed her eyes as she made the decision to take Mark off the drugs that were his only hope of keeping him alive. She could not watch him suffer like this for one more minute. She knew in her heart, she had to set him free from his suffering and it started right now.

"April's right, Tom. Mark's body is on overload right now." Dan took pity on his niece, knowing the difficulty of her decision to fight for her husband, knowing the consequences of her decision.

"Let's give his body a break, at least six hours drug free. The drug I gave him will be out of his system in forty-five minutes," Dr. Price advised as she reviewed Mark's chart with Tom and Steven.

Both agreed it had to be the medications making Mark behave the way he was. With Mark's long history of drug reactions and allergies, every drug they combined with other drugs was sure to cause some sort of unusual allergic reaction. Exactly what kind, they would never know until Mark experienced the reactions firsthand.

"Keep him on the monitors, oxygen, and IV fluids, but no drugs, CBC in four hours," Tom ordered Beth who had just come on duty and joined the fleet of doctors.

The drugs were stopped to give Mark's body a chance to bounce back to whatever was normal for him. An hour later, he was awake, but drowsy as he laid there in April's protective arms, deep in thought.

What happened to me earlier, and why? Why did I act that way? Did I yell at everyone, including April? This has to stop. I can't live like this. His behavior profoundly bothered him.

It was not long before his disposition was back to normal, and he sincerely asked everyone to forgive him for the way he had insensitively acted towards them.

Eve came in and got Mark's water jug. "I'm just helping Beth out. I'll bring you some fresh water." Although this seemed like an act of kindness, Eve's expression seemed harsh to April.

Mark's heart broke thinking of the stress he had put on April. *She did not deserve any of this. This was not part of the deal when I married her.* Mark was determined that if the drugs were going to make him act unpleasant, *he might just have to do something about that.*

He held April in his arms as he thought about how he was going to make up for his illness and bring joy back into her life. As soon as he could get out of this hospital, he had a big surprise waiting for her at the ranch.

He tearfully asked her forgiveness and accepted her answer with his lips. She smoothly ran her fingers through his hair as he fell back asleep.

She wanted to take him home as much as he wanted to go there.

Chapter Twenty-Nine

Finding a Smile

§§

At noon, Mark's CBC test results came back; it was not encouraging. Tom took the results straight to Mark and let him decide what he wanted them to do.

Mark agreed to a blood transfusion, with Benadryl and Tylenol. He wanted something for the pain in his stomach. He asked Dr. Price to give him something to clear his mind and alleviate his anxiety. Four medications went back into his system.

Tom felt confident Mark's mental state was improving as the hours passed. Mark affectionately held April against his chest as he dozed. After taking his vital signs, Beth told Tom that Mark had a low-grade fever. Fearing an infection, three antibiotics were given to him.

Dr. McGuire came back in to check on his heart rate and even though he was holding a steady heartbeat, she was feeling uneasy that he was off his heart meds. She was thankful he was able to sleep off and on peacefully. She instructed Beth to keep a closer watch on his heart before she left him in the hands of the two women.

Later, Mark's strength returned after he received the blood and a shot for pain. This time Dr. Stevenson freed him of the monitors and oxygen and helped him over to the recliner so he could sit up and view the scenery outside the window. April joined him by sitting on his knee and wrapping her arm around his bare shoulder.

"One hour, then it is back to bed, Mark," Tom told him sternly. Mark shook his head in agreement. "I have a surgery scheduled in a few minutes. I'll be back later to check on you." Tom patted Mark on his shoulder as his heart reached out to the young man. *If only I could figure out a way to help him*, Tom thought despondently as he headed to the OR.

Mark was ready to test his newfound strength and get on with living the way he should. It was time to find some enjoyment in this horrible situation. The morning had been awful, but he was determined to take back the remainder of the day from the devil, and make something positive happen.

He passionately kissed April and whispered words of his love for her as he kissed the lobe of her ear. His hands explored her neckline and traveled down her smooth arms, as he distracted her with the fullness of his mouth. Just as he was contemplating his next desire with April, his new victims entered his room. He let a wide smile consume his face as they came through the door.

When Teresa and Kathleen came in, he begged them to take him to the physical therapy room so he could really work out. Their answer was a firm no. He could not leave the Unit yet, not with his low white cell counts.

He pretended to pout and told them they were both being "bad cops" today, but they saw his hidden smile behind his turned up lips and laughed.

"Mark Sanders, don't give me that look. I know you still love me. So get over it, you are not going out of this room," Teresa informed him warmheartedly as she patted the bed for him to come.

Kathleen and April gently helped him stand up, and he stiffly walked to the bed. His sweatpants looked two sizes too big on him, from the weight he had lost. His bare torso remained firm in all the right places, but he needed to add back the weight he had lost.

"I know you loved my good looking legs, ladies, but it is sweatpants from now on, so get over it," he threw out at Teresa, giving her a dose of his medicine. He was, however, glad, he did not have to wear that airy hospital gown anymore.

"Whoever invented hospital gowns should have to parade down Main Street wearing one, on a windy day," he chuckled.

"Mark Sanders!" April exclaimed as she turned red and was thankful for the two professional women standing there eyeing Mark. "Go ahead, be my guest, slap him."

"Believe me; I would, if he still had on his gown," Teresa remarked with a sly smile. Kathleen hid her face, thinking about the question her son Matthew asked her.

"Mom, what is Mark Sanders really like?" She pondered that answer, as she looked straight into his mischievous face and tried not to laugh.

Mark continued testing his facial expressions, as he lay flat on the bed so they could begin working on his legs.

They laughed at him as they stretched his muscles in different directions, but as his facial expressions turned to pain, their faces showed concern for him. The new drugs had caused even more joint stiffness and it was painful for him, but Mark tolerated the workout without complaining.

They let him get back out of bed and walk around as they stood inches from him, until they noticed he was struggling. Fearful of a fall, they had him sit down on the recliner to catch his breath.

Mark thanked them when they finished fussing over him and gave Teresa two autographed footballs to give to her sons. "As soon as they let me out of this prison I will take your boys to the stadium to meet some of the other players."

"They would love that, Mark."

"I'll get Pete season tickets as soon as I can get my hands on four of them," he pledged. "But first you have to get me out of here. Next time you come in here bring me the key to the door." He poked fun at her and she gave his cheek a squeeze as she stood over him.

He promised Kathleen he would have Jeff bring him another football for Matthew, but in the meantime, he autographed his unused bedpan Beth gave him that morning.

"Tell Matthew he can get a good price for this bedpan on E-Buys on the internet. What's a Mark Sanders' bedpan worth these days? It's gotta be worth more than my bobble-head doll."

Kathleen laughed at him. "Mark Sanders, you're so ... so ... so bad!" He was just an overgrown teddy bear with a funny sense of humor.

"At least you have one less object to throw at the nurses," she chuckled as she looked at the signature he had written on the pan and read it out loud.

"King of the throne, even when I am sitting down. Mark Sanders #12." They all laughed as Mark grabbed his pillow and held it against his painful stomach.

When they left, April sat down on Mark's knee, wrapped her arms around his neck and kissed him. Their lips melted together as Mark held his warm hand against the middle of her back and drew her body to him.

April realized she was playing with fire as she felt his wandering hand against her bare skin, claiming her as his. It took both her hands pressing against his shoulders to hold him back.

"Mark, we need to stop, before you can't."

"King Mark, wants his princess April." He claimed a lock of her soft hair in wishful thinking of more to come.

"I am going to go visit with Sunny for an hour at the penthouse, since you seem to be feeling much better."

"I'd like one hour with you at the penthouse, myself." Mark grinned and she gave him a consolation kiss on his forehead and helped him over to his bed. He unsuccessfully attempted to detain her next to him.

"You stay in bed and behave yourself while I am gone, and I just might think of something to reward you with when I get back," she blushed as she undid his craving fingers from around her waist.

"I'll be waiting," he grinned, but he knew nothing could compare to what he had in mind for them at the penthouse.

She shook her head at him, "Just remember what Dr. Stevenson said about the Foley catheter. If you have to go, call Beth to help you to the bathroom. Otherwise, well, you know what will happen."

She blushed as she left the room, leaving Mark sitting there with his mouth half open contemplating that undesirable thought. That was certainly not what he had in mind to do with April, he laughed as he ran his fingers through his hair.

Beth brought in Mark's food tray and begged him to try to eat something. He opened the lid, looked at the *soggy* mashed potatoes and shook his head no.

"I can't, Beth, really. My stomach is still upset from yesterday." She took the tray out of the room and returned with a new bedpan.

"April said you gave away the one I gave you this morning." She was professionally trying not to smile. "I am going to go on my break. Eve's at the desk if you need anything."

"What's with Eve? She doesn't seem to like me."

"Sorry, Mark, she already has a boyfriend. To be honest, he's a tad too old for her, if you ask me. I met him once in the hospital-parking garage. He made the hair on my arm stand up. But Eve seems crazy about him, so I guess he is a nice enough man."

"Is it just me, or is she unsociable with all her patients?"

"As far as I can tell, the other patients seem to like Eve. She doesn't interact much with the staff, but she is great with the kids in the Unit. She is a good nurse, just strong-headed, like some of our doctors around here."

Now just who was she referring to, hmmm, Mark smiled, *surely not me.*

"Nothing personal, but they can have her. I like my nurses just fine. So hurry back before she tries to kill me," he chuckled.

Beth playfully shook her head at Mark and thought, *what's not to like about Mark, hmmm. Thank goodness for the happy drugs Gina gave him earlier*, she smiled at his eye-catching face. *Yes, we all love Mark.*

Mark was glad April and Beth were gone. He had the whole room all to himself, and he could do whatever he wanted, just like a little child. His rebellious mood erupted as he got out of bed, taking his faithful IV pole with him.

"Come on, Stanley; let's see what we can find to do, 'Doctor thinks he knows it all' is in surgery," he spoke to his IV pole as he walked around stiffly.

His sense of humor abruptly stopped as he felt the pain increasing in his legs. *I have to keep my legs limber*, he thought seriously, as he pushed himself harder to keep walking around. *I will never make it to the game if I can't move my legs.* That was not something he was going to joke around about. He was going to do whatever it took to get back in shape, no matter how painful it was.

His legs were not his only problem as he staggered in the direction of the bathroom to be sick.

When Beth returned from her break, she noticed Mark's pale face and asked him if he had been sick again.

"No, but my stomach is upset. Can you get me something to calm it down?" She returned with all the medications he needed and a fresh jug of ice water.

When April returned, she found Mark throwing objects like footballs across the room into the trashcan, testing his throwing arm. It was all April could do to get him back in bed and keep him there.

"What kind of drugs did Dr. Price give you, Mark? You are being so bad, Mr. Sanders. Now get back in bed, before Dr. Stevenson comes in here to check on you."

Nevertheless, she was thankful for the fight he had in him. He asked a million questions about her visit with Sunny. Then as soon as his energy level subsided, he fell back asleep for the next two hours, as she lay next to him.

She took pleasure in running her fingertips across his firm chest, knowing it was safe to satisfy her longing to touch him without causing him to be aroused.

As the hours passed, April had mixed feelings. His sleeping gave her a few hours of peace, but it also reminded her that Mark had a long uphill road ahead of him to recovery.

She softly ran her fingertips across his cheeks and outlined his lips. She missed his smile already as he slept. She took his hand and held it to her heart.

"Mark Sanders, I love you. Thank you for making me smile today when I know all you wanted to do was cry. *"My heart belongs to you, Mark,"* she whispered, as she thought of the letter she had written just in case it was needed someday.

It would take many more laughs and smiles if Mark was going to survive his stay in this hospital. She cuddled up next to him, wrapped him in her arms, and fell asleep next to the man *she would give her own life for, if it meant he could live.*

Chapter Thirty

Extending Compassion

§&

While Mark was asleep, Willy, a worker from the hospital cafeteria, came to check on Mark. He was an older man of small build, in his late fifties, yet he looked worn out for his age. It was obvious he suffered from a rough life. He had a cut over his left eye and a swollen jaw indicating he had been in a recent fight.

Mark had treated Willy in the emergency room after Willy had been beaten up over a gambling debt he owed from betting against Mark's football team.

It did not matter to Mark that Willy bet against his team. Mark felt compassion for his patient, who seemed down on his luck. It hurt Mark's heart that his winning a simple football game had caused this man to be in the ER suffering. God spoke to Mark's heart to bless Willy.

Mark helped Willy get into an alcohol treatment program. He generously gave Willy the money to get back on his feet. He got him a job working in the hospital cafeteria as a cook. He even co-signed on a mortgage with Willy at his bank.

But most importantly, Mark had invited Willy and his wife, Wendy, to his church. Wendy quickly got involved with the children's ministry. However, Willy, not having any self-worth, shied away from the men of the church. Mark did his best to draw Willy into the heart of the church without making Willy feel uncomfortable.

Willy sorrowfully watched Mark sleeping. His eyes were teary; he nervously wrenched his fingers together.

"I'm mighty sorry, Mark, that I'm makin' you sick. You see, I ain't got no choice," Willy whispered before he turned and left in despair.

If'n it had just been me that they were uh threatenin' to hurt, I would uh let them. But Willy could not let anything happen to Wendy. He had to choose, either Mark's life or Wendy's.

He touched his swollen eye, which was a reminder of what they would do again if he did not do what they said. Willy's heart felt sick. He prayed Mark would continue to refuse to eat the hospital food. He intentionally made it look uninviting so Mark would refuse to eat.

Then he thought of the bowl of jello, and tears once again filled his eyes. He had heard that Mark had eaten the jello. *Thank ya, God, for lookin' out for poor old Mark, if'n he ate the whole bowl, he'd be . . .*

Mark's blood tests came back. There was no increase in his levels, in fact, they had dropped slightly. Immediately after receiving his blood transfusions, Mark's counts would increase, but soon afterwards, they would drop. Logically, it did not make any sense.

What is causing Mark to stay anemic? Frustrated, Dr. Stevenson was forced to try again to give Mark medications to bring up his falling blood cell counts, knowing Mark would have to suffer from the side effects.

Mark put up a brief fuss, but when Tom showed him the report, he asked Mark what he would do if he were the doctor and not the patient.

"Dr. Sanders, give me your professional opinion. How would you treat this patient?" Mark reluctantly told Beth what she needed to put in his IV and what to inject into his thigh; he even added Benadryl to the order.

"Dr. Sanders, someday you might just make a good doctor, but I doubt you will ever make a good patient."

Beth returned with the syringes and handed one to April. Mark lay back on the bed so April could inject the syringe into his thigh muscle. He teasingly played the "wounded soldier role" to get a sympathetic kiss from his "hot" nurse. April was quick to accommodate him; however, Beth left the room with blushed cheeks after she gave him the shot from her syringe.

Tom shook his head at the playboy and waited with crossed arms to see how Mark would react to the medications.

To Tom's surprise, Mark was able to tolerate the side effects. He had a mild headache, some muscle tension, threw up twice, had a slight fever, but no violent mood swing. He felt better in an hour and was able to fall asleep.

This puzzled Dr. Stevenson. What had been the difference in the three attempts? If only he could figure out why, then he would know how to treat Mark. Nevertheless, it was decided to continue Mark on this lower dosage.

April went to the ranch to have dinner with Sunny while Mark slept from the Benadryl.

The "Angels" appeared at 4:30 and woke Mark up. For the first time, they saw him hesitate about getting out of bed. He was not his usual bubbly self as he took his hands and assisted his legs over the side of the bed, unable to hold back his moans of pain.

"Mark, do you want me to get you something for pain?" Kathleen asked. Mark shook his head no. He decided to see how long he could go without the pain medication. When he was in pain, he was determined no one needed to know. His plan was to taper the dose down so he could go home.

Mark was stiff from the medication April had given him, so they let him walk up and down the hallway to work out his cramped muscles. Teresa held one arm as Kathleen held the other, both encouraging their quiet patient to take another step forward.

One more step to the Super Bowl. I can do this. Another step to the Super Bowl. I should have taken the pain med. He looked down the corridor and frowned.

"I have to stop," his voice low, "I can't make it. My legs are cramping."

Mark held the hand railing on the wall while Kathleen quickly got a wheelchair for him. Without protesting, he sat down with difficulty. The despondent expression on his face broke their hearts.

"Wait right here, Kathleen." Teresa eyed her sister and went to ask Dr. Stevenson's permission for something.

Kathleen knelt down to face Mark and placed her hand on his knee. "I know how difficult this is for you, Mark, but God has special plans for your life. I believe that for you. Try to hold on to that thought when you are feeling defeated."

Their eyes held a special bond of compassion, as Mark thanked Kathleen for her kind words. Kathleen thought of Mark more like a son than a patient. He had won her heart.

Teresa came bouncing back, her face glowing. "Dr. Sanders, we are taking you for a ride. But first you must put this facemask back on." She helped Mark tie the strings, as she winked at Kathleen.

They took him to the physical therapy room and turned on the whirl-pool. Jeff and Dan arrived, just before Mark was about to bashfully object to the two women helping him undress.

Kathleen handed Jeff the towels, then she gave Mark a warm blushful smile and handed him a hospital gown as she remembered Mark's comment about "airy" hospital gowns.

"At least we are not parading down, uh, Main Street, Mark." Kathleen blushed as she teased him and gave him the smile he was lacking. This time the gown was a welcome cover-up for the bashful doctor. Mark removed his facemask and was all grins.

The jubilant smile on Mark's face warmed their hearts and Mark topped it off, when he stood up with their help and planted kisses on their cheeks.

"Thanks, Angels, you are the best," he thanked them sincerely. He felt humble before the two women.

"How about getting us tickets to the Super Bowl?" Teresa inquired, with a hopeful smile.

"Only if you talk Dr. Stevenson into letting me play in the game," Mark joked back. Or was he joking?

Teresa knew, however, Mark's desire to be at that game was strong, and if she could have made that happen for him, she would have. Mark needed to be made whole again, to have his life back the way it should have been. In her profession, too many of her patients never got that chance. She prayed Mark would be the exception.

"Gentlemen, he is all yours," Kathleen told the two doctors waiting to dunk Mark in the swirling warm water.

When Beth brought in his supper tray, Mark promised to eat something but when she left, Mark deceitfully dumped the food in the toilet and put the empty tray back on the table.

When Beth came in later to get the tray, she noticed the food was missing. She grinned at Mark to let him know he was not as smart as he thought he was.

When April returned from the ranch, she brought him homemade soup broth from Martha's kitchen. Mark ate half a bowl and kept it down. Thirty minutes later, he ate the homemade biscuits and the remaining soup as everyone watched over him. *Don't they trust me?* Although frustrated, he kept a smile on his face and pretended to be enjoying every bite.

He was finally hungry, they thought with relief. Everyone rejoiced that he had finally eaten something other than packaged crackers.

Mark, on the other hand, was regretting the meal he had consumed on a stomach that felt like a hot exploding volcano. The pain was now worse than ever. If only he had not felt pressured to eat something in front of everyone, he would have left the soup in the bowl.

That night, Dr. Stevenson continued with the new drug. He ordered a strong muscle relaxant and was relieved the only reactions Mark had was a slight fever and stomach cramps. Tom was still puzzled why the first dose had made Mark so violently sick and stiff.

Nothing made any sense when it came to Mark's illness. One day he was violently sick, the next day he was fine.

It just did not add up, but then nothing added up when it came to treating Mark.

Chapter Thirty-One

Testing Limitations

§ ᘒ

B y the next morning, Mark was feeling much better and was acting more like himself. Tom had increased Mark's pain medication during the night and continued with the muscle relaxant, due to his muscle pain after his workout with his "Angels".

Mark was concerned about the amount of pain medications the doctors kept giving him. The last thing he wanted was to sleep all day from them. But he knew the pain meds were the only way he could make it through the day. He knew he had to keep moving forward to get where he wanted to go. He also knew he needed to taper off them if he wanted to go home sooner than his doctors' projected date.

When Teresa and Kathleen arrived early, they took him to the physical therapy room to work on his leg and arm movements. They let him get in the whirlpool. Jeff and April stood on-duty to assist the "Angels."

Mark wanted Jeff to tell him how things were progressing as a second year resident. April saw the look of yearning on Mark's face to be back as a doctor. Jeff made light of his new position, in consideration of Mark's feelings. They both knew how much Mark wanted his life to return to normal.

"You'll be back, Mark. Your vacation time is just about up, and then you will be back having your good-humored fun down in the ER." Jeff half-smiled; his heart was wishing Mark was on duty right now beside him in the ER, where Mark belonged.

"Yeah, I'll be back, *sooner* than you know." Mark grinned to relieve Jeff's tension, as he held back his true feelings. He saw the compassionate look on the Angels' faces and knew they understood exactly how he felt about not being a doctor.

The more time Mark spent with these two women, the more they understood how he truly felt. Humiliated, embarrassed, defenseless, weak, exposed, out of control, and vulnerable were just some of the feelings this illness had inflicted on him over the last few days. Feelings that he had turned over to God, not willing to let them take away his joy.

However, with Teresa and Kathleen working with him two or three times a day, he had exposed those innermost feelings of his, in their conversations when April was out of the room.

Teresa and Kathleen were his human safety nets, his ropes to hang onto when he felt the weight of his life hanging on by a thread and had to vent. What he valued most about them was that he did not have to pretend with them anymore.

With April and Jeff, he could not express his true feelings without the fear of upsetting them. If he did not feel like smiling, he had to smile for them. He loved them too much to make his pain be their pain. His illness was not all about him; it was about what it did emotionally to all those he loved.

His relationship with God was a constant battle. As he claimed healing, others called him sick. As he claimed victories, others reminded him of his setbacks. As he turned to faith and prayer, he was seen as arrogant. He knew the missing piece to his healing was because he was not allowing God in his room as much as he should have.

What he really needed was some quiet time alone with his family in a place that did not smell like a hospital, and he had just that place in mind. He could not wait to show April his surprise when he got out of this dungeon.

Once Mark was back in his room, Beth took his vital signs and hooked him back up to the monitors. She was thankful Mark did not protest the lead wires she placed on his chest.

April was thankful Mark's disposition was more relaxed. He was cheerful and in good spirits. His time with the "Angels" always improved his mood. She just hoped they felt the same way when they left him.

Dr. Price came in with Beth to check on Mark before going to her office. Dr. Price explained to them the different mood swings Mark would experience as he went through his long-term drug treatments, hospital stays, and the limitations of his activities.

"Your life as you knew it will never be the same, Mark, but that does not mean your new way of life will not be as fulfilling."

Mark held his tongue; he was claiming an even better life than he had before. He was not settling for the half-a-life he felt Gina just offered him.

Gina suggested Mark stay on the anxiety medication she had prescribed for him yesterday. Mark was agreeable and Gina gave Beth the order.

Mark wanted more information about his illness for his family and friends to read. If they were more informed, maybe they could understand what he was experiencing was normal: his different mood swings, his reactions to the drugs, and whatever else was thrown his way by the devil himself. He would continue to seek the only true answers from the "real book" for the cure to his ongoing emotional problems – his Bible.

Dr. Price gave him the Aplastic Anemia and MDS International Foundation, Inc. website. She suggested April get in touch with other families with AA for support. "The PNH organization has a wonderful support group on the Internet. Many of their members have or had AA and can provide you with valuable information." Then Gina told Mark she would check on him later that afternoon.

After a phone call to Sunny, April laid in Mark's arms as they watched the early morning show on TV. Beth came in with Dr. Megan McGuire and injected the medication Dr. Price ordered.

Sherry Grooms hooked Mark back up to the heart monitor during the night. Megan was pleased his heart rate was back to normal. She was convinced that his high blood pressure was from the pain he had been in before Tom medicated him.

"If you are in pain, Mark, I want you to make sure you take your pain meds. Otherwise, your blood pressure will go back up."

She removed the leads from his chest. She told him that every four hours she wanted him on the monitor for an hour, no exceptions. She went to finish her morning rounds.

Mark felt better now that he was only tied down to Stanley. He and Stanley were fast becoming best friends. He pulled his legs over the side of the bed and stretched them for a few minutes.

He jokingly danced with Stanley on his way to the bathroom. April followed close behind him to make sure he did not fall; she smiled at his playfulness.

With a broad grin, Mark asked April to call Dr. McGuire back and see if she would grant him medical clearance so he and she could do a little dancing of their own. It was hard to ignore the wide grin and the wink he gave her, as she blushed like a new bride.

"Robert Mark Sanders, the third, I am not going to call Dr. McGuire and ask her if you can have s..." Before she could finish the word, Dr. Steven Martin entered the room.

"Ask Dr. McGuire what?" Steven asked as he picked up Mark's chart and read the latest reports from the other doctors.

"Uh," April turned a bright shade of red.

Steven took notice of her embarrassed face. His face widened and he chuckled. "I should have known what Casanova wanted. Mark, get out of that bathroom right now! I know you are hiding from me."

Mark came out with a guilty look on his face; he tried not to smile at Steven. He and Stanley headed to his bed, but before he got there, he got lightheaded. Steven grabbed a hold of him, keeping him from falling, and helped him over to the bed.

"On the bed, Mark, right now," Steven instructed him firmly, noting the painful look on Mark's face. "Do you need something for pain?" Mark shook his head, no, but in truth, he should have said yes. "I want to take a look at your incisions."

Mark was somewhat dazed, lay back flat on the bed, and was quiet. April pulled Mark's football jersey shirt up to his collarbone so Steven could have a look. She put on her sterile gloves and removed the dressing.

The incisions were not healing as quickly as Steven had hoped. He told Mark that the stitches were not ready to be removed. He handed April a tube of medicated cream to rub on Mark's incisions.

"Mark, as long as you show signs of lightheadedness, you cannot get out of bed unless someone is standing with you." Steven wrote notes in Mark's chart. "I am dead serious, Mark, not one foot out of this bed unless the nurses or the 'Angels' are here. And as far as asking Dr. McGuire your question about reinstating your love life, I will personally let her know what I think." He turned and was out the door before Mark could whole-heartedly protest.

April finished applying the medication under Mark's attentive eyes. He was wishing she and he could be doing something far more exciting then rubbing cream on his abdomen. His hands soon found places that were off limits to the nurses, and April playfully slapped his hand.

"Behave, Mark. Beth might come in here," April said in a hushed voice. She was not about to be caught twice discussing what Mark had in mind right this minute.

As predicted, Mark was not listening to anything anyone had to say. He knew he felt better, and he was anxious to test his limitations. April quickly moved away from the bed when Mark decided not to behave himself with his cravings for her.

Mark was bored; he had never been one to lie around and do nothing, not even when he was sick as a child. He always found something interesting to do. He smiled thinking about the time he had the chickenpox when he was four, and he decided to let the chickens out of the hen house and give them a bath for giving him their poxes. Poor Pedro, he was chasing chickens for a week. Mark laughed thinking about the repercussions he'd suffered after that stunt.

He called Sunny and had a long talk about her cat, Hannah and her dog, Madison. Sunny informed Mark that Madison was getting way too fat. "What do ya thinks wrong with Madison?" Sunny's innocent voice asked Doctor Mark.

Mark eyed April; his heart wishfully prayed April would soon announce she was in the same condition as Madison. He wanted April to go get Sunny and sneak her in for a visit.

April just grinned at him. She would have to think of something to occupy Mark, before he got himself into real trouble.

Then April noticed Carlo, Jerk, and Justin at the window making eye contact with Mark. *Oh, great, a fine time for those knuckleheads to show up and influence Mark.*

Carlo held up a football, and Mark grinned as he made a move to exit the bed. April grabbed his arm firmly. "Mark, don't you dare go out there with those guys!"

"Just for a few minutes, what's a few minutes going to hurt?" She held firm and stood her ground as he continued to protest.

Beth appeared and spoke with the men. She was shaking her head, no, as they protested. Finally, they gave her the things they had for Mark, and she brought them into Mark's room.

"You would think this was the White House and Mark was the President. He has enough bodyguards surrounding him," Carlo commented loudly enough Mark could hear him.

"Well, at least they are pleasing to the eyes. Bet old Mark is having a grand time teasing the nurses," Justin laughed, as his twin brother's face lit up.

A clever thought occurred to Jerk; maybe they should teach Mark a lesson about messing around with the nurses. *Oh boy.* A wide grin crossed his face as he told Carlo his brainy plan to teach poor old Mark a lesson on how to behave with the nurses.

"Let's just give Mark a honeymoon with a nurse he will never forget," Jerk laughed with the anticipation of things to come for Mark. *The nurse they planned to surprise him with would not be April.*

Beth handed Mark the football and the football cards the men had given her. He was sulking as he put them on his table and pulled the covers back over his legs.

"If I am the President, then why am I in this concentration camp?" His humor was short lived as his eyes suddenly showed pain. "Ahhh, man," he expressed in pain as he moved to find a comfortable position.

"Mark, do you need any pain medication?" she asked as she witnessed the strained look on his face when he moved on the bed.

"No, I'm fine," he lied, willing to tough it out with the pain for as long as he could.

"April, would you like to have a cup of coffee with me?" April followed Beth to the nurse's station. Beth told April she thought Mark was throwing his hospital food away. "We need to keep a closer eye on that husband of yours."

Sure enough, when Mark sent April to get him another sports drink out of the vending machine, his breakfast disappeared while she was out of the room. This time he had April to deal with, and she was not as forgiving at his deceitfulness, as he begged for mercy.

The "Angels" made their second morning appearance. Mark wanted to know if Matthew was a millionaire from selling his "Mark Sanders" bedpan on E-buy? They all laughed. Mark gave Kathleen the autographed football and some signed football cards from the players.

April took this time to take a shower and get her thoughts together. Mark was in excellent hands. She was more worried about the "Angels."

They did their usual workout with his legs and let him walk the halls. They disappeared in embarrassment when Mark wanted to know if they would put in a good word for him with Dr. McGuire about resuming his love life with April. Sometimes he was way too honest about what he wanted!

Mark was ready to lift weights and get back in shape. He was exercising his biceps with anything he could pick up. He talked Jeff into bringing him arm weights. Dr. Stevenson quickly took them away. Mark's incisions were not healing, and he did not want Mark busting them open.

Julia brought Mark more of Martha's soup and biscuits, and he quickly ate them for lunch. April was standing guard over him making sure he really was eating them. She smiled at him with each bite he took.

Mark seemed to be enjoying himself as he teased her with his twinkling eyes. She knew what he really wanted for lunch, and it was not those biscuits. She would have to keep her distance from him. She went out to the nurse's station to have a word with Beth. Mark disappeared in the bathroom while she was gone.

Jeff was not helping any when he brought Mark another football, and they tossed it around the room and in the hallways. April frowned at them but they continued to act like schoolboys. *Well, at least Mark has on a facemask this time.*

Dr. Stevenson took the football away. He frowned at the two and sent Jeff packing. "I swear, Mark, you belong in the children's ward." Mark thought that would be better than this place. He could really have fun there. Well, at least Mark had his sense of humor back. They were all thankful for that fact.

Dr. Stevenson secretly added a light sedative to Mark's IV to keep Mark from overexerting himself. His blood cell counts were still not high enough to let him leave the hospital. Mark needed to stay on his new medications. How much longer could he keep Mark under wrap?

Tomorrow, Mark would regret he had done so much today, Dr. Stevenson thought with just a slight hint of satisfaction to teach Mark a valuable lesson. That would be one way of keeping Mark where he belonged, in his bed.

The sedative kicked in and Mark fell asleep. Dr. Stevenson explained to April that Mark would have highs and lows as his counts went up and down. Every time he overexerts himself he will crash and then sleep. He told her not to worry unless Mark showed other symptoms such as a high fever, sweating, pain, or a mood change.

Mark woke up later that afternoon from a long nap, stiff and sore. He did not want to move a muscle. He was not about to admit it to anyone. He would suffer on his own. He pretended to be interested in the "chick flick" movie April was watching on TV.

Mark did not fool her. She went out and got him his pain medication that would help him fall back asleep. She lied and told him it was his antibiotic as she injected it into his IV access device, hoping that he would not notice she had not given him an IV Piggyback of antibiotics. *Two can play at his game*, she smiled.

Just this once she was thankful he had fallen back asleep as the romantic scene in the movie heated up. She knew his desires to resume their honeymoon were stronger than ever.

She looked over at the man she loved and smiled. *Soon, Mark, we will have our own precious moments where we will love each other and nothing, nothing, will take away our passion*, she vowed.

Chapter Thirty-Two

Pay Back

§§

When the dinner tray arrived, April woke Mark up. Mark pushed it aside and went back to sleep. April pulled his blanket up over him and kissed his forehead.

That evening, Jeff called and asked April to come eat with him in the café downstairs. She looked over at Mark; he was sleeping soundly. She kissed his forehead and went downstairs. What April did not know was that Jeff had removed her from the room so Mark's teammates could have some fun with him.

The gang showed up and begged Christy to give into their plot to get Mark. "Come on, payback for the stunts he has pulled on the staff," Carlo grinned. "We promise not to hurt him and Jerk will wear a mask."

Jerk was dressed as a 300-pound nurse. Mark told Jerk in the locker room he did a good impersonation of a woman. Jerk was up for the challenge. Jerk had on a shaggy black wig and was dressed in a nurse's uniform. He put a mask over his face and rubber gloves on his hands. The guys were already laughing hysterically as they sat on the floor to view the monitor.

They turned on the surveillance video camera Robert had installed in Mark's room so they could see and hear what was going on in his room at the nurse's station. Mark was sleeping so peacefully. The guys looked at each other and smiled; this was going to be fun. Justin gave Carlo a high five and laughed.

Jerk went in and stood over Mark. He comically waved at the camera. He noticed Mark's dinner tray and lifted the lid. *I bet this tastes good.* He dipped his fingers in the mashed potatoes, pulled down his mask, and sucked on his fingers. He made an awful face and the guys all laughed. Then he replaced his mask and shook Mark's shoulder.

"Mr. Sanders, honey, it is time to wake up," he whispered like a woman into Mark's ear. Jerk was glad he had on a mask. It was extremely hard to keep a straight face.

Mark slowly opened his eyes and focused on the odd-looking nurse in front of him. *What? Who is she?* He appeared puzzled as he rubbed his sluggish eyes and then he opened them wide when he realized he was not dreaming. He inquisitively looked around the room for April. He sat up slightly, leaning on his elbow, staring at the nurse in front of him. *What's she doing in here*, he wondered.

"I've heard you have been a very bad patient, so I am going to whip you into shape!" Jerk articulated like a woman drill sergeant.

"What?" Mark sleepily asked her as he tucked his pillow under his head. He rubbed his eyes again. Was he hearing her right? *Maybe if I close my eyes she will go away*, he thought with anticipation that she would leave him alone, but that disappointingly was not the case.

Jerk shook Mark's shoulder again, and Mark opened his eyes, and then he quickly closed them, praying she would get the hint and go away. *Maybe I am hallucinating*, or at least he prayed he was, or *maybe I am dreaming. I just think I am awake.* Then he heard her rough voice near his ear.

"Dr. Stevenson said you have not been following his orders. He sent me in here to straighten you out," Jerk told him sternly as he shook Mark's shoulder. Mark looked up at him with disbelief on his face.

"Uhhh …OoooOk," Mark said slowly as he looked again for April or Christy to rescue him. *Where'd April disappear to?*

Jerk picked up Mark's chart and pretended to read it. "Let's see, it says here, that you are not allowed out of this bed without someone at your side at all times. My, my, it says here, you need a shower tonight. Let's me and you go get that shower, honey." Jerk winked at Mark and pulled Mark's covers back.

Mark's eyes got big and he snatched the covers back. *What does this woman think she is doing?* It was not her size or looks. He had not even allowed Christy or Beth to physically touch him, let alone stand there watching him take a shower! It was April or no one!

"I am not taking a shower with you!" Mark stated firmly but was careful not to offend the nurse. "I'll just wait on my wife," he told her as his eyebrows knitted together.

"Honey, your wife has gone home for the night; it is just you and me." Jerk took the sheet and pulled it again, and Mark tugged back. The guys at the nurse's station were rolling on the floor laughing.

"Really, I don't need a shower," Mark insisted in a panic.

"Have it your way. I will just give you a sponge bath then." Jerk picked up the pan off the nightstand. Mark's mouth dropped.

"Oh, no way, that is not going to happen!" Mark raised his eyebrows sternly at her. "What do you think you are doing?"

"You and I are about to get to know each other real good," Jerk said as he got up in Mark's face with the sponge. The guys covered their mouths to keep from being heard. They were laughing so hard.

"You're not serious … are you?" Mark asked frantically as he pulled the blanket up to his chin and backed away from her, drawing his knees up to his chest.

"What's the matter, honey? Don't tell me you are shy?" Jerk winked at Mark. Mark took note of her awful thick bushy eyebrows.

Mark reached his hand up and ran his fingers through his hair, trying to think of some way out of this. "Really, I promise you; I don't need a bath," Mark said, shaking his head no. *There's no way I'm leaving this bed with her!* The guys had tears streaming down their faces as they tried not to laugh so hard Mark would hear them.

"Honey, you ain't got nothin' I haven't seen before," Jerk said as he yanked the blanket off Mark. Mark kept a firm grip on the sheet. He pulled his knees up tighter to his chest. He was glad he had on his sweatpants, because he was not taking anything off for this insane nurse.

"Lady, you are crazy if you think you are giving me a bath!" Mark busted out at her. *April, where are you?*

Jerk chuckled softly and reached into his pocket, pulled out a syringe, and held it out in front of Mark's face. "Maybe this will calm you down; turn on over and show me a cheek," Jerk told Mark with wide eyes.

Mark's face turned red as he put his hands over his face and rubbed his fingers down the sides of his face. He tried to smile as he shook his head in disbelief. "I'm outta here!" Mark told her as he jumped off the bed and stood facing her from across the bed. He was ready to battle this crazed woman to keep her away from him. He pointed to the door. "Get away from me before I have to hurt you!"

"Come on, honey, come to momma," Jerk commanded and made kissing sounds.

She's insane! She must have escaped from the mental floor. Oh, God, you gotta get me out of this mess! Mark held his hands up to protect himself from this wild woman who smelled like bad after-shave lotion. Then Mark saw the video camera, with the light blinking, meaning it was turned on, and he smiled brightly.

Those bushy eyebrows, her awful smell, hmmmm, oh ok ... he knew he had been had by the guys. He had fallen head over heels, right into their little plot. The prankster came out in him as he shook his head and laughed. *Real funny, you guys*, he thought as he planned a quick revenge on this unsuspecting nurse.

Mark went over to Jerk and pushed him backwards on the bed. He grabbed the nurse's face with both hands and gave her a kiss through the mask. Jerk was kicking his legs and flopping around on the bed trying to get away from Mark.

April and Jeff walked into the room. April could not believe her eyes. She was shocked, her mouth wide open, as she watched her husband attacking some poor nurse with a kiss she obviously did not want! "Mark Sanders! What are you doing?" she asked him smartly. Mark turned around and faced her disbelieving eyes. Jeff was laughing hysterically. Jerk flopped off the bed to his feet.

The guys were standing at the sliding glass door laughing uncontrollably. Mark went over to the door and shook his fist at them. Jerk exited the room and ran to the elevator. The guys ran after him. "Got ya, Mark!" they yelled back. "Now leave the poor nurses alone!"

Mark fell backwards onto the bed, grabbed his pillow, held it tight to his abdomen, and then he laughed until tears were rolling down the side of his face. When he finally stopped laughing, he grabbed April's arm and took her into the bathroom. He took a quick shower with April standing there. *He was not taking any chances that insane nurse was coming back!*

Chapter Thirty-Three

A Change in Plans

§§

During the night, Mark got up and removed his oxygen mask so he could walk around with Stanley. He was stiff and it was apparent his incisions were bothering him. But he decided not to ask for any more pain medication.

It made him smile, thinking of the good laugh he had earlier. Those guys would pay for that one, he grinned. They brought some fun to him in the midst of his pain and he loved them. He gave thanks for his great friends.

Mark sat on the recliner and watched the late night sports channel. It was all about the upcoming Super Bowl Game. Right away, his heart started beating faster. Since he was a little boy, he dreamed of being in the Super Bowl. That dream was just days away. Disappointment filled his heart. *I was so close to having my dream,* he thought despondently for just a few seconds and then, true to his form, he thought positively.

I can be ready to play by Sunday, he thought, unwilling to give up his dream. *Maybe just one or two passes, just so I could say I played in a Super Bowl game. Or maybe three passes, at least one touchdown throw. Hmmm. It is not as if my spleen is going to bust again. Been there, done that, I do not wanna do that again.* He contemplated that thought with an uplifted eyebrow.

They showed clips from the AFC Championship Game, including Mark's pass to Carlo that had won the game. For the first time he got to witness the joy on his teammate's faces as they won the game. He had spoiled the excitement of the win for them when he fell half-dead on the field. Recalling that moment bothered him deeply. That was not the memory he wanted his teammates to have of that win.

If I had not played in the game, we would have lost. That memory would have been much worse.

He was thankful they did not show the clip of him lying on the field. He had already seen it, and it reminded him how close he had been to death. It reminded him of the pain his family and friends had suffered as they stood there watching him die. He bit his lip with his front teeth as his stomach twisted into a knot. He would have done anything to erase that memory from everyone's minds.

The commentators talked about Mark, about his season, the records he set. They looked out and said, "Mark, if you are watching this, everyone here at the Sports Center is wishing you a fast recovery."

Mark was getting extremely anxious. He looked at the sleeping pair, his prison guards. Jeff was out cold on April's bed. Mark began to plan his exit from this prison cell.

What do I have to do to get out of this place? I have to get off these drugs, all of them, every last one of them. But how can I do that with the amount of pain that I am in?

His second step would be getting April to join forces with him against Dr. Stevenson. That was not going to be an easy task. She had already proven she could match him point for point. Despair invaded his heavy heart, thinking he would never get out of this place in time for the game.

April stirred on the bed, opened her eyes, and saw him. She sat up and stretched. "Mark, what are you doing? Come lay down with me," she said sleepily as she patted the bed beside her.

He shook his despondent head no. He had a somber face, like a little boy who had lost his puppy. She got up and went to him. "What's wrong, honey?" she asked sympathetically as she bent down beside the recliner and put her affectionate hand on his arm. She looked up at him with her warm blue eyes.

"I can't stay here. I've got to get out of here," he faintly told her as he looked into her understanding eyes and brushed back a lock of her hair from her face. She took the remote from him and turned the TV off.

"You have to stop watching the sports channel; it will drive you crazy," she told him with a compassionate voice. Her heart felt heavy for him, knowing how he felt.

"The team leaves Wednesday. I am going to get out of here and join them," he calmly told her. "I am their quarterback, April. My place is with my team." She looked into his sad eyes and understood how desperately lost he was feeling.

"It's been seven days. I should be able to go home tomorrow. I should have been out of here two days ago."

"Mark, you know you are not a normal surgical patient, you almost died ... you have aplastic ..."

"April, stop," he begged her with his longing eyes for her to comprehend what his heart was feeling, as he searched for her to join him in his faith. "I am healed. Please, April, believe that with me. I don't need to be here. Can you understand how I feel?"

April took a deep breath; she knew he was right. It was time to believe God had worked a miracle in Mark's body. It was time to let him go on with his life. There would be no stopping him from going to that game, as determined as he was. Dr. Stevenson would have a fit, but Mark would win this battle; that she was sure he would do.

"Sunny and I will go with you. We will have a mini vacation," she smiled warmly at him. She was the most incredible woman he had ever met and she belonged to him. His thoughts were now consumed with her, his wife of seven days.

April instantly cheered him up. Mark kicked Jeff out of the room and closed the window shades to the room. He threw his blanket over the video camera with a smile. *No one is watching this night*; he grinned and looked at April with his irresistible smile.

They had been married one week today. Mark planned to make it special even if they were in the hospital together. He took his AFC Championship ball cap and hung it on the outside door handle. It was a habit his college roommates did when they had a girl over and they did not want to be disturbed. Finally, it was his turn. He had the girl of his dreams standing right there ready to turn his life around.

Just how far she would go with him was still up for debate, he ginned optimistically.

Sunday morning he refused his pain medication, surprising everyone. "I feel great." But the pain remained in his stomach and muscles, only now, without the meds, he knew just how bad the pain could get.

While he was in the bathroom, he took a few minutes to worship with the God he knew was his only escape from this place. Then he washed his face in cool water, put on a smile and got back on the bed with his bride.

Roses arrived to honor their first week together. However, the flowers were not allowed in his room. It did not matter; the most important thing was the woman he still held in his arms.

225

She tipped her head back as his lips kissed the nape of her neck. Her heart fluttered as he kissed her soundly. When she opened her eyes to his, there was no mistaking the mischief that sparkled within.

As a gift for their first week together, Tom had let Mark have the night off from his new regiment of drugs. Therefore, Mark had slept the whole night through for the first time in a week without being sick. Well, maybe not the whole night, but at least it was not the drugs keeping him awake this time.

Jeff came in holding Mark's ball cap. "Uh, Mark, you might just want to hide this cap before Dr. McGuire shows up," he grinned at the two on the bed and took pleasure in making them blush.

Jeff told Mark that Jerk was down in the Emergency Room getting fluids for a bad case of food poisoning he had gotten during the night.

Mark joked that Jerk must have eaten in the hospital cafeteria last night. Mark wanted to know if the hospital had supplied the *rotten eggs* the team had eaten the day of the Championship game.

April frowned as Mark continued to tell Jeff that he was "dead serious" about the sorry food the hospital served. "I need to go have a talk with Willy and see if he's back on the liquor bottle."

Then he thought of David, another one of his alcoholic rescues from the ER. David was now supplying the team with his laundry service, thanks to Mark. Mark was his Alcoholics Anonymous sponsor. *I have fallen short of my commitment to David,* Mark thought with regret and promised himself he would give David a call and see how things were going.

Mark got special permission from Dr. Stevenson to have their lunch brought in from Nathan's Restaurant. As long as Mark ate something, Tom was not concerned with where he got the food as long as it was on Mark's approved food list.

They pulled the window shades and ate lunch by candlelight. The shine was back in his twinkling blue eyes as he admired April's beauty from across the table. They held hands as Mark blessed the meal and gave God thanks for his speedy recovery. Then he leaned over the table and gave April a scrumptious kiss. Mark gave April a necklace with a heart he had purchased from **Main Street Jewelry and Gifts**, where he had Penny Reddick help him pick out their magnificent wedding rings.

His heart was forever hers, and she was never to forget that. She cried tears of happiness when she saw it. She got up, sat down in his lap, and embraced his neck with both her arms as her lips melted into his. She was seriously thinking about letting him throw his blanket over the camera again, and this time, well, she might just give him what he really wanted.

Sunny arrived with Mark's parents. They had expected her visit would be limited to speaking to Mark on the intercom, but to their welcomed surprise, Dr. Stevenson allowed Mark to hold Sunny in his protective arms.

She was a priceless gift, which brought new hope into his life. She nestled her head against his shoulder, her gaze settled on Mark, as a tiny tear weaved its way down her cheek.

Mark was consumed with joyful tears as he held Sunny with such love, his whole face glowed. She was the healing medication he needed. It was amazing to Mark that this little girl wrapped up in his arms was his very own daughter. He had missed the first five years of her life, and he planned to make up for that lost time.

Mark's parents waited outside the glass door and watched the family together. How precious they were, laughing, hugging, and making this time special as a family. Robert wrapped Julia in his arms as they continued to watch Sunny love all over Mark.

Robert knew they were taking a chance legally with the visit, but this was a special day for April and Mark. This was truly a day no one ever thought this couple would have. Everyone was thankful Mark continued to improve. Mark had remarkably beaten all the odds against him, *so far.*

The dreaded court hearing was set for this coming Thursday morning at 8 a.m. Robert would break the horrible news to Mark and April tomorrow about the court hearing they were facing to achieve custody of Sunny. Today, Robert did not want to spoil their time together as Mark and April loved the miracle Mark held in his arms.

Robert affectionately hugged Julia next to him. He was thankful he had given his life over to God. Everything in his life, including his marriage and his relationships with people, had dramatically improved since he made that heartfelt decision to seek God.

No longer was Robert depending on his best friend, Dan, to fill in as a father to Mark and Rebecca. He would always be grateful to Dan for loving his family when he chose to be a workaholic.

In addition, the secret that Julia and Dan had kept for 25 years, Robert now took full responsibility for it. He rightfully blamed himself for what had almost happened the night he went off on a business trip, leaving his distraught wife in the arms of Dan.

Twenty-five years ago, while looking frantically for a tie one day, Robert came across a letter that Julia had written to her mother, Victoria. It was then he realized his marriage was in serious trouble. He realized he was the only one who could change the outcome of his failing marriage. Instead of dying to himself and doing the right thing, he put Julia and Dan into a vulnerable situation to test their loyalty to him.

Rebecca was three and Julia was tired of being left alone while Robert was working relentless hours trying to prove himself to his father. For the last two years, Julia had begged Robert to have another child with her but he refused her request.

In the letter, Julia admitted to her mother her marriage was falling apart. She was losing her high school sweetheart to a man she barely knew. If it had not been for the encouragement of their best friend, Dan, she would have ended her marriage. She wondered if she had chosen the wrong man for her husband, she wrote.

Dan had been Julia's reliable friend in high school, while Robert was the bigger than life president of their school, handsome, big blue eyes, rich, dream-of-a-catch man Julia had fallen head over heels in love with.

Dan, on the other hand, was the sports hero of the high school, handsome and strong, deep brown eyes, yet humble and in love with the Lord. When it came time for Julia to choose the man she loved, she chose Robert. Dan gracefully stepped aside and remained the best friend.

But Robert put them to the test on a harsh wintry night when he had a horrible fight with Julia over the baby she so desperately wanted. Unfortunately, for Dan, he walked right into the middle of the fight.

"If you want a baby so bad, let Dan father it for you! He's the one you really love," Robert yelled as he stomped out of the room and left town on a business trip.

Dan had certainly been a better man than Robert would have been, given the same circumstances. Things would have turned out so differently for all of them if Dan had not chosen to honor their friendship that night when he was left alone with a grieving Julia, the only woman he truly loved.

Robert took a long look at Mark, the child he had not wanted, the child that could easily have belonged to Dan. How wrong Robert had been that night he left another man alone with his grief-stricken wife, to console her, and to make love to her.

Yet a day later, fearing he had lost Julia to Dan, Robert came rushing back on his hands and knees begging Julia for forgiveness, and she compassionately took him back into her arms and into her bed.

Nine months later, a son was born. When Robert arrived at the hospital, Dan stood beside Julia's bed, holding the baby in his arms and he heard Dan say, "He's going to make a fine son."

Robert thought, *whose son, my son or Dan's son?* That thought had bothered him for the last nine months. Robert thought only twenty-four hours separated the two men from loving Julia. Which one of them had produced the child Dan held in his arms?

Dan turned to Robert and faced him. Then Dan looked down at the tiny baby, his heart aching, knowing he had done the right thing that night. But at this serene moment, he wished with all his heart that the baby he held was his, not Robert's. Robert did not deserve this precious baby boy. This baby should have been his son.

If God had not given him self-control that night, with the only woman he had ever loved, Mark would have been his son.

Dan looked up at Robert, their eyes met. Dan's brown eyes were tearful as he hugged Mark to his heart. He went to Robert and held Mark out for his father to take him.

"You don't deserve this baby. He should have been mine, but he's not, he is yours. Julia loves only you. She always has and she always will. However, Mark will be my son in my heart until the day I die. I will love him as if he were from my seed. Someday, I will tell him the truth about the night you left his mother alone with me to conceive him."

Dan handed Mark to Robert and left the room. Robert looked down at the blue-eyed baby boy and knew Dan was right. Mark should have been Dan's son. He did not deserve such a precious gift of love from his wife. Mark was indeed the heir to the Sanders' empire. He would be the pride and joy of Robert Senior, his namesake.

Although Robert wondered what really happened between Dan and Julia that night, he knew in his heart that they must have been faithful. He knew they had a secret but they owed him no explanation. Dan's friendship and loyalty remained strong as the years passed, and Dan fulfilled his role as Mark's Godfather. Mark would always be Dan's son in his heart.

If only Robert had not let his anger at his father get in the way of loving Mark when he was younger, Robert would not have lost those precious years with Mark, years that belonged to Dan and Julia. Dan had every right to call Mark his son. Robert had failed Mark as a father.

Godly men had surrounded Robert back then, but he was too blind to see, too prideful to acknowledge, and refused to see all the blessings he was missing with his family. Nevertheless, Robert had plenty of time to reflect back on those times with regret after Mark nearly died from his motorcycle accident.

Because of Mark, Robert was no longer warming the pew he sat on. He was sitting on the edge to learn more about God. Mark had shown him the power of forgiveness, mercy, and the grace of a wonderful God.

Now if Robert could just grasp the supernatural healing miracle revelation that Mark claimed, he could let go of his fear for Mark's health and Mark's life.

Sunny was the miracle child sent down from heaven. If Mark's health continued to improve, Dr. Stevenson planned to approach the transplant board and get approval to start Mark on his chemo treatments the following Monday. Tom had not yet been informed that it would have to wait until the following week, when Mark got back from California.

Mark hated the thought Sunny would have pain from the removal of her bone marrow. He arranged to keep her in his room with him on the day of the transplant.

This would be their first journey together as father and daughter.

Chapter Thirty-Four

Hidden Secrets

ॐॐ

Sunday afternoon, Mark was weaker. April noticed he took no interest in anything but sleeping. He had progressed so fast over the last few days; now she was afraid he had relapsed. He developed a fever and chills. April covered him in blankets and held him close to her.

Dr. Stevenson increased the doses of the three preventive antibiotics Mark was currently taking to ward off an infection. He ordered tests and increased Mark's IV fluid intake, fearing Mark had an infection.

Mark declined his pain meds, insisting he was not in pain. Tom did not buy it. Mark's strained face told a completely different story. He added pain meds to his order. This setback would delay the beginning stages of his transplant, Tom thought with growing frustration.

Mark knew what was happening to his body. He was aggravated and depressed this setback would mean he could not go home today. *That was, unless he did something about it.* He contemplated that thought and waited for his lab work to come back.

Just as Mark thought, his lab work showed his blood cell counts dropped slightly. The drop was not significant enough to be making him feel as tired as he was. That fact confirmed his private diagnosis.

A new annoying side effect had developed that Mark was determined to handle himself, for the time being. *Nothing can interfere with my plans this week,* he thought with determination. He thought long and hard about how he was going to handle his care on his own or with Jeff's help if he absolutely had no other choice.

Dr. Stevenson concluded that the drugs Mark was taking were not working. They were just making him sick from their side effects. This time, Dr. Stevenson chose to wait one more day before giving Mark another blood transfusion.

Was it too much to ask that his counts level off and stay there? Dr. Stevenson shook his head in frustration.

Mark's workout with the "Angels" was a little more encouraging. His muscles appeared to be more flexible as they stretched them. If only Mark had shown more interest in working out, they could have made more progress. Mark was being all too quiet.

Teresa pondered Mark's strained face. *He is up to something.* She turned her head sideways and tried to figure out just what it was he was hiding from them. When they came in for their second visit, Mark just wanted to sleep. Even their offer to take him to the physical therapy room was not tempting to him. They stood at his bedside and watched him restlessly drifting off and on, and then they began working on his ankles. His muscles were much more relaxed, and they were thankful for his progress.

Mark let out a moan and opened his eyes as Kathleen stretched his leg and bent his knee upward. She was surprised at his response of pain. Their eyes met, and she was just about to question him, when he closed his eyes again, and turned on his side. The two women faced each other with a suspicious look; something was not right. Mark was definitely hiding some sort of pain. The question was where?

After a few more moans, Mark told them he was not feeling up to a workout, and he just wanted to sleep. They felt sleep was the best thing for him and told him they would give him the rest of the night off. He was too subdued for their liking, and they went to speak to Dr. Stevenson about their concerns.

Mark's food trays remained untouched, but he kept up with his fluid intake by drinking bottles of water and by the IV fluids Dr. Stevenson ordered.

Later, he talked with his friends briefly on the phone as he lay in bed. His last call went to Sunny to tell her goodnight. Jeff stopped in for a visit. Mark sent April for another bottle of water. He asked Jeff to go into the bathroom with him.

Afterwards, Jeff left the room with a concerned look on his face, as April reentered the room with the bottle. Mark drank the entire bottle, turned over on his side, and fell back asleep.

Dr. Stevenson did not seem overly concerned since Mark had been over-exerting himself. Tom reminded everyone about Mark's highs and lows. "Tomorrow, Mark will be up and running again and we will all be sorry." He made light of the situation to give Mark's family some peace of mind, but he was not convinced that he should not be worried about Mark himself.

Everyone prayed that would be the case and waited to see what Mark would do on Monday. Later that night, Mark was restless, and he sent April for another bottle of water. While she was gone, Mark called Jeff and asked Jeff to do something for him. Jeff showed up and they went back into the bathroom and closed the door.

During the night, April had a horrible dream. Her wild movements and faint screams woke Mark up. He cradled her in his arms. "What's wrong, April?"

April looked in Mark's concerned eyes. It was clear she was frightened. "We were driving on an icy bridge and, and, we were in an accident." Her voice was shaking, afraid to tell him the outcome of the dream. She thought of her letter and tears formed in her eyes.

"Shhhh, it's ok, April. It was just a *dream*."

Dr. Stevenson came in early Monday morning to have a serious talk with Mark and April. He broke the news to them that they had not been able to harvest enough of Mark's stem cells the night before the game. Mark's blood counts dropped during the night. Mark took this news with a frown.

The new med were not working as well as Dr. Stevenson had hoped. Tom was afraid of making Mark sicker by using the other drugs used to treat aplastic anemia patients, which they had tried in the very beginning of his treatment. Even though the drugs were unsuccessful, they debated about trying the drugs once again at a smaller dose.

If they stopped all the drugs, Mark's life would be dependent on blood transfusions until they could do the transplant. Both men knew the more transfusions Mark received, the less his chances would be of a successful transplant.

Nevertheless, his counts were in the danger zone again, and there was no way to avoid another transfusion. Mark's own immune system was destroying his blood cells. There was no other explanation for why the transfusions were not lasting longer. Even as early as it was in the morning, Mark's father was donating right now in the donation room. The Brown's were on their way to the hospital. An anonymous donor had agreed to come donate if needed.

Dr. Stevenson told Mark and April that Sunny could also donate her stem cells instead of her bone marrow. They could start that procedure today. Tom would give her twice-daily injections of G-CSF under the skin, just as he had given Mark.

After five or more days of injections, she would come in and have a double lumen catheter placed in the vein in her neck. This would require her to be given a general anesthesia in the bone marrow operating room. Then they would do the collection, which would take about 4-5 hours. It might take several days of this before they could collect enough stem cells. Mark shook his head no, as he listened.

"No, that's too much for her. I am not going to put her through all that," his voice agonizingly clear.

"Just listen to me, Mark, and then you can decide."

Dr. Stevenson wanted to start Mark's chemo in a few days after his counts stabilized again, and then in ten days they could do the transplant. Mark listened to all the information given. A look of dissatisfaction was written all over his face. April took his hand in hers. She understood how upset he was feeling about Sunny, as she tenderly rubbed his fingers in compassion.

Mark looked Dr. Stevenson squarely in the face. "Sunny's not doing the stem cells. I am not going to allow her to go through it." Tears formed at the corners of his eyes. "That drug has horrible side effects and makes your muscles stiff and painful. I am just getting over the side effects from it. Seriously, I am about to cancel the whole bone marrow thing," Mark said in a painstakingly quiet voice as he looked away. He could not justify his daughter suffering any more pain because of him. That was more than he could allow, even though it meant he could die.

"I understand how you feel, Mark, but Sunny is the only link we have to saving your life. Without her, you do not stand a chance. You have rejected everything else we have tried. There is nothing more we could do for you than continue you on weekly blood transfusions," Dr. Stevenson told him with compassion. Mark already knew those facts.

"Mark, I don't want Sunny to have to go through pain either, but she loves you. When she is older, she will want her father. You have to let her do this for you," April reassured warmly, hoping to convince him, but his face remained torn and tired.

Mark looked away. He was thinking about the appalling time he had found Sunny in the park, all dirty, cold, and scared. He had caused her enough pain already. When Sunny shed a single tear, the guilt he felt was intense. It was his job to protect her, not cause her pain.

234

Mark stared out the window in the far distance, yet his eyes saw nothing, his mind too deep in thought. Without turning around, he spoke softly, "No. I'll continue the transfusions today and tomorrow, but I am out of here on Wednesday. That's it, no more," he said with a remorseful voice, his eyes weak, knowing he was risking his health. He had no other choice; he had to do this. Sunny was no longer a part of the equation to saving his life.

April and Dr. Stevenson exchanged despondent looks. April shook her head indicating for Tom to remain speechless. She touched his arm, led him to the door, and went with him into the hallway.

"Sunny is my daughter. Have Julia bring her here. Do whatever you have to do to get those stem cells," April insisted, her eyes determined this was the way it was going to have to happen if she was going to save Mark's life. "Call me when she gets here so I can hold her."

"What about the chemo?" Dr. Stevenson asked her, knowing Sunny's stem cells were useless without Mark doing chemo and radiation treatments.

"Not this week," April expressed sadly. "Mark needs a break from here. We are leaving this week to go to California to be with his team. The chemo will have to wait until we get back next Monday."

"What? Mark cannot risk leaving this hospital, certainly not now. He has an infection and his blood counts have dropped. The removal of his spleen has put him in danger of many types of bacterial infections. Mark needs more time to heal."

"Tom, we know all of that, but Mark needs to do this. He needs to finish this chapter in his life, even if he cannot play. What do you have to offer him here, nothing but side effects and pain? It is time to give Mark a break and let him do what he needs to do. After we get back, I will convince him to start the treatments. He will be in a much better frame of mind and easier to deal with."

"I don't like this. Are you sure Mark does not plan to play?" Dr. Stevenson asked her with uncertainty in his voice, knowing how determined Mark was about football.

"I plan to handcuff him to my wrist. Mark is not setting one foot on that field," she assured him in a stern voice. "The fact he is there has to be enough for him."

"That sounds like a plan, but are you forgetting who you are dealing with?" Dr. Stevenson questioned her, knowing Mark would not give up easily, if his mind was set in stone on playing.

"We have to let him feel in control to get around him. He has to be there with his team," she reasoned with him. "He earned this Super Bowl, Tom. He lived when most of us had already buried him. I am going to ask Uncle Dan and Jeff to go with us. They can keep a close eye on him."

"I understand, April, but that does not mean I agree." He took a deep defeated breath. "I'll have Christy bring in his first bag of platelets. Can you handle it?"

"I can do it," April assured him and gave him a hug. "Pray for Mark, Tom, he's suffering inside."

Just how much Mark was suffering was Mark's silent secret.

Dr. Stevenson walked back to his office. He felt deep compassion for Mark. As his medical condition continued, Mark would have many hard decisions to make. Tom just prayed Mark would make the right ones and not *risk his life* for the sake of others.

Mark had a lot to think about if he planned to have any future with his family.

Chapter Thirty-Five

A Calculating Mistake

April went back into the room. Mark stood staring out the window. Absorbed in deep thought, he twisted his *medical alert bracelet*. She sat down and respected his need to be alone.

He is just physically tired; once he gets some sleep, he will be fine, she told herself, feeling guilty about their night together.

Christy entered the room with the platelets, a saline bag and handed them to April. "Mark, I need to take your vitals." Mark reluctantly went over to his bed and sat down on the edge as Christy took his vitals.

Christy noticed Mark's subdued behavior as she cared for him. She knew the last thing he wanted was to be treated like a patient. When he was like this, it was better for all of them if April took care of him.

Christy and April checked the platelets with Mark's ID band and signed the paperwork. Mark walked back over to the window and stared out. Christy gave April a supportive look. She knew better than to ask Mark to come back over to the bed so they could hook his central line up to the platelets. She would leave that task to April.

"April, I will get Mark's meds ready and put them in his basket at the nurse's station. I'll give you a minute with him and when he is ready, I will give his meds to him." Christy looked at her watch and told April she was going off duty in a few minutes, and the other floor nurse, Eve, would be coming on duty in Beth's place.

"Eve's been working the other half of this Unit, but she is going to start taking care of patients on our side now. Mainly, she'll take care of Mark and two other patients."

April thanked Christy for her kindness and patience with Mark. "I'll be right out to get his meds, as soon as I get him back in bed. You don't have to wait on me. Just leave his meds in his basket, and I'll give them to him." Christy agreed, trusting April would give Mark his meds.

April felt uncomfortable being around Eve; she did not seem friendly. She wondered how Eve and Mark would get along. The two strong-headed personalities would surely butt heads. She said a quick prayer she was wrong in her intuitions about Eve.

April hung the bag of platelets and the saline bag on the pole. Mark continued to stare out the window. She went and touched his shoulder gently. He turned and was captured by her soft sincere eyes. She could melt his heart instantly.

She was a victim of his illness, and he wanted her to forget they were in this hospital, if only for a moment. He took her in his arms and kissed her, thankful she was so understanding of his moods. Her affection for him as they kissed took him into an imaginary world, making him forget everything around him but her.

Eve came in and saw them embracing. She frowned at them with disgust. Eve was not a very pleasant looking woman, somewhere in her early thirties. "Your breakfast is here," Eve obnoxiously said.

Mark and April did not hear a word she said as they continued to embrace each other in their passionate kisses.

"Fine, I will leave them on the table," Eve said smartly, as she dropped the two trays carelessly on the table and left the room. It was more than obvious she disliked Mark for some *unknown* reason.

April led Mark over to the bed and pushed him back while kissing him. Mark laughed; she was indisputably a better kisser than the nurse his teammates had provided. They were not in his castle, but with her, she was a princess no matter where they were. He was ready to remind her of his magical ability to romance her.

When she moved off him, he grabbed her arm and pulled her back on top of him. She finally convinced him to let her go before someone came in the room. She hooked up one of his central line lumens to the bottom of the "Y" shaped tubing connected to the platelets and hooked up the saline into one of the central line lumens. She ran the saline first to clear the line, and then she started the platelets.

Mark was rubbing his chest where she had laid. He felt a sharp pain in his lower back and jerked. He took a slow deep breath, trying to convince himself he could make it without having to go into the bathroom. She put his pillow under his head and kissed him.

"I will get you your pain medication," she told him as she kept far enough away he could not grab her again. She knew those eyes of his and knew what he really wanted for breakfast. He did not object to the pain med this time, knowing he needed the relief it would offer him.

April went to the window and discovered Christy had already gone. She called on the intercom and asked Eve to bring her Mark's antibiotic and pain medication from his basket.

Dan came in the room for a morning visit. Mark was happy to see Dan, but what Mark really wanted to do was throw the blanket over the camera again and spend some quality time with April. He winked at April and she returned a blushing smile.

Dan optimistically told them Mark's x-rays were very encouraging; his ribs had healed nicely. Once Mark's blood counts got higher, Dan felt certain Mark would be able to go home before his transplant. Mark and April shared a good-humored look, knowing they had to tell Dan about California.

Eve came in the room and gave April the IVPB antibiotic and Mark's pain medication. April took them over to Mark's bed. Just as she was about to check the label on the bag, Mark distracted her by grabbing her for a quick kiss. "Mark, behave yourself," she teased him as she hung the small plastic bag up and connected it. Mark continued his playfulness with her as she injected the pain med into another lumen. Eve stood there watching her do it.

Eve gave Mark the food tray with his name on it. He opened the lid and closed it again. "You need to eat this food!" Eve said as she frowned at Mark and opened the lid for him, and then she left the room mumbling.

Dan was not impressed with Eve's temperament with Mark; he exchanged a concerned look with April. "What's up with her?" April shrugged her shoulders and shook her head.

Mark closed the lid with a playful frown. He would wait for his mother to bring him some of Martha's home cooking. He was not eating those *runny eggs*! That reminded him; he needed to go visit Jerk on the third floor, where Jerk had been admitted for food poisoning. The guys had gone to Bryan's for pizza after the stunt they had pulled on Mark, but strangely none of the other guys had gotten sick.

Mark was upbeat, so Dan said nothing more about Eve. If anyone could handle a bad tempered person, it would be Mark.

April sat down next to Dan at the table, and they started to talk about their plans for California. Soon Mark's voice sounded hoarse, and he complained he had a lump in his throat as he started coughing. He rubbed his throat and coughed harder.

April thought that was odd. He looked strange to her; he was flushed. She got up to check on him. He had not eaten so he was not choking. She handed him his sports drink. He drank it with difficulty. He started wheezing and complained of his chest tightening.

Dan jumped up from the table; he had seen Mark do this many times before. He knew instantly Mark was having a severe reaction to the medications April had just given him. "Stop the antibiotic infusion!" Dan shouted and April quickly obeyed.

Dan quickly went into the hallway and ran to the Unit's crash cart. He grabbed the epinephrine from it and pushed the cart to the doors of Mark's room. He headed back into Mark's room. Mark was now having difficulty breathing. April had placed the oxygen mask over his face. Mark complained of abdominal cramps as he cradled his stomach.

Dan injected the first dose of epinephrine. Dan told April to stop the platelet infusion, run the saline wide open and get another liter bag of saline. She quickly followed his instructions and then rushed out of the room. She saw Eve, who was just sitting at her desk reading a book. "Eve, we need your help!" April frantically yelled over to her as she pushed the cart into the room to help Dan.

Eve stood up and watched through the glass door for a few minutes. She entered the room and stood there, pretending to be concerned.

Dan checked Mark's blood pressure; it was very low. His pulse was rapid. Dan attached the cardiac monitor leads to Mark's chest. The reading was not good, and the alarm sounded. Dan waited an agonizing ten minutes, and it did not improve. He injected the second dose of epinephrine and prayed it would work. He turned the oxygen level up as Mark continued to struggle breathing.

April had already hooked up the other saline bag and started its drip wide open. Her heart was pounding. *What happened? Why is this happening to Mark?*

Just before Dan was ready to call a code blue, Dr. McGuire arrived and began assisting Dan. Megan told Dan that Mark's heart monitor results were sent directly to her office monitors. Her nurse practitioner, Vivian, had alerted her. She told her that Mark's monitor had been reconnected and was beeping.

Ten minutes and no change. Dan frantically injected the third dose. April got the intubation kit off the cart and held it in her shaking hands. She prayed Dan would not need to use it to restore Mark's breathing. Mark responded to the third dose of epinephrine. He had a rash on his chest and arms. Dan ordered an injection of antihistamine and corticosteroids. Eve got the drugs from the cart and injected them into his central line.

Dan and Megan were very angry. *What had happened?* Mark had been given this same pain medication and antibiotics for the last seven days, why the allergic reaction today?

Dan reached up and looked at the antibiotic bag hanging on Mark's pole. To his horror, he discovered the bag was labeled for the boy in the next room. The drug was ***penicillin***. Shock crossed his face.

Mark is allergic to penicillin. He wears a bracelet on his wrist with the warning not to give penicillin. How did that antibiotic get mixed up with Mark's medications? Dan turned and questioned Eve.

Eve claimed she had gotten the medicines from the container labeled Mark Sanders that Christy had prepared before she left the floor. "Christy said to give them to April."

"Eve, did you double check to see if the medications were right before you gave them to April?"

"Well, they were in his basket. I thought Christy had them right," Eve answered smartly.

"That's no excuse for not double checking them! You should have double checked them before giving them to April. Eve, your mistake could have cost Mark his life!"

"Well, April was the one who gave them to Mark, not me. This is her fault; she did not double check them."

That was not the attitude Dan expected; he was fuming. He stared Eve in the face but was too angry to say anything as he picked up the phone. Dan called Christy to find out what she had done. She swore the correct antibiotic was in Mark's basket. She knew Mark was allergic to penicillin. His basket had a warning label on it. She had been Mark's nurse for over a week and nothing like this had happened.

Did Eve take it out of the wrong basket? Dan would never know exactly what happened. He was fuming.

April was beside herself. She knew this mistake was as much her fault as it was Eve's since she had not double checked the label either. Dan had every right to blame her, too.

Mark was still sick to his stomach so Dan prescribed something to calm his stomach. Dan told April to keep him on all the treatments until he came back. He went to call Dr. Stevenson, who was in a meeting downstairs.

Dr. McGuire told April to leave Mark on his heart monitor, and she would check back with him in a half-hour. She called and asked for CICU nurse, Sherry, to come monitor Mark's care, since April was so upset and Eve was on the defensive.

April lay next to Mark and held him in her arms, as Sherry entered the room. *Another brush with death, when will this ever end for Mark? How much more will he have to suffer?*

Eve came in the room later and told April that Dr. Stevenson wanted her in the donor room and then she abruptly left the room. Dan came back in the room and said he would sit with Mark. Sherry was attentively taking care of Mark's medical needs.

Mark was asleep, so April slipped out of the room. When April passed by Eve, she was sitting at the desk reading a book. April gave her a disapproving look.

Charlie called the room to check on Mark. Charlie told Dan he had another one of his uneasy feelings about Mark. Once again, Charlie had been right; Mark had been in danger.

Dan's reassuring voice, however, did not erase the feeling Charlie had that Mark was still in serious danger.

Chapter Thirty-Six

The Love of a Child

❦❦

April went into the donor room. Julia had Sunny sitting in her lap. Julia noticed the distressed expression on April's face and wondered what had happened. April volunteered no explanation for her trembling hands. How could she tell Julia she had almost killed her son?

April sat down beside Sunny, put her in her lap, and cuddled her. April explained to Sunny that Mark needed her blood if he was going to get better. Sunny was very brave and wanted to help Mark. "I will do it. I will save Mark."

Dr. Stevenson came in and made friends with Sunny again. He explained to her what they needed to do. He was very gentle and patient with her. When he injected her, she did not cry. They all fussed about how brave she had been for her daddy.

Dr. Stevenson explained to April and Julia that he would need Sunny to come twice a day for the injections. He gave Julia a medication to give to Sunny for any pain she might experience with her muscles. They would have to watch her for reactions, as they all knew who her father was. "Let's pray she is nothing like her father," Tom told the two women.

Julia said they would come in the morning and stay at the penthouse until Sunny had her second dose, then they would go back to the ranch if she had no reactions. The plan was put into action.

Sunny wanted desperately to see Mark. At first, April told her no, but then she decided Mark needed to know how brave his daughter had been for him. April was not sure how Mark would react to her deceiving him. In his weakened condition, she hoped he would not have much to say.

April put a little facemask and gown on Sunny and took her into the room. Dan told her Mark was doing fine; he had slept the entire time she was out of the room. He gave Sunny a warm hug and tickled her. Then he went to speak to Julia.

Sherry finished checking Mark's vital signs and left the room so April could be alone with her husband.

April sat Sunny on the bed near Mark's head. Sunny gently touched his face with her hand and claimed his earlobe between her fingers. Mark stirred and opened his sleepy eyes. He was surprised to see Sunny and hugged her to his chest. He did not care that her elbow caused him pain. Mark looked at April with a question on his face, as he pulled Sunny's mask down to her chin so he could see her brilliant smile.

"Mark, I am going to save you," Sunny informed Mark with a prideful smile.

Mark took the oxygen mask off his face. "Really, are you going to give me *a wish*?" He teased her, remembering the time Sunny had given him his wish of having a little girl back when they were at his apartment.

"No, silly. I am going to give you my blood," Sunny said proudly and giggled, as Mark's eyes widened.

"Oh, really? How is that?" Mark inquired as he looked directly at April with a disapproving face, knowing exactly what he was about to hear. His throat was still sore; he pointed at his hospital water jug sitting over on the table.

"Dr. Steve said I will make you all better, if you take my blood," she told him with a big smile and rubbed his cheeks with her tiny hands.

"Oh, he did, did he?" Mark gave April another disapproving look as she handed him a drink of water. He took a slow sip making sure he could swallow without choking. He drank half the jug while he listened to Sunny.

"Yup! It didn't hurt at all."

"I bet you were very brave," Mark smiled at her as he pushed her long hair out of her face and planted a wet kiss on her forehead.

"Yup! Just like you." She laid her head down on his chest and hugged him. This time he put her to his heart. Mark returned the hug, wishing that Sunny did not hold him up so high on a pedestal. He loved this little bundle in his arms. He kissed the top of her head. A tear escaped from the corner of his eye as he thought of all the years he had missed.

"Sunny, you don't have to give me your blood. I will be fine," Mark tenderly told her.

She pointed her finger in his face as she spoke firmly. "Dr. Steve said, you gotta get my blood if you are gonna get better, Mark. I think you better listen to him. He looks real smart." She giggled at him as she made her point.

Mark laughed. *She is every bit as domineering as her mother. Oh, great. I do not stand a chance against these two overpowering women in my life. So it is a good thing I love them with all my heart.*

Sunny wrapped her arms back around him to assure him of her love for him. Her unselfishness would save his life. Sunny's excitement to save him convinced Mark he needed to do the stem cell transplant procedure. She was brave beyond her years, and he was proud of her. It was decided Sunny would donate her stem cells. She gave a loud joyful cheer when Mark told her he would let her give him her special blood.

Eve came into the room in a huff. "Take that child out of this room at once! You know the rules, Mark Sanders!"

"But I don't want to go," Sunny whimpered.

"April, I am not going to ask twice. You know the rules about kids being around Mark."

After April took Sunny into the hallway, Eve and Mark exchanged debating words. April could see through the glass door that Mark was not happy with Eve's temperament, but he was trying his best to patiently reason with her. Eve stormed out of the room and plopped in her chair at the desk. "Mark Sanders, you just wait!"

April did not have Mark's meekness; she wanted to give Eve a piece of her mind. Eve's lack of professionalism was inexcusable! April was surprised Eve had not been dismissed from her duties as a nurse, if this was how she had treated her other patients.

April did not trust Eve with Mark's care. *Did Eve poison Mark on purpose by giving me the wrong meds, um ...o... ok, that is enough of my mind running wild,* April thought as she glanced at Mark and chills ran down her spine, thinking Eve had almost killed her husband.

April hugged Julia tightly, told Sunny goodbye, and went back into Mark's room to face Mark's disconcertment of Eve. The first thing April did was put him back on oxygen to calm down his breathing.

Julia took Sunny back to the penthouse with her and watched her closely for any type of reactions. Thankfully, the injection sight was not even swollen. Julia called Mark to tell him the good news. Just like her father, Sunny wanted to go back to the ranch and go to the stable to be with Charlie who was fast becoming Sunny's favorite person at the ranch.

Mark received his blood transfusion, and a few hours later, he was feeling much better physically. Eve did her best to challenge Mark mentally. The test of their strong wills was about to come to a head-on collision.

Mark instantly had a dislike for Eve's determination to have unwarranted authority over him. She insisted on doing things her way and made April feel uncomfortable. Eve had no compassion for his need to be with his daughter or his wife.

Even after he protested and told Eve that Martha's soup was the only thing he was going to eat, she took away the soup and threw it in the toilet. She had the nerve to order him jello, even after he told her he would not touch it with a ten-foot pole.

"April, you need to stop buying him drinks out of the vending machine and make him drink his water out of his hospital water jug. It's a waste of good money."

"Why should you care? It's not your money. If Mark wants bottled water, then that is what I am going to give him." Eve crossed her eyes at April and left the room.

"She makes me so mad, I just want to …"

Mark laughed, "Now, sweetheart, you need to calm down before I have to sedate you."

"That's not funny, Mark," she puffed.

When it was lunchtime, Eve placed his tray in front of him and stood with her arms crossed, demanding that he eat. "You have to eat, Mark. Stop wasting my time and eat."

"I told you before, I am not hungry." He pushed it away; she pushed it back at him. April was afraid the whole tray was going to end up on the floor, or worse, Eve would end up wearing it.

They were both rescued when Dr. McGuire came in the room wanting to know why Mark's heart rate was up on her office monitor. That settled that; Megan had the tray removed.

"Mark, I know your stomach is upset from this morning, but tomorrow, you need to start eating," Megan told him as she listened to his heart before she left.

Eve gave Mark a condescending look thinking she had won that battle. *Tomorrow I will make sure he gets a double dose of the hospital food*, she thought cunningly.

Mark liked the nurse his teammates provided much better. Eve made his skin crawl. He was glad Eve stayed out of his room for most of her shift, after he politely informed her he was absolutely not wearing the hospital gown she wanted to help him change into. *Nor was she ever going to undress him or touch any part of his body without his permission first.*

Who's going to sedate who, now, Mark? April held her breath as Eve's eyes glared at Mark. He took a deep breath and said a silent prayer, as he calmed down under April's watchful eyes.

You just wait, Mark Sanders! Someday, I will have control over you, and there won't be anything you can do about it, Eve thought with blood-thirsty eyes and pushed together lips as her mind formed a plan.

"Nothing personal against you, Eve. It's just that I am a public figure and I have to protect myself. Not that you would unprofessionally say anything to the media about me. But I would rather not put you into that compromising position with the media paying big bucks to know what's going on with me right now."

"Why should anyone care about you, Mark? Now give me your wrist."

Uh, did you not just hear what I said? Don't touch me. He did not even want Eve taking his pulse, but he held his tongue as she snatched his wrist and held it. *She's doing this on purpose to make me mad. God, I am going to kill her, if she doesn't let go of my wrist!*

When he saw the red light flashing again on his heart monitor and the phone rang, he knew he had gone too far with being fed up with Eve's power struggle over him. Dr. McGuire was not too thrilled Mark continued to set off his alarm over a conversation with a nurse.

After an upsetting phone call from April, Dr. McGuire came to the Unit and asked Eve to step into Dr. Stevenson's office. There Megan spoke to Eve and told her that she needed to respect Dr. Mark Sanders, as a doctor and as a professional athlete.

"We are bending the rules slightly to assist Mark through this difficult time in his life. It is your job to help him feel more comfortable with his long-term surroundings. Mark is a very sick young man. Whatever we can do to keep him calm needs to be done. I suggest that you begin by listening to his minor requests. After all, Mark is not being unreasonable in his requests," she stressed to the unreceptive Eve.

"It's not fair to the other patients."

"Each individual family has their own special needs in this Unit that we strive to accommodate if at all possible. We have rules that must be upheld, but there are rules we can bend from time to time as long as it does not harm the patient."

Eve didn't seem to be absorbing her instructions, Megan felt, as she continued her speech in a firmer voice.

"Mark has his doctor's permission to wear whatever makes him feel comfortable as long as the clothing comes straight from the cleaners

wrapped in plastic. Right now, whatever he will eat within his food allow-
ance is acceptable and welcomed. Mark has lost at least 30 pounds in the
last month. April is his wife and she is a nurse. She is capable of handling
anything delicate that he needs done. Your job is to supervise his care, not
necessarily do it for him. It would be in your best interest to comply with
these orders, as I do not plan to interrupt my busy day coming back to
this Unit again to settle an argument between you and Mark. Have I made
myself clear?"

Eve was steaming when Dr. McGuire left the Unit. *Mark has all his
doctors wrapped around his little finger and it will be a cold day before I
join them*, she thought angrily as she stormed back to her desk to plot her
revenge. She made a quick phone call to her *boyfriend*, careful not to let
anyone hear what she had to tell him.

Mark told April they needed to pray for Eve's attitude toward life in
general. "Anyone that unpleasant must have a deep-seeded reason."

Then he considered his own attitude and started praying he could
somehow reach out to Eve and befriend her. He started with telling her he
was sorry he was being disagreeable. She tossed her head and left the room
icy cold and did not return.

Jeff came in the room, and when April went into the bathroom, Jeff
quickly took a syringe from his jacket pocket and injected it into Mark's
central line. He turned and gave Mark a frown and left the room hoping
Dan or Tom would not find out he had written Mark another prescription.
Mark took a minute to reflect on his choice of treatment. His stomach
turned, but what else could he do but take charge of his own care? Nothing
Tom did for him was working.

Teresa and Kathleen heard what happened that morning and came to
offer Mark and April their support. Mark was back on the monitors so they
worked with him while he lay in bed. He tired quickly and they let him fall
asleep on them as they continued their workout.

Mark had lingering effects of the poisoning from the penicillin and had
to pray extra hard about not taking back his promise to befriend Eve. The
pain in his stomach was intense, but he never said anything. He thought
about calling Jeff again but chose to tough it out until Jeff came back in
four hours.

April continued to bring him bottled water, and Dr. Stevenson increased
his IV fluids when April told Tom she was concerned Mark had not been
out of bed since early that morning.

Christy came on duty and talked to Mark and April about what had happened to him. Christy said she had been very careful not to mix up the medications knowing that Mark was allergic to the penicillin.

They all knew it had been Eve's mistake *or was it a mistake*, Mark wondered. Something in his gut told him that Eve was evil, and he needed to not only pray for her but he also needed to watch her carefully.

Beth called to talk to April that night and let her know that she was upset with what had happened to Mark. Mark's temperament did not improve once he learned Beth had taken time off to care for her cousin who had terminal cancer, and Eve would be her replacement.

Tom came in with Dan and told Mark he needed to keep at least three doses of epinephrine on him at all times. "You never know what hospital you will end up in or what someone might mistakenly give you."

April took the epinephrine auto-injector EpiPens from Tom and put one in her purse and two into *Mark's leather jacket.* Dan made sure they understood how to use them.

"Hopefully, you will never need to use them," he expressed to the couple. *Hopefully he was right.*

Chapter Thirty-Seven

Gone Astray

৪৾

Tuesday morning, Robert got a call from Judge Thompson. Robert was ordered to stop the treatments being given to Sunny. The Judge reinforced the fact that Sunny did not belong to Mark and April; she belonged to the State. They had no legal rights over Sunny.

Judge Thompson made it clear it was only speculation that Sunny was the biological daughter of Mark and April. There were no birth records. He summoned an informal hearing to determine the legitimacy of Mark and April's claim.

Robert called Dr. Stevenson and told him that no more medical procedures could legally be done on Sunny without a court order signed by the judge. This was not good news. Tom was beside himself; Mark was scheduled to begin chemo the following Wednesday. He did not want to deliberate over what would happen if the court refused to let Sunny donate her bone marrow or stem cells to Mark. He made an urgent call to the National Bone Marrow Donor Registry, placing Mark's name back on the list.

When Sunny did not show up, April went to find out why. She called the ranch from the nurse's station as Eve sat there reading her usual book. Eve only had three patients, including Mark, but still, she should have plenty to do other than sitting there reading a book. April frowned at her as she waited for Robert to answer the phone. Eve listened carefully to April's conversation with Robert.

Robert reluctantly told April what was going on with the court order. April became fearful she and Mark might not get Sunny back, but Robert assured her that would never happen. Her hands were trembling as she placed the phone back on the receiver and looked over at Mark's room.

How was she going to tell Mark this devastating news? She took a deep breath and headed in his direction.

The minute Mark saw her downcast face he knew something was wrong. He removed the leads to his heart monitor and turned off the machine. He sat on the edge of the bed waiting to find out what it was that had April so upset.

He fearfully thought something awful had happened to Sunny. "Is something wrong with Sunny? Did something happen to her? April, tell me!" April had no other choice but to tell Mark the awful news, as much as she feared what it would do to him emotionally.

"Sunny is not coming. The judge called your dad. He said . . . oh, Mark, he said that Sunny is not ours. She can't donate her bone marrow to you."

"What are you talking about?"

"We have to go to court and prove she belongs to us."

She told Mark everything Robert had told her. Mark became extremely angry. How could the state keep him from his own daughter and who had told the judge they were harvesting Sunny's stem cells? He was up pacing the floor, pulling his IV lines to their limit. April threatened to sedate Mark, in order to make him calm down.

"This is insane! How can they deny us of our own child?" Mark grabbed Stanley and went in the bathroom, sat on the floor, and took his frustrations straight to the Lord.

April nervously waited for him to come out. Finally, she opened the door and saw him sitting on the floor, with his head between his knees, his hands wrapped around his knees and folded together in prayer. She joined him on the floor and wrapped him in her arms.

"It's going to be ok, honey, we will get her back."

Mark's heart was heavy. He told April it was inconceivable he had not had the chance to hold Sunny as a baby. "I never got to hold her in my arms the day she was born." His tears fell as he felt as if his heart was going to break in half. "Now, they want to take her away from me, again. April, I don't think I could live … if I ever lost her," he spoke with a heavy heart.

April quickly broke down and sobbed. Mark regretted telling April how he felt. "April, oh God, I am so sorry, please don't cry." He kissed her tears from her face. "I am so sorry, sweetheart. I didn't mean to make you cry."

He never wanted to cause April any more heartache than she had already been through. She had been the one to suffer all these years, not him. He held her against him and reminded her of his unending love for her.

"I love you, April, so much. We will get through this together. I promise you that. No one is going to take our daughter away from us, no one. We are a family."

Then the words Mark least expected came spilling out from her. April confided in Mark that Sunny had not replaced Jessica in her heart. Jessica was just a baby when she was taken from her arms, and in April's heart, she still felt an emptiness for her baby Jessica. Her baby was still missing. Through her tears, she told Mark, "Jessica is still out there missing. We will never get her back."

"Oh, April, sweetheart, that's not true."

"Yes, it is. We lost everything our baby did, her first steps, her first words." With tears streaming down her face, she let it all out. "Oh Mark, who did she call Mommy ... and Daddy?" she cried, tearing Mark's heart in a million pieces knowing he could not bring back the last five years they had lost of Sunny's life. "Our baby is gone and she is not coming back."

April loved Sunny with all her heart, but Sunny was Sunny, not Jessica. Mark had never known Jessica. His heart completely belonged to Sunny. He wanted what he had missed with Sunny as a baby. His heart had fallen in love with Sunny without knowing she was his child. Sunny was Sunny. April was right; Jessica was gone forever. They could not bring her back.

Mark understood April's need for the baby she was forced to let go of so long ago. He had suspected April had not been dealing with her feelings towards Sunny.

April was afraid to love Sunny completely for fear of losing her again. Mark was fearful himself of losing Sunny. The kidnappers were still out there. *Would they make a second attempt at kidnapping their daughter?*

Worse than that, April had to bury baby Jessica in her mind, before Sunny could take her place. How could she?

He had heard of cases like this. When a child is kidnapped and returned years later, there was a big adjustment for the parents and the child to make. Including letting go of the past they missed and being set free of their painful emotions in order to start a new beginning. It was not as simple as everyone perceived it to be, to reunite as a family. It took time to heal.

He also knew Sunny favored him over April, but he was not about to share that distressing information with April. *Maybe Sunny blames April somehow for giving her up.* With all that had gone on, the subject had never been discussed. *How is Sunny feeling towards April,* Mark pondered with a heavy heart. *Does Sunny really love her mother?*

He suggested they talk to Pastor Evan; he could help them work through their feelings. Mark held April's hand and they prayed together for the healing of their hearts.

Then Mark reassured April of his love for her as he gathered her in his lap and kissed her. He loved her so much his heart hurt. He silently thanked God for April and continued his promise to love her with his entire soul. *God, let April's heart find our daughter in Sunny.*

April went to get them both a change of clean clothes. Then they showered together, renewing the love they had for each other as the water gently sprayed over them. Mark added another prayer request, for a baby, as he took pleasure in loving his wife's amazing body.

Mark received another transfusion after another disappointing CBC report. The drugs continued to make him sick, in more ways than he let anyone know. He insisted this time he no longer needed April to follow him into the bathroom. His feet were steady, he assured her. April granted him his need for independence.

Later, while she was in the bathroom, he made a quick call down to the ER to Jeff. When she came out, she could have sworn Mark had a guilty look about his face. But that look was short lived as he gathered April in his arms and kissed her, sending her mind back to their satisfying moment in the shower.

Even though his counts were not up, he was feeling stronger. With the reluctant help of Jeff, the pain in his stomach was just a dull sensation now. His leg and arm muscles felt better as he increased his physical activity.

He really wanted to spend the rest of the week at the ranch before they left on Friday. He did not care what the state had to say about Sunny. He was spending time with her whether they allowed it or not. He justified his reckless plan to make things happen and blocked out any common sense he had as a doctor.

Dr. Stevenson reminded Mark he was not getting enough nutrients through his IV and told Mark he had to start eating the hospital food before he could go home.

"Eat it and keep it down and you can go home." Mark frowned at him, but Tom crossed his arms and stood firm in his decision.

Nevertheless, when the breakfast tray arrived, Mark took one look at the soggy eggs and closed the lid. April stood over him like a mother hen. "Mark, you heard what Dr. Stevenson said; you have to eat."

"There is no way that food is going in my mouth!" he firmly told her as he pushed the tray to the edge of the table. He grabbed his bottle of water and drank it. It was the fourth bottle he had downed that morning.

Mark would only eat the pre-packaged foods on his tray, such as the crackers. He really thought someone was trying to poison him with the hospital food, but no one would take him seriously. Eve was on the top of his list, and he was thankful she was staying clear of him for the time being.

Mark called his mother and asked her to bring him something from the ranch. When she arrived, he ate enough to satisfy Dr. Stevenson. He cut his visit short with his mother and asked April to go down to the gift shop and buy him the latest newspaper on the Super Bowl. He cleared the room of people just in time, as his feet barely hit the floor before he was in the bathroom with Stanley, his IV pole.

Later Mark's blood test came back, and his counts had gone back up from the transfusions. Dr. Stevenson thought that explained why Mark was feeling so much stronger as the morning progressed. He watched Mark juggling the pre-packaged pudding and jello cups Julia gave him and shook his head before leaving the room.

"Mark, stop playing with the jello and eat it." April sat down on the recliner to begin reading her book.

"You are no fun," he teased as he juggled the cups.

When Jeff came in, he discreetly handed Mark something, and Mark went in to the bathroom. April briefly eyed Jeff, who stood next to the bathroom door, as if he was standing guard. His mannerisms seemed odd to her. Jeff seemed uneasy as he tossed her a broad smile before she went back to her reading.

When Mark came out, he whispered something to Jeff, and Jeff frowned at him. Mark gave him a playful punch in his chest and laughed. "Lighten up, Jeff, old buddy. Let's have some fun."

Mark tossed Jeff a pudding cup. They began tossing them around, using them as basketballs, ringing the trashcan, until one busted open, and splattered all over the wall. They both laughed as April frowned at them. *There's that teacher look again,* Mark thought as he looked at April's disapproving face and laughed.

April knew she did not dare ask Eve to clean up the mess, so she called housekeeping and Carolyn arrived soon afterwards.

"Mark Sanders, did you make this mess just to get a hug from me?" she teased him as he encased her in his arms. Mark knew underneath her mask was one of her brilliant smiles for him.

"You know I have missed you. Tell me what's going on at church. How is your sister, Bette?" he inquired and she informed him of all the latest details.

Mark asked, "Carolyn, what has happened to Marty? I haven't seen him around lately."

Carolyn looked at Mark with a puzzled expression. "Marty is not assigned to this floor. This is my floor. Christy informed housekeeping that the nurses would take care of this room," she told him as she cleaned up the mess.

Mark thought that was odd, but his thoughts were sidetracked when Jeff tossed him another pudding cup. Carolyn looked at Jeff sternly. "Next time, Jeffery, you can clean it up, yourself." She looked at April. "How do you put up with these two monkeys?" They all laughed.

Kathleen and Teresa were impressed with Mark's steadiness and the return of his strength in his legs. His stiffness was not as bad. The drug causing his stiffness must finally be out of his system. Even though it did seem a little bit too early for that to have happened, they thought. *Could Mark have gotten another miracle?*

He did several laps around the Unit to prove to them that he was ready to go home and work out on his own. Both pampered him and took up his prayer that soon he could return home. They gave Tom a good report on Mark's progress.

He wanted to go to the gym but Steven would not give him the clearance to lift more than five pounds. Another check of his incisions was proof enough that Mark needed to take it easy. His low blood counts were not allowing the incisions to heal as quickly as they should have.

Sherry came to listen to his heart and lungs. Mark teased her as she placed her warm hands on his chest. "Keep it up, Mark, and next time I am going to stick my hands in ice before I come in here." They both laughed.

As the morning continued, Mark's health and mood improved. Even Eve did not ruffle his feathers with her demands on him to eat something. He tried his best to win her over. He invited her to his church, but that invitation sent her out of his room for the remainder of the day, leaving April to do her job.

What is it about that woman that made her dislike me so much? Mark wondered.

Chapter Thirty-Eight

This is Who I Am

❦❦

Jeff offered to go with Mark and April to California. Jeff wanted to take Ashley with him. Mark arranged for his family and friends to take the company jet.

Since Robert donated the jet to be used to transport patients from out of state, it had the oxygen and medical equipment on it Mark might need while flying.

With Steven, Dan, Jeff, Rebecca, Faye, Ashley, and April, he would also have a full medical staff watching over him. Any freedom Mark thought he would have on this trip would be nonexistent with the watchful eyes of all of them. He was outnumbered and that was not a thought he welcomed.

Mark was busy making unique plans for the trip. He had some other surprises up his sleeves for special friends. He grinned when he got off the phone with his travel agent, Pat.

Dr. Stevenson reminded Mark that he could not go swimming in the ocean. He wanted Mark to continue with the preventive antibiotics and the new drugs while he was gone. Mark kept a straight face during Tom's lecture. He wasn't about to lose his chance to gain freedom.

Tom told Mark he needed to stay away from as many people as he could. "You need to wear a facemask at all times if you are going to be in a crowd of people."

"Sure, whatever you say."

Tom sternly reminded Mark of what Dr. Martin had told him, "You cannot pick up anything that weighs over five pounds and you cannot drive."

Mark was agreeable to Tom's instructions yet Tom held an untrusting look on his face as he eyed Mark. He cautiously knew Mark's creative mind not to be submissive to the rules.

Julia brought Mark some homemade soup and biscuits for lunch, and he devoured them in front of April. "April, I want some new magazines. Can you get me some?"

But it wasn't long before Mark's stomach regretted every bite. He quickly went back into the bathroom for over fifteen minutes. When he came out, he crawled back in bed, laid in the fetal position and held his stomach.

His door opened and April reentered the room with a handful of sports magazines and a sandwich for herself. She set them down on the table and sat down.

"Sorry I took so long. I bumped into Rev. Smith. He sends you his prayers." She said a prayer, took a bite of her sandwich and opened one of her magazines.

"He's a good man." Mark was glad she was facing away from him. He quickly regained his fake smile, determined that no one would find out how he was really feeling. He returned to his good-natured self.

"I really appreciate all Rick has done for us."

"I'll give Rick a call and thank him."

"I'm sure he would enjoy hearing from you."

He looked at the bathroom door and said a quick prayer that his stomach would calm down.

Eve entered the room and gave him one of her evil looks.

The fact that Mark had eaten again pleased everyone, except Eve, who made a revolting face at Mark as she picked up his untouched hospital tray. Her look was enough to make his stomach stir again. However, he was determined to keep his humor with her.

"How's your day going, Eve?" he asked.

"Like you would care. You think you are so special you don't have to eat what the rest of our patients do," she mumbled as she left the room in a huff.

Mark ignored her statement and grinned at April with dancing eyes. *Freedom was looking pretty good, no more Eve.*

"What was that all about?" Teresa asked as she walked in the room. "Is that woman mad at my favorite patient?"

"Shhhh, don't say I am your favorite patient too loud. I am trying my best to get kicked out of here," Mark teased. "Hey, where did the bad cop go?"

"If you are referring to Kathleen, she went home to stay with Matthew. Seems his classmates teased him yesterday about you, and he refused to go to school this morning. His classmates did not believe him when he said his mom was the one making you better. They called him a liar."

Mark's eyes got wide. "Where are my jeans, April? We're going on a class field trip today to Matthew's school!" Mark declared as he looked around for something other than sweatpants to wear.

April and Teresa exchanged looks and joined forces.

"Oh, no, you don't, Mark. You're not going anywhere just yet," Teresa stressed as she held onto his arm.

"But my favorite fan needs me. I am going to show those good for nothing classmates of Matthew's ...."

"Not today, Mark. How would it look if you walked in Matthew's classroom and fell flat on your face?" she interrupted him. "We have lots of work to do today to get you back in shape before you can take on the school bullies."

"Well, then, call Kathleen and tell her to bring Matthew here and tell her to bring her camera. I'll call some of my teammates, and we'll just show Matthew's classmates who rules."

Teresa admired Mark's desire to help Matthew out, but first she had to make sure that Mark could hold his own before she let him go.

He made a quick trip to the bathroom while Teresa was talking to April. *I have to do something about this stomach. I can't keep throwing up everything I eat.*

Teresa took Mark to the physical therapy room, and they worked out for over an hour. Mark proved he was ready to work out on his own and go home.

Mark got permission from Dr. Stevenson to go outside in the garden when Matthew arrived. "Wear your mask until you get down to the garden, and you can go."

Mark gave Tom a thankful hearty hug and got on the phone with his friends. Then he took a nap with his favorite cheerleader.

When Kathleen and Matthew arrived, Mark spent some time getting to know Matthew. He was a great kid and they were soon pals.

Then Mark gave his first public appearance since his accident as he took Matthew out to the garden area and tossed the football with him. The throws were all underhanded and not more than five feet apart. He was able to do it without causing any pain. Dr. Stevenson kept a close eye on Mark as he sat on the patio with Kathleen, April, and Teresa.

Carlo, Justin, Kevin, Jerk, and Craig joined them for pictures, as the press bombarded Mark with questions.

"Mark, are you going to the Super Bowl? Mark, are you planning to play? Mark ..."

He waved at them to be silent as he pointed to Matthew and said, "This is my friend, Matthew, and he is my number one fan. So all you kids at Ford Middle School, eat your hearts out." They snapped more pictures and continued with questions but Mark ignored them.

Dr. Stevenson escorted Mark back to the Unit when he felt Mark had had enough excitement and put him back to bed. Tom ordered an infusion of IV nutrients for Mark. Five minutes later, he was asleep and for the next two hours, he did not move.

Good news came when he woke up. Mark's counts were up, and they looked like they were holding steady. Even his ANC had reached 450. Tom wanted to increase Mark's dosage from one fourth to a half and see if they could get his count over 900. Mark was apprehensive about the increase, but if it meant he could go home, he agreed to try it.

Later that afternoon, Mark and April were watching TV when their show was interrupted with a special news report. There had been a devastating pile up accident on the freeway. The news crew showed live action chaotic scenes from the accident.

Mark leaned forward as he intensely listened to the report. Their hospital was calling in all their off duty nurses and doctors to help with the injured.

Mark wanted to go down to the ER and help, but April reminded him that he was no longer on the rotation schedule in the ER.

"I'm not on the schedule, but I'm still on the payroll. I'm on vacation, remember? These people are injured. They are not sick; they don't pose any danger to me," he argued. "Trauma is what I do best."

She kissed his forehead and told him to stay right where he was while she went to see if she could help.

Mark waited until he saw April get into the elevator. He grabbed his jeans and quickly changed. He darted past Eve, who had her nose buried in her book, to the stairs and went down to the ER.

His heart was racing thinking about the injured people that needed his help. Each step down he prayed for the injured, the medical staff, and the families.

He quickly went into the doctor's locker room and went to his locker. His scrubs and lab coats were still hanging inside his locker. He hurriedly put on a scrub shirt and his white lab coat.

Mark reached up, got his name badge off the top shelf, and held it in his hands as reality hit him. "Dr. Mark Sanders" it read. *This is who I am. I am not a patient; I am a doctor*, he thought humbly. Mark put the badge proudly in place and headed out the door. With all the wild confusion going on, he just might get away with helping.

There were many new faces as the new rotation of ER interns and medical students had arrived. No one questioned Mark as he took on his first patient. It was a seven-year-old boy with a broken arm and a large cut on his forehead. An attending Mark had not met came in the room. Mark reviewed with him what he needed to do and got his paperwork signed.

When Mark finished treating the boy, the attending asked Mark to assist him with a woman with chest trauma. Her name was Monica Morton. She needed several units of type A+ blood. Mark and the attending worked on her for an hour before they sent her to the OR. After they finished, the attending introduced himself to Mark as Dr. Aaron Brower.

They shook hands. "Dr. Sanders," Mark informed him.

"What year resident are you, Dr. Sanders?"

"Call me Mark. Second year; this is my first day on duty. ER rotation so far," Mark said as he drank from a bottle of water and seriously thought he was physically able to go back on duty full time. *Forget the transplant. I am going back to work where I belong.*

"Mark, that was a great save. I thought you were at least a third year by your excellent skills."

"You're new here?" Mark half-asked with a smile.

"Second day, transferred from Atlanta, Georgia. I am taking over the Chief of Surgery position soon. What about you? What are your future plans as a doctor, Mark?"

Mark slyly smiled. "I want a position in trauma surgery. And then I want your job."

Aaron laughed at Mark's honesty. "I'd be glad to recommend you for the surgical trauma rotation. I would like a chance to work with you," Aaron announced sincerely. "But I plan to keep my job, Mark."

Mark smiled wide and laughed. "Thanks, Aaron, I will consider that offer. Let's go see what is on the board."

Obviously this guy never watches football or reads the paper, Mark thought with a sly underhanded grin. *I guess I am not as famous as I thought I was, at least not in Atlanta, Georgia*, he chuckled.

Mark continued to take patient after patient for the next two hours, working closely with Dr. Brower. He had to dodge Jeff, Dan, and Steven several times. He never did see April. The other nurses he worked with knew him, but they never thought anything about him being there. They took orders from him just as they had always done just a few weeks ago.

He thought he saw Sister Jessica standing at the nurse's station as he came out of a trauma room. He turned back around for a second look.

Jessica was being led away by Erin; it appeared she was crying. Mark knew Erin from his church; he had helped her get into nursing school. Erin led Jessica into Rev. Smith's office. *I wonder what that was all about?*

Mark noticed Becky and Bonnie from the small country doctor/hospital office where he and Jeff had gone after their accident in the mountains. *What are they doing here*, he wondered.

Then he saw William Triplett round the corner, falling straight into Becky's arms. Mark grinned, but his grin widened as Becky appeared to be introducing Bonnie to Dr. Stevenson. Matchmaking sparks went off in his head. *Hmmmm. I will just have to help Becky out with Tom and Bonnie.*

He would have loved to talk with Becky and Bonnie, but he stayed hidden out of Tom's sight. He felt a touch on his shoulder and nervously turned around. "Mark, we have another trauma," Aaron told him.

Finally, the patient load was down, and Mark felt exhausted so he went back into the locker room. Mark rounded the corner and ran face to face into Jeff. Mark grinned and Jeff smiled back. They gave each other a zestful high five.

"I should have guessed you would be down here. Now I know who the mystery signature was on the patient board. It was you, Dr. R-M-S," Jeff laughed as he shook his head back and forth.

"Guilty," Mark laughed. They gave each other another high five.

"Who did you get to sign off for you?"

"The new guy, Dr. Brower." Mark smiled, thinking he was pretty clever tricking the new guy into helping him.

Jeff laughed, "Wait 'till Dan hears about this; he will hit the ceiling. I would love to be a fly on the wall when he chews you out, Dr. R-M-S."

"It won't be the first time, and I am sure it won't be the last time I get chewed out," Mark grinned and Jeff laughed.

"Just make sure you tell Dan I had nothing to do with this. You've already got me in enough hot water as it is. And if Tom finds out that you and I are …"

"Hey, I'm still on staff here. They called in all off duty doctors, which definitely includes me," Mark comically interrupted, hoping he was right.

He remembered the chewing out he and Jeff had gotten when they did the aspiration without an attending present. And as far as Tom finding out what he and Jeff were up to right now, well, that wasn't high on his priority list either. Not unless they both planned to take a long, long vacation due to unemployment.

Mark had to hurry before Dr. Stevenson discovered he had left the Unit. He quickly changed out of his lab coat and hung it up.

I will be back, Mark thought as he set his nametag on the shelf. If he got in trouble, it had been worth it. He had saved several patients.

"I am a doctor, not a patient. They will just have to deal with it because I plan on being back on rotation very soon." He meant every word as he closed the door to his locker, with the initials, Dr. R.M.S. Jr.

Jeff handed Mark a small medication bottle. "I was going to bring it up to you later. This is it, Mark, after this you are on your own. Mrs. Freeman is going to get suspicious and start asking questions about why I am one of your doctors."

"Thanks, Jeff. I got everything under control. This should do it. Every doctor in this hospital is writing prescriptions for me. Don't worry so much, our secret is safe."

Jeff ran interference and Mark took the stairs back up to the Unit. Mark felt great. He needed to be a doctor and have his life back. It was time to reclaim his life. He planned to be back on rotation as soon as he finished chemo and had the transplant.

He stopped on each floor and took a deep breath, and rubbed his painful legs. It was a lot easier going down the stairs than going back up them. He prayed Teresa and Kathleen would let him have another turn in the whirlpool bath when they showed up for his last workout.

Mark opened the door to the Unit and headed to his room. He should have known that April and Dr. Stevenson would be standing there at the door waiting for him.

Both were looking at him with their disapproving teacher faces. Mark smiled just as he had done as a boy, giving them that innocent look of his, which he had perfected over his many years of mischievous deeds.

"What? I went for a walk."

It was worth it, thought Mark. He wanted his life back and for those few hours in the ER, he had felt completely useful again. *I am Dr. Robert Mark Sanders, Jr.. I am not patient 61134.*

Chapter Thirty-Nine

Spending Time With God

§§

After receiving a shot of the new drug at an increased dose, Mark took a shower alone. As the water sprayed down his firm back, he humbly thought about his life as a doctor.

"God, I am washing all sickness from my body. I need You, God, more than ever right now. The devil is messing with my body and my head, Lord."

He wrapped himself in a towel and awkwardly stepped out of the shower, grabbing his lower back and letting out a moan. He gripped the toilet bowl rim and threw up.

This increased dose is not working. The only thing it is good for is making me sicker. These drugs mess with my emotions. I'm sick of them.

The growing pain in his stomach and back demanded relief. *I can't deal with this pain. I've got to do something about it.* He clutched the bottle Jeff had given him in his hand before opening it.

The bottle angered him, yet he was already regretting what he was about to do. *I hear you, Lord; deception in any form is still deception. You think I want to do this, well I don't.* He tried reasoning with his indecisive thoughts, trying to justify them.

Why, God, do I have to feel so guilty for trying to save myself from the destruction of these drugs? I don't have a choice. I have to do this. I am not giving up my plans this week because of my pain. I am going to do whatever it takes to get out of this hospital.

He removed the pills from the bottle into his open palm. He said a heartfelt prayer for immediate healing and then he popped the pills in his mouth. But remorse quickly spread over him.

Did I just speak to God with an attitude? I am so sorry, God. I'm so tired of all of this, forgive me. You see what I mean, God, the drugs are the devil's way of controlling my actions and my thoughts.

After he finished in the bathroom, he fell across his bed exhausted. April was on the other bed. She had fallen asleep while he was taking his shower.

I've worn her out, Lord. She doesn't deserve any of this. I can't keep doing this to her. What am I going to do to keep from hurting her? He turned away from her. For the first time, he wanted to be alone.

He slept off and on restlessly as his mind battled with his earlier actions. He thought about getting up and going to April. He knew she would provide the comfort he needed to fall asleep.

He also knew he and God had some unfinished business to take care of first. He'd had a slight taste at a normal life today, and he wanted desperately to have his freedom from this illness. It was robbing him of gaining back his life to the fullest.

"The devil is not going to rip me off by sending me this pain. The devil is a liar. He is trespassing, Lord; it is time to shut him down. Has he forgotten I belong to You? You own me. Let's just remind him who bought me by dying for me. I am not for sale. The devil is not going to steal my health."

Mark was once the indestructible man who now found himself with this awful illness. It was stripping him of everything he had ever known. He went from the successful doctor and professional football player to a patient who had to depend on daily medications and transfusions to live.

Mark's belief in God had carried him through the beginning stages of his illness. He faithfully tried to prove to everyone around him that he would find joy and laughter in every situation, no matter how awful it might be. He was trusting God's promises and would not back down from his beliefs.

He thought about what he had done earlier in the bathroom and an uneasy feeling swept through his stomach. His pain was a reminder the devil wanted control of him. He realized the longer he remained sick, the devil would continue honing in on him to try and steal away his joy and make him do things he never would have done otherwise.

I must fight harder than I have ever fought before if I am going to win this battle against the devil so I can regain my life as I once knew it, Mark thought as he turned over on his other side and glanced over at April. Sadness filled his mind.

"I am healed," he whispered, "I am a doctor. I am a football player. I am a little boy's hero. Do you hear me, devil?"

And that's the way it is going to be from now on. So find someone else to pick on, 'cause you ain't messing with me anymore. I won't let you win! You cannot touch me without God stepping in and protecting me. God has stamped me, His.

He fought the urge to throw up again.

I have people counting on me, Lord. I can't be sick another day of my life, so I am ready to claim what You promised me.

Mark had touched the lives of so many people. He thought of Matthew and the kids in the Pediatric Unit. *If I am sick, I can't be a blessing to others.*

He had given unselfishly of himself to all those he had come into contact with. Now he realizes he must depend on others to give back to him.

I'm supposed to be a doctor and helping others, not the other way around. I've got to get things back under control before things get way out of hand.

Then he thought about the hardships and heartaches Job had in the Bible story.

How much more will I be able to tolerate of the devil before I reach my breaking point? What more must I endure before all of this craziness ends? Will I be like Job? Will I be faithful to the end of all of this? You know, Lord, I am a fighter for You. I don't want to throw in the towel. So, why am I feeling this way, tonight? It's the drugs; it has to be the drugs.

He stretched his stiff muscles and reshuffled his pillows under his head and around his chest.

God, You promised me You would restore my life better than it was before, just as You did with Job. By the stripes and the blood on Your back, Lord, I believed the answers to all my questions will be answered as You show me Your grace and mercy and healing.

Mark knew he had to hang onto God's promises and remember it is all about his love and his relationship with God that will keep him strong in his faith. He knew he could do nothing without God in his life.

God, You are my shield against all that will come against me. I believe that.

It's just hard when everyone around me wants to try and talk me out of my dreams. I will not listen to what they have to say, Lord. I will believe in what You have to say to me. You and I have a covenant.

Let everyone think that I am being arrogant when I say I'm healed. I'll show them that it's my faith I am standing firm on, not me. This isn't about me. I need to surround myself with believers and get back on track with what I know is the truth.

Mark knew he would receive his healing through his eyes of faith and that he needs to see it on the inside of him before it will come to pass on the outside of him. *I cannot waver, Lord, I know that.*

Again a wave of pain struck his lower back as he moved. Mark knew it was the devil trying to have the last say in this argument. But he refused to give in.

Stop the devil from telling lies about me to those that love me, Lord. Make them understand, I am healed, because I can't do it right now. They don't see me healed, Lord; they see me as a sick man.

He thought of all the unnecessary tears that were shed because of him.

Those who do not share in my faith or supernatural healing will be closely watching me. Lord, let them seek to have the same kind of relationship I have with You and believe with me, when I say, I am a healed man of God.

I know I can't mess up now; too many people are watching me. Too many people think I am going to give in and let aplastic anemia beat me.

But Lord, You know my heart for You; even if I am messing up right now, You know how I really feel. You understand when I do what I have to do in order to survive. Show me grace, Lord. I need it.

I just want one more moment in time when all my dreams will come true. I want those around me to stop suffering because I appear sick. I'm searching out Your plan for my life. Help me, Lord, tell me what to do.

Tonight, questions about his future kept him from drifting back to sleep. He grew restless as time passed and his mind and body continued to attack him.

When will I finally find victory from this illness? When will You give back what the devil has stolen from me?

It wasn't a matter of if God would do it for him; it was a matter of when God would.

God, help me find the patience to wait on You. I am ready to move on with my life and be who You want me to be. Use me, Lord, not doing my will, but Yours. I am ready; just tell me what I can do for Your kingdom.

He thought about the dark night he had spent sitting beside his grandfather's grave when he was a teenager.

I should have died that night in the cemetery. But You shielded me from the cold, Lord. You kept me alive until someone found me.

He knew then it was God's plan to do more with his life than play football. God gave him a heart to help the sick, the injured, and the hurting animals at a very young age.

He learned first hand how strong God planted those feelings in his heart when he shadowed behind Dan at the hospital. God gave him the gift of compassion for people, too.

It was then he had to make a decision between being a football player, veterinarian, or a doctor. Two of those choices were nonnegotiable.

But why was it he really wanted to be a doctor and not a vet? He had never shared his painful reasons with anyone. They remained hidden all these years with the rest of his unspoken heartaches.

His past was what had made him into who he was today or who he never wanted to become. But tonight, there was no avoiding the thoughts of his past. His grandfather had come for a visit in his mind.

Grandfather, I know you thought I wanted to become a vet. I did. But when you died . . . I wanted more than saving animals.

I wanted to prevent little boys, just like me, from having to tell their grandfathers goodbye when they were only eight years old.

I miss you, Papa, so much. Not a day goes by that I don't think of you. It's not fair, Papa, you should still be here with me.

Tears filled his eyes. *I saw you on the football field waiting for me to die so we could be together again. At first, I wanted to go with you. But then, I felt April touching me, reminding me of our love for each other. I had to go back to her, Papa. That doesn't mean I love you less. She needs me, Papa, and I need her.*

Do you remember the day I fell in the mineshaft? I was all alone down there. I didn't know God was with me. I never want to feel that way again. I wish I could forget what it was like being trapped in that horrible mine. But I can't. I can't stop the nightmares. I pray God will erase those memories from my mind. There has to be a greater reason I can't forget. I don't know.

It was you and April who got me through that awful time. But you're gone . . . and she is here. She's my rock, Papa. She's the half of me that makes me whole. I feel as if I can't breathe if she's not with me.

Thank you, Papa, for letting me go that day in the OR when you came to get me. You sent me back . . . to April when she came into the OR to be with me.

A tear slid down his cheek.

If she hadn't come, Papa, would you have taken me with you? I don't understand why you are still holding your hand out to me to take me when I close my eyes when April is not at my side?

That thought opened the door for his next question. *Did God send you to get me, and you followed your heart when you saw April with me? Did you let me stay here with her? Is that what happened? Is that why I didn't die?*

More tears escaped softly down his cheeks. *Are you trying to take me from her because I am on borrowed time now? Is that it? Does God still want me? Maybe it's not His plan to heal me. I am confused; you are confusing me.*

No. I do believe God is going to heal me, Papa. I am claiming healing. I can't believe God is ready for me.

If you come again, I am not going with you. My life is with April and Sunny. Don't make me choose, Papa. Go back up to heaven and leave me here. I will come to you soon enough. I will always love you . . . but I am letting you go. This is goodbye.

The tears steamed down his face, and he let go of the man he dearly loved. He was sending his papa away as if he had been in the room with him. His heart was breaking. He felt as if he were eight again. His pain was as great as it had been on that tragic day in his grandfather's bedroom.

It was finished; his talk with his grandfather was over. Whether it was all in his imagination or real about his grandfather's visits, he might never know, but he had said what he had to say. He prayed that would be the end of his fear of being taken away from the woman he loved.

I have to continue being a doctor, Lord. If that's what You have put in my heart to be, Lord, then that is what I am going to keep doing; nothing will stop me.

His eyes fell on April again, and his thoughts turned to Sunny.

You have more for me, Lord. I am a husband and a father. I am not a person dying from aplastic anemia. You know it and now I know it, so that's it, Lord. I am speaking healing and I am out of here tomorrow.

He looked around for his Bible and held it between his fingers. He read and searched for the places that held answers for him.

He knew it had been far too long since he had this private time alone with God. He was quick to repent and turned to the Book of Job.

After reading a few passages, God spoke to his heart. Mark obeyed and went to April and cradled her in his arms and found peace.

God had answered him. He wanted him to be with April. "Thank you, God," Mark whispered, before falling asleep.

Chapter Forty

Freedom at Last

§§

The next morning, Dan went down to the café to get a cup of coffee. He noticed his new Chief of Surgery sitting at a table reading a medical chart. Dan went over to him. Aaron looked up and held his hand out for Dan to shake.

"I heard you had quite a remarkable day yesterday in the ER. Unfortunately, I did not get a chance to work with you myself," Dan expressed.

"I am sure we will get the opportunity soon. By the way, I worked with one of your second year residents. His work was very impressive; therefore, I'd like to move him from the ER rotation to my surgical trauma rotation as soon as possible."

"You must be talking about Dr. Jeffery Kirkland. Yes, Jeff would be an excellent choice for your surgical rotation."

"No, he wasn't Jeff. Although, Jeff is a fine doctor. I was referring to Dr. Mark Sanders."

"Uhh, what? You worked with Dr. Sanders yesterday?" Dan asked, somewhat puzzled with a lifted eyebrow. "Are you certain he was Mark Sanders?"

"Yes, Sir. Blue jeans, cowboy boots, light sandy brown hair, built like an athlete."

"U-mmm, yes, that does describe Mark perfectly."

"I was very impressed with his excellent skills under pressure. I would like to have the opportunity to train Mark in trauma surgery. I see a promising career ahead for him."

"Well, as soon as I am done breaking both his arms, he is all yours," Dan replied. "If you will excuse me, Dr. Brower, I have some unfinished business I need to attend to, right away, on the sixth floor."

This might be a good time to say a prayer for Mark. I have the feeling he is going to need it, Aaron grinned.

After Dan finished chewing Mark out for his stunt in the ER, Dr. Stevenson promised to release Mark from the hospital into April's capable hands. For all it was worth, Tom gave Mark strict orders to follow. Mark was flying high, excited to be going home.

"Here is your bottle of pain pills. There should be enough to last you two full weeks. If you need them, Mark, take them, otherwise leave them in the bottle." Tom gave no thought that he had just handed Mark a ticking time bomb. Mark flipped the bottle in the air, caught it, and put it in his pocket with his other bottle.

"Before you leave here, there's a meeting in the boardroom you must attend," Tom informed him with a stern face.

"You mean a gang-up-on-Mark session?" Mark joked, only Tom was not laughing when he left the room.

April went to get Mark a water bottle. Christy came in the room. "Mark, there was a call from David for you at the nurse's station. He wanted to know if you could come to an Alcoholics Anonymous meeting downstairs with him this morning. I told him I would let you know about the meeting."

"Thanks, Christy; I'll get ready to go," Mark said as he quickly pulled off his sweatshirt and grabbed a dress shirt out of the closet.

Mark might be her patient, but she couldn't help but admire his well-defined upper body. She blushed when he turned and caught her looking at him. He grinned, knowing exactly what she was thinking, as he slid into the shirt and began buttoning it up.

"You know, Mark, I never thought I would see you drink, until I saw you do it the night of the State Champion Game. You really tied one on that night, in front of all the players and cheerleaders. Except for April, of course; she wasn't there."

Mark's face took on a serious look. "You remember that? Because, I don't." That was one memory he was not disappointed he didn't remember.

"You were on a one-way mission to destroy yourself for some strange reason. We all thought you and April had a big fight. I guess you were kind of lucky Jessica Morton got her claws into you and took you away with her, so you would stop drinking. But you know, you would have thought Jessica got your message loud and clear, you didn't want to be with her, when you called her April by mistake, in front of everyone. Anyways, she finally did manage to convince you to take a walk with her. She told you you needed to stop drinking and walk it off."

"Really, Jessica did that?" Mark felt uneasy.

"Yeah, the two of you disappeared for about an hour. You know, I always wondered what the two of you were up to, off by yourselves, alone?" She gave him a playful teasing smile even though she knew Mark's unblemished reputation back then. She knew the answer to her own question; she just wanted to tease him. Mark wasn't finding any humor in this conversation.

"Jessica sure had her eyes on you, and you were pretty tanked, Mark. You were still staggering when you two came back to the house. To tell you the truth, Mark, I am glad you came to your senses and made up with April and gave Jessica the shaft. Jessica just never seemed to fit in with our group. She was a wanta be April, if you asked me. And she was way too sweet on you. Who would have figured she'd become a nun, though?"

Mark had a puzzled look on his face. He had gotten some of his memory back about that night, but he definitely did not remember being at Carlo's cousin's house.

"Fortunately for me, Christy, I don't remember much about that night. But I do know I made a poor decision to drink. I don't regret for one minute that Sunny is a result of my drinking. But, Christy, if I could do it all over again, I never would have taken that first drink."

Mark took a deep breath. "God has shown me grace and mercy for what I did, and I am going to use that awful experience to witness to teenagers about drinking. People like Willy and David just need someone who cares and understands them without judgment. They need someone who is willing to support them through their difficult time. It's the least I can do. It's my responsibility to help them. I plan to speak at the high school about drinking when I get over my transplant. Youth look up to me; I have to honor that responsibility."

"You are a good man, Mark. You always have been. I was just teasing you. I know nothing happened between you and Jessica. I remember how you stood up for the underdogs at school and Jessica was definitely one of them. We all mess up. Why should you be any different from the rest of us? I am glad you haven't let fame go to your head and you haven't forgotten about us little people." Her words brought a smile to them both.

April came in the room just as Christy got a warm hug from Mark. She smiled, *every time I leave the room, I come back to find Mark in the arms of another woman.*

Did she have any reservations about Mark's love for her? Absolutely not and when Christy left the room, Mark made that point perfectly clear - she was the only woman in his life. Home was looking pretty good right this minute. He could not wait to continue what he had started with April before she blushed and gave him her usual, "Behave yourself, Mark" line.

Mark went to the meeting with David, and afterwards he promised David he would get together with him.

Willy had also been at the meeting, but he acted strangely when Mark approached him. Mark felt something odd was wrong and concluded Willy must be feeling guilty because he had started drinking again. He looked rough around the edges, and he would not look Mark straight in the face when Mark spoke to him. *Well, that explains why Willy can't cook,* Mark thought sadly.

When he got back to the Unit, he went to the nurse's station and asked Eve to get him the phone book, a pen and paper. He looked up the number to his bank and underlined the number before writing it down. Eve suspiciously watched him, noting the page he was looking at.

"Thanks, Eve." He smiled as he handed her the stuff back. She rolled her eyes at him. Mark turned and went to his room. Eve quickly turned the page back to the bank section, copied down the information to Mark's bank, and slipped the paper in her pocket. *Someday, Mark, you will pay!*

She turned on the monitor to Mark's room and listened as Mark made a phone call to his banker, Colin Lambert. Mark was checking to see if Willy was behind on his loan. "Just take the money out of my account to cover the payments." Eve heard Mark tell a Mr. Lambert.

Kathleen and Teresa came to bid Mark farewell. April was finishing the packing as Mark was finishing phone calls he had to make. Mark was definitely in a great mood, despite the fact Tom made him do another IV infusion of nutrients.

"We heard you are breaking out of here," Teresa teased him with a broad smile; thankful this day had come.

"Not without saying goodbye to my two favorite "Angels". Here's a token of my gratitude for putting up with me." He handed them each a bedpan wrapped in red ribbon.

"That's very sweet of you, Mark, thank you," Kathleen half grinned. *As always, Mark has selected us to be his last victims with his joking around*, she thought. She looked over at Teresa who looked like she was going to faint.

"Oh, my gosh, oh my gosh, oh cool!" Teresa kept repeating as she held up something she had taken out of the bedpan.

"What?" Kathleen asked and Teresa pointed to the inside of her bedpan.

"Oh, my gosh, oh my gosh, oh Mark, are these real?" Kathleen asked as she held up three Super Bowl tickets and three VIP ground level passes.

"Ladies, I know I have pulled some pretty bad jokes on you while I was here, and I hope you will forgive me."

"Pete is going to have a heart attack."

"Oh, my gosh," Kathleen started all over again as she pulled out three first class airline tickets.

"Oh, cool," Teresa followed up when she took out four tickets to Disneyland and four tickets to Sea World and hotel accommodations.

"Your plane leaves in twenty-four hours. Dan made all the arrangements for your vacation time. I hope Pete can get off without losing his job."

"Pete will quit his job if he has too. Mark, this is too much, how can we thank you?"

Ok, so maybe Teresa should have known better than to ask Mark that loaded question. A wide grin formed on his good-humored face. "When I am on chemo ...."

"Oh, no you don't, Mark Sanders. You are going to follow the rules when you get back in here." Kathleen gave him one of April's teacher looks.

"Dang, what's a guy gotta do to earn some respect around here?" he laughed. Ok, so maybe he should not have asked the two of them that question, as they reached up, grabbed his cheeks, and lightly pinched him.

He arranged to meet them when he got out there on Friday. "Sell the bedpans, and you'll have some extra spending money," he joked, but inside an envelope were traveler's checks. His travel agent, Pat, had seen to every detail, just the way Mark wanted it.

Sherry and Vivian came to listen to Mark's heart and lungs one last time before signing off on his release forms.

"Don't go giving your heart away to any of those California hot nurses," Sherry joked with him.

Mark assured Sherry she was the only one he would let touch his heart. He planted a kiss on her cheek and gave Vivian a hug. "That *touchdown pass* I am going to throw will have your name written all over it," he whispered to Vivian with a broad grin.

They promised they would be watching the game and cheering him on if he got to play. But in their hearts, they knew Mark would not be throwing any touchdown passes on Sunday. Tests Dr. McGuire had run on Mark's heart confirmed his heart was still enlarged.

All of Mark's doctors gathered with Mark and April in the boardroom to discuss a treatment plan for Mark while he was "temporarily" out of the hospital.

Did they have to stress, temporarily, Mark thought as he sat sideways in his chair and felt helplessly surrounded by the domineering doctors about to determine his future fate.

Fearful of complications while Mark was out of the hospital, they prepared two medical bags with medications Mark might need in an emergency. They included an emergency container of oxygen and other supplies Mark might require.

Dan would keep one bag with him at all times when he was with Mark. The other bag would travel with Mark wherever he went. A double check system was put into place.

Dr. Price was deeply concerned about Mark's anxiety level over the pending court hearing and included medications to calm him down if they needed to do it.

"I want you to remain on your anxiety medication, Mark." *The only anxiety I have is from this hospital*, Mark silently grinned.

Dr. McGuire included medications Mark might need to control his heart rate and high blood pressure. She went over the medications with everyone, making sure April understood which ones to give Mark if they were alone and Mark was unable to tell her what he needed.

I plan to give my heart a good workout, alone with April, Mark thought as he winked at April and chuckled to himself. *She's blushing; she got my message*. Then he got her message to pay attention.

A third bag contained all Mark's daily medications with instructions for him to follow. Tom gave Mark eight bottles of medication to take each day, along with his IV medications, a box of facemasks, and instructions.

Jeff and Dan would watch over him on his trip to California. With the game plan in order, Tom signed Mark's release papers. Then everyone gave Mark a hug and wished him well.

When they went into the hallway, Dan handed Mark a bottle of pain pills. "I know you have weaned off of them, Mark, but take these to California just in case you should need them," Dan instructed Mark, not knowing about the bottle of pain pills Tom and Jeff had already given him.

Mark inconspicuously placed the bottle next to the other two and gave thanks his jeans hung loose on him so no one would see the outline of the three bottles.

Super Bowl – here I come, he thought as his feet hit the sidewalk outside of the hospital.

Chapter Forty-One

The Homecoming

§ò

April and Mark flew out to the ranch. Everyone was outside to welcome Mark home. They all tearfully fussed over him.

"It's so good to have you home, Master Mark," Thomas expressed for the entire group. "And you, Miss April, welcome to your new home."

"Mark!" Sunny was the first to claim his outstretched arms as she jumped up and held tight around his neck, claiming his earlobe between her fingers. "I've missed ya so much!"

"I missed you, too, Sunny."

His grandparents, Victoria and Everett, tenderly hugged him. The jubilant staff each wanted a hug and a kiss from him. Mark gladly accommodated them, thankful he had so many people that loved him.

Mark felt a tinge of sadness, as his heart instantly missed his Grandfather not being there to welcome him home. The next time his papa would welcome him home would be in heaven.

What a wonderful reunion that will be, Mark thought, with peace in his heart thinking about his recent conversation with his grandfather in the hospital. *Remember what I said, Papa, it's not time.*

Mark gathered his Grandmother Ella into his arms and warmly hugged her. Sunny wrapped her arms around both their necks.

Mark noted the moisture of tears in his grandmother's eyes and kissed her forehead. Together the three walked inside the house.

A big welcome home sign graced the entrance. It was uplifting to be home. Mark set Sunny down, and she ran to April for a hug.

Mark turned his attention to Ella. Her eyes seemed drawn, and there were dark circles under her eyes. Mark anxiously thought about her heart condition and concern settled over him.

"You look tired, Grams. Are you taking care of yourself?" She touched his cheek with the palm of her hand to bring him reassurance.

"I am just fine, now that you are home, Mark. My heart has missed you." Her tears were evidence of that truth. She pulled out the handkerchief Mark had made for her for "happy tears."

Mark gathered her back in his arms and fought back his own tears. *God, I love this woman. Please, God, let her be all right. Don't let my illness have damaged her heart.*

"Indulge me, Grams; let's go to my office. I want to have a look at you just to make sure." He tenderly led her by the arm to his makeshift doctor's office where he treated the ranch hands and staff.

He helped her up on the exam table. He took his stethoscope that was hanging from the hook on the wall and placed the eartips in his ears. His touch on her chest was gentle as he listened to her heart. Relief showed on his soft face as he focused his loving eyes straight into her eyes, expressing his deepest love for her.

This is the young man that has been missing from our household. Our compassionate doctor that everyone loves deeply is finally home. Thank you, God, for bringing Mark home to us.

Mark went over the medications Dr. McGuire prescribed for her and was satisfied everything was in order with his grandmother's care.

"Everything looks great, Grams," he expressed with sincere kindness that softened her heart.

"I knew it would be the minute you came home, Mark." She didn't have to ask for the hug she melted into as her grandson claimed her in his loving arms. This time she wiped his happy tears.

Sunny peeked in the room, ran to Mark, and encased her arms around his legs for a hug. It was obvious to Mark how fond Sunny was of his Grams by the affectionate look they exchanged with each other.

"Mark, ya are my hero for taking care of my Grams." *Mark would never let anything happen to my Grams*, Sunny thought with high-esteem for Mark. She loved the stories Grams told her about Mark and his grandfather's relationship and all their many adventures when Mark was a young boy. Now it was her turn to be Grams' favorite great-granddaughter and make some memories of her own.

Together they went into the family room, where everyone was waiting anxiously to talk to Mark.

"Mark, we are so glad to have you home. After you scared us half-to-death there on the football field, we never thought this day would come," Everett expressed.

As the unnerving questions began, Mark turned to Sunny with concern. *She should not be listening to this kind of talk.* "Sunny, run in the kitchen and get me a bottle of water."

She ran off, eager to please Mark. She returned with the bottle and handed it to Mark before taking ownership of his lap.

Mark was cordial and happy to have his family around him, but he grew restless. Their well-meaning attention was overwhelming, causing him to feel anxious. They focused on the fact he almost died. When the words "chemo" and "radiation" were mentioned, those words did not sit well with his *already unsettled* stomach.

He sent Sunny for another bottle. This was not a conversation he wanted Sunny to hear. When she came back with the bottle, he encouraged her to find her cousins and play, while the adults talked. She unwillingly left the room and hid just outside the doorway and listened.

"I have heard so many dreadful things about chemo. I just hate this for you, honey. We will all be here to support you through this, honey ...," Victoria tearfully said as she leaned her head on Everett's shoulder and dabbed her tears.

"I'll be fine. I am not about to let a little chemo take the zest out of me," Mark responded with unconvincing words hidden behind the tense smile he painted on his face as the questions about chemo continued.

He began twisting his stiff fingers together as the word "death" was mentioned again. He struggled with the cap to the bottle, unable to open this one. This was not the first time April had seen tremors in his unsteady hands. She sensed his need to unwind and have his freedom from this conversation. He had come home to get away from his illness, not to be reminded of the unpleasant treatments he had yet to endure.

Sunny slowly reentered the room with a long sad face that caught Mark's attention, and he opened his arms out to her. *I hope she wasn't listening.*

April thought of a way to give Mark an opportunity to excuse himself from the room. She abruptly changed the subject.

"Everyone, I'm sorry. I hope you don't mind if I steal my husband for a few minutes. Mark, I'd really like to start unpacking our things so you can get some rest before lunch. Can you show me to our bedroom?" Her plan worked; his face brightened knowing she had rescued him. He thankfully winked at her.

Another encouraging thought crossed his mind. *That's right; April has never seen my bedroom.* Mark was glad for the interruption in more ways than one. He stood up and took April's hand in his. *I'd be more than happy to show you to my bedroom*, he grinned, thinking of possibilities to come for his new bride.

Unfortunately, for him, his mother and Sunny followed them.

Julia turned down the sheets on Mark's bed so he could rest, but Mark insisted he was fine. Mark was tired of looking at walls. His room had a French door that opened out to the pool deck. Before Julia could say anymore, Mark ducked out the door. Sunny stayed inside with April to help her unpack her clothes.

Mark sat on the pool deck for a while and rested. He managed to open the bottle of water and drank the entire bottle. He could not stop thinking about the game on Sunday. For as long as he could remember he had watched the Super Bowl, now here he was, an NFL quarterback whose team would be playing in the game. Just thinking about it raised his adrenaline level.

He went in search of Sunny and another two bottles of water. Then he took Sunny down to the stable to play with the new kittens.

Sunny surrounded herself with the kittens on the hay, but Mark turned his attention on Thunder. *I've missed riding you, boy*, he thought, as he stroked Thunder's moist nose and decided he would take Thunder out for a spin with Sunny.

He was immediately reminded of his stitches when he bent down to pick up Thunder's saddle. He could not lift it without the searing pain and tearing of his incisions. He took a deep breath as he once again unsuccessfully attempted to lift the saddle on Thunder's back. He felt frustrated as he dropped the heavy saddle on the ground and hugged his painful abdomen. "That hurt, oh, man."

He was reminded of the five-pound rule and frowned. Defeat was not in his vocabulary, but this time, he knew better than to attempt the task again.

Charlie was quietly watching over Mark. He was thankful Mark's motorcycle was still out in the woods somewhere gathering rust.

He saw Mark take a bottle of pills out of his pocket and shake some into his hand. He swallowed them with a swig from his water bottle. He put the bottle in his jacket.

Charlie stood with a heavy heart, observing Mark as he walked around in circles restlessly for a few minutes before he joined Sunny on the hay, acting as if he was pain free. Charlie did not like what he witnessed. *Mark ain't well; he's just pretendin'*.

Mark took Sunny back to the house and went to see what April was doing. Maybe he could get lucky and eat lunch alone with her in his bedroom. Now that was something positive to think about doing. He carelessly set his jacket down on the dining room table.

He went into the kitchen to gather supplies. Martha looked over when Mark opened the refrigerator. He grabbed another bottle of water. Martha frowned, *isn't that the third or fourth bottle he has gotten out of the refrigerator in the last hour?*

"Mark, what are you doing? I am making your lunch," she inquired cheerfully, glad for the opportunity to be serving Mark once again.

"Where are the grapes and the strawberries?" He turned and looked at Martha. Her disapproving face, one that he had seen many times as a teenager when he had raided the refrigerator, met him.

"Mark, you know you can't have fresh fruits," Martha reminded him with a kind heart.

Mark shook his head back and forth. *Great, now I have a food monitor*, he laughed to himself as he smiled at Martha. He knew her intentions were well meant, and he excused her protectiveness over him.

"I thought April would like some for lunch."

"April and your grandmothers just finished eating a light lunch. They are in your bedroom," Martha informed Mark as she handed him a sandwich that was on his list of approved foods.

"Thanks, Martha." Mark kissed her cheek and left the room. *There are three too many women in my bedroom! I will just have to eliminate them.*

Mark went to his bedroom and set the sandwich down on the dresser. "Sunny, Martha made you a sandwich." Sunny was quick to pick up Mark's sandwich and took a big bite.

Mark eyed his jacket on the dresser and picked it up. *Who moved my jacket in here?* A lump filled his throat as he thought about what he needed to do again to relieve the pain he was still feeling from picking up the saddle. *The pills I have are not strong enough; they are not working. I am going to have to take more.*

April was busy talking with his mother as his grandmothers looked on. Julia insisted they redecorate Mark's bedroom so April would feel more like this was her home. Sunny agreed with a big smile, before she left the room with her sandwich.

April held up a color chart in front of Mark. "Which colors do you like best, Mark?" April inquired and was met by Mark's "*are you really asking me*" look.

"Whatever makes you happy, Babe." Mark forced a smile to accommodate his bride. Mark wanted nothing to do with decorating the room. He did not care what the bedroom looked like as long as April was the only one in it. Frustrated, he went into the bathroom with his jacket and fifteen minutes later, he came out. He went to see where Sunny wandered off without him.

Robert called to see how Mark was doing. Julia reported that Mark was extremely restless. Robert said he would take care of Mark when he got home in a few hours.

Robert Sanders and William Triplett had a serious business meeting they had to attend. The AFC Championship Game win resulted in severe complications for one California businessman that was now related to Mark. Robert would have to explain the situation to Mark as soon as he felt Mark was up to the grueling conversation.

That, however, would not be any time soon.

Chapter Forty-Two

Finding His Way Back Home

Mark was feeling better by the time he went into the playroom. In fact, he hardly felt any pain at all. He playfully grabbed James Robert up off the floor and flipped him over his shoulders onto his back.

"Uncle Markie!" James laughed as Mark tickled him. Sunny squealed in delight when her turn came.

Rebecca and Steven arrived home from the hospital. Rebecca had not been the same since the night of the football game. The trauma of Mark's accident had emotionally scarred her. She seemed to be avoiding Mark. Her visits to his hospital room had been few.

Rebecca came in the playroom. Mark was on the floor with her two boys wrestling and laughing. Brad was on top of Mark's chest. James Robert was pulling Mark's feet, and Sunny was cheering loudly.

"Mark! What do you think you are doing? Boys, get off of Uncle Mark right now before you hurt him!" she fretfully yelled.

Rebecca quickly grabbed them up away from Mark and told them not to wrestle with their Uncle Mark anymore. She herded them out of the room. They loudly protested, as they loved playing with their Uncle Markie.

"Oh, Mommy, we wanta play with Uncle Markie!" James complained loudly.

Steven came in the room when he heard Rebecca's frightened voice. "What's going on?"

Rebecca took one look at Mark lying on the floor and had a flashback of him lying half-dead on the football field. She let her reserved tears fall and swirled around to leave the room. Steven grabbed her arm to stop her. "What's wrong, sweetheart?"

"Nothing, I don't want to talk about it."

Mark sat up on the floor and tried to speak to her. "Please, Beck, we need to talk."

Without making eye contact with Mark, she told him, "I have to take a shower before dinner."

"Come on, Beck, talk to me," Mark pleaded as he stood. She broke Steven's hold on her and left the room.

Steven patted Mark on the shoulder and told him to have patience with her; she would eventually come around. Her rejection hurt Mark's heart deeply. How could he get back their relationship to the way it was before, he wondered.

Then Steven chewed Mark out for wrestling with the boys and reminded him of the five-pound rule.

"Why is everyone always chewing me out, come on, give me a break?" Mark pleaded his case to his unreceptive brother-in-law as he guiltily thought about the pain pills he had taken.

Sunny went to help Maria and Martha in the kitchen to assist in making Mark his favorite dinner. Since her heartbroken outburst the night of Mark's game, everyone had done his or her best to keep Sunny busy so she would not miss Mark as much.

There was nothing for Mark to do. He was bored and feeling awkwardly misplaced in his surroundings. This house was now his "temporary" home. *As soon as I get back from California, it's back to the hospital.* He had other plans for a home and a big surprise waiting for April, when the timing was right. But first, he had to restore his family.

He went into the exercise room and contemplated working out. *Maybe I can lift weights with my legs*, he thought, but after doing five, even that hurt his stomach muscles and now his lower back was twitching.

He felt his clammy forehead and knew he had a fever. He made another trip to the bathroom to find some Tylenol. Then he went back outside on the pool deck and walked around slowly, eyeing the inviting water.

The pool was heated, but he knew he could not get his stitches *wet* with the pool water without getting an infection in his central line. What was there left to do? Mark was not used to having nothing to do; this was going to drive him crazy.

He took the *binoculars* off the wall by the pool and looked out over the fields at the cattle. *Branding season is coming up. Pedro will need my help. Lord, I got a lot to do in the next few weeks. And being sick from chemo is not on that list. Let's just fast forward to the chapter of my life where I am a healed man.*

April came and told him she was going to take a shower and get ready for photographer who was coming to take some pictures of them in their wedding attire.

"Rebecca loaned me her wedding dress for some outside shots of us. I wanted more of a flowing wedding dress for those pictures. Is that okay with you, honey?"

"Whatever makes you happy, Babe, is fine with me." Although he had planned this photo session for her, right now, he wasn't in the mood to be taking pictures.

April wanted him to come in the house and get out of the cool air before he had to get dressed in his tuxedo.

He cleverly followed her to the shower. Now that was definitely something he was in the mood to do; he grinned as his spirits lifted. At last, they could be alone.

Once the pictures were taken, Mark found himself bored again. April was looking at a photo album with his mother and Sunny. They were all giggling at Mark's baby pictures.

Mark shook his head and left the room. *What I need is some guy time doing guy stuff. I can't swim, lift weights, ride my horse or go to football practice. Lord, I am not feeling joy right now.*

Robert arrived home with the gang: Jeff, Carlo, Kevin, Craig, Justin, Jerk, William, and Dan. Craig was Steven's younger brother.

When Mark walked into the dining room and saw all of them there, he smiled wide and gave each one of them a fist to fist high five. *Now this is what I was talking about, Lord. Guy time it is.* Mark looked around for the nurse and was thankful the group had not included her.

"What? No nurse?" They all laughed. Mark had forgiven them for the stunt they had pulled on him in the hospital. However, he was still planning his revenge on them.

None of them would reveal who the mystery woman had been. Mark told them he could identify the woman by her awful after-shave lotion. They all looked at each other and busted out laughing.

Justin reminded Mark that they still owed him a bachelor party. Mark half smiled at them. "That should be real fun; I can't wait." Mark stared them down with his smart look of, "*I just dare you guys to do anything else to me*" and they laughed.

"We promise, the woman we get to jump out of the cake will look better than the nurse we provided for you in the hospital." Jerk laughed, as he thought about how he would look dressed in a two-piece swimsuit with a padded bra. He chuckled.

"What now?" Mark asked with squinted eyes.

"Never mind, Mark, I was just thinking about something." Jerk grinned.

"Well, knock it off. It's my turn to get you guys back."

Just eleven days ago, they thought they had lost Mark forever. Now they planned to enjoy every moment they could with him. Mark's smiles and the sound of his laugher brightened their hearts. They did not know Mark planned to join them for the Super Bowl Game, so no one mentioned the game. They knew it would be a painful subject for Mark.

Tonight, they would board the team plane without him. Only Carlo would remain behind for the custody court hearing tomorrow before he left for California.

They had a deck of cards ready and Robert was clearing off the dining room table. Mark was thankful he had gotten another chance to have his friends around him.

Martha and Sunny came out with the finger foods and colas. Sunny gave Mark a bottle of water. The rest of the family ate in the informal dining room.

The group was soon laughing and having a good time playing cards. It was just what Mark needed. He was tired of being sick, he was tired of the hospital, and he missed hanging out with the gang. It was time to start living again, and he planned to do just that.

April was glad Mark had a distraction. Tomorrow was the court hearing and they were both concerned about its outcome.

April gathered Sunny in her arms and held on tight. Everyone was concerned about Mark's heart condition, but right now, it was her heart that was anxious. Could she open her heart up completely and let Sunny own the part that belonged to Jessica, without fearing someone would take her baby away from her again?

Sunny was Sunny, not Jessica, and April could not bear to lose Sunny, too. She fought back her tears as Sunny nestled against her breasts. She knew at that moment there was no denying what her heart was telling her. It was too late; she had already fallen deeply in love with Sunny.

There was no stopping her succumbing tears as she let Sunny know how she felt. "I love you, Sunny. I always have and I always will. You will always be my little girl."

Sunny buried her face against April and put her thumb in her mouth. *Then, why did ya give me away? Why did ya take me away from Mark?*

She brushed back her tears. *If Mark thinks he loves ya after what you did to me, then maybe I can. I wanted ya to be my mother before I found out ya really was, but I just don't know if I can forgive ya.* She let a few more tears fall and sucked on her thumb.

April suddenly thought about her twin sister, Allison. She had died the night they were born. She remembered her Mother taking her to Allison's grave when she was five. She hugged Sunny and thanked God Jessica was alive and she was holding her in her arms.

After the men went home early, the family gathered in Robert's office to discuss the court hearing. Robert sat down next to Sunny and gently explained what would happen to her tomorrow in the courtroom.

Sunny sat quietly on Mark's lap and listened carefully. Robert explained to her that she would have to answer questions from the judge. Sunny got teary eyed and held tighter to Mark, taking a hold of his ear for security.

"Please, Mark; don't make me talk to them people." Mark combed her hair with his fingers.

How can I allow this to happen to her? She is scared and wants my protection. He looked over his shoulder. Sunny wasn't his only concern; April stood behind him in tears.

"You don't have to say anything, if you don't want to. Robert will do all the talking for you, ok, Sunny?"

"I guess, but after it is over, will I be yours, Mark?" Oh, the fibers she just tangled up in Mark's heart at that moment, leaving him searching for an answer. No more promises, no more breaking her heart. How could he answer truthfully without making her afraid? No words were spoken from his heart or his mouth.

"Sunny, you have nothing to worry about. I am going to take good care of you tomorrow," Robert volunteered the promises Mark could not make.

Julia and April took Sunny to her room and read to her until she fell asleep. Mark stood in the doorway and watched, as his eyes filled with tears of love for the two women on the bed with his precious daughter.

Then he went outside on the pool deck, looked up into the heavens, and gave his heart to his Father.

When Mark finally came in his bedroom, April was waiting for him. She was sitting in bed, trying to read a book. Mark fell across the bed laying face down. April put her book down and ran her fingers through his hair.

"Mark, did you take your medications yet?"

"Not yet, I am too tired."

"Do you want me to give you the injections?" She volunteered as she teased his hair between her fingers. Mark rolled over and looked up into her face.

"No, I'll do it," he told her as he rolled off the bed and reluctantly went into the bathroom.

He opened the medical bag and got the medications out. He took off his sweater. He carefully measured the dose in the syringe and injected it into his central line. He repeated it with the second medication. He undid his belt buckle and removed his jeans. He took the pre-filled syringe, pinched the skin on his thigh, and injected the syringe with a swift motion. "Dang."

Then he opened each bottle and took out what he needed and downed them with water. April watched him as he looked in the bathroom mirror at himself with frustration on his face. Her heart hurt for him, knowing what he was thinking. He shut off the light, came out into the bedroom, and looked at April.

Even though it was April and Mark's first night at the ranch together, Mark insisted Sunny sleep in the bed with them. He wanted both his women close to him tonight. April whole-heartedly agreed and made a spot next to her for Sunny.

Mark went into Sunny's room, gathered her gently in his arms, carried her into his bedroom, and placed her on the bed beside April. He cuddled next to Sunny and held his hand out to April.

His family was all he needed as he drifted off to sleep. Thirty minutes later, he was in the bathroom sick. He spent most of the night on the bathroom floor. His stomach would not calm down.

Mark knew he could not continue to be sick like this if he was going to go to California on Friday. He wanted to make this trip as pleasant as possible for the two women he loved more than his own life. He could not do that if he was sick to his stomach and running fevers from the medications. *He only had one choice to make and he made it.*

During the night, the house alarm went off. Mark left the bathroom and went with his Dad to investigate; they found no one. Anthony came and checked around the outside of the house, but he did not find anything out of order.

Only the bedroom window in Sunny's room was slightly open, and Mark thought the women must have forgotten to close it when they had been cleaning in there.

Mark crawled back in bed with his family and was able to fall asleep for about an hour before he found himself back on the bathroom floor.

Old Charlie got little sleep that night.

Chapter Forty-Three

Heading into the Lion's Den

ᔕᔓ

Thursday, everyone was up early and felt the tension of the events about to unfold that day. April noticed Mark looked tired, but he did not say anything. He played with his breakfast and drank two glasses of water, as he eyed Sunny across the table.

"Did you take your medications this morning?"

He looked at April with a frown. "April, let me handle my medications."

"I just thought …" She looked away, and Mark quickly touched her hand and brought her fingers to his lips.

"I'm sorry, April. I didn't mean to hurt your feelings. I know you are just trying to keep me straight. That's why I love you so much." He reached over and kissed her lips and Sunny giggled.

"Mark, can I go play with the boys before we have to go to the court-house?" Sunny asked as she got up from the table.

Mark sat staring at her. His reserved thoughts crowded his mind, leaving him unable to speak. He had already lost her once. What would happen today in the courtroom if he lost her again? A huge suffocating lump filled his throat.

April replied after Mark sat silent, "Go ahead, Sunny. But just for a few minutes. Then we need to get dressed to leave."

"Ok." She gave them one last look. *Mark does love her, that's for sure. If she makes Mark happy, then I'm happy she's gonna be my mom.* With that thought, she went to find the boys.

Mark was thankful Sunny did not seem to be worried about the court hearing. He'd had a hard time emotionally listening to his father as Robert prepared Sunny for the court hearing last night. Something else was bothering him; Sunny continued to refer to him as Mark.

Why won't she call me, daddy? Is it because she thinks I will never be her daddy? And why doesn't Sunny tell April she loves her?

Robert was in his office going over last minute details for the court hearing. If he did not win this case and get the judge to grant custody of Sunny to Mark there would be no bone marrow transplant. Mark's life depended on him winning this case today. There was no time for a formal hearing that could take months to settle.

He looked up when Julia entered the room with a cup of fresh coffee. Their eyes met, both understanding what was at stake today. Robert had shared his conversation with the judge earlier that week with Julia, a conversation that had not gone as well as he anticipated.

Legally, Sunny was a ward of the state, with an adoptability status. The Stanleys had filed a petition to adopt Sunny. Robert's first job would be to establish that Sunny was no longer available for adoption.

The Stanleys had acquired a prominent lawyer who was up for reelection, and this was just the case he needed to gain himself some first-class publicity. But how was it possible the Stanleys were paying for a lawyer of this magnitude? What could the Stanleys possibly want with a child when they could not afford to feed themselves? Something was definitely wrong with the whole picture.

Robert angrily held the morning newspaper in his hands and read the front page to Julia. "Attorney Jackson Vicks is challenging NFL Quarterback, Mark Sanders, in court today, in a case to determine the legitimization of Mr. Sanders' claim to the paternity of a child Sanders claims he fathered six years ago with his current wife, April Morgan Sanders."

"Oh, please, Robert, I cannot bear to hear the rest. Has Mark seen the paper?" Julia worried.

Robert crumbled the paper up and threw it in the trashcan. "Not that I am aware of. Have you seen Mark this morning?"

"Mark and April are eating breakfast with Sunny. Robert, Mark looks so pale. I am so worried about him."

Steven and Rebecca entered the breakfast area. Steven was drawn to Mark's pale face. Before he could say anything, Rebecca reached out and felt Mark's forehead for a fever.

"Mark, you have a fever."

Mark jerked away from her angrily, got up, and left the room abruptly. April apologized and chased after him.

April found Mark in their bathroom splashing cold water on his face. She decided to leave him alone. She sat on the bed and twisted her hands together. If she hadn't been so concerned for Mark, she would have wrapped the bed sheets around her and cried, just as she had done five years ago, when she had lost Sunny to her father.

Sunny came in their bedroom holding the dress Mark bought her for Christmas. The bounce in her steps was missing. Mark could see her pitiful reflection in the bathroom mirror, as she despondently held up the dress and asked April if she could wear it today. Mark moved over to the bathroom door and closed it. He hit the floor with his knees and prayed.

The entire family flew into the city for the court hearing. Mark held Sunny in his lap as they flew. He sat in prayer, as he held her close to his heart. Every beat of her heart echoed against his arm.

Sunny sort of understood what was going to happen. Although everyone pretended things would go just fine, she felt their apprehension. She gathered Mark's earlobe between her fingers and resisted sucking her thumb. Mark kissed the top of her head as April reached out and took her hand in hers.

April searched Mark's face just as a single tear slid down her cheek. Mark reached up and gently wiped it away. They did not have to say anything as their hearts spoke to each other.

April's face suddenly looked concerned. "Mark, did you remember to put your emergency medical bag in the helicopter?"

Mark shook his head. "I forgot. It's okay, I'm fine." April wanted them to turn the helicopter around and get the bag, but Mark assured her that he would be fine.

Once they arrived at the helipad, they got into a limo with Dan and drove to the courthouse. When they arrived, the media tried to get an interview with Mark as soon as he stepped out of the limo. Robert's hired bodyguards and Anthony kept the media and paparazzi back. Mark ignored the persistent media as he sheltered April and Sunny next to him.

In the courtroom, Sunny was required to sit at the defendant's table with Robert, Julia, and Mrs. Wilson. Mark and April sat next to each other in the front row, and held hands for support. Jeff and Dan sat next to them on one side. Rebecca sat between April and Steven.

Reporters had been prohibited from the courtroom, since the hearing involved a minor child. Robert had seen to that detail earlier in the week with Judge Thompson.

Mark had the feeling the judge disliked the Sanders' family because he had been so strict with them. He took a slow deep breath and held himself together. Maybe they should have gone back for the medical bag, he thought with concern, as he touched his sore chest. He said a quick prayer his heart would remain steady throughout the hearing.

Sunny turned around to face Mark and April. She was frightened of this awful place, and she wanted Mark to hold her in his protective arms. Julia and Robert spoke gently to her, trying to bring her comfort. Still, she kept her eyes on Mark who was doing his best to reassure her with his silly faces. Jeff joined in and soon Sunny was smiling at the two comedians.

Debbie and her husband, Phil, and her mother, Tammy, sat three rows behind Mark and April. While Mark was in the hospital, they had gone out to the ranch to spend time with Sunny. Tammy was saddened that Sunny seemed so lost without Mark. All Sunny wanted was her Mark.

Tammy understood why Sunny was feeling overwhelmed by all her new family members. Nevertheless, she wondered why Sunny was not asking more about April.

Tammy had not heard anything from Paul. There were signs he stayed at their old house with Todd before the wedding. Tammy decided to stay with Debbie and Phil when she first arrived in town. She just could not face Paul after what he had done. They all feared Paul was off stewing. What would he have to say when he resurfaced, they worried?

Paul's bankers had made contact with Tammy and said they needed to speak to Paul right away. *Was Paul in some kind of trouble with his bank?* she wondered.

Robert needed vital information from Paul for the court hearing. He asked Tammy if she could contact Paul and get that information. Tammy, instead, left messages on Todd's answering machine, telling him what Robert wanted. She was hoping Todd could get through to his father and stop all of this nonsense for the sake of April and Sunny.

Todd had not returned any of her messages for the last few days. Worse than that, Todd had not shown up for the court hearing today to support his sister. *Had Todd joined forces with Paul?* That thought ripped through Tammy's heart.

The Stanleys self-assuredly walked into the courtroom with their high-powered lawyer. They had petitioned the court for custody of Sunny.

Their lawyer, Mr. Jackson Vicks, would contend that Sunny was not the biological child of Mark Sanders or April Morgan Sanders. This was just a conspiracy of Mark Sanders to obtain custody of a child the court had already ruled could not be adopted by him.

In addition, if Robert established Sunny was April's biological child, Jackson fully intended to provide evidence that April had abandoned Sunny, therefore severing all her parental rights as Sunny's mother.

Mr. Vicks intended to prove Mark Sanders was an unsuitable candidate for guardianship of Sunny. This informal hearing would determine Sunny's eligibility for adoption by someone other than Mark and April Sanders. Once that was established, Jackson would seek custody of Sunny for Sara and Bill Stanley.

Mr. Vicks was a man that gave lawyers a heartless, manipulating, ruthless reputation. He gave no consideration at all to the small child sitting across the courtroom from him. His goal was to bring someone as legendary as Mark Sanders to his knees.

With the Super Bowl just days away, all media attention was focused on Mark Sanders and his team, and Mr. Vicks planned to do whatever it took to cash in on that media attention.

Chapter Forty-Four

Tormenting Testimony

§§

The informal court hearing began as Robert stood up to begin his questioning of April.

When Robert called April to testify about giving birth to Sunny, Julia and Rebecca took Sunny out of the courtroom. Standing in the hallway was John, Sunny's friend from the park. Sunny instantly ran to him and they hugged.

"What are you doing here, John?"

"My mom's here for something. She made me tag along, cause my real dad is working. Why are you here, Sunny?"

"I might get adopted by Mark," she said flatly, as if her heart already decided it might not happen.

"I hope you get Mark as a dad; he seems really nice."

"He is, but I can't call Mark my daddy yet. My heart won't let me, 'cause ... it would just break in two ... if I lost Mark again ... I would die if I lost my ... daddy." Tears sprinkled down her rosy cheeks and John compassionately hugged her.

Julia and Rebecca gave each other a consoling look. So that is why Sunny is not calling Mark, daddy.

"It's gonna be ok, Sunny. You and me, we're tough. Remember when my Dad almost died in that fire last year trying to save that baby? Well, I prayed real hard and God made him better. God can fix this too, Sunny. He'll give you a daddy. I know He will. You have to believe." Sunny did believe in John's words. She believed God and John had a direct connection.

"Sunny, we have to go sit in the waiting room. Tell your friend John goodbye," Julia spoke softly to her.

"John's daddy is a fireman. He is brave like Mark," Sunny bragged to Julia and Rebecca. John stood tall with pride.

"A fireman is very brave. I know you must be very proud of your father, John," Julia spoke to John with a warm smile. "Sunny, we have to go."

"I will try to come to the park, and we can sit on '*Mark's bench*' and talk. But I gotta go now, bye, John." She leaned forward and hugged him. John took her hand in his and held it briefly as he transferred his heart over to her.

"Bye, Sunny. I'll see you around." His compassionate eyes reached out to her as their hands dropped. *God, please give Sunny whatever she wants.*

John stood still as he watched Sunny be led away by Julia. Sunny turned back and waved at him just before she went into a room. John whispered three little words from his heart as he waved back.

April took the witness stand, and Robert gently questioned her, as Mark looked on nervously. He felt the small Gideon Bible he had placed in his pocket and said a quick prayer.

"April, how old were you when you became pregnant with a baby girl you later named Jessica Parker?"

"Eighteen." Robert established April was of legal age when she and Mark had an intimate relationship with each other.

"April, is the father of your child, Jessica Parker, in this courtroom?"

"Yes."

"Tell the court his name and identify him by pointing to him."

"Robert Mark Sanders." She pointed at Mark and joined her eyes and heart with him.

"April, was Mark Sanders aware you were pregnant with his child?

"No, I never told Mark, not until recently."

"Did Mark Sanders know you later gave birth to his child?"

"No."

"Did Mark Sanders sign any legal papers giving up his legal rights to his child?"

"No, Mark never would have signed away his legal rights to his child."

"April, why did you choose not to inform Mark you were carrying his child?"

"My father threatened to kill the man that had been with me. I had to protect Mark from my father. If I had told Mark … he would have done the right thing ..., married me ..., and raised our child. But my father never would have allowed that to happen. So I was forced to keep my pregnancy a secret to protect Mark."

"April, did you willingly give up your child?"

"No, my father forcefully took my child away from me."

"April, did you sign any legal documentation giving up your parental rights to your child, Jessica Parker?"

"No, I never would have done that."

"April, did you make any attempt to find your child?"

"Yes, everyday for the last five years, I have looked for her, hoping that I could get her back."

"April, I want you to tell this court what happened the morning you gave birth to Jessica Parker."

April cried the entire time she was testifying how her father had taken her child away from her.

Mark was restless and anxious as she spoke of her ordeal. He twisted his fingers together. He felt the guilt build up inside of him as April cried. *This is all my fault. I did this to her.* His stomach was churning as April continued telling the emotional story.

Mark leaned forward and covered his face with his hands. His heart was breaking for April as she continued to cry. Jeff moved over and sat closer to Mark. He placed his hand on Mark's back to offer support.

Tammy cried against Debbie as she felt her daughter's deep pain. *How could Paul have done this to our daughter? His actions are unthinkable. He knew what it was like to lose a child. We buried our little Allison. I don't know if I will ever be able to forgive him for taking away my grandchild.*

"April, is it your desire to have custody of your child, Jessica Parker, known as Sunflower or Sunny?"

"Yes, please, your Honor. I want Jessica returned to Mark and me, so we can raise her and love her as her parents."

"April, thank you for your testimony."

"Your Honor, April Morgan Sanders was of legal age when she conceived a child by Mark Sanders. She has testified she was not an agreeable participant in the illegal abduction of her child. She has testified that Mark Sanders did not give up his parental rights to his child. There are no legal documents signed by April Morgan Sanders or Robert Mark Sanders, giving their child, Jessica Parker, up for adoption or for placement in a state-operated children's facility. Your Honor, it is April's desire to have Jessica Parker, Sunny, placed back into her custody along with her husband

and father of her child, Robert Mark Sanders. Your Honor, I petition for this court to honor that said request."

"So noted, Mr. Sanders. Mr. Vicks, you may question the witness."

Mr. Vicks took a stab at tearing April's story apart: first, that there never was a baby, it was a story she invented to help her new husband gain custody of Sunny. Secondly, he tried to prove April willingly gave her baby up so she could run back to her lover, Mark Sanders.

Jeff had to hold Mark back as Mr. Vicks unmercifully interrogated April.

"Wow, what an unbelievable story! You want this courtroom to believe your father forced you to give up your baby, his grandchild, and that this man, Lewis Richards, took your child from your arms and took her thousands of miles away to a children's home here in this county?"

"Yes," April cried, "it's true."

"You gave birth to a baby in your bedroom, unbelievable?" Jackson said sarcastically.

"Yes."

"Did you have prenatal care?" he intensely inquired.

"No, my father ..."

"Did a doctor deliver you?" Jackson shot out at her.

"No, a midwife did."

"What about a birth certification; do you have one?"

"No."

"Come on, Mrs. Sanders, isn't it true that if you had a baby at all, in your bedroom as a teenager, you willfully gave that baby up?"

"No, I loved my baby."

"Did you love Mark Sanders in high school?"

"Yes."

"Did he love you?"

"Yes."

"Did you tell him you were pregnant with his child?"

"No."

"Why not? If Mark loved you, as you said, why did you not tell him you were carrying his baby?"

"My father would have hurt him."

"That's right, your father did not approve of Mark Sanders. You said he would have killed Mark. I have a daughter. I would have said the same thing, given the same circumstances, but I would not have killed him, maybe made him wish that he was dead. But you actually believed your father would have carried through with his threats and killed Mark Sanders?"

"Yes, he would have ..."

Mr. Vick's tone rose; he had April flustered. "But yet you continued seeing Mark Sanders anyways, knowing your father hated him! Knowing your father would have killed him! You blatantly disregarded your father's threats and disobediently continued your relationship with Mark Sanders, behind your father's back! You were willing to risk Mark's life and have sex with him! But on the other hand, you were not willing to risk Mark's life and tell him he got you pregnant because your father would have killed him. Is that correct, Mrs. Sanders?"

"We were ... just friends ... we never dated alone. I never wanted Mark to ... to fall in love with me ... it just happened."

"You slept with your friend, resulting in a baby. You must have been alone with him or is that a lie?"

"No ... it just happened once ... we didn't plan..."

"Do you make a habit of sleeping with all your male 'friends,' April?" His accusing voice clearly made it appear as if she was some sort of lying tramp.

"No, I would never do that."

"You just testified Mark Sanders was your friend, and you never sleep with your male friends. But yet somehow, you got pregnant by Mark Sanders? A man you did not sleep with!"

"It was an accident ... we didn't mean for it to happen," she cried out. Tension filled the courtroom.

"Let's just assume you were pregnant. Mark Sanders was only eighteen years old and had a promising career ahead of him. College scouts and professional football teams were making him offers to play football. You were fully aware of the career path Mark planned to take with his life. Isn't that correct, Mrs. Sanders?"

"Yes."

"Surely, you knew a baby would have messed that all up for him. You were smart enough to know he would have chosen his football career over being a father to a child he did not want. Isn't that true?"

"I . . . I don't know . . . No, he would have done the right thing, if I told him."

"He would have been very angry if he found out you were pregnant. He would have blamed you for trying to mess up his life. Is that the real reason you did not tell him you were pregnant? Because the baby was an accident and you knew Mark Sanders would not want a baby messing up his career?"

"No, I was scared … I didn't know what to do."

"You never planned to keep the baby and wreck Mark's life. Therefore, you did not inform him about the baby because you were willingly going to give the baby up for adoption, hide the truth from him, and not wreck his life. Isn't that true?"

"No, I wanted to tell Mark. I wanted to keep our baby. I wanted us to be a family."

"Oh, really, a family? I believe you pretended to be pregnant on purpose. That way, you thought your father could not stop you from being with the man you loved because you were supposedly pregnant with his child. As you said, just so you could be a family. And then later on, after you had what you really wanted, Mark Sanders, you would have claimed a miscarriage. So then, is it not true, April, that you were never pregnant!"

"No, I was pregnant … it just happened."

"You didn't really want a baby! Did you, April! You wanted your lover, that man!" He pointed at Mark with a straight-arm and heatedly hollered out, "Mark Sanders! Your deceitful plan to lie to your father about being pregnant to trap Mark into a relationship with you backfired when you realized your father would kill Mark instead of letting you be with him! Isn't that the truth?" He screamed at her tormented face.

"No!" April cried out in anguish and Robert was immediately on his feet. Jeff grabbed Mark's arm and held firmly. The crowd was buzzing with contempt.

"Your Honor! Mr. Vicks is badgering Mrs. Sanders! His barbaric attitude is uncalled for!" Robert stormed angrily.

"Mr. Vicks, this is an informal hearing. Your brutal line of questioning is out of line. Continue your questioning in a more civilized manner."

Mr. Vicks gave the judge a discerning look but nodded his head in agreement. He gave Mark a calculating stare and grinned before he turned his attention on April. The harshness of his voice with April as he continued proved otherwise; he did not intend to show her any mercy.

"When you moved back here, did Mark Sanders still love you?"

"He did."

"Oh come now, April, that is a lie. Isn't it true Mark Sanders did not even remember who you were? In fact, the two of you had not seen or spoken to each other since high school. For six years, he had absolutely nothing to do with you. Isn't that true?"

"Yes, but …"

"Mark did not even remember you, but you were still madly in love with him. In fact you were obsessed with him, isn't that true?"

"I loved Mark, when he was ..."

"Thousands of women were in love with the NFL's most eligible bachelor, Mark Sanders. What made you think he would choose to love you over all of them – he didn't even know who you were?"

"I ... I ..."

"So you came up with a plan to win him. And what better way than to tell him he fathered a child with you six years ago. Was that your scheming plan to capture him?"

"No ... I didn't tell Mark the truth right away. Not until after I found out the truth about Sunny. By then, he had already fallen in love with me."

"Is it true Mark Sanders loved Sunny more than you?"

"At first, but then he fell in love with me." Tears continued to trickle down her distraught face.

"Mark planned on adopting Sunny, and he informed you that was his plan?"

"Yes, Sunny is everything to him."

"That is correct. Mark loves Sunny enough that he would do anything to get custody of her. Isn't that true?"

"Yes, but not what you are implying."

"So tell this court, why was Sunny removed from Mark's apartment?"

"I am not sure."

"Oh, come on now, Mrs. Sanders, isn't it true that Mark was a single male and in order to adopt Sunny he had to get married?"

April looked away, knowing where this question was leading.

"Answer the question, Mrs. Sanders, and remember you are under oath. Did Mark Sanders have to get married if he wanted to adopt Sunny?"

"Yes, but that is not why we got married."

"It is true! Mark Sanders had to get married to get what he wanted: Sunny! And conveniently for Mark, you loved him so desperately you were willing to marry him, even though he did not remember anything about you! You gave Mark what he wanted, Sunny, by agreeing to marry him! Isn't that true?" Mr. Vicks stormed.

"No, that's not what happened ..."

"You are correct; there is more to this story. This is all just one big scheme to give Mr. Sanders the child he found and wants to adopt! You made up this whole concocted story about having his child and claimed that child was none other than Sunny, so he would marry you. He gets Sunny and you get him in the deal, NFL Superstar, Mark Sanders, your lover from high school?"

"No, Sunny is my baby!" April covered her tear-swollen face in her hands. Mark quickly stood up angrily as Jeff held him back and advised him to sit back down.

"Your marriage is nothing more than a marriage of convenience to give Mark Sanders a child that does not belong to him or to you! Once this court gives Mark Sanders custody of Sunny, he will not need you! Will he, Mrs. Sanders! He'll have what he wants and he'll divorce you, isn't that the real truth? Jackson exploded at April as he leaned inches from her face.

"No . . ."

"Did Mark Sanders pay you to marry him so he could get custody of Jessica?" he howled out.

"Oh, God, how can you say that?" April burst out crying. Robert was back on his feet, and Mark was standing in the aisle with Jeff and Dan ready to help Mark tear Jackson Vicks to shreds. The entire courtroom was angrily protesting.

"That's a lie! I love my wife!" Mark screamed out as Robert grabbed the front of him and held him tight.

"Your Honor, those remarks of Mr. Vicks' were inappropriate, vindictive lies! I strongly oppose Mr. Vicks' conduct in this courtroom!" Robert protested, and then he quickly whispered in Mark's ear, to calm down. "Let me handle this, Mark." Mark took a step away from his father.

The judge was hammering his gavel against the wooden block on his bench, trying to restore order in the courtroom. The bailiff was standing in front of Mark, with his hands firmly against Mark's chest, pushing Mark backward.

"April, I am right here. I love you!"

"Everyone, please be seated, now! Or I will clear this courtroom! Mr. Vicks, there will be no more harassing the witnesses. Do I make myself clear, now continue!"

Mr. Vicks eyed Mark and gave him a manipulative grin. Dan and Jeff escorted Mark back to his seat. April was crying into a Kleenex.

"Your Honor, there is no proof April Sanders gave birth in her home. There is no birth certificate, no county records and no doctor visits. There was no baby born to April Sanders! Therefore, there would be no need for documentation of adoption papers signed by April Sander to give up her rights to her child."

Mark shook his head. He could not believe what he was hearing. April hid her face with her hands as Mr. Vicks continued.

"April Morgan is scheming with Mark Sanders to gain custody of this child we are referring to as Jessica Parker, as a replacement for the child we should be referring to as Jane Doe, because that child does not exist! Jessica Parker is not the child in this courtroom today."

April looked over at Mark. *Oh, Mark, how can this man tell such lies and get away with it?*

"Furthermore, if it were true April Morgan did give birth to a child, she discarded that child, knowing full well Mark Sanders had a promising career ahead of him, and he would not have sought to be a teenage father. April Morgan Sanders wanted Mark Sanders, not a baby. April Sanders has not established anything here today other than a fabrication of lies to gain custody of a child that does not belong to her or to Mark Sanders. I hereby petition this court to deny any future custody of said child, Jessica Parker, to Mrs. Sanders or Mr. Sanders. I am finished questioning Mrs. Sanders, she can step down."

Mark's face was pale, his breathing labored. Mr. Vicks had shot him right through his heart. Sunny was slipping through his fingers, and his heart was ripping apart.

Chapter Forty-Five

Haunting Courtroom Testimony

Mr. Vicks had destroyed April. It was up to Robert to turn it back around in their favor.

"Mr. Sanders, do you want to cross examine your witness?"

"Yes, your Honor." Robert stood up and gave April an encouraging smile to calm her down. April searched Mark's eyes and took a deep breath to consume her threatening tears.

"April, is everything you testified in this courtroom today the absolute truth?"

"Yes, Sunny is my child. Mark is her father. We love each other and want to be a family."

"April, how do you know Sunny is without a doubt your child?"

"I gave my baby the class ring Mark Sanders gave to me in high school. I wrote a letter to Jessica and hid it in her baby sweater just before she was taken away from me. Mark and I found that letter in a file at the children's home in a file under J.P. and Sunny had Mark's ring. I named my baby, Jessica Parker."

"Your Honor, I will provide testimony to support these findings later in this hearing. April, if Sunny were not your child, would you still desire for this court to grant you custody of her?"

"Yes, I loved Sunny before I knew she was my child. I did not use Sunny to win Mark's heart. Mark did not marry me to gain custody of Sunny. You have to believe that, your Honor. We both love Sunny, she is our daughter. Please find it in your heart to give her back to us," April wept as she spoke. Tears filled the courtroom.

Finally, April was finished. Mark stood up, gathered April in his arms, and led her out of the courtroom. Jeff followed behind them. Robert asked the judge for a brief recess.

Mark held April against his body and spoke comforting words to her heart as she continued to cry on his chest. Jeff brought them both a cup of water. April's hands were still trembling.

Debbie and Tammy stood watching Mark attentively calming April. As much as Tammy wanted to take her daughter in her own arms, Tammy let Mark comfort her. If only Paul could see for himself how much April loved Mark, Tammy thought, maybe Paul would change his mind and welcome Mark into their family.

Mark gently wiped away the tears from April's face. He held her face with his palms and looked deep into her eyes before he bent and kissed her.

"We will win this case, April. We have to have faith God will defeat our enemy." He took her hand and led her back into the courtroom.

Robert called Tammy to the stand. She testified April was pregnant before they moved to California. She explained that Paul was devastated and wanted to keep the pregnancy a secret. He wanted to give the baby up for adoption, but April was against it. When the tension in the household became too stressful, Paul sent her to Paris.

Mr. Vicks broke a pencil in two before standing up and facing Tammy. He paced back and forth in front of her, as if to intimidate her.

"Did you ever take your daughter, April Morgan, to a doctor to confirm she was indeed pregnant?"

"No, she took a home pregnancy test."

"Did you see the results of that test?"

"Well, no, April told us she was pregnant. I wanted to take her to a doctor but her father would not allow it."

"Why? Why would he deny his daughter medical attention? No father in his right mind would do that!"

"He did not want anyone to find out she was pregnant and … disgrace our family."

"Is it possible April lied to you about being pregnant?"

"She was telling us the truth, she was pregnant."

"Your daughter was pregnant; you must have wanted the father of her child to take responsibility for what he did to your daughter. Did April tell you who the father of her baby was?"

"April refused to tell us. My husband was very angry ... she was afraid."

"Surely, you knew it had to be her boyfriend, Mark Sanders, that got her pregnant?"

"We did not know she was dating Mark."

"Why not? Your daughter was apparently having sex with him. How could that happen and you were unaware she was seeing him?

"She never told us about Mark."

"I see, she never told you about Mark, hmmm. Then it was possible April was seeing other men behind her father's back as well, besides Mark Sanders. Isn't it likely any one of them could have been the father of her child and not Mark Sanders?

"Uh ... April was not allowed to date at the time. There were no other boys."

"She apparently lied about Mark, so who is to say she did not lie about seeing other boys, too. You just testified you knew nothing about her dating Mark. So it is possible then that she got pregnant by someone else other than Mark Sanders, and in order to trap Mark, she claimed it was his baby. Isn't that a real possibility, Mrs. Morgan?"

"No, she loved Mark."

"How do you know that! You just testified that you knew nothing about Mark Sanders?"

"Uh ... well ..."

"Your husband, Paul, disliked Mark. He even forbid April to see Mark, why?"

"My husband's dislike for Mark had nothing to do with Mark. Paul and Mark's father were business rivals."

"Romeo and Juliet. I get the picture. Father forbids daughter to see her lover. Another twist here. Did your daughter think if she were pregnant with Mark's child, her father would have to allow them to be together, so she lied about being pregnant in order to be with Mark?"

"No, April was pregnant. She refused to tell Paul the truth about the father of her child."

"You mean she lied to her father?" he yelled at her.

"Only to protect Mark!"

"So Paul Morgan takes his family, moves them across the country to hide the shame of his daughter's affair with a man he forbid her to see?"

"Yes."

"And then he sends you off on a holiday to Paris, right in the middle of all of this?"

311

"It was not like that."

"You left your pregnant daughter to go on vacation! What kind of mother would leave her pregnant daughter and go on vacation?"

"I had no choice; Paul sent me there."

"You went off to Paris because you knew April was not really pregnant?"

"No, I told you. Paul sent me away."

"Surely you planned to be back for the birth of your grandchild?"

"Yes, I planned to return. I wanted the baby."

"But you weren't at the birth, why?"

"Paul told me April miscarried the baby."

"You believed your husband was telling you the truth about the baby's death?"

"Yes, at the time ..."

"Your husband told you your grandchild was dead and you believed him?"

"Yes."

"Do you believe everything your husband tells you?"

"Uh, yes, but . . ."

"Did April tell you she had lost the baby?"

"No, we never talked about it, she ..."

"Unbelievable, your daughter was pregnant, you leave the country, she miscarried the baby and you never talked to her about it."

"She didn't tell me, because the baby was alive."

"Was there a baby when you returned home?"

"No ..."

"You want this court to believe your daughter had a baby somewhere out there, and for five years, she never mentioned her baby to you, her own mother! She let you believe the baby, your grandchild, was dead!"

"She ... she was afraid."

"Mrs. Sanders did not tell you about the baby, because there was no baby! She faked the pregnancy and she faked the miscarriage, isn't that the real truth?"

"No, she had a baby!"

"There is no way you could have known that. You were not there. And if she did have a baby, you just testified the baby she had was dead. That is what you believed to be true for five years! And low and behold, the baby is suddenly alive. How convenient for April!"

"I did not know the baby was alive. I just found out the truth." Tammy stood up and faced Mr. Vicks with a killer look.

"That will be all, Mrs. Morgan."

"But it is true! Sunny is my granddaughter. You are a mean man, Mr. Vicks!"

"I said, Mrs. Morgan, that will be all!" Vicks stormed at her, trying to shut her up.

"How dare you hurt this innocent couple and fill this courtroom with lies about them!"

The courtroom crowd agreed and voiced the same opinion and again the judge had to silence the courtroom. "Quiet! Quiet in this courtroom! Mrs. Morgan, please be seated."

"Your Honor, clearly none of Mrs. Morgan's story makes sense. If April Morgan was even pregnant, she clearly lost that baby. Mrs. Morgan just testified that April's child is dead! April is trying to replace that dead child with Sunny, to win favors with Mark Sanders. There are so many contorted twists to this whole story. But clearly, Jessica Parker, the child abandoned at the children's home is not the child of April Morgan."

He turned and glared at Mark. "And as for Mark Sanders, well, let us just say, he was just one of many men who could have fathered a child with April Morgan, if she had a child. April did not tell Mark Sanders she was pregnant with his child, because the truth is, the baby was not Mark Sanders' child!"

Gasps were heard. Jackson faced the judge. "No baby at all or a dead baby, or who knows who April's baby's father is, pick your choice, your Honor. I have no further questions for Mrs. Morgan. Furthermore, based on this information, I request that Jessica Parker is declared eligible for adoption by this court."

Robert realized questioning Tammy any further would make her story even more unbelievable. *Mr. Vicks has done a damaging job,* Robert thought, as he focused on regrouping.

April was devastated; her sorrow tore Mark straight down the center of his heart. Each breath he took hurt his chest. He whispered to Jeff that he could not catch his breath. Jeff stood up and tapped Robert on the back. When Robert turned around and saw Mark desperate for air, he knew.

"Your Honor, we need a recess!" Robert abruptly requested.

"Twenty minutes." The judge stood up and left his bench.

Then Robert discreetly assisted Jeff in taking Mark out of the courtroom into a room across the hall. April grabbed Dan's arm in a panic.

"Dan, we forgot Mark's emergency bag!"

"I have mine in the back of the limo; he's going to be fine, calm down." Dan went to get Mark the bag. *It was a good thing Dr. Stevenson prepared two bags.*

"Dad ... this hearing ... is not going too good ... I am going to ... lose Sunny." Mark gasped at air, as he struggled to catch his breath. Robert and April helped Mark to a chair. "I can't ... lose Sunny ... I can't."

"Mark, it's not over by a long shot. We are not walking out of this courthouse without your daughter; do you understand me?" Robert held Mark's shoulder as April took his hand and laid her head on his knee as she knelt beside him.

"Mark, remember what you told me. God is here fighting for us. He has to be ... here."

"He is, April. He is here . . . we will believe together.*" April is the half of me that makes me whole and now she claims my faith when I falter.* He took her in his arms and joined their hearts.

Dan returned with the emergency bag and took out the oxygen. He quickly placed the mask over Mark's face. He took his stethoscope and listened to Mark's heart. Jeff went to get Mark a glass of water. Dan took out a syringe and vial from his medical bag. He measured the dose.

"Mark, I am going to give you something to calm your heart down." He undid the buttons to Mark's dress shirt and injected the medication directly into Mark's central line. "You need to calm down, Mark, your heart is racing."

"I'm trying." Mark gently caressed April's hair to offer her comfort. Nothing more was said as they waited for Mark to recover.

Jeff returned with the water and Mark gladly drank it. Then Jeff handed Robert a large envelope with Robert's name on it. A cross was drawn under his name. Robert thought that was odd.

"The clerk said this was left on her desk by a man, and she asked me to give it to you."

Robert opened the large envelope, pulled out the paperwork, and scanned it. A miracle was in his hands. He looked at those waiting anxiously for an explanation.

"It's the documentation of April's home birth and a statement from the midwife that delivered April's baby. There is also a statement from the housekeeper stating Lewis Richards had taken the baby from April and left the house with the baby."

Mark cuddled April into his lap and they both cried. Then they all did what they should have done earlier, they joined hands and prayed. They knew God was there ready to fight their battle.

Robert took the documents and went to the judge's chambers to speak to him about the documents. They all prayed the judge would allow Robert to enter the documents into the hearing as evidence.

It was their only chance of winning this case.

If Mark lost Sunny, his life would be over.

Chapter Forty-Six

A Child's Wish

§§

Dan wanted Mark to wear a facemask, but Robert was concerned it would give Mr. Vicks leverage that Mark was too ill to obtain custody of Sunny. This whole hearing was not about Sunny. It was about Mr. Vicks defeating Mark Sanders and gaining publicity for his election campaign.

Robert had planned to call Mark to the witness stand next, but he decided Mark's heart was not up to the intolerable questioning of Mr. Vicks. Robert was not about to let Mr. Vicks cross-examine Mark. Doing so could cause his son to have a heart attack by infuriating him even more than he already was.

Instead, Robert asked the judge for permission to enter into evidence the documentations that would establish Jessica Parker was the biological child of April and Mark Sanders. The judge granted Robert permission.

Robert produced the documentations of the home birth and the statement from the woman who had delivered Sunny. He furnished the judge with the notarized memorandum from the housekeeper, stating April Morgan had given birth to a baby girl, and Lewis Richard as ordered by her father, Paul Morgan, forcefully took the baby from April.

To top it off, Robert provided undeniable proof Sunny's DNA was a match to both April and Mark Sanders.

Mr. Vicks made an objection to the documents. "There is no proof these documents are not fabrications. Mark Sanders could have paid these women for their statements!" He did not challenge the DNA test results. He did not want to bring additional attention to those results.

Although Lewis and Blanche Richards were the key to the transportation of Sunny from California to the children's home, they had not been located. They were up on kidnapping charges. The police record of the kidnapping was entered in as evidence. The kidnapping was proof Lewis and Blanche Richards were in some sort of conspiracy involving Sunny. Most likely, they planned to demand a ransom from the Sanders.

Robert pointed out that Lewis worked for Paul Morgan and it was his sister Blanche that ran the children's home. It was highly possible Lewis took Sunny to his sister's, with intentions of some kind of illegal plot for later on when Sunny was older, such as kidnapping Sunny and demanding money for her return from either the Morgan family or the Sanders family.

Mr. Vicks pointed out the distance between California and the children's home. How did Lewis bring a newborn baby all that way by himself, he asked the judge?

"We have no proof the child April gave birth to in California is the same child found here, hundreds of miles away. There could be two babies out there, one in California and one here."

Robert had wanted to subpoena Paul, but Mark wanted nothing to do with Paul right now. The incident at the church was still fresh in Mark's mind, something he had decided not to tell April. Mark had no way of knowing if Paul was ready to accept him as his son-in-law or kill him. He did not intend to tell April about the cross and falsely get her hopes up her father had opened his heart to their marriage.

Mark was fearful that if Paul testified he would lie and tell the court April had made up this whole story to give them custody of Sunny. He was afraid that Jackson Vicks was hired by Paul to take Sunny away from him. Would Jackson call Paul Morgan to testify against his own daughter?

Mark did not want April to have to confront her father about what he had done to her as a teenager, in a courtroom filled with people. Mark desperately prayed April was pregnant, and he did not want anything to upset her. Paul had already taken one baby from them. Mark vowed he would never allow Paul to hurt them again.

Robert called Sister Jessica Morton to the stand. She tightly linked her fingers together and fought to keep a straight face as she avoided looking in Mark's direction.

Sister Jessica told how she found Sunny in the basket at the children's home. She said she had been the one to call the police, not Blanche. She found April's note in Sunny's sweater and turned it over to the police officer.

"In the note, Jessica, tell the court what the baby's name was listed as."

"Jessica Parker."

"From that day on was the baby known as Jessica Parker?"

"Yes, Mrs. Wilson let her keep her real name."

Sister Jessica testified April was pregnant before April left for California. She said April told her Mark Sanders was the father of her child. She told the courtroom she had watched over Sunny for the last five years.

During the questioning, Mr. Vicks noted the likeness between April and Jessica. Either one of them could easily have been Sunny's mother. *Hmmmm.* Mr. Vicks was ready to reexamine her testimony.

"For five years then, you took care of Mark Sanders' child, and yet you never told him. Why?"

Jessica made direct eye contact with Mark as she sat quiet in a daze. She thought about the real reason she had not told Mark about his child. There was no way she could tell this courtroom of people of her deep seeded love for Mark.

"Jessica, answer the question. Why didn't you tell Mark Sanders you thought he had a child at the children's home?"

"Uh, because, Paul Morgan would have hurt him." Tears formed in her eyes.

"Isn't that what April told you? She put that false fear in you, to keep you quiet?"

"Yes . . . she told me that and I believed her story."

"Five years is a long time not to tell a man he fathered a child. With Mark's prestige in this community, surely he could have fought against Paul Morgan to claim his child if indeed he wanted his child. But you did not give him that chance. Why, Jessica? Did you believe Mark Sanders would not have wanted a baby at eighteen?"

"I ... I don't know."

"Or maybe you knew the child was not his. Other than April's word, you have no way of knowing who the father was, or if April was even pregnant, is that true? Is it possible April lied to you and she is lying to this court?"

"I am not sure, I mean, April told me she was pregnant and Mark was the father."

Mr. Vicks noted the attention Jessica was directing at Mark. Her longing sad eyes told him something was going on between Jessica and Mark, and he had a gut feeling he knew exactly what secret they shared.

319

"Jessica, you were caught at the front door of the children's home with the basket containing Jessica Parker in your hands. Is that true?"

"Yes, I was …"

"You dropped out of high school and became a nun. Is that true?"

"Yes, but …"

"Jessica, may I remind you that you are under oath. Is Jessica Parker your child and not the missing child of April Morgan?" The courtroom got very quiet.

Once again, Jessica looked at Mark and said nothing as tears fell from her eyes. *Sunflower is mine; I was the one who loved her, not April. She is my baby.*

"Jessica, please answer the question."

"No, she's not my child," Jessica answered quietly, as she wiped the tears from her eyes.

Jackson absorbed the obvious attention Jessica was giving Mark. One look at the stunned expression on Mark's face confirmed his next line of questions.

"Why are you crying, Jessica? Is it not true that you were the one pregnant, not April Morgan? That is why you dropped out of school and became a nun? It was you who was standing there holding your own baby in the basket when Katie opened the door. Is that the truth?"

"No."

"Isn't it true you and Mark Sanders conceived a child together, and that child is none other than Jessica Parker, your namesake?"

"No." She was in full tears now as Jackson hollered at her, trying to force the truth from her.

"April did not name the baby; you did! You placed that note in the baby sweater. April is covering up for you; by saying she was the one pregnant!" Mr. Vicks stormed at her, "and that is why you secretly raised Jessica. You hid her out at the children's home so no one would find out the truth!"

"Your Honor, I object to Mr. Vicks personal opinions and his leading questions!" Robert screamed out angrily.

"No … no, that's not true. Oh Lord, no, no, I am a nun!" Jessica covered her stream of tears with her hands.

"Your Honor, Mr. Vicks is clearly harassing this innocent young woman. I object to his line of questioning!" Robert appealed to the judge in a flurry.

"Your Honor, it has just become clear to this court that the biological mother of Jessica Parker is none other than Sister Jessica Morton, not April

Sanders! I demand a DNA test of Sister Jessica. I can assure you she will also match Jessica Parker!"

Again, the courtroom erupted and the judge had to bring back order.

Mark could not believe what he was hearing, and thoughts about that night at Carlo's cousin's house invaded his uncertain mind. What had happened while he was so drunk he could not even remember his own name the next morning when he woke up?

One thing he did know, the cheerleaders had all been there, and Jessica had been a cheerleader. Only April had been missing from the party. He had left her in the park alone after he and she had been together. That part of the night he did remember.

A few days ago, Christy told him she could not believe he had gotten so drunk at the party. Christy had said he and Jessica had gone off together, but she did not know what they had done or where they had gone, and neither did he.

Sister Jessica was the only one who held on to that secret. It had not been important to him until now, until Jackson Vicks put doubts in his mind about what he might have done.

April held strong to his hand, but this time he could not look her in the eyes, knowing it was possible he had betrayed her with another woman. He shook his head no and begged God with all his heart it was not true.

"Sister Jessica, what is your blood type?"

"O negative."

"Your Honor, Jessica Parker is also O negative."

Robert stood up and talked out of turn. "Your Honor, both Mark and April are O negative, their DNA matches perfectly to Jessica Parker, I already established that fact."

"So noted, Mr. Sanders, be seated."

"You have an O negative father, who shacks up with an O negative mother and bingo, you have Jessica Parker. But just which one of these women is the real biological mother?" Jackson questioned.

"What a coincidence that both women are O negative? Your honor, I demand a DNA test done on Jessica Morton immediately."

"So noted, continue with your questioning."

"Jessica Morton quits school after she finds out she is pregnant, and April Morgan moves to California because her father thinks she is pregnant. How convenient for Mark Sanders if he is indeed the father of both babies. We really don't know who fathered these children. April's baby dies, and Jessica disposes her baby at the children's home in a basket. She wrote the letter, not April Morgan. I believe Sister Jessica used April to cover up her own pregnancy. Tell this court, that is the truth, Jessica!"

"Your Honor, Mr. Vicks is out of line; this is all hearsay!" Robert shouted out before Jessica could answer.

The judge called a recess and took April and Jessica into his chambers and asked them to write certain words on a piece of paper.

Mark paced back and forth in the courtroom, still pondering the night at the party. Dan warned Mark to calm down before his heart stopped.

There is no doubt in my mind that Sunny is my child, by April. But is it possible that . . . no, it's not possible. It's just not possible. Mr. Vicks is playing with my head.

Tammy was overcome with a distressing thought back to that horrible wintry night when she had given birth to twin girls. She and Paul rushed to a country hospital because Paul's secretary, Monica Morton, had been in an awful accident with her husband, Roger.

By the time they got there, Roger had died and Monica was in premature labor with Jessica. Paul stayed with Monica during her labor while Tammy struggled with her own onset of labor. Then when things went terribly wrong and Tammy began bleeding heavily, Paul joined her. When Tammy woke up later, Paul had compassionately told her one of their babies had not survived.

"Mom, are you alright?" Debbie asked her, interrupting Tammy's uncertain thoughts about that night.

Monica lost her husband and Tammy lost her daughter, Allison. Because of that, Jessica held a special place in Tammy's heart. She and Paul thought of Jessica as the child they lost, April's twin sister. Tammy felt compassion for Jessica as Jackson Vicks tormented her.

April's letter in Sunny's file was compared to April and Jessica's handwriting. It was clearly April's handwriting that had written the letter, and of course, Mr. Vicks objected to that, saying Jessica was not writing normally because she did not want her secret exposed.

The judge had had enough at this point and turned to Jessica. "Young lady, you are still under oath. Is Jessica Parker your child?"

"No," she said tearfully.

"You can step down now."

The police report from the day Jessica was left at the children's home was entered in as evidence. Mrs. Wilson confirmed the note was the same one found the day Jessica was found at the children's home.

Mr. Vicks pointed out that the police mentioned no ring in their report.

Katie testified what she knew about Sunflower. She explained how she had found the class ring hidden in Sunflower's sweater and hid it. She explained how she looked in the yearbook and found out the initials M.S. on the ring could only belong to Mark Sanders. She told the judge Sunflower told Blanche Mark was her father and that was when Blanche took Sunflower away.

Mr. Vicks badgered Katie into saying Sister Jessica was holding the basket when she opened the door and Sister Jessica had a special bond with Sunflower more so than she did with the other children.

He contended that Mark could have given his ring to Sister Jessica and she was the one who hid it in the sweater.

Carlo took the stand and testified Mark gave his class ring to April the night of the championship football game in the park, and April and Mark had gone off on their own to, uh, be alone.

"Just because they were together does not mean they conceived a child, Your Honor. I believe April gave the ring to Jessica when she found out she was carrying Mark's child."

Robert said he had several other witnesses that would testify Mark gave the ring to April and she was seen wearing it on a chain around her neck before she moved to California. Judge Thompson said he had heard enough.

Dan remembered the ring around April's neck the night she said her final goodbyes to Mark in the hospital, before she moved away with her father the next day. He remembered his odd conversation with April.

I knew she was hiding something. She knew then she was pregnant. And that ring was on a chain around her neck the night of his motorcycle accident, too.

Mr. Vicks got up and told the judge Mark had violated the court's restraining order. He enlightened the judge that Mark should be doing jail time for his court ordered violations. He angrily pointed over at Mark.

"Mark Sanders thinks he is above the law! He is not suitable to raise a child!"

Robert spoke quickly in Mark's defense. "Your Honor, Mark did not take Sunny from the children's home or visit her there, as the restraining order warranted."

"Mark Sanders knew what the restraining order was referring to and he chose to ignore it!"

"Under the circumstances of Mark's illness, it was important Sunny spend time with Mark, and that is why Mark continued his relationship with Sunny before this hearing."

"Is Mark Sanders above the law?"

"Mark thought he was dying, and he wanted to spend as much time with Sunny as possible."

"Your Honor, that is garbage! What gives Mark Sanders the right to break the law? Just because he is an NFL player, he thinks he can disregard the laws to suit himself!"

"A court order was all that separated Mark from his child. I do not feel it was fair to punish Sunny by keeping her away from her father!" The crowd clapped their hands in approval.

"Your Honor, Mr. Sanders broke the law! He belongs in jail!"

"If April had been honest with Mark in the very beginning Mark would have raised Sunny from birth. Mark was not a willing participant in Sunny's placement at the children's home. Mark has been denied his rights as Sunny's biological father."

"I have heard enough. Mr. Vicks, do you have anything else to add to this hearing."

"Yes, your Honor. In fact, I want to point out that Mark Sanders has an illness that could cause his premature death, therefore not making him a suitable father."

"Your Honor . . ."

"Mark's got one foot in the grave! This child deserves to have a father to walk her down the aisle at her wedding, not one she's going to have to bury!"

Once again, he pointed at Mark. "All that man wants is a lab rat! He wants to take that girl's bone marrow, a very painful process I might add, and use experimental procedures on her to save his own skin." Then he sat down with a huff. The courtroom became extremely quiet. The only sound was April sobbing as she hid her face against Mark.

Robert was adamant Mark had an 80% chance of a normal life after he received his transplant from Sunny. "A person without an illness could die from an accident just as easily," Robert challenged. "No father or mother is guaranteed a lifetime with their child. Mark's illness is not a legal reason to deny Mark Sanders his child."

Robert established Mark's loving relationship with Sunny. He produced pictures of Mark and Sunny at the wedding. The final picture was of the three of them: Mark, April and Sunny, the perfect family, Robert called them.

Robert and Mr. Vicks battled back and forth, about why Mark should or should not be allowed to achieve custody of Sunny. Mark continued to pray for favor and held April's hand in his as the two lawyers battled their case before the judge.

Judge Thompson ordered Robert to bring Sunny back into the court-room. Julia led Sunny in the room. The judge asked for Sunny to take the stand. But when Robert took Sunny's hand, she refused to go up there. She tried to pull away from Robert and started crying.

"I don't want to go." Sunny was scared; she cried out for Mark. "I want my Daddy!" She reached her arms out for Mark to take her as Robert tried to hold her back.

"Dad dy … Dad dy … hold me!" she tearfully cried out for him. "I want my Daddy!" Her arms were reaching out as far as she could stretch them in Mark's direction. "Give me my Daddy!"

Mark stood up quickly and hurried to Sunny. She fell into his arms, wrapped her arms around his neck and cried.

"I want you to be my Daddy." April knelt with them and tried soothing Sunny's fears. Mark stood up with Sunny in his arms. "Please, Daddy, take me home," she cried, her face damp with tears. "Take me home …

Sunny had called him "daddy". That extraordinary word entered into Mark's heart and joy exploded, tears made their way down his cheeks as well. *I am her daddy.*

Mark pitifully looked straight at Judge Thompson with all the love he had in his heart for Sunny, as tears raced down the side of his face.

The entire room felt the compassion Mark had for this beautiful little girl. Many tears started falling as this touching, heart-wrenching scene took place. There was no doubt the child belonged with the man who held her in his arms, never wanting to let her go. The man she had called, daddy.

Judge Thompson ordered the three to step forward. Mark begged the judge with his desperate teary blue eyes to do the right thing. Mark's swollen throat made it hard for him to swallow the lump that had formed in the back of his throat. Nevertheless, his passion for this small child was evident in his tearful eyes.

"Sunny, I want you to look at me," the judge spoke softly to her. Sunny turned her dampened face towards him as she kept her grip tight around Mark's neck. Mark brushed her wet strands of hair away from her tear-swollen face as he walked closer to the judge, with April holding tight to his side.

Judge Thompson gave immediate attention to the blueness of their eyes. Sunny was the mirror image of Mark and April. The DNA test results were 99% conclusive Mark Sanders and April Morgan Sanders were inevitably Jessica Parkers' biological parents.

"Sunny, do you want to live with Mark Sanders and April Sanders for the rest of your life?" the judge asked her.

Sunny's face lit up and she shook her head yes and kissed Mark's cheek. She held her tiny hand out to April. "Yes, Sir, please may I live with my Daddy ... and April?" she begged with her whole little heart.

Judge Thompson smiled and winked at Sunny. "I have heard enough evidence today to support the claim that Jessica Parker is the biological child of April and Mark Sanders. Mark Sanders was denied his parental rights as the biological father. I believe April Sanders was forced to hand her child over to her father and she made every reasonable effort to locate her missing child."

"Therefore Jessica Parker is no longer eligible for adoption by this State. She is, however, still a ward of this State pending my decision to place her with her biological parents or to continue her care in a suitable foster home."

"Your Honor, Sir," Sunny interrupted and he stopped and smiled at her.

"What is it, Sunny?"

"That's too many words for me to understand. Can you get to the part where Mark is my new daddy? I want to go home."

The judge gave her a wide smile and laughed. "So be it. Jessica, Sunflower, Sunny, Parker is hereby ordered by this court, to live the rest of her adolescent days with her new parents, Mark Sanders and April Sanders, as Jessica Parker Sanders." He hit the gavel on the bench to make it final. Then he winked at Sunny. "Mark is your new daddy, Sunny."

"Yippee!" Sunny shouted with joy as she planted a wet kiss on Mark's teary cheek. She reached out to April with both hands and gave her a hug.

Everyone in the courtroom cheered, clapped, and hugged each other. No one was without tears. The three hugged each other through their tears of happiness. They would be a family. Julia and Robert joined them and their friends each came forward and congratulated them.

Mark looked in the back of the courtroom for Old Charlie. Instead, his eyes caught a man sitting in the back of the room, with a large oversize hat and sunglasses. The man promptly stood to leave the courtroom, but not before he removed his glasses and made direct eye contact with Mark. Once out of the courtroom the man made a quick phone call.

"Lewis, I want you to listen to me carefully. That nurse friend of yours, I need her to pull Mark Sanders' medical records ..."

Chapter Forty-Seven

Celebrating the Family

The family had a huge celebration at the ranch that morning to celebrate the addition of Sunny to the family. Robert and Steven grilled out by the pool for lunch as their family and friends gathered around the outdoor patio. Martha had made a huge cake for Sunny.

Mark and April shared the joy of having their little girl officially reunited with their families. They had a lot to be thankful for today. Everyone gather around Sunny as Mark placed a heartfelt blessing and divine protection over her life.

Rebecca seemed to have relaxed with Mark as she generously hugged him and planted kisses on his rosy cheeks, letting him know he was once again embedded in her heart. Even when Mark chased the boys around the pool, she smiled at him with approval.

Mark picked up four-year-old James Robert and pretended he was going to throw him in the pool. It was so good to see Mark full of life and acting his usual energetic self, everyone thought as they laughed at the squealing little boy, as Mark held James sideways over the water.

"Mark, put James down!" Steven protectively yelled over at him. His concern was not for his son, but for Mark and the incision that ran the length of his abdomen. "I am not stitching you back together today."

"Swing me again, Uncle Markie!" Mark tousled his hair and told him they would play later.

April frowned when Mark started tossing the football to six-year-old Brad. Mark was tossing it under handed at first but then he started tossing it over his shoulder. Brad was only about 10 yards from Mark, so April was not too concerned. She would keep a close watch on him, as she knew his mischievous mind all too well.

When Carlo saw Mark with the football, he ran out for a long pass. "Throw it to me, Mark!"

April held her breath as Mark threw the football over 25 yards right into Carlo's arms. "Touchdown!" Mark yelled out. "Great catch!"

April waited for Mark to scream out in pain, but he just smiled and raised his eyebrows cleverly to acknowledge his newest physical achievement since his illness. Carlo threw the ball back and Mark caught it with ease. "I'm back!" His grin widened. "Go forty, Carlo!" Mark waved for Carlo to go back further.

April jumped out of her seat as Mark held his arm up to throw the ball to Carlo. "Mark Sanders, don't you dare!" she screamed at him and captured the attention of all their guests.

Mark stopped abruptly and looked over at April's stern face. He looked back out at Carlo, as he held the ball up with the support of his other hand. He looked once more at April. This time the stern look on her face meant business. He smiled at her with a full-blown grin. Then he turned towards Carlo and Brad and he under handed it to Brad. Carlo gave Mark a wave goodbye as he headed in the direction of his car to go to the airport.

Mark looked over at April. She had her hands crossed over her chest and was frowning at him. Mark looked her square in the eyes with his sly eyes and came at her. She did not back down until he grabbed her around the neck and pulled her face to his for an engaging kiss.

"You are so bad, Mark." She loved him with her whole heart and the sweetness of her lips against his was proof of her love.

"Only you can get away with telling me what to do," he jokingly whispered into her ear and hugged her. He was such a tease and she loved every inch of him. She anticipated their next romantic time alone.

Julia wrapped her arm around Robert's waist as her attention focused on Mark and April. "It looks like April has Mark under control." Robert agreed with his wife. April would be Mark's angel on earth. Her love for him would see him through each day of their lives together.

Thomas came out to the pool with the cordless phone and handed it to Mark. Mark took it and said hello. "This is not over with!" The *unfamiliar* voice angrily said and then there was a sharp click.

Mark stood puzzled, but before he could give much thought to the strange message, Sunny was pulling on his shirt and pointing towards the driveway. Sister Jessica and Katie were walking toward them. "Come see my cake!" Sunny pulled Katie's hand and they ran off in the direction of the food table.

"Thank you for inviting us. After what happened in the courtroom, I was not sure if you would ever want to see me again," Jessica said to April, yet she looked up at Mark as she spoke.

Mark had a perplexed look on his face as he made eye contact with Jessica. He was pondering a thought; one he was not quite sure how to handle.

"You did nothing wrong; it was not your fault, Sister Jessica. That awful lawyer was searching for something against Mark and he used you to try to get it. We are so sorry you had to go through that." April hugged Jessica and received another unexpected cold hug in return.

"I appreciate your kindness," she said softly.

April and Mark had discussed the change in Jessica since her last visit to the hospital. Sharon told them that Jessica left high school, took her GED, and then she took administrative classes at the college while she was at the convent. She left the convent to take a job at the local Catholic Church to help Father Paul O'Hare in his office. She volunteered at the children's home in her spare time.

"Sit down, Jessica, beside me. I want you to tell me all about Sunny's childhood," April said with a heart ready to accept Sunny as her baby Jessica. Mark felt his chest tightening as he worried about April's emotional state, not sure if April was ready to resign herself to the missing years of their daughter's life without them.

Sister Jessica sat down beside April and began talking about the cute things Sunny did growing up. Mark stood behind April's lounge chair and listened to all they had missed as parents. He gently placed his hand on April's shoulder to offer support.

Sunny interrupted the conversation just as April dabbed her first tears. Sunny wanted to introduce Sister Jessica to all her new cousins. "Ok, Sunny, let's go meet everyone." Jessica stood up, once again her eyes settled on Mark and then she went with Sunny. Mark slid into Jessica's chair, took April's hand in his, and wrapped their fingers together.

"We can't get back what we have lost, April. We need to focus on our future with Sunny." She melted in his warm understanding eyes. He leaned over and kissed her. She knew she could count on Mark to be strong for her and get her through this transitional time in their lives.

While Mark was in the hospital, Pastor Evan told them they had to accept without regret or bitterness all of the things they missed when Sunny was a baby and instead concentrate on all the new things they would share in Sunny's life that would bring them joy.

Pastor Evan felt April needed to call Sunny by her given name, Jessica. April had to train her brain and heart that Jessica was Sunny.

Mark felt it was not fair to Sunny to make her become someone she had never been. They planned to take Sunny to their next meeting with Pastor Evan and listen to how Sunny felt.

Sister Jessica came back with a glowing Sunny. She climbed in Mark's lap and hugged him. "I love you, Daddy," she whispered into his ear and kissed his cheek. He gladly returned her kiss, as he looked into her mother's tearful eyes and gave her a wink.

Sister Jessica stood silent as she witnessed the love the family had for each other. Mark noticed Sister Jessica's reserved look and wondered why she looked so detached.

Then Mark looked deep into Sister Jessica's blue eyes as she focused on him. He looked over into April's eyes. The two women shared an uncanny likeness, the same eyes, same color of hair, and the same smile.

"I really have to go. Sunny, I am so happy for you," Sister Jessica spoke and Mark added the same voice to his list of things the two women shared in common.

Mark stood up and faced Jessica. It was time for some answers to the questions that troubled his mind.

Chapter Forty-Eight

A Forbidden Love

§§

"Sister Jessica, do you like horses?" Mark questioned.

"Oh, yes, very much."

"April, I am going to take Sister Jessica down to the stable to see our horses."

"I want to come, too," Sunny stated with bouncing excitement.

Mark knelt down to her. "Sunny, this is your party. You need to talk to everyone and thank them for coming. Why don't you start with Uncle Jeff."

"Oh, all right." She ran off with Katie following her.

Mark gave April a kiss on her forehead. "We'll be right back. I love you." She touched his face with her hand.

"I love you, too, honey."

Mark led Sister Jessica to the stable. It was a quiet walk, a time Mark used to reflect on what he was going to say. When they went into the stable, Mark gently grasped her arm and calmly spoke to her.

"Jessica, I want you to come clean and tell me what you did not tell everyone in the courtroom today." He caught her off guard. She turned away and pulled her arm away from him. His eyes appeared painfully sincere in wanting a truthful answer from her.

"You lied to me on Christmas Eve. You completely turned white when you saw me walk in that church with Sunny. I want to know why; what are you hiding?"

"Mark, don't do this, please," she pleaded in a soft shaky voice as her eyes watered, knowing she could never reveal to Mark her true feelings for him.

"I'm a pretty good judge of character, Jessica. Your eyes give you away when you look at me. You are in love with me."

He might as well have crushed her lungs, because the room was spinning and she felt faint. He took a hold of her again, to prevent her from falling. But this time she did not resist him. Instead, she wrapped her arms around his waist and hugged him as she laid her head against his firm chest. Mark's arms dropped instantly to his sides in response to her indiscreet affection.

"Oh, Mark, I did love you, a long time ago, back in high school." She was crying now as she let him go, aware of his opposition to her holding onto him. Feeling embarrassed and awkward, she dropped her chin to her chest as she cried softly.

Her tears gained Mark's instant compassion for her, and he gently lifted her chin so their eyes met. He softly wiped away her tears with the palms of his hands. *Her tears are somehow my fault*, he thought in despair. Their lips were close enough for a kiss but Mark resisted her impulsive advance to kiss his lips in this vulnerable moment. Mark lifted his face away from hers.

"Did I love you back, Jessica, before my accident? Is there something I do not remember about you and me?" Mark sincerely asked in a serene voice that melted her heart.

Mark had always been the perfect gentleman, which was one of his special traits that had attracted her to him back in high school.

She let him go, looked into his innocent uncertain eyes, and gave him the answer he was desperately seeking. "No, Mark. You loved April. You never even noticed me. You only saw April after she walked into your life, and you forgot all about me. I, and every other girl in the school that fantasized over you, became nothing more than a blur in your eyes, when April Morgan came into your life."

"But you told me that night in the church that we danced together at my birthday party, that we were friends. Now I know you were at Carlo's party the night I was so drunk. And Mr. Vicks, what he said in the courtroom today, got me thinking about what might have happened that night between you and me?"

His eyes held a tormenting stare; their meaning was all too clear. He wanted to know if he had betrayed April with her.

Had Jessica's intense love for me brought us together that night while I was so drunk? he feared after he had left the courtroom today. *Was it possible Jessica pretended to be April? Christy told me I had called*

Jessica, April. In my drunken state of mind, it could have been possible I mixed up the two women. Is it possible I have a child with Jessica, too? He still could not remember anything about the party or that night. Jessica was the only one who could tell him the truth.

"Mark, you may have danced with me, but your distressed eyes were searching the room for her. It was April you wanted in your arms, not me. You were faithfully devoted to her. Mark, you did nothing dishonorable at the party with me. I do not know you, like you know April, if you know what I mean." Tears once again escaped her eyes.

Mark knew what she was sensitively trying to say. He had not been with her. He looked released of his torment. Yet questions still flooded his mind.

"Why did you become a nun?" his voice tender with her, noting the pain this distressing conversation was causing her. She was relieved he did not press her for more information about the party.

"Because you were lost to me forever when April told me she was pregnant with your child. I knew then, there was no future for you and me. I dropped out of school when it became too painful to see you at school and not have you love me back."

"I am sorry, Jessica. I don't know what to say."

"I've only loved two people in my life, you and God. I could not have you, not after you had been with another woman, so I chose God." Mark heard the bitterness in her pained voice as she poured her heart out to him.

"I love God, Mark, I really do. But I am not completely over you even though you hurt me. I have truly tried to stop loving you, but it is impossible, and seeing you with April, it hurts."

"And Sunny, did you keep your secret about her all these years to punish me for not loving you back?"

"Not you, Mark. It was April I wanted to punish. She had taken you away from me, when she slept with you. When I found Sunny that day in the basket, I knew Sunny belonged to you. I secretly had a part of you. I had your baby and I loved her, Mark, with all my heart, as if she was ours. I thought about telling you when you found Sunny. But you would have run back to April, and I did not want to lose Sunny or you. Oh, Mark, you have to forgive me."

"You wanted us to be a family, you, me, and Sunny?" he questioned her as his mind tried to absorb her story.

"Yes, Mark, but not as husband and wife. No, I belong to God now. But together we could have raised Sunny. I thought if you adopted Sunny, then I would have to be a part of your life, because Sunny loves me. I have been her mother, not April."

"And April, what about her?"

"I never thought she would come back here. I thought she would go on with her life after she gave Sunny up to the children's home. She had everything growing up. I was just the child of her *father's secretary*. I did not have the big house, the fancy birthday parties, or a devoted father. I was jealous of her. I know that was wrong of me, but ever since we were little, she got what she wanted. I even had to share the same birthday with her. My Dad died the night we were both born. So I guess her parents took pity on me. My mother insisted I be April's friend because she worked for her father, Paul."

"Jessica, that was not April's fault. Her father gave her many things but he never gave her what she needed most, his love. I know; I grew up with her, too. She begged for her father's attention, and he never gave it to her."

"But Paul was always so good to her at the parties I went to, her car, her clothes. I got her hand me downs, not that I needed them. My mother was well paid at her job with April's dad. But I was nowhere near her royal standards. She was the princess, and I was her understudy."

"It was all just a show, the perfect businessman, husband, father; it was all just a lie. Jessica, April was never a snob, in fact, she was very shy, and she thought she was your friend. She told me she treated you like her sister. Why did you really dislike her?"

"April was like my sister when we were little, but she always wanted to go out to the ranch and be with you. You took her away from me. Then when you two went off to private schools, I was left here alone. When you came back to high school, I fell in love with you. But April ruined any hope I had with you when she came back. She got you and I wanted you."

"I am sorry if I hurt you in anyway, but you cannot blame April because I fell in love with her. Jessica, that was God's plan; we just obeyed it. I love April and I thank God everyday that she is my wife. I will never love anyone like I love April. *Every beat of my heart belongs to her.*"

Mark touched his heart with his fist as he sincerely tried to make Jessica understand, there would never be another woman in his life and that included her.

Jessica's eyes watered. "And Sunny, she's like my child, Mark. Please don't take her away from me."

"That will never happen, I promise you. Sunny loves you, and as long as you can find it in your heart to let go of your resentment toward April, I will make sure you can continue seeing Sunny."

"I am praying daily for God to release me of my sins, my thoughts of you, and to help me let go of you. You have to believe me, Mark."

"Jessica, I want you to understand. Just because I am allowing you to see Sunny. I am not a part of your relationship with Sunny. After today, you and I will never be alone together. You and Sunny can be together, but I am not a part of that equation. Satan can have no stronghold over us, do you understand?"

Mark was firm. Jessica was too vulnerable with her feelings for him. He definitely would not put them into any compromising situation that would lead her to believe he had any feelings for her. He would not allow her to use Sunny to have a relationship with him.

"And April, what will you tell her?"

"The truth; April and I will always be truthful with each other. You and I have done nothing wrong. She will understand your love for me, and she will understand your heart's desire to continue loving Sunny. There is no reason the two of you cannot become good friends again."

"Mark, you are being very generous."

"I love God, too, Jessica. I am so proud of you that you have chosen to devote your life to serving Him. But are you sure you did it for the right reasons?"

"I admit God was my second choice, but now, God means everything to me. Even if I knew ... I could have you, I would still choose Him." *Maybe I could honor those words, if I tried harder,* she thought, as she felt dizzy.

"I'm glad. God is so much worthier than me, Jessica. I wish you the best in your service to Him."

Jessica fell forward, as if she was about to faint. Mark quickly grabbed her with both hands and held her.

"Jessica, are you alright?" She was pale.

Jessica caught her breath. "I am fine. I gave blood a few days ago, and I am still feeling kind of weak." He led her to a trunk and helped her sit down.

"Is there anything I can do for you, a glass of water?"

"No, I will be fine. You can help me with something else. I have been asked to take over the children's home. Now with Blanche gone, the girls have all been displaced, and I want to bring them back together again. I would be honored if you and April would help me make that possible."

"The children's home was Sunny's home for five years; those girls are like her sisters. I'll tell you what, you bring them home, and I will get my accountant, Suzy, to meet with you this week. Whatever you need financially, don't hesitate to ask me for it."

"Thank you, Mark." She wiped a tear. She would find comfort in diverting her attention away from the man she so admired. He would always own a special corner of her heart.

Sister Jessica would continue her work for God by providing love for the girls in the children's home as their new administrator. Father Paul O'Hare would have to find a replacement at the rectory, someone that would volunteer to help her at the children's home. She had just the young nun in mind, Sister Charlotte.

Mark took his wallet out and pulled out a business card. "This is Suzy's number; give her a call. She will be more than happy to help you with the accounts at the home."

"Thanks, Mark."

Jessica asked Mark to pray for her mother, who had been in an awful car accident. He joined hands with her, and together they prayed for the healing of her mother.

"Lord, Mark and I come together to ask You for the healing of my mother, Monica." Mark had heard that name somewhere before, but his thought returned to the prayer.

"You promised us that if two or more come together in Your Holy name, You will honor us. Thank You, Lord, that Sunny is home where she belongs, with Mark and April. Bless this family as they start a journey together to honor You in all they do. Amen." Sister Jessica and Mark shared a goodbye hug that day in the stables, one neither would forget.

During Mark's walk back to the house, he thought about Monica Morton, Jessica's mother, and realized he was the one who had saved Jessica's mother in the ER. For some strange reason, he remembered that her mother's blood type was A+. *That's odd; Jessica is O negative. That must mean her father was O negative.*

Jessica donated her blood to her mother and it is possible she could donate blood to me, Mark thought with mixed emotions. *I wonder if she realizes that? Was she tested to be bone marrow match for me? Surely, she would have. And how odd is it that Jessica and April are both O negative?* He added that to the list of things the two women had in common.

By three o'clock, everyone had gone home. Mark helped Martha and Maria clean up around the pool. They thanked him kindly with kisses to his cheeks. Sunny and April went inside to take a nap. April wanted Mark to join them, but he said he wanted to go down to the stable and visit with Charlie for a while. He claimed he was feeling great and insisted she take a nap without him.

April was concerned Mark had already overexerted himself. She had seen Jeff take Mark aside for a private conversation, and then the two of them disappeared for about fifteen minutes.

After Mark finished cleaning up, he went down by the old barn, with a bottle of water and the football in tow. *The cat is asleep, and the mouse is going to play,* he smiled at himself, thinking he was about to pull one over on April. He was going to give the old tire swing and football a good work out.

His life as a quarterback had started with this old tire swing when his father had punished him for falling in the mineshaft. He planned to resume his life as a quarterback, and once again, he would use this tire swing to prove to himself that his goal was obtainable.

His mind was working overtime thinking about the trip tomorrow to California. How do you spell Super Bowl? Each time he threw the ball through the center of the tire, he called out a letter. S – U – P – E – R, it took him 10 throws to spell Super Bowl.

Mark was cleverly smiling to himself. It had been 3 weeks since he fractured his ribs and 12 days since his surgery. By Sunday, he would feel even better. It might just be possible for him to play in the Super Bowl. Well, maybe not really, but it sure was worth thinking about. A miracle could happen between now and then. He was after all a "Mighty man of God."

He thought of Ms. Carolyn Taylor, from his church, and he smiled. "Yes, Ms. Taylor, I am a mighty man of God. That I do believe."

When April woke up, Mark was nowhere to be found in the house. In a panic, she hurried down to the stable to see if he was still with Charlie.

Charlie was busy cleaning a stall. When he saw April, he smiled and pointed to Thunder's stall. April went over to Thunder's stall and looked over the door.

Thunder was lying in the hay with Mark resting against him. Both were sound asleep. What a touching sight, the man and his horse. April smiled warmly. She loved Mark so much whether he was the man or the little boy trapped in a man's body.

She rubbed her tummy and prayed for a baby boy, just like Mark. "Oh, please, God, give us a baby."

Then April went to Mark and gently touched his shoulder to wake him up. He sleepily opened his eyes, but once he saw April kneeling over him in the hay, he quickly grinned. He was wide-awake and had a grin on his face.

Chapter Forty-Nine

Flying High

§§

Early Friday morning, April handed Mark his medication bag and a bottle of water. Mark took the bag and bottle, went into the bathroom and closed the door.

April turned around puzzled and looked at the closed door. Mark never closed the door to the bathroom when it was just the two of them, she thought baffled. She started to go to the door to see what he was doing behind that closed door. Knowing Mark all too well, she knew he might just be up to no good.

Sunny knocked on the bedroom door and came bouncing in the room with excitement. April turned around to see what Sunny wanted as she jumped up on the bed next to the suitcases. "I am ready, let's go!"

Mark came out of the bathroom, grabbed Sunny up into his arms, and asked her if she was ready to go to California and have some real fun. Her bright smile and giggles were the exact answer he was seeking. Mark ran his fingers through her silky hair and kissed her forehead.

"I love you so much, Sunny. I knew the minute I met you that you belonged right here in my heart." He placed her tiny hand on his chest over his heart.

The new Sanders' family boarded the family jet along with Jeff and Ashley, Julia and Robert, Rebecca and Steven and their children, James Robert and Brad. Debbie, Phil, and their boys also came along. Jeffery was four and Michael was two.

April had gotten permission from Mrs. Wilson to take Katie to California. She wanted this to be a real treat for Sunny. Hopefully, Sunny would spend time with Katie and let Mark get some rest between the activities Mark planned for them.

Dan brought along Faye Wilson as his guest. Mark arranged for Faye and Dan to have a romantic time by themselves while he took the kids to Disneyland. Dan was not the only one who could play matchmaker. Mark had plenty of surprises for the two of them up his sleeve.

If Mark's illness had any purpose, it was bringing those he loved closer to each other and having them realize the value of their time together. Life was a precious gift from God. Each moment of each day was very important to Mark, and he was not wasting one minute of it feeling sorry for himself.

Before the AFC Championship Game, Mark rented an entire floor of a hotel for three days in anticipation that his team would be playing in the Super Bowl, and he would be taking his family there to watch him play.

He never said anything to anyone about the rooms, just in case something did happen to him in the AFC Championship Game. After his spleen ruptured and it looked like he would miss going to the Super Bowl, he remained quiet about the rooms, not wanting to disappoint his family or have them feeling sorry for him.

Mark's team was staying two floors below. The players and the media still had no clue Mark was going to be there. Mark even kept his plans secret from Carlo. This way the media would leave his family alone while he spent time with them.

Mark had the team's schedule for the week, but he did not plan to join them in any of their practices. He planned to devote his attention to his family until Sunday just before the beginning of the game.

While Sunny played with the boys and Katie on the plane, Mark and April laid on top of the comforter on the bed in the bedroom suite of the plane. Mark had to stay on oxygen during the flight, and they rested together in each other's arms peacefully.

Tomorrow would mark their second week of marriage, another miracle celebration of their life together. Mark planned to make it very romantic for the woman he loved. He was very thankful for the blessings God continued to send his way. April was the best blessing of all.

As the rest of the group on the plane were busy keeping the children entertained, no one seemed to noticed how much Dan and Faye were enjoying talking to each other as if they were the only ones on the plane.

For many years, they had worked at the same hospital and attended the same church together, but the thought of their close friendship advancing to another level just never occurred to them. That was until Mark had gotten involved and made them see each other as more than special friends.

Dan finally realized the love of his life had been right there in front of him all these years. Faye had gone through some of the most trying times of his life with him. He depended on her friendship, and he was sure he had provided her with a shoulder to lean on throughout their years as friends.

Mark's matchmaking had been successful. Dan realized he needed to sever his apron strings with the Sanders' family and move on to begin his own family. He could not wait for the plane to land so he could be alone with Faye and tell her how he truly felt about their newfound relationship.

April fell asleep, but Mark lay restless with thoughts that invaded his mind. He struggled with what he was going to do about the game on Sunday. This was the Super Bowl after all. He had dreamed of playing in the Super Bowl his entire life, and he had risked his life to get his team to this game. It did not seem fair to walk away from what should have been his. He restlessly continued to contemplate his decision.

He rubbed his sore stitches. They quickly reminded him of all he had suffered by playing in the AFC Championship Game. If he had it to do all over again, he knew he would have played in that game.

It was not a matter of what he wanted to do at the time. It was a decision that involved his loyalty to his team. Being their quarterback was a job he had been paid well to perform. They had needed him, at that critical time in the game, to be their quarterback. There had been no other choice for him to make. The decision to play had been made for him when some crazy person poisoned his teammates.

He had tried to call in sick that day, but unfortunately, his game plans changed when Kevin became too sick to play. This left Mark with a job to do and he did it. It was just that simple or was it? Some viewed Mark as a hero, while others criticized him. There was a huge debate going on within the National Football Organization. Had he recklessly endangered his life, or had he sacrificed his life for the benefit of the team?

Mark's agent, Charlie Ryan, was fearful Mark could be suspended or put on probation. Charlie and Robert were meeting with the commissioner of football on Mark's behalf after the Super Bowl game.

Mark had another big decision to make and so little time to make it. He had called and talked to his coach about the game. It still might be possible for him to play; however, the coach made him no promises.

On Saturday, Mark's name would be removed from the ineligible list and put on the active roster, opening the door for the opportunity to play.

However, he knew it was more of a courtesy that he was being taken off the list.

Mark heard the reality of his playing time in his coach's despondent voice. There was not much of a chance he would see any playing time.

Mark frowned in disappointment of the whole emotional situation. His feelings were not solely based on the fact he might not get to play. His feelings stemmed from the fact that his situation was causing everyone so much stress about whether he should play or not. His sitting out this game was not a relief to his family. It was seen more as a letdown to what should have been for him.

The pressure was on Kevin Brown. All media attention was focused on the underdog quarterback. Mark had spoken to Kevin on the phone several times and encouraged him to stay clear of the media.

"You have to focus on the job ahead of you, Kevin. Don't let the media attention play with your head. Don't let them compare the two of us and take away your self-confidence. You have a great team behind you. All you have to do is believe in yourself, and the team will do the rest. I was not a one-man team; it was all of us players that got us to this game. Get yourself right with God and listen to the tapes I sent over to you."

Mark had a great passion for the game and his teammates, but he had an even greater passion for his new life, which included the only woman he had ever loved, and the sweetest little girl in the whole world. A wide smile crossed his face with that thought.

Mark moved closer to April and placed his hand on her belly. He was looking forward to finding out if she was pregnant. He had missed her being pregnant with Sunny, and he did not intend to miss this pregnancy or the birth of his next child. "God, please let April be pregnant."

He wanted this baby far more than any playing time in this up coming Super Bowl game, and if he could trade a Super Bowl ring for a baby, he would be at the front of the line ready to make that trade. That is just how much he wanted this baby.

His first time with April had given them Sunny and his second time with her ... *oh, please, God, let us have conceived a child on our wedding night.* Mark knew that was the only night it possibly could have happened for them.

He remembered his lecture with Sunny weeks ago when he first met her, "God does not make deals, Sunny. God has a plan for you and he knows what is best."

As it turned out, God did have a plan for Sunny and for him. Mark quickly gave thanks for that plan; it turned out better than he could have ever dreamed. God gave him April and Sunny, doubling his blessings. "Ok, God, put the icing on the cake for me; let April be pregnant."

His hand retraced her belly and he prayed deep within his heart that underneath his hand was the child they had created together in the richness of their love for each other.

Mark started thinking about the thrilled look Sunny would have on her little face when she finally got to meet her favorite Disney character, Tigger, at Disneyland. Mark laughed; he had never been to Disneyland as a child, and so he wanted to meet Tigger as much as Sunny.

His deepest desire was to make this a weekend Sunny would never forget, because no one knew how his transplant would go when they got back home. Nothing would spoil this trip. He was determined to make that happen, at all cost.

At last the plane landed. Sunny was so excited she could not wait to get off the plane to start having fun with her new daddy. And as for her new daddy, well, he was ecstatic and ready to live his life to the fullest with the family God had blessed him with, yesterday, today, and tomorrow.

Chapter Fifty

Surprises All Around Us

ॐ

They took two limos to the hotel. Mark got all the hotel keys and handed them out. Everyone went to their rooms to freshen up and unpack their things.

Julia and Faye stopped to look at the outfits in the hotel dress shop while Robert and Dan went up to their rooms. When the women went upstairs, they agreed to meet later to have dinner together as a group.

April and Mark unpacked a few of the clothes that needed to be put on hangers. April handed Mark his medication bag and reminded him it was past time to take them. He took the bag into the bathroom and closed the door.

Sunny was bouncing around the room like Tigger and telling everyone to hurry up. Mark came out of the bathroom. They got the girls together and went out the door. Rebecca and her family met them in the lobby. Debbie, Phil, and their boys were already there.

Faye went into her room. She looked around at all the beautiful flower arrangements that graced the room. It was very romantic. *Mark must have done it*, she smiled, *he is so thoughtful.*

Strangely, she thought she heard water running in the bathroom and opened the door to investigate. Just as she did, Dan came out of the door wrapped in a towel. She let out a frightened gasp before realizing it was Dan.

The two looked at each other and smiled, knowing the culprit who set them up. At the same time, they said it. "Mark!" Both shook their head in agreement.

"Will Mark stop at nothing to put the two of us together?" Dan shook his head and grinned. He went over to the table and held up two tickets for several of California's most romantic sightseeing places. Mark set them up for a weekend of romance.

"Mark's mind must have been working overtime planning this room mix up. I will be sure to speak to him about that." Dan humored Faye, but right now, he felt like a schoolboy caught with his girl behind the shed.

Faye nervously stood there. Dan looked down at his towel. "I will be right back." *Mark Sanders ... I am going to ...* But Dan couldn't help but grin at the thought of his mischievous son. *What's not to like about Mark, hmmmm.*

Faye sat down on the couch and tried to catch her breath. *Mark is nothing but a romantic*, she thought. *No wonder his heart beats too fast.* She felt her flushed face. *I'll just have to give him a great big hug when I see him*, she thought with a blushful smile.

When Dan came into the room, he sat down beside her. He looked her in the eyes and exposed how his heart truly felt. He told her he was sorry it had taken him so long to realize how much he cared for her. "I want to be with you, Faye, for the rest of his life."

Faye looked into his eyes warmly and told him it was about time he realized the two of them belonged together. "I almost gave up hope on you."

Dan gently took her in his arms and kissed her. Then he got down on one knee, took her hand in his and looked into her dark brown eyes.

"Faye, I love you with everything I am, will you marry me?"

Faye was not expecting a proposal. She took a slow breath, smiled at him, and told him, "Yes." They embraced and sealed it with a kiss.

Faye would make Dan's life complete, just the way Mark prayed she would. Life was too short, and Dan took Mark's lead and popped the question spontaneously. There was no doubt that Dan's best man would be Mark.

Meanwhile Mark was having the time of his life with April, Sunny, and Katie at Disneyland. It was everything he thought it would be for Sunny. She was laughing and having the time of her life.

He knew right then what he had to do about the game. However, he would worry about that later; he wanted to meet Tigger.

When Mark took Sunny and Katie on the kiddy rollercoaster ride, April refused to go with them. She sat down on a bench to watch. A group of young children and adults walked by her. They all had on matching shirts, which read, Make-A-Wish Foundation. Her heart sunk to her stomach as she thought of Mark.

She tried not to cry but the tears softly fell as she thought how close she had come to losing Mark. She wiped the tears away and prayed this would not be Mark's last wish.

Then a thought came to her. If Mark did have one last wish, would it be to play in the Super Bowl? Suddenly her heart wanted him to have that moment, a moment that belonged to him. She wanted Mark to complete his dream on Sunday.

When Mark, Sunny, and Katie came off the rollercoaster, they were laughing and ran to her. April quickly fell into Mark's arms and hugged him, never wanting to let him free from her arms.

Mark noticed her red eyes and knew she had been crying but he said nothing. Something had triggered her tears, and it probably had to do with him, he thought with guilt.

"Mark Sanders, I love you." She affectionately kissed him. Mark held her closer and returned the kiss much to Sunny's delight. April was standing in front of one of the world's biggest storybook castles and she was his princess. That he made perfectly clear to all those that passed by them.

When they sat down for a late lunch, April caught Mark rubbing his back and moving uneasily in his chair. He drank an entire bottle of water. She knew he needed to go back to the hotel and rest. They had been out in the sun too long.

She looked at her watch to see if it was time for his medications. Dr. Stevenson would have a fit if he knew Mark was at Disneyland without his facemask on and that he was not taking his medications on time. April thought anxiously as a group of dads and their children gathered around him wanting an autograph. Any one of them could have a cold Mark could catch and end up with a life-threatening illness.

Earlier, Mark informed her that the mask would remind Sunny he was sick, and it would spoil her fun with him. He wanted them to forget he was sick; this weekend was about living, nothing else. This was his special time to be with all his family and friends he loved, and he planned to celebrate this time with them to the fullest. That was the end of their conversation on the facemask.

"Let's go have some fun."

With all the children in this amusement park, there was a high chance Mark could get an infection. That thought sent chills down her spine. It was time to take Mark back to the safety of their hotel room.

When April told Mark it was time they all went back to the hotel, he shook his head and told her he was having too much fun. Sunny agreed heartily with him, and they were off for more excitement before April could protest. Mark held Sunny's hand as they skipped down the sidewalk to the next ride.

April and Katie had a hard time keeping up with them. Mark never let on how much pain he was in, but April was watching him carefully and saw his strained facial expressions when he thought no one was looking.

Mark acted like a child and was having a blast. Sunny glowed with her love for him. Sunny's laughter reminded April she should trust God. This trip was just what Mark needed; April finally realized, as she lightened up and laughed at the two of them. No medicine could fill his heart with the kind of love Sunny had for her father.

When they got back to the hotel, there was a message on their phone. When Mark pressed play, Dan's stern voice said, "Mark Sanders, I need to speak to you, right now!" Mark grinned and chuckled a few times aloud; he knew what Dan wanted.

April looked Mark straight in the face and questioned his mischievous grin that indisputably told her that he had done something under-handed to poor Dan. Mark continued to smile and said he would be right back.

She heard him laughing in the hallway. *Mark Sanders, what have you done now,* she wondered, as she joined him in an unavoidable laugh.

Mark hesitantly knocked on the door to Dan's room or was it Faye's room; he smiled wide and chuckled. Dan opened the door and saw Mark standing there grinning. Mark desperately tried hard not to laugh. Dan pulled Mark in by the front of his shirt and closed the door. Then Dan embraced Mark and thanked him for the mix up.

Mark was overjoyed when Dan and Faye told him the fantastic news of their upcoming engagement. Mark went over to the flower arrangement, removed a silk bag, and handed it to Dan with a smile. Dan felt the ring inside the bag and looked at Mark with such admiration.

Mark whispered, "I had Teresa find out her ring size, and **Main Street Jewelry and Gifts** shipped the order here to the hotel, you know, just in case you might need it."

"Thanks, son."

They warmly embraced each other. Mark was his son. If ever a man could have a son, his son was Mark. Tears filled Dan's eyes as they stared at each other. Mark smiled in agreement, and then he turned and humbly left the room.

Mark leaned back against the wall in the hallway and thanked God for Dan. Life was about loving the friends God had put in his path. Dan owned a big part of Mark's heart long before Mark overheard his mother talking to Dan about their night together twenty-five years ago. If things had been different, he would have been Dan's son, and that would have been just fine with him.

Dan told Faye that if they married she would be inheriting Mark as a son. That could be a scary thought sometimes, he warned her with a full smile.

Faye was more than willing to include Mark in her new family. She would be proud to have Mark as a son. Mark was the kind of son every parent would treasure, she told Dan and he agreed.

At five o'clock, the entire group had dinner in the fine dining room. Mark was cutting up with everyone, making sure they were having a good time. It felt so good to have all his family and friends around him.

April noticed Mark did all the talking but ate nothing but a few bites of his roll. She noticed he had his water glass refilled five times during the meal. *Why is Mark drinking so much water?*

When they finished eating, Katie, Rebecca, and Debbie took the kids swimming. The other women decided to go to the mall to do some shopping. Mark gave April his credit card and told her to buy something for everyone.

Just like Mark, he spared no expense to make sure everyone was having a great time. His kiss on her lips was priceless, as he winked at her to let her know there was more to come when she got back, something the credit card could not buy.

Mark was right, he was going to take pleasure in everything there was to enjoy in life.

Chapter Fifty-One

Unable to Escape

§§

Jeff, Steven, Phil, Robert, and Dan kidnapped Mark and took him out for some masculine fun. It was his belated bachelor party, and he was at their mercy as they entered the western establishment where there was plenty of clean-cut entertainment.

They were having a great time laughing and enjoying the scenery. Mark was thankful for all these great guys surrounding him as they sat at a round table. In this moment of fellowshipping, he was able to forget he was supposed to be sick. Being out in the sunshine today had tanned his face and smoothed his stress lines on his forehead, so other than his loose fitting jeans he looked in perfect health.

Jeff got up, toasted Mark with his soft drink, and made Mark laugh. None of the men were drinking alcohol. They were just overly happy to be celebrating Mark's life and his marriage to April. Mark's bright smile was what this evening was all about, a time to relax and enjoy life with special friends.

Mark jokingly commented on Jeff's bachelorhood, as an inviting woman, dressed as an eighteen hundred's saloon barmaid, made appealing passes at Jeff and wrapped a purple-feathered boa around his neck.

"Go for her, Jeff," Mark teased and they all laughed at Jeff's willingness to play along. She made her way to Mark and he held up his hands to playfully refuse her advancements.

"Sorry, but I am taken," he grinned and they all laughed as she claimed Mark's cheek for a kiss.

"The cowboy's been out of his saddle too long." Jeff made Mark laugh again, and when he did, Mark inhaled the soda bubbles up his nose. Mark sneezed hard several times and started coughing. The blood vessels in his nose ruptured and his nose poured blood.

Mark quickly grabbed up a cloth napkin and held it to his nose. The men quickly tried to assist him.

"Hold on, Mark, we are going to help you," Dan reassured Mark, not believing the shocking situation as it unfolded.

Mark's blood quickly soaked through the napkin and started seeping through his fingers. With his low platelet count, it was possible his blood would not clot and he could bleed to death.

Taking control of the urgent situation, Steven asked the waiter to get him their first aid kit. Dan held Mark's head in his hands as Jeff replaced the first blood soaked napkin with another one.

Mark was trying to pinch the soft tissue of his nose together. He was struggling breathing out of his mouth.

Jeff looked at his watch to keep time as Mark held his nose shut. After 5 minutes, Jeff told Mark to release his nose. When Mark let go, the blood continued to pour out, running down his chin and dripping onto his shirt and jeans. Mark bent over the table, got the water pitcher, and spit up blood into it.

It was clear Mark was swallowing blood and he was sick to his stomach. Mark was sweating and pale, no longer was he the picture of health. He was unable to escape the illness that had ownership of his body at this time.

Steven told the men to grab Mark under his arms and get him on the floor. Robert hurriedly knelt on the floor, and the men swiftly positioned Mark so he was leaning back against Robert in a sitting position. Mark's weak ashen face bobbled forward as he passed out on them, just as Steven feared Mark would.

Dan firmly held Mark's head up so Mark would not drown in his own blood. Steven knew the bleed was posterior, and he needed to act quickly to stop the flow of blood. Steven asked if anyone had nose spray. He was handed nose spray. He squirted the spray into Mark's nose and held pressure on his nose for 10 minutes, as the others seemed to hold their breath waiting anxiously for the bleeding to stop.

Steven told the waiter to get him a bag of ice and towels. He did a second squirt of nose spray into Mark's nose. Jeff applied the ice to Mark's nose and cheeks. Robert and Phil protected Mark from the onlookers.

Mark slowly came to but he was disoriented as he looked around at his surroundings and gathered his uncertain thoughts about what was happening to him.

Mark thought the guys had gone crazy, holding him on the floor and putting ice on his face. He knocked Jeff's hand away from his face.

"What do you think you guys are doing to me?" he asked. The last thing he remembered was a woman with a purple boa, wrapping it around Jeff's neck.

The guys all looked at each other. Mark tried to stand up but was unsteady on his feet. Robert and Dan grabbed his arms and helped him to a chair.

"Did you guys put something in my drink?" he accused them. He was feeling lightheaded and nauseated.

"Mark, you had a bloody nose. You lost a lot of blood. We need to get you to the hospital, stat," Dan said. Now Mark knew they were crazy.

"First, I can't have sex on my honeymoon, and now you want me to spend my bachelor party in the hospital. Will you guys get a life and leave mine alone."

Mark looked down at his shirt and saw all the blood covering it. When he saw the bloody tablecloths lying on the table in front of him, he knew they were telling him the truth. His desolate situation sunk in with a devastating force.

Suddenly, the nauseating blood churning in his stomach made him extremely sick and he stood up in a panic. The blood drained from Mark's face as the nausea grabbed him and sent his head spinning.

Jeff and Dan grabbed Mark under his arms and rushed him to the bathroom, just in time before the besieging wave hit him.

Steven told Phil to have the chauffeur bring the limo to the back of the restaurant. Steven joined Jeff and Dan to help take care of Mark.

Jeff swiftly grabbed Mark's jacket off the back of his chair as they were leaving the building. Jeff did not notice the *objects* that fell out of the pocket of Mark's jacket onto the floor.

The next stop was the hospital. They pulled the limo up to the ER sliding glass doors and helped Mark out of the car. Jeff rushed inside and got a wheelchair. They helped Mark slide into the chair and rushed inside.

"We need some help here!" Jeff shouted.

When the nurse saw all the blood covering the front of Mark's shirt, she thought he had been shot. She immediately told them to follow her to the trauma room.

"Get him on the stretcher, fellows. Was he shot?" she asked Jeff.

"No, he had a bloody nose. He's lost a lot of blood."

"I can see that. Let's get him undressed."

Jeff reached under Mark's arm and helped him stand up. Dan grabbed his other arm and they helped him up on the stretcher. Mark was dazed from the loss of blood as he surrendered to the situation he could not avoid.

An overzealous intern came in the room and witnessed the men standing there by Mark, helping him take off his bloody shirt and jeans.

"What's going on in here? Who are all these men?" the intern asked the nurse who was assisting Dan and Jeff. She handed Jeff a hospital gown for Mark.

The intern looked over at Mark. "Oh, man, is that Mark Sanders?"

"Yes, now get your attending in here, stat!" Dan instructed him impatiently. "Get a blood draw for a CBC," Dan instructed the nurse who had taken charge of Mark's care.

"And you are, who?" the intern asked Dan arrogantly.

"Do you not understand English, kid! Dr. Morgan asked you to get your attending, now do it!" Phil told the intern with firm eyes. "You tell anyone that Mark Sanders is in this hospital, and I will personally wrap your stethoscope around your arrogant neck."

The intern turned white as he stared in Phil's annoyed face. "You're, you're, Phil, Phil Johnson, the pitcher for…"

"Jason," Phil took the intern's nametag in his hand, "Get your attending in here now!"

"Yes, sir, right away. Oh man, Mark Sanders and Phil Johnson are in our ER," Jason muttered as he left. Two other nurses rushed into the room to assist.

The first nurse touched Mark's shoulder and lifted his left arm up, taking note of the medical alert bracelet around his wrist. "Hello, Mark, my name is Kaley. I am going to take blood, and Blair will hook you up to the monitors, as Kathy takes your vitals."

Mark turned over on his side, his legs bent at his knees. His pale face indicated he was feeling nauseated. Steven picked up a plastic container and held it for him. Mark leaned on his elbow as he threw up more blood into the container.

The attending came in and focused his attention on Mark. "Good evening, gentlemen. I am the ER attending, Dr. Cody Lawton. What is going on with our patient?" He watched Mark vomit. Kathy wrote Mark's vitals down and handed Dr. Lawton Mark's chart.

Dan extended his hand out and the two men shook hands. "I am Dr. Dan Morgan, chief of staff at our hospital. This is Dr. Steven Martin, surgical fellow; Dr. Jeff Kirkland, resident; Robert Sanders, Mark's father; Phil

356

Johnson, Mark's brother-in-law. Your patient is Dr. Mark Sanders. Mark has severe aplastic anemia and just suffered a posterior nose bleed."

Mark laid back down as the nurses were attending to him. The loss of blood had left him too weak to protest the attention he was receiving.

"I've heard all about Mark Sanders. In fact, I have tickets for the game Sunday. Mark, it is an honor to meet you in person." Cody shook hands with Mark, who was wishing he was anywhere but in this hospital.

Dan exchanged Mark's medical information with Cody and they began immediate treatment. They pumped out Mark's stomach, gave him a unit of blood, a unit of platelets, IV fluids, and placed him on oxygen.

Cody wanted to admit Mark because his blood counts were low, and he wanted to run other tests once he discovered Mark had a low-grade fever. Mark protested and refused to let Cody do any more tests. He just wanted the blood and set free.

Dan and Jeff promised Cody they would take care of Mark as soon as the transfusions were completed.

At first, Cody could not believe these three doctors would allow Mark to be released from the hospital in his condition. Dan took Cody aside and explained everything Mark had already been through in the past few weeks and all Mark had coming up once they returned home.

Dan told Cody that Mark needed to spend as much quality time with his daughter as he could in case his transplant was not successful. Staying in the hospital while they were in California would not provide Mark the precious time he needed to be with his daughter, Dan argued.

"Mark is on borrowed time," Dan stuttered with a downcast face. No one had dared to say those words before, but they all knew the words were the truth.

Dan looked over at Mark on the gurney and was thankful Mark had fallen asleep. They would let him sleep for the remaining three hours they were there, while the blood dripped into his central line.

"I've followed Mark's dreadful situation. I cannot imagine how degrading this illness has been for Mark. He is in the prime of his life, a promising surgeon, NFL quarterback who has led his team to the Super Bowl, married less than a month, and a father, and now aplastic anemia threatens to take all of that away from him. It is unimaginable. How does he handle it?"

"Mark is strong-willed, pulling strength deep from within his soul to survive. Not for himself, he lives for all of us. His unselfish love for his family and friends helps him fight through all the unpleasant aspects of aplastic anemia that holds his body hostage." Tears swelled in Dan's eyes as he poured out his soul to Cody, who gained new respect for the young man lying helplessly on the stretcher sleeping.

"Dan, we have an excellent bone marrow team here at this hospital. Is there anything we can do for Mark? We would be honored to assist Mark in his treatments."

"Thank you, Cody. I will have Dr. Stevenson give you a call, and he can compare notes with your staff here. But honestly, I doubt there is any treatment we can offer Mark if his transplant is not successful. He is in God's hands, and that is exactly how Mark has always wanted it to be."

The other men had gathered in the waiting room and were watching the late night sports show on the countdown to the Super Bowl Game. They looked at each other with sadness knowing there was no physical way Mark would be strong enough to play in the game.

"I don't understand! This is maddening!" Phil fumed as he paced the floor below the TV where Mark was now the main subject of the sports show. "None of this makes any sense! What are we doing here? Mark should be off with his teammates tonight, not stuck in this darn hospital!"

Phil's words were the unsaid thoughts of the others, who were also wondering why Mark could not have just one day without a reminder that his life was being held hostage, with no escape of his impending bondage any time soon.

"How are we are going to face Sunday? The biggest day of Mark's life, and he is going to be sitting on the stupid bench? It would be like me missing the World Series." No one had any answers to give Phil. He would just have to wait for Mark to show them all how he would deal with his unattainable lifetime dream.

Robert went to the mall and bought Mark a new shirt and a pair of jeans. He saw Julia and April and had to duck into a rack of clothes so they would not see him.

Mark made them all swear they would not tell anyone what happened. It was almost one a.m. when Mark finally slid in bed beside April. She turned over and sleepily kissed his cheek. He took a deep breath, thankful she did not want more from him, as he gathered her in his arms and held her as she drifted off to sleep.

His disturbing thoughts of what had just happened to him consumed his troubled mind as he laid there beside the woman he loved. He swallowed hard. His promise to be honest with April would be impossible to keep. Not if the truth caused her heart to ache for him.

From this moment on, he vowed his main goal in his life would be to bring sunshine into her life, at any cost. He would freely do it for her with all of his heart. She was the answer to his prayers, and for as long as he lived, he would love her with *every beat of his heart.*

Chapter Fifty-Two

Looking Over the Horizon

§§

The next day everyone did his or her own things. Mark and April entertained the girls at Sea World. Jeff and Ashley joined them. Jeff was keeping a close eye on Mark, knowing as his blood levels dropped again, Mark would become weaker and Jeff did not want a repeat of last night.

However, Mark seemed to have more energy than he'd had in a long time. It was hard to tell if Mark was one of the kids or one of the adults. He never stopped smiling the entire day. True to his form, Mark made sure everyone was having a great time.

April stood with Ashley as Mark and Jeff ducked into the men's room and were gone for over fifteen minutes. Mark claimed a long line. Ashley laughed, "You men don't know what a long line is, try the ladies' room sometime."

After they got back to the hotel, Mark insisted he take Sunny and Katie swimming while April took a quick nap. He smiled as he reminded her that she was taking a nap for two. April prayed she was carrying the precious child Mark so desired in his heart.

When they got to the pool, they were the only ones there. "Look at me, Daddy, I am swimming," Sunny proudly announced as she let go of the side and flopped around in the shallow water. Mark anxiously watched her. Katie was jumping off the diving board. Mark felt tired and his eyes became heavy, as he watched the girls. He lay down on a lounge chair.

"Sunny, stay in the shallow end, ok?" he warned her, not sure how well she could swim. *I really don't know much about my own child.*

"Ok, Daddy," she waved at him. As hard as Mark tried to keep his eyes open to watch her, he found himself drifting off. He would jerk back awake and quickly search for her.

When he opened his eyes, he noticed that a man had joined them across the pool. He had on a wide hat and sunglasses. He held a magazine in his hands as he sat down on one of the chairs and faced the girls.

Mark eyed him, and then he eyed Sunny. A feeling of protectiveness came over him, and he moved his lounge chair closer to the shallow end.

"Sunny, stay where I can see you," he told her as he forced himself to keep his eyes open.

"Ok, Daddy. Are you watching me swim?"

"You are doing great. Kick your feet. That's it. Come back to shallow end. You are drifting out too far."

"Look at me! I'm doing it."

After awhile, Katie came up to him, hobbling on one leg, the other leg bleeding.

"Mark, I cut my knee." Mark looked around and saw a first-aid kit against the wall by the bathrooms. He picked her up, carried her over to the wall, took down the kit, and searched for a band-aid.

"That should do it, Katie. I'll put another one on when we go upstairs." He turned to tell Sunny they needed to go. His face turned pale as he searched the pool area. Sunny was gone! A quick search revealed the man was gone, too. Mark grabbed at his chest, as his heart began pounding.

"Sunny!" he screamed in terror. "Sunny!" He ran to the edge of the pool as his heart raced. *Oh, God, please don't let her be at the bottom of the pool.* He reached the edge and frantically searched the bottom of the pool. Sunny was not there. His next thought, the man. *The man took her!* "Oh, God, help me, help me find her!"

He turned around in slow motion, his head spinning. His teary eyes caught movement near the towel hut. "Sunny!" She turned around and waved at him. He rushed to her; his feet must have flown across the floor in his hurry to snatch her up in his arms, because he could not remember touching the ground.

"Sunny, don't ever do that again!"

"What, Daddy, what did I do?"

It was four o'clock when Mark returned with the girls to the room. He failed to mention his scare with Sunny. April swiftly put the girls in the shower. She got them dressed for dinner, while Mark went to take his shower.

Mark told April to go ahead and take the girls downstairs while he finished dressing; he would join them in a few minutes.

Once Mark was alone, he reached in his jean jacket and removed the new bottle of pain pills he had gotten at the hospital the night before. He opened the bottle, took two of them out, and popped them into his mouth as he grabbed his water bottle and took a drink to wash them down.

He rubbed his hand across his bare back and groaned as he bent down to pick up his slacks on the bed. He fell forward on the bed and cuddled his legs up to his chest in a fetal position, and there he prayed God would give him just a few more days with his family.

When the family met for dinner downstairs at five, Mark was missing. The emptiness of his chair was unsettling to those sitting around the table waiting for Mark to join them.

April waited a few minutes and then she excused herself and went to see what was taking Mark so long.

Everyone was concerned as the room fell silent. The men in particular exchanged discerning looks with each other. Jeff started to stand up to follow April, but Dan gently touched his arm and motioned for him to sit back down.

April rushed upstairs and there she found Mark asleep on the bed, his slacks beside him. She stood over him as her heart poured out to him.

"Oh, Mark, I love you so much. I could never live without you, never. You take my breath away when you love me like you do. If only we could have forever … Mark. If I did not have you in my life, I would have nothing. So don't give up. Fight for us, Mark, fight."

She covered him up with a blanket, and then she kissed her fingers and gently touched his forehead with her moist fingers. She went back downstairs to tell everyone he was sleeping.

The adults ate quietly. They knew Mark had been overexerting himself for everyone else's benefit. They knew Mark was giving them *one more moment in time* with him. April's heart was upstairs; all those that noticed her silence and read her forlorn face, felt compassion for her.

Rebecca generously asked April if Sunny and Katie could spend the night in their room with the boys. April hesitantly agreed; although, she was not sure how Mark would feel about that. He was very protective of his time with Sunny. If the girls were out of their room tonight, maybe Mark would continue to sleep and get the rest he needed. With that thought, she agreed to let Rebecca take the girls off her hands for the night.

Everyone agreed Mark would want them to go out that evening to do fun things rather than to sit around at the hotel moping. April refused to leave Mark alone in their room.

Dan and Faye offered to stay with him. They were both tired and said they could use a night off. April finally agreed to go with Debbie and Rebecca, to take the children to see a movie.

Dan and Faye took April's hotel key and went upstairs. Dan looked in on Mark and found him still asleep on the bed. Phil was right. This whole situation was unimaginable. Nothing had turned out as Mark had planned it when he had first been drafted into the NFL.

Dan joined Faye on the couch, and they watched TV, keeping the volume down in case Mark woke up and needed them.

At seven o'clock, Mark appeared in the doorway to the living room. He leaned against the frame of the door and looked awful. "Where's April and Sunny?" he weakly asked.

Dan jumped up and quickly went to him. Mark was sweating, flushed, and lightheaded. Dan helped him back to the bed. Faye got a washcloth and wiped Mark's face off with cool water.

Dan went to get his medical bag out of his room. When Dan returned Mark was back asleep. Dan listened to Mark's heart and lungs, took his blood pressure, pulse, and his temperature.

Dan knew Mark had an infection somewhere in his body. He went into the bathroom and went through Mark's medicine bag. He read the instruction list Dr. Stevenson had given Mark. It did not take Dan long to figure out that Mark had missed several doses of some of his medications and he had increased the dose of some of the preventive antibiotics. Deep concern washed over his face.

Dan would have to increase the strength of Mark's antibiotics and give them by injections in order to fight the infection Mark was developing. Dan called the hotel doctor and asked him to call in three particular antibiotics and a medication for Mark's fever.

He thought about forcing Mark to take his other medicines, but decided against it, taking only the Benadryl into Mark's bedroom. He would need the Benadryl once Dan gave him the injections.

Half an hour later, the doctor came to the room with the vials and the syringes. Dan injected one of the medications directly into Mark's catheter. The other two he gave to Mark in his hip. Then he covered him up with just the sheet. Dan sat down in a sofa chair next to the bed and silently prayed.

An hour later, Mark was awake and his fever was down. Dan chewed him out for not taking all his medications.

Mark lied and claimed he had only missed a few of them. "If I take the meds, then I have to take the Benadryl and the other meds, and I can't stay awake if I take all of them."

Mark begged Dan not to tell April what he had done with his meds. "I don't want to spoil this trip for her."

Dan reluctantly agreed but only if Mark came to him to get the injections of the antibiotics during the night and in the morning.

"I can't trust you, Mark. You have to take these antibiotics, if you want to fight this infection you have."

Dan was preaching to the doctor, who was feeling more like a five year old. Mark had no choice but to give in. He hated it that he had lost Dan's trust in him. He may have lost Dan's trust but the love between them was as strong as ever.

Faye came in with a tray of soft foods. "I ordered up some food for Mark." She sat on the bed beside him as Dan stood over him. Mark rubbed his forehead with his hand in frustration and shook his head back and forth.

"I can't eat, really, I just can't," Mark admitted to Dan with weak eyes. "My stomach is so messed up. Everything goes straight through me when I eat."

"Mark, you have to eat something."

"I'm starving, but I can't eat, Dan, not here, not now. We only have one more day, and then we will be home. I just have to make it through one more day."

However, from the desperation in Mark's voice, Dan knew that one more day was entirely too far away. Mark needed to be back in the hospital getting IV infusions.

Faye got up with the tray and put it on the dresser. While the group had feasted on their luscious meals, Mark had been starving himself, afraid of being sick.

Dan shook his head but he gave in to Mark's reluctance to eat. Dan now understood just how profound Mark's sacrifice was to make sure they were all having a grand time while he silently suffered.

"At least you have been drinking water."

"I'm trying hard not to get dehydrated." Mark looked away, knowing he could not tell Dan anymore than that without risking another quick trip to the hospital.

"Mark, you look exhausted. You have to slow down." He sat on Mark's bed beside him.

"Dan, I can't slow down. I only have one day at a time to live, and I want to live each day to the fullest with Sunny and April." He tearfully leaned forward and let Dan take him in his arms for an embrace.

Dan's heart ripped in two. He could not make it better for Mark. He reflected on the many scraped knees he had put a band-aid on for Mark as a child, but this time, a band-aid would not fix his problem.

Faye shed tears as she watched the two men share in this emotional moment. Dan's love and desire to protect Mark was touching. Dan was as much or more than a father to Mark, than Robert. She understood the depth of Dan's relationship with Mark.

Dan understood Mark's need to bring joy to them all. He just hoped Mark would not risk his life to accomplish that task.

Why couldn't this trip have been uneventful? Mark deserved to have three days to enjoy his life with his family without being sick.

Mark had never admitted it to anyone there was a strong possibility he might not recover. Although Mark did not say it tonight, Dan read into Mark's discouraging eyes and knew the reality of aplastic anemia was revealing itself to Mark. *Mark is finally accepting he is a very sick young man.*

Just when Dan conceded to his despairing thoughts, Mark wiped back his tears and smiled. "I haven't given in, Dan, I am not sick. I am just tired of the devil messing with me. So stop worrying about me and go cuddle up on the couch with Faye and do what I wish I was doing with April right now."

As a familiar grin formed on Mark's face, Dan found a new fondness to Mark's mischievous thoughts. Dan gave Mark a wink and went to find Faye, just to make Mark happy. But Dan left his heart in Mark's bedroom, with him.

When Dan came back ten minutes later, Mark was peacefully sleeping. Dan gently placed his hand on Mark's forehead. His fever was gone. A tear slid down Dan's cheek. "Thank you, God. Thank you for healing my son."

When April came in later, Dan and Faye were cuddled on the couch asleep. *Mark must be proud of himself*, she thought as she admired the couple wrapped in each other's arms and smiled.

She gently woke them up. "Ok, you two lovebirds, it's time to go."

Her smile disappeared the minute Dan looked into her face. She knew something was wrong. His superficial smile and compassionate hug confirmed her suspicions.

"What's wrong with Mark?"

"He's sleeping comfortably."

When Dan saw her worried expression, he knew he had to break his promise to Mark and tell her the truth.

"Mark had a fever. He is better now." He chose not to tell her Mark was not taking his medications because of Sunny and her.

"I knew it! He never should have gone to Disneyland with all those kids!" she responded as if she were a guilty parent who had just put her child in danger.

"April, this is not your fault. Mark knew the risks and he chose to ignore them. You cannot put Mark in a glass house; you know that, sweetheart. Mark needs to live his life to the fullest. You have to stop trying to protect him and let him make his own choices. Mark acts from his heart ... he does what he feels is best."

Dan's words gave her little comfort. She knew what Dan was really trying to say to her. Mark had risked his life for Sunny and for her.

"Mark needs another dose of his meds at midnight, four a.m. and at eight a.m.." He gave April the vials out of his pocket. He told her what she needed to give Mark.

"In twenty-four hours, he'll be fine, so stop worrying, and go be with him." Faye and Dan each gave her a supportive hug before they left for *their separate rooms.*

April undressed and lay down beside Mark and cuddled him to her. He would always be her endless love. She held him close in her arms to keep herself warm.

She closed her eyes and thought about that magnificent snowy night when they had gotten married in the park. That night was a fairytale Mark had made come true for them. Mark, her gallant prince, the father of her child, had made her magical promises, and on nights like tonight, she would still believe in those promises.

With that thought secure, she kissed his lips like Snow White and was rewarded briefly by his twinkling eyes upon her face before they both drifted off into a land of enchanting dreams.

Chapter Fifty-Three

A Dream or Living Life

§♭

S unday morning, everyone met downstairs for breakfast and started discussing the big game. Everyone was still curious as to what Mark would do. They impatiently waited for Mark and April to come down.

Mark got up to take a shower. He saw the vials of medications and the used disposable syringes in a plastic water bottle on the bathroom counter. He knew April or Dan must have continued his medications during the night while he slept. He felt his forehead for a fever and quickly took some Tylenol.

April came into the bathroom; she wrapped her arms around his bare waist. He jerked slightly in pain from her tight squeeze. He bent and kissed the back of her neck, hoping she had not noticed his discomfort. "Good morning, sweetheart. I love you."

"I love you too, honey. How are you feeling?"

"I'm fine. I'm about to show you just how great I feel." He teased her with his touches.

"Dan told me you were running a fever last night. He asked me to keep up with your injections during the night," she told him as she invited him to kiss her awaiting lips.

He gladly bent his head to meet the softness of her lips and satisfied her with the fullness of his mouth upon hers. Then he undid the belt to her robe and slid it off her shoulders as he encased her warm body to his. "The only fever I have is for you." He playfully slid the thin straps of her silk nightgown off her shoulders to midway down her arms. His fingertips glided tenderly down her smooth arms, causing her to quiver. When his hands reached her fingers, he intertwined his fingers with hers and held on as he drew her next to his bare skin.

"The things you do to me, Mrs. Sanders."

"Mark . . . oh, Mark, I love you so much." His tender lips claimed the curve of her neck as he freed the gown from her and led her into the shower with him. He would show her exactly how much strength she bestowed upon him to face the world today.

Forever he would love her and bring her unimaginable enjoyment in their union as husband and wife, in this private moment that belonged exclusively to them.

By the time Mark and April appeared at the table with the family, most of them had already finished eating. "Daddy!" Sunny jumped up and ran to him. He placed a kiss on her forehead.

April's face glowed as she led Mark to the table. They sat down inches from each other acting like teenagers in love. Mark placed his hand on her neck and drew her to him for a kiss. Her fingertips claimed his cheek as she returned the kiss.

Their affection for each other brought smiles to those around the table. Robert tapped his plate with his knife to get Mark's attention.

"Good morning, Mark and April." Mark broke the seal on his kiss and turned to face everyone with a wide grin.

"Good morning, everyone. Isn't this going to be a great day?" Mark was under the watchful eyes of the others sitting around the table. April gave a confirming wink at Dan to let him know everything was fine with Mark. Her blushed face brought a thankful smile to Dan's face.

Mark looked tired but he never let on he was. Once again, Mark had picked himself off the floor, overcoming yet another setback, and made his life into something magical with his bride. Dan thought warmly as his heart filled with thanksgiving for Mark's constant belief to live his life to the fullest no matter what obstacles he had to endure.

There was no denying the romantic exchanges that passed between Mark and April as they sat there admiring each other as if no one else sat at the table. The sparkling of their eyes told of their undeniable love and it radiated around them.

Robert gave a silent sigh of relief as Mark leaned over and tickled Sunny. Mark's laughter and Sunny's giggling were priceless sounds to everyone.

April noticed Mark's plate went untouched as he and Sunny teased each other. She did not say anything about it. She watched as he downed an entire glass of water in one breath before he snatched Sunny up out of

370

her chair, placed her on his lap, and tickled her until she was roaring in laughter.

"Daddy, stop!" She giggled in her wiggling to free herself from Mark's good-humored attention. Mark obliged and gave her a soft kiss on her forehead.

Sunny and Katie told everyone how much fun they had at Disneyland and at Sea World. This trip had been the best few days of their lives, they both agreed. Sunny gave Mark's ear a thankful twist between her fingers. It warmed Mark's heart to know he had been able to bring joy to Sunny's life.

Sunny's smile and giggles were worth the physical pain he had been going through to make these three days possible. The pill bottles he kept hidden were just about empty. But his heart was overflowing with the love his family had provided him with during this trip.

Mark picked up a water pitcher with one hand, poured water into his glass, and drank the entire glass. Jeff passed another pitcher of water to Mark. April thought she witnessed a disapproving expression on Jeff's face as Mark accepted the pitcher from Jeff.

Julia and Robert looked around at their beautiful family and told everyone how blessed they were to be a part of each other's lives. "We are blessed to have Sunny as our new granddaughter."

Sunny smiled and said she was blessed too because God had supplied all her needs when "her Mark" found her in the park. Sunny bounced up and down on his knee and said, "Now I have a big family, too." She held both hands out at arms length to include everyone sitting at the table.

Only Rebecca noticed the sadness of Katie's face as Sunny giggled with her father. *Poor Katie, she's never had a family, and I've never had a daughter.* She looked over at Steven as her mind began to think about the possibilities.

Mark winked at Dan. "It looks like our family is growing, isn't it, Dan?"

Dan smiled, letting the joy in his heart cross his face. "Yes, I asked Faye to marry me and she said yes. Thanks to Mark for the room mix-up, I might add." Dan gleamed as he looked at Mark with a commendable smile.

Mark laughed, "Anytime, Dan, anytime."

Sunny hopped off Mark's knee and jumped up and down yelling, "Yea, Dr. Dan and Dr. Faye are getting married just like my Mark and April did!" Everyone congratulated the couple on their up-coming marriage. Faye proudly showed everyone her sparkling ring.

They took the limos to the morning church service. Mark seemed fine as he signed a few autographs before going into the church.

He held Sunny up in his arm as they sang. Together they made a joyful sound. April admired how handsome he was as he winked at her and squeezed her hand. Her heart skipped a beat wondering if he was feeling better, or was he putting on a convincing show for all of them?

After the service was over, they went to eat at a restaurant next to the ocean. Mark had been quiet during the ride, giving an occasional smile when someone said something to him.

Mark sat next to the big bay window and stared out at the ocean. No one said anything as they watched him sitting there in deep thought. As they ate, Mark kept his attention on the rolling waves.

Life has dealt Mark an unfair hand. How is he going to make it through the day? Robert wondered.

April touched Mark's shoulder to get his attention and offered him a piece of her steak on her fork. He said nothing as he denied the fork she held to his mouth. Instead, he leaned into a kiss. It was too brief to satisfy her concern for him.

His attention turned back to a *dove* that landed on the ledge.

When it's time, Grandfather, I'll come to you, Mark thought, as a lump formed in his throat. *I'm not ready. But I am glad you came for what should have been the most important day of my life.* This time no tears fell from his soft eyes.

Robert thought of the past when Mark was ten. Mark had come into his office. Robert looked up and saw the anticipation on Mark's face. "Did you get the tickets to the Super Bowl, Father?" It was a promise his father had made him on his birthday.

"No, Mark. I have an out of town meeting that weekend. Maybe next year we can go," Robert told a disappointed boy as he picked up the phone. "I have an important call to make, Mark." That ended another broken promise.

"Someday, I am going to play in the Super Bowl. I hope you will have time and come watch me play, Father."

Robert shook his head in agreement. "I'll be there." His father waved his hand at Mark to shoo him out of the room. "William, how is it going? Any word on the merger?"

Robert watched as Mark hung his head and left the room looking rejected. Mark stood in the doorway and looked back at him.

"You just wait, Father. I will play in the Super Bowl someday! I will be the quarterback! You just watch me! Then maybe you'll go to the game with me, yeah, to see me play!" Mark stormed at him.

"Mark, I'm on the phone, go on. Sorry, William, that was just Mark. Now when do you think the deal will be finalized ... great?"

Oh, God, if I could only take back that day and make it right, Robert thought as his tearful eyes fell on Mark. He pushed his plate away. *How can I eat, with Mark hurting the way he is right now?*

Mark stared at the blue sky above the ocean. The bright sun stung his eyes and made them water. Memories flooded his mind as he watched the whipping white waves splash against the beach and then flow back into the ocean. He thought of the day he had stormed out of his father's office after his father had disappointed him.

"Fine, Father! Finish your stupid phone call with William. See if I care!" *I'll make my dreams come true without you. I don't need you! And don't think I will cry over you, Father! I won't!* he thought as he ran from the room.

After their conversation, determination set in and Mark's dream continued for years as he drove himself to greatness in every aspect of his life in hopes his father would finally find him worthy of his attention and notice him. Mark wanted his father to share in his dreams.

Would it be too much to ask, Father, to notice how successful I have become in high school sports? He walked into his father's office. Robert hung up the phone and looked up at Mark.

"I'm playing in the State High School Championship Football Game. Do you think maybe you could come, Father?"

"I will be there, Mark. Listen, I have a lot of work to do. Can we talk about this later?"

"Sure, Father, just let me know when we can talk."

I guess a high school game is not important enough for him. Someday, I will play for the NFL and win a Super Bowl game, and then maybe I will be the man my father can be proud of, he thought, with a downcast heart as he walked out and closed the door.

I can't sit here and dwell on the past. It's over. My life is ahead of me. I have been so blessed since high school. Mark thought about the first time he heard his father tell him he loved him. It had taken a motorcycle accident to open his father's eyes. God had moved in his father's life and they had become best friends. *Did I ever tell You, thank You, for changing my dad's heart, Lord? Thanks for giving us a second chance to be father and son.*

Mark had won a Rose Bowl game in his senior year of college, and then he was drafted into the NFL as a first round pick. Mark's life changed the moment they called out his name at the draft. He turned to his father and they shook hands.

"I made it, Dad! You and me, we are going to go to the Super Bowl together." Then he felt his father embracing him and patting him on the back. It felt so good to have his father's approval. That day had been their triumphant moment as father and son.

Mark knew he had finally earned his father's respect as they stood there embracing. However, Mark's grateful eyes fell on the special man that stood behind his father.

It was Dan who had loved and supported him unconditionally for all those years. Dan waited patiently with tears in his eyes to hug Mark and congratulate him on his lifetime dream.

"You made it happen, Mark. You are an NFL quarterback. I am so proud of you, Son."

Now fourteen years later, after that day in the office, Robert was sitting here watching his son's dream floating out to sea as Mark stared out the window.

They never made it to a Super Bowl game. In the last few years, Robert had offered to take Mark, but Mark wanted to wait until he was the quarterback playing in the game, and then they would go together.

Robert wiped a tear from his eye. Their day had finally come. *Only today, Mark will be sitting on the bench dying: emotionally and physically. There is no taking back the time I did not spend with my son.*

Mark's dream of playing in a Super Bowl was over. The moment had come when he had to face reality. There was no way to avoid the sadness that fell over his heart for that brief moment as he accepted things for what they were.

He looked over at his dad and saw the tears, knowing why they were there. *We made it here, Dad. I am so sorry I am breaking your heart. This is not how I wanted it to be, either.* He took a deep breath and looked back out at the sea.

He watched a couple walking across the sand, holding the hands of their small child between them. He smiled. *Now that is living, the perfect woman and a child. I have that. Lord, did you just send me a visual to wake me up?*

It is a beautiful day to be alive, he thought. *The ocean is God's glory, a reminder of how wonderful God is.*

He felt April's hand on his thigh. His thoughts turned to her, as her love for him commanded his attention. As always, Mark turned his focus on what was important and a smile crossed his face.

New dreams, my life will be made up of new dreams, and I look forward to each one of them. Starting with this incredible woman and my little sunshine.

He sat quietly thinking about that. He was taking in the magnificent scene of the ocean and the warmth that remained on his leg. *Life is about new dreams, not old ones,* he thought, as he gave thanks to God for the brilliant reminder in front of him.

Then Mark realized everyone was extremely quiet. He turned and faced them and saw their concerned faces. He smiled and started cutting up with them. He soon realized he was the only one smiling as the family continued to worry about him.

A wide smile formed on Mark's face. "I am going to go jump in the ocean!" he announced as he jumped up from the table and headed toward the door all in one leap.

"Mark Sanders, don't you dare!" April called as she chased after him. Mark ran down the steps to the beach and headed toward the water. April stopped to unfasten her high-heeled shoes so she could run through the sand.

Those at the table stood up and watched out the window. Mark reached the edge of the water. He pulled off his sports jacket, threw it up into the wind. He lifted his dress shirt over his head, and threw it in the sand. He undid his belt and pulled it out of his slacks.

Then he reached down to take off his boots. He hopped on one foot, trying to pull the boot off with both his hands. Just as he got the boot off, April tackled him to the sand. He lost interest in the water as he found her enticing lips.

"Oh, Lord, what are we going to do with that boy?" Robert asked as he gathered Julia in his arms and they exchanged a look of passion and kissed.

Everyone at the table sat down and smiled. No one spoke; they just grinned in shades of red. Which is just what Mark Sanders had hoped would happen. Just like Mark, he made everyone laugh and smile, when they all felt like crying.

Jeff held Ashley's hand under the table and gave it a squeeze as he looked in her sparkling eyes. He looked around the table and noticed his hands were not the only ones missing from the table. Mark had spread the feeling of love among them all.

Robert turned slightly to get a glance out of the window. Julia waited for his response. Robert gave her a wink and asked the waiter to bring them a second round of coffee.

Chapter Fifty-Four

Treasure the Ones You Love

The group went back to the hotel for the afternoon. Mark and April disappeared as soon as the limo arrived. Mark muttered something about getting the sand out of April's hair.

At five, the family met in the dining room for dinner. Mark and April arrived locked in each other's arms and sat down. Mark looked well rested. He cuddled next to April and held her hand under the table.

Mark noticed everyone at the table was keeping a sharp eye on him. *They are all just waiting for me to keel over.* He knew it was up to him to cut the tension at the table once again.

He looked over at Jeff and they exchanged mischievous looks. Mark gave Jeff a wink. They were ready to begin their usual comic act to lighten the tension.

"Do you remember the time in first grade when you were throwing a biscuit at me and you hit Principal Quarterman in the back of the head?" Jeff asked Mark. They laughed remembering that moment.

"I thought I was dead when he picked me up by the ear and dragged me to his office. He tore my tail up that day." Sunny laughed at Mark's story.

Jeff stood up and reenacted the pass, making arm movements to tell the story. "Mark's biscuit flew from the first grade table, over the second grade table and then over my head at the third grade table. It was Mark's first touchdown throw. Right into the back of old Quarterman's head. Bam!"

"Yeah, and you missed the throw and got me in big trouble," Mark grinned. Dan remembered picking Mark up from the principal's office that day.

"Sunny, did you know your daddy had a chair in the principal's office with his name on it, and at least once a week, he went to visit it? The problem was when he came out of the principal's office, sitting was the last thing he wanted to do." Jeff and Mark laughed. Even though Sunny was not sure what Jeff was talking about, she laughed too.

Maybe it was a good thing his father sent him off to boarding school when he was eight, Mark thought as he remembered his frequent visits to see Mr. Quarterman.

"Wonder what the buzzard thinks of me now?" Mark laughed and Jeff joined him. "Can you imagine the stories he must tell about me, now that I am famous? 'I spanked Mark Sanders when he was a boy.' I bet he feels honored."

When Mark and Jeff started messing around, tossing biscuits across the table at each other, April frowned and moved the breadbasket out of Mark's reach.

"Ok, Mark, stop it. When Sunny gets in trouble at school, it will be you that has to go to the principal's office. Because if I have to go, I will tell them she acts just like her father." She broke a smile as Mark laid on his irresistible charm and kissed her.

"I love you, too, Babe," he said sarcastically.

"For your sake, Mark, I hope old Quarterman has retired," Jeff chuckled. The results of their story produced smiles and laughter throughout the rest of the meal, as Mark led in another one of his tactics of keeping everyone at ease.

Mark counted his many blessings sitting before him. His father and mother were hugging his precious daughter, as Sunny drew them deeper into her heart.

The transformation in his father was apparent as he now worshipped his time with his family. His grandchildren were the focus of his attention the minute he arrived home from his office. Julia's eyes beamed with love as she glanced at Robert and placed a kiss on his cheek.

Faye and Dan exchanging lovesick looks made Mark laugh. *Life is great, when you have what I have right here at this table*, Mark thought with adoration. He looked forward to many more moments like this one with his entire family and friends. Nothing else mattered; living each precious moment of his life was all that was important to him and that, he intended to do.

It was finally time to go to the game. Everyone got in the limo and sat quietly looking at Mark, wondering what he would do. Sunny got on Mark's lap, and put her arms around his neck, "I love you, Daddy."

If Mark's mind was not sure what to do earlier, it was now. Mark thought, what could be any better than hearing the words, *I love you, Daddy*. He planted a kiss on Sunny's forehead, leaned over, and brushed April's tender lips. His actions brought reassurance to those that watched him relish in his family.

When they arrived at the stadium, everyone stood by the limo and wished Mark well in his decision. None gave him their unspoken opinions.

Sunny told Mark she had a big surprise for him. "Oh, you do, kiddo, I wonder what it is?" Mark teased her and gave her a kiss and a bear hug that left her giggling. Then he turned to April with curious eyes.

April shook her head; she was not telling Sunny's secret, no matter how persuasive Mark was with his enticing hands around her body as he held her in his arms for their final moment together before he left her with the others.

He placed both his hands on the sides of her neck and faced her. "I have to go join the team in the locker room. I don't want you to worry. Unless something happens between now and when the team takes the field, I will not be playing."

He gathered her in his arms and embraced her. "I love you, April, more than anything in this world and that includes football. One *second* on the field playing today could never bring me the joy that a lifetime with you will bring me."

April held onto him, as his engaging words conveyed his love, and she whispered through her tears. "Mark, you are my endless love … my heart belongs to you … we are one heart joined together … and if you want to play in this game, go ahead. Don't ever let me stand in your way of reaching your goals. Let me be a part of your dreams. Don't let me be the one to take your dreams from you."

His hands lightly encased the sides of her cheeks as he gently brushed back her hair, leaned down over her, and kissed her lips so passionately in appreciation of her selfless love for him.

"I love you, April, more than my own life and more than this game," Mark reassured her as he lifted her chin up so their eyes met. "Thank you for supporting me in my dream today, but honestly, April, my dream is not this game. My dream is loving you for the rest of my life. I am looking forward to having you in my arms tonight as I make love to you." He smiled until she blushed and then he kissed her forehead and was off to the locker room.

April joined the rest of the family and their friends. Dan took her in his arms to reassure her that everything was going to be just fine. "Mark knows what he is doing. We all know he loves football and the team, but April, he loves you and Sunny more."

"I just want him to be happy ... the disappointment he has to be feeling right now."

"April, Mark knows in his heart that everything happens for a reason. He'll draw strength from knowing that. Mark gave you his words. Now it is up to you to believe in them with all your heart."

"Mark Sanders *owns my heart*, it belongs only to him."

The locker room was full of excitement and the anticipation of the upcoming game. But there was definitely something missing in their joy, as a reserved feeling spread across the room. They all knew it was because Mark was not there with them to share in this significant moment.

Mark was the one who got them to the Super Bowl and for Mark to miss this game entirely seemed unfair, unthinkable. They felt heartbroken for him wondering if he was home watching the pre-game coverage on TV, feeling miserable that he was not here with them.

Carlo duct-taped Mark's jersey number to his helmet and the others were doing the same. This game would be dedicated to Mark. Mark would be the driving force they needed to come out of this game with a victory.

All of a sudden cheering broke out by the door to the locker room. Mark's friends watched as Mark enthusiastically came busting in the room with his hands raised in the air giving high fives to the players as he made his way through the locker room.

Mark stood in front of Carlo, Kevin, Jerk, Justin, and Craig with a wide grin on his face. They were silent for a few seconds and then they broke out in cheers as they hugged him.

Mark looked at them with his beaming grin. "You guys didn't think you could come to California without me, did you?" He smiled at them. The guys were thrilled to see him and were in awe at his cheerful disposition. *For a man who is not playing, he sure is happy*, Carlo thought. *What is he up to now?*

Mark told the guys how much he loved them but he told them that after seeing Sunny at Disneyland, he knew he could not risk playing. "I'll be back next year; you can take that to the bank," he promised them and was surrounded by their buoyant embraces.

"You had me going there for a minute. I thought you'd come to play." Carlo patted Mark on the shoulder.

"Nope, not a chance."

Mark led the team in prayer before they went out onto the field. The team was thankful Mark was alive and here with them on this special day. Mark earned this day and it would not feel right leaving him on the sideline when the game started. Mark was upbeat and showed no signs of regret as he pumped his team up before they rushed out onto the field. He was a true team leader in every way possible.

Mark went out onto the field with the guys in his team jersey, and he took his place with them for the National Anthem. He stood proudly as the reality of the moment sank in.

Wow, I am standing on the field, the turf underneath my feet, with my teammates, at a Super Bowl game, and my entire family is here to witness this moment with me!

A small voice echoed from the microphone. "Daddy, I told you I had a surprise for you," Sunny said with a giggle.

Mark looked up surprised and saw Sunny staring at him, and he smiled as chills ran down his spine. *I love you, little girl.*

"Please stand, while my Grandmother and I sing the National Anthem, in honor of my new daddy, Mark Sanders," she said in a grown-up voice. Tears formed in his eyes as his mother and Sunny sang beautifully. They enhanced his thoughts of a great day.

After the song was finished, Sunny said, "Daddy, I love you. I told you, God would supply all our needs."

She said that wonderful word, "Daddy," Mark thought with such love in his heart for his precious little daughter, tears of love for her softly warmed his cheeks. Mark knew in his heart that no matter what hardships were sent in his direction, he could conquer them all with the love of God and the love of Sunny and April.

As team captain, Mark went to do the coin toss and then he went up to the announcers' booth to do the commentary play by play of the game. When asked if he had any regrets about not playing, Mark replied, "Absolutely not, I have learned to count my blessings. Just being alive today is enough. Having a second chance with my family is more important to me than playing in this game. I will never take my life with them for granted."

Mark reminded the fans they needed to be tested for a bone marrow transplant donor. He reminded them how important it was to donate blood. Giving that message was more crucial to him than playing.

April and Sunny sat beside Mark in the booth. April looked into Mark's eyes and thanked him for giving up the game for them. Mark looked at his two girls and said.

"No, thank you. It is because of you and Sunny that I take a breath of air each day and that my life is complete. I don't need anything but you two. I feel so blessed you are my wife and you put up with me." With that said, she fell in his arms and kissed him like there was no tomorrow.

It did not matter to Mark if the team won or not. He was already a winner. The greatest ring in the world was already on his wedding ring finger. The Super Bowl ring was nothing more than a bonus.

He had his *one more moment in time*.

Chapter Fifty-Five

Fulfilling His Dream

ৡৢ

With five minutes left in the game, the phone rang in the booth. Howard handed the phone to Mark, who listened carefully and then hung up.

"They need me in the locker room. Doc is having mild chest pains. I better hurry." He got up quickly, gave April a kiss, tousled Sunny's head, and headed to the door, where the security guard met him with a golf cart to transport him.

"Mr. Sanders, I'll escort you to the locker room." Thoughts and prayers filled Mark's head as the two men rushed in the cart to the locker room. Mark jumped out as soon as they reached the door.

April gathered up Sunny and smiled at Howard.

"Sunny, we have a big surprise for your Daddy. We have to hurry. Thanks, Stan and Howard, for everything."

"Good luck with Mark. We'll be keeping him in our prayers in the coming weeks," Howard expressed.

Mark rushed into the locker room fully expecting to see Doc lying on the exam table. When he opened the door, several of the players pounced on him. They grabbed at his shirt and pulled it up over his head. Someone was undoing his belt buckle and the zipper to his pants.

"Hold on, guys, what's going on; what are you doing?" Mark asked in a state of confusion, as they pulled his team t-shirt over his head and pulled it down. "Where's Doc?"

"He's fine; he is on the field waiting on you."

"What?"

383

"We had to tell you something to get you to the locker room in a hurry," Justin informed him.

"You guys just about gave me a heart attack!"

"Sorry, Mark, it was Jerk's idea." Mark should have guessed it was Jerk who came up with this lame-blasted scheme.

"You have a game to play, Mark. The team needs you," Justin added as he put on Mark's shoulder pads and tightened them.

"What? You guys don't need me. Kevin is doing just fine. We were ahead by 10 points when I left the booth."

They lifted him up, sat him down on the table, and started removing his boots and his pants.

"Guys, come on, you're kidding, right?" He was defenseless as they hurriedly undressed him and then redressed him. They lifted his arms up and his team jersey was pulled down over his shoulder pads. Next came his pants and his cleats.

Mark took it all in with a laughing attitude, what else could he do. These guys had a plan and they were not backing down. Finally, they grabbed him by the front of his jersey and stood him up for inspection.

"Yep, he looks like a quarterback," Justin expressed with a teasing glow as he handed Mark his helmet. "Let's get Mark on the field, men. Mark, you have a Super Bowl game to play."

At half time, the team players had gathered together and came up with a plan for the end of the game. Dan had gone up to the booth and filled April in on their plan while Mark was giving an interview down on the field.

When Mark came out on the field, the players were waiting for him. They stood in two straight lines and as Mark walked between them, they clapped and cheered in a round of congratulations.

"Way to go, Mark!" "This is your night, Mark!"

Their plan was successful. The grin on Mark's face was heartfelt by all those standing there in his honor. His entire family and friends stood at the end of the row ready to cheer him on to a victory.

The coach approached Mark and shook his hand. He handed Mark the football. "Four plays, Mark, as soon as our defense shuts them down, the ball is yours."

Mark looked up at the clock, when he smiled wide and laughed, knowing he was taking the field with less than one minute left to play. His team was ahead by ten points. The game was already in the bag. All Mark had to do was take a knee and run out the clock.

"Very funny, guys," he laughed as he exchanged a grin with the players. He loved them for including him in the game, even if it was for just one minute.

A quick kiss on April's cheek joined their hearts in unison. It was evident how proud she was of him as she touched his face before sending him out to collect his victory.

When he stepped on the field, the crowd went absolutely wild chanting his name. He waved his hand in appreciation. Both teams stood clapping their hands as he went to join the huddle for his honorary last play.

Excitement over the impending win, just a minute away, and the exhilaration over Mark joining them for the final play of the Super Bowl, filled the huddle.

Mark held up his hands to get his teammates attention. All stood ready as they waited for their faithful leader to call the obvious play: he was taking a knee as soon as the ball was hiked into his hands. Surprise soon crossed their faces as they heard what Mark said instead.

"First and ten, boys, go deep, Carlo, my pass is going all the way to the end zone!" Mark grinned wide; a sly smile held his face as he pointed straight out at the end zone.

"We're going for the touchdown!" Not a sound was heard as the players contemplated Mark's final call and watched him smile. "We are about to rock this stadium!"

"Are you serious, Mark?" Carlo asked what they were all nervously thinking.

Was Mark really going for the touchdown? Knowing Mark anything was possible. It would be just like him to have the final say.

Mark grinned and laughed at them. "I finally got you guys back!"

"That you did, Mark!" They all laughed, thankful for their faithful leader's sense of humor to the very end.

Mark's face became serious, and the men stood at attention to hear what Mark had to say.

"I have waited my whole life for this moment. I realized this week there is more to life than this big game." He glanced over at April and his family and his eyes watered. Everyone he loved was all around him.

"Today is about victory. God has done so many miracles to get me this far, and I don't want to take advantage of that by putting myself in harm's way. I am taking a knee, and I am taking it with pride and gratefulness to

God. We have won the Super Bowl, and that is victory enough. But the real victory is having each other."

The end of the game came, and Mark was surrounded by all those that loved him, in a celebration of his life, in the celebration that he had fulfilled one of his lifetime dreams.

His *one more moment in time* was nothing more than a miracle from God who had indeed supplied all his needs once again.

This time, Mark kept his promise to love April with his entire heart as he took her back to the seclusion of their hotel room and continued where he had left off that morning. The amazing union of their hearts, once again, blessed their honeymoon time together in their *endless love* for each other.

April was the magnificent gift God had placed in his life to treasure, and he wanted much more than their "One More Moment in Time." He wanted her to be "Forever in His Heart."

The End. Amen. Be blessed in your life.

Book Three of the Endless Love Series - **Forever in His Heart**

To order - Contact - *endlesslovebookorders@yahoo.com*

§§

Donate Blood, Platelets, or Marrow

Your donation of blood, platelets, bone marrow, or umbilical cord blood help patients stay alive – compare that value to any other use of your time!

There are very practical ways you can help patients with bone marrow diseases. Many patients depend on blood transfusions until their treatments become effective. Some patients rely on blood transfusions for many years. You can donate blood, platelets, bone marrow, or umbilical cord blood to extend and improve the lives of those suffering from these diseases. Another vital way of promoting the cause is by encouraging and recruiting other donors within your family, community, and at your place of employment.

Contact your local hospital to find the nearest blood bank. Employees and volunteers at your community blood bank are able to provide you with general information on donating blood and platelets. More information can be found through the American Red Cross at www.redcross.org or America's Blood Centers at www.americasblood.org

Bone marrow transplant (BMT) is the only curative option for bone marrow diseases. However, not all patients are eligible for this procedure for a variety of reasons. Those who are eligible for a BMT may not have a matching sibling donor. The National Marrow Donor Program (NMDP) Registry will assist patients in finding a matching donor who is not a biological relative. Donors of all ethnic groups are desperately needed but according to NMDP: "Of utmost urgency is the need for more minorities – specifically African Americans, Asian and Pacific Islanders, Hispanics, and American Indian/Alaska Natives – to become volunteer donors. Transplants require matching certain tissue traits of the donor to the patient; because these traits are inherited, the most likely donor will come from the person's same racial or ethnic group." To volunteer, contact your local NMDP center or recruitment group at www.marrow.org.

Another opportunity to support this endeavor is through the donation of **umbilical cord blood** that is used for stem cell transplants. Cord blood transplantation is an investigational therapy for bone marrow disease. You can encourage expectant parents to contact a local cord blood bank.

Who can be a Double Red Cell Donor?

If you meet the requirements for donating blood, you probably can give Double Red Cells. Donors must have Type O or Type B. They must be at least 18 years old - be in good health. Males: weigh at least 130 lbs, and height at least 5'1. Females: weight at least 150 lbs, and height at least 5'5.

How does the Procedure Work? Blood is drawn from your arm with a disposable needle, connected to a disposable collection bowl, called a "set." The blood is mixed automatically with an anticoagulant, and drawn into the spinning centrifuge bowl, where it is separated into red cells and plasma. The plasma (about 250-300 ml) is collected into a temporary storage bag. When the bowl is filled with red cells, the plasma is mixed with sterile saline and returned to the donor. The red cells are transferred automatically from the centrifuge bowl to a storage bag. This process is repeated one more time, to yield two units of red cells.

My book series has a purpose as you might have guessed. I am trying to make the public more aware of the need for blood donations and for bone marrow donations. I give blood as often as possible, and I am honored to be able to help someone like Mark Sanders.

Recently, I gave my first Double Red Cell donation. The entire time I was donating, I felt like I was doing it for Mark. It was a very personal experience that left me feeling humble.

I encourage my readers to donate blood, bone marrow, or help out with your local blood drives. – Elizabeth A. Ryan